TANDEM

The Rival Monster

None of the islanders doubted that some strange
creature had arrived on the shores of the two
Toddays. Young Kenny Macroon had met it
when laying lobster pots off Little Todday.
Archie MacRurie – the Biffer – saw something
most alarming on the west coast of Great Todday.
Whether they were the same monster, whether
either or both was indeed the unhappy refugee
from Loch Ness, the islanders knew they had
acquired a valuable asset.

A certain amount of rivalry was inevitable: was it
Great Todday's monster or Little Todday's?
But the islanders can be relied on to make good
use of whatever providence chooses to send to
their shores, and when reporters, folklorists and
scientists descended on the Toddays to
investigate the monster, it was clearly going to
be an extremely profitable tourist season.

KEEP THE HOME GUARD TURNING and
ROCKETS GALORE, two more of Compton
Mackenzie's famous Island comedies, are also
available in Tandem editions.

D1470891

Map of the Islands

Fearvig
PILLAY

Bàgh Mhic Ròin

The Coolish
Ardvanish
Sròn Ruairidh
Knockdown

Traigh Vooey
Gerryboo
Loch Skinny

LITTLE TODDAY
Ben Bustival

Carraig
an Ròin
Snorvig
Loch Bob

Ben
Sticla

Kiltod
Bobanish

GREAT TODDAY

Traigh Swish

Ben Pucka

Ard Swish
A Sloc

Traigh
Veck
Watasett

Traigh
nam Marbh
Loch Sleeport
POPPAY

Roade

The Rival Monster

Compton Mackenzie

TANDEM
14 Gloucester Road, London SW7

Originally published in Great Britain by
Chatto & Windus, 1952
Two impressions

First published by Universal-Tandem
Publishing Co. Ltd, 1972

© Compton Mackenzie 1952

Made and printed in Great Britain by
C. Nicholls & Company Ltd

Contents

To
Harold Raymond, Ian Parsons
&
Norah Smallwood
from an
Affectionate Author

March 12th, 1951

Chapter 1

THE LETHAL SAUCER

ON an afternoon in March when the world was supposed to be at peace again Roderick MacRurie, the landlord of the Snorvig Hotel on the island of Great Todday, and Joseph Macroon, the postmaster and principal merchant of Kiltod, the metropolis of Little Todday, emerged from the meeting of the Inverness-shire County Council and walked along together in the direction of the Porridge Hotel, the renowned hostelry of the Northern capital.

Big Roderick MacRurie's bulk, of which the austerity of a long war had not robbed him of an ounce, seemed to bound as lightly along the pavement as a balloon; his black tufted eyebrows stuck out as aggressively as two Sitka spruces planted by the Forestry Commission on some really good grazing land; he was humming to himself the refrain of the song *Red Rory's Galley*, which celebrates the piratical exploits of his clan in the days when Scotland really did stand where it did. The reason for Big Roderick's lightness of foot and heart was that he had succeeded in persuading his fellow councillors to make a grant for the construction of a pier at Garryboo, a crofting township whose exposure to the full fury of the westerly Atlantic gales had been a grievance for years and had led at the last County Council election to a unanimous vote against the hotel-keeper, who was accused of always favouring Snorvig at the expense of the rest of the island.

"Ah, well, well, Choseph, it's the people of Garryboo will be pleased when Cheorge Campbell puts my telegraph up on the school door to say the pier has been granted to them. Ay, ay, they'll be ferry well pleased right enough."

"Ay, I believe they will," Joseph Macroon agreed without warmth. Joseph was a much smaller man, but this afternoon he seemed to weigh twice as much as Roderick, so unwontedly did his trim white moustache droop at the corners.

"It was a pity right enough about the lobster-pool for Little Todday," Roderick went on. "Every member from the islands voted for it, but these stink-in-the-muds from the

east of the county crudge us every farthing. Ay, ay, chust a
parcel of skinnyflints."

"You had your pier," Joseph Macroon muttered
sombrely.

"Ach, you had your new school at Kiltod two years ago,"
Roderick reminded him.

"Not before the old one was a pure disgrace to the county.
A Dhia, if Hitler had invaded us I would have been ashamed
for the man to see it."

Joseph Macroon walked on in silence; the more he
thought about that pier which Roderick MacRurie had
extracted from the Council, the more depressed he felt
about his own failure to extract a lobster-pool.

"All the priests were after voting for you, Ruairidh," he
said at last.

"Ay, they did that," the hotel-keeper agreed.

"But some of the ministers were not after voting for me."

"Och, I wouldn't say it was a religious matter at all,
Choseph," Roderick protested. "*A Chruitheir*, what religion
at all has a lobster? No, no, it was chust a piece of what
they call economicality."

"And lobsters fetching six shillings each from the buyers
if we can get them fresh to market. What economicality is
there in that?" Joseph demanded sternly. "*A Dhia*, it's
a wonderful price. There never was such a price for lobsters."

By this time the two Islandmen had reached the entrance
of the Porridge Hotel and as they passed in to the lounge
they were greeted by John Maclean, the dapper porter.

"A lovely day we've had. I hope to-day's wind-up of
the Council was successful."

"Ay, it was pretty successful right enough," Roderick
declared.

"It wasn't successful at all, at all," declared Joseph
simultaneously.

"We all enjoyed the film, Mr Macroon," the porter said.
"I went three times myself."

"Is it *Whisky Galore* you'll be talking about?" Joseph
asked indignantly. "What kind of a fillum is it that was
after turning me into a Protestant and never had so much as
one view of Little Todday from one end of the fillum to the
other? I don't call that a fillum at all. Just a piece of
ignorance."

"Ah, well, Mr Macroon, it gave us all a good laugh in

Inverness," the porter insisted. "And the monster has been very lively this month. I believe we will have a splendid season. We're booked right up from July on."

"It was pretty queer nobody in Inverness saw the monster when the war was still going strong," Joseph observed sardonically. "I suppose the Military Permit Office wouldn't give her a permit to be showing herself."

"They reckoned the monster was disturbed by the depth charges they were dropping on these submarines, and laid up for the duration," the porter pointed out. "But it's lively enough again now. Two of the monks at Fort Augustus saw its tail last week, which would appear to be forked."

"Ay, it would be," Joseph muttered.

"And the very same evening Willie Bayne, who's taken on Charlie Macintosh's job as traveller for Duthie's Dreadnought Sheep Dip, heard what he thought was the water boiling in his radiator just before he came to the road up to Drumsticket and when he pulled up the bonnet it wasn't his radiator at all. No, no. It was something snorting at him from the lochside, but it was too dark by then to make out just what it was. Oh, yes, and Ben Nevis was telling me only this morning he saw it the day before yesterday for the twelfth time. Near Tummie it was. He got quite annoyed with Colonel Lindsay-Wolseley because the Colonel said it was an otter he'd been watching for the last month. 'Otter?' Ben Nevis shouted. 'Do you think I've lived to be seventy this month to start imagining at my age that otters are eighty feet long? Don't be ridiculous, Lindsay-Wolseley.' Yes, that's what he said to the Colonel. 'Don't be ridiculous.' I don't believe the Colonel was too pleased."

"Look at that now," said Joseph Macroon. "You wouldn't think that a man who's after seeing the monster twelve times would be grudging the people of Little Todday a lobster-pool. But he voted against us this afternoon."

The two Islandmen, after a much needed couple of drams, entered the car which the kind-hearted ratepayers provided for their long journey to Obaig, where early next morning they would board the *Island Queen* for Snorvig. With them was Father Macintyre, the priest of St Bunian's, Drumsticket, who gently chaffed Joseph Macroon in Gaelic about the ignoring of Little Todday in the film *Whisky Galore*.

"I never would have believed that Roderick here was

such a Hitler. No wonder he managed to get that pier for Garryboo this afternoon."

But Joseph Macroon felt too strongly about Roderick MacRurie's success over the pier and his own failure over the lobster-pool to smile. He withdrew into that vagueness which was always his refuge against the inconvenient demands of the present.

"Ay, ay, Father," he murmured, and gazed from the window of the car at the steely water of the loch.

It was twilight when the car reached the Chapel House in Drumsticket; immediately Father Macintyre alighted he was surrounded by a small crowd of excited parishioners who had been waiting for his arrival.

"Father, Father, the monster has been killed," he was told.

"He wasn't shot by the Colonel or Sir Hubert," the priest assured them, "for both guns were at the Council meeting."

"No, no, it was killed by a flying teapot."

"Sure as death, it's true, Father. It was Coinneach Mór who saw it happen."

Joseph Macroon turned gloomily to his companion.

"Ach, let you and I be getting on our way, Roderick. It's all stupidity on the mainland. Not enough sense in them to keep lobsters fresh and keening now for a dead water-horse. Good night, Father, we've a long road before we get back to the West."

"And civilisation," the priest added with a chuckle. "*Beannachd leibh.* And I hope the monster's ghost won't be on your tracks."

It was not until the *Scottish Daily Tale* of two days later reached the islands of Great and Little Todday that the two Councillors realised how near they had been to the epi-centrum of an earth-shaking event on that March evening.

LOCH NESS MONSTER HIT BY A FLYING SAUCER?

GROAN HEARD BY DRUMSTICKET MAN MAY HAVE BEEN DEATH AGONY

AMAZING STORY

'The people of the remote Inverness-shire village of Drumsticket some ten miles from Fort Augustus were on tenterhooks yesterday when a representative of the *Scottish Daily Tale* arrived to investigate the amazing story told by Mr Kenneth MacLennan, head stalker on the Cloy estate of the well-known sportsman, Sir Hubert Bottley, Bart.

Mr MacLennan, a fine figure of a Highlander of the old school, gave our representative a vivid account of the amazing occurrence.

"I had been over to Tummie House to see Colonel Lindsay-Wolseley on a matter of business, and finding that the Colonel was in Inverness at a Council meeting I was walking back home when just before I came to the turning off the lochside road to Drumsticket I was aware of a bright light travelling at great speed down the loch from the direction of Inverness about twenty feet above the surface of the water. As it drew nearer the front of the missile became a sort of orange-red. I was reminded of the end of a cigar when it is being puffed."

"It was not a circular disc then?"

"Definitely no," replied Mr MacLennan. "But that doesn't say it was the shape of a cigar. I would prefer to compare it to the spout of a teapot. Well, to cut a long story short, just after this flying spout passed close to where I was standing, out of the loch came something I can only describe as a huge horse's head on top of a snaky neck. At the same time I heard a kind of loud hissing noise, but whether this was made by the monster or the flying saucer as you can call this spout I wouldn't care to say. Then suddenly there was a blinding flash and I heard a groan like a cow in agony but much louder of course. I must have shut my eyes for a moment, for I don't mind admitting I was extremely scared, and when I looked again there was nothing there except a quantity of bubbles on the surface of the loch."

"Do you think the monster tried to attack this flying saucer, Mr MacLennan?"

"I wouldn't care to express an opinion on that. All I'm prepared to say is that it's a possibility."

"Had you ever seen the monster before?"

"Never," Mr MacLennan answered emphatically. "In fact, until to-day's amazing occurrence I was inclined to disbelieve in the monster, which only goes to show how wrong anybody can be."

"And had you had any previous experience of flying saucers?"

"Only in the newspapers," Mr MacLennan replied.

"But this flying object was definitely not like a saucer?"

"As I've said, it more nearly resembled the spout of a teapot."

Comment in Drumsticket and Cloy on this amazing story told by Mr Kenneth MacLennan testified warmly to his reputation as an accurate observer of nature.

Anxiety about the fate of the monster is of course widespread on Loch Ness side where, ever since the first alarming stories of its ferocity had been demonstrated to be devoid of credibility, it has long been regarded with the genuine affection that is typical of the 'true and tender North.'

Provost Hugh Macpherson, O.B.E., said last night:

"If the monster has indeed been killed Inverness will have suffered the greatest blow since the Battle of Culloden. We are hopeful, however, that the monster succeeded in diving to safety in time. It will indeed be an ironical stroke of fate if a creature in whose existence many presumptuous persons affect to disbelieve should be lost to Loch Ness by the action of a phenomenon which many other people do not accept as an established fact."

The *Scottish Daily Tale* is privileged to offer its readers a symposium of public opinion collected from various prominent Invernessians and others:

MacDonald of Ben Nevis

"I do not believe in these things called flying saucers and therefore I do not believe that the Loch Ness Monster, which I saw for the twelfth time less than a week ago, is dead. I consider that Kenneth MacLennan, whom I have known for years as one of the finest stalkers in the North, was dazzled by the sudden appearance of the sun just as the monster emerged."

Sir Hubert Bottley of Cloy, Bart.

"Coinneach Mór (Big Kenneth) as we all call him is not the kind of man to spread a fairy tale. I am satisfied that the eyes of a man whose professional powers of observation have never been at fault since I have had the privilege of enjoying his services as head stalker would not have been deceived. At the same time Coinneach Mór definitely refuses to commit himself to the assertion that this flying saucer or teapot spout, as he insists it resembled, actually hit the monster. The groan he heard may easily have been an expression of rage at the unwarranted attack made upon it."

Dr Angus Macfadyen, the famous Celtic historian

"I am not qualified to express an opinion about the destructive powers of these mysterious phenomena generally known as 'flying saucers,' but I hesitate to believe that an animal which has existed since the days of St Columba at least would at this date fall a victim to a 'flying saucer.' This is to stretch the long arm of coincidence too far for even the most credulous historian. While I have no doubt whatever in the existence of the Loch Ness Monster I am not yet completely satisfied that the 'flying saucers' have been identified as such and I deprecate any premature theories about their possible provenance in the present state of our knowledge. It will be a sad day if the existence of the Loch Ness Monster is finally established in the teeth of sceptics by its failure to appear again and I hope that a stricter watch than ever will be maintained all along Loch Ness. The reappearance of the monster shortly after V day was to many of us a sign that peace had indeed come again to our distracted world."

Professor Andrew Fleming, the great biopsychical expert

"My researches into biopsychics have led me to recognise what are vulgarly called 'flying saucers' as an attempt by highly developed insects from the planet Mars to communicate with our planet. Unfortunately for reasons which we are unable to explain at present these devoted emissaries become incandescent as they approach the Earth and finally vanish altogether. I might put forward, very tentatively, a suggestion that Mr Kenneth MacLennan enjoyed the privilege of witnessing the 'blinding flash' which accompanies the moment of dissolution. I wish I could be equally convinced by the evidence hitherto adduced in favour of the reality of the Loch Ness Monster. How then, it may be asked, did Mr MacLennan, who has so accurately observed the phenomenon of a flying saucer, imagine the appearance of the monster? I venture to put forward an explanation which may be startling to many at first but in my opinion deserves the fullest consideration. If, as seems certain, the flying saucer is the vehicle of a super-insect it may be that Mr MacLennan enjoyed the unique experience of actually seeing one of these insects desperately attempting to counter the effect of its passage through space by magnifying its own corporeal entity, and thus appearing to resemble the popular conception of the Loch Ness Monster. I make this suggestion with the greatest reserve, for the science of biopsychics is still in the empirical stage. We are, indeed, at present groping in the dark."

Mr Hector Hamish Mackay, the historian and topographer

"I refuse to despair. I believe that the Loch Ness Monster succeeded in avoiding the flying saucer. It may well be that its mane was singed as the saucer passed over it which would account for the loud groan heard by Mr MacLennan. As readers of the *Scottish Daily Tale* are aware, I have long been convinced that there are two monsters, a male and a female, the latter of which lays her eggs on a shelf in the submarine passage between Loch Ness and the North Sea. If by misfortune one of the monsters *has* been killed by this flying saucer I feel sure that the survivor will seek a mate in the 'dark, unfathomed caves of ocean' and that it may not be long before we hear of a 'sea-serpent' having been sighted off our coasts. Verb. sap.'"

"Och, it would be fine right enough if we could be seeing one of these Verb Saps off Great Todday," Roderick MacRurie observed to his wife that evening after he had read the article in the *Scottish Daily Tale*.

"What are you saying, Roderick?" Mrs MacRurie exclaimed. "I never heard tell of a Verb Sap before. Is Joseph Macroon after getting one for Little Todday?"

"What would a Verb Sap be doing in Little Todday?

It's no place at all for the crayture. But there would be a beautiful run for it up Loch Sleeport or Loch Bob."

"I don't know at all what you're talking about, Roderick," his wife said.

"Ah, woman, you're icknorant right enough. A Verb Sap is a huge great monster,—a kind of *each uisge* but bicker."

"We're wanting no Verb Saps or water-horses on Great Todday," Mrs MacRurie declared firmly. "It's bad enough with the children all turning into Hitlers and Hoolickans."

"Do you mind how many towrists were coming last summer to hear the seals singing on Poppay and Pillay? Choseph was for effer sending the *Morning Star* to bring them over to Little Todday. Ay, and the Biffer would always be taking parties in the *Kittiwake*. 'I would be ashamed, *a Bhiffer*,' I was after saying to him once, 'I would be townright ashamed to be showing off the seals on Poppay and Pillay to towrists and you a Great Todday man and a MacRurie and your great-grandfather the brother of my own great-grandfather.' Ay, and Mr Hector Hamish Mackay himself who's a good friend of my own likes to blow about these tam seals." *

"*Isd, a Ruairidh*, I wish you wouldn't be using such terrible bad words," his wife protested.

"Ach, it would make the Minister use bad words the way Choseph Macroon will always be sniffing around for towrists like a dock after pitches. . . ."

"Roderick!"

"It's chust the plain truth, wife, I'm after telling you."

"Too plain indeed."

"And that's why I'm after saying it would be fine if a Verb Sap would be seen off Great Todday. That would be putting the noses of these tam seals out of their joints."

---

* 'But hark! What is that melodious moaning we hear in the west? It is the singing of the seals on Poppay and Pillay, the twin small isles that guard the extremities of Little Todday, their fantastic shapes standing out dark against the blood-stained western sky. Would that the present scribe possessed the musical genius of Mrs Kennedy Fraser that he might set down in due notation their melodious moanings.'
Faerie Lands Forlorn, by Hector Hamish Mackay.

Chapter 2

BEN NEVIS INVESTIGATES

MANY an anxious eye was turned towards the waters of Loch Ness during the weeks that followed Kenneth MacLennan's remarkable adventure, but not even the ebullient optimism of Ben Nevis was able to imagine that the monster had been seen again. The head stalker himself, a tall lean man with dark hair now grizzled, a big aquiline nose and a headland of a chin, never wavered in his account of what had happened on that March day.

"I haven't the slightest doubt you saw the monster, MacLennan," the Chieftain assured him when he and the Laird of Cloy paid the head stalker a visit in his little house, soon after the event which had roused an interest unequalled since the monster appeared about ten years before the outbreak of the Second World War, and seemed likely to make it a better public-relations officer for Inverness than ever.

"Yes, I'm sure you saw the monster," the Chieftain went on fervidly, "but this flying saucer . . ."

"It was more like a spout, Ben Nevis," the stalker put in.

"Well, flying teapot, spout, or whatever it was," the Chieftain barked, "I think you were so excited at seeing the monster—and I don't blame you, I've seen it twelve times now, but I'm just as excited as I was when Johnnie Macpherson, my driver, heard me see it the first time—yes, I think you were so excited that when the sun suddenly came out over those beastly deodars planted by these Forestry nincompoops on the other side of the loch you thought it was a flying teacup. I mean, all this flying crockery has been worked up by the papers. That's why these Communist fellows are always dodging behind the Iron Curtain into Russia."

"I don't quite get that one, Donald," said Sir Hubert Bottley, looking more than usually plump and florid between the eagle countenances of Ben Nevis and Coinneach Mór. "Are they trying to dodge the flying saucers?"

The Chieftain guffawed genially.

"No, what I mean is everybody's paying so much

attention to these flying saucers that they get away with those atom bomb secrets. Suppose you and I, Bertie, had gone off on the scent of flying saucers when the war was on? We should have made even bigger fools of ourselves than all those Military Permit Office nincompoops."

"I didn't believe there was a monster in Loch Ness till I saw him with my own eyes, Ben Nevis," MacLennan affirmed gravely. "And I didn't believe in those flying saucers till I saw one with my own eyes."

"You're a bit of a Doubting Thomas, what?" Mac 'ic Eachainn woofed.

"I can only mind one peculiar thing like that happening to me before," said MacLennan. "Did I ever tell you the story of the fox that carried off my deerstalker cap, Sir Hubert?"

"No, you never told me that one, Coinneach."

"Well, it was when I went as an obligement for a couple of seasons to Sir Simon Mackenzie of Battledore over in Wester Ross."

"I never knew you were ever with old Battledore, Mac-Lennan," the Chieftain put in. "Grand old boy! We don't produce them like that to-day."

"Och, I wouldn't be saying that, Ben Nevis," said Coinneach Mór with the faintest hint of an approving smile upon his lean, stern countenance.

"Ah, I'm afraid you're a bit of a flatterer, MacLennan," said Ben Nevis, who was nevertheless obviously pleased by the compliment. "But I interrupted your story."

"Well, one day in October when the wind was blowing hard from the west I was out on the braes of Meall Oona and I lifted my gun to a fox that was moving quickly through the heather about fifty yards below, but just as I fired the wind got into the deerstalker cap I was wearing and carried it away down the brae."

"Like a flying saucer, what?" the Chieftain guffawed.

"Well, I missed my bold fox," MacLennan continued. "And what's more I missed my cap, for when I went down to look for it it was nowhere to be seen. It had just clean vanished away. I was a bit annoyed because I was pretty fond of that cap. Well, the winter passed away and when it came to spring I was walking again on the braes of Meall Oona and I saw a fox again slinking along the way they will. I thought he was carrying a rabbit in his mouth, and this time I got my bold fellow. But what do you think he was really carrying in his mouth?"

"Your deerstalker, I suppose," the Chieftain woofed.

"Ay, it was my deerstalker right enough, Ben Nevis."

"It was? Extraordinary!"

"And what do you think I found in my cap? Ten eggs he must have stolen from the chicken-runs at Battledore House."

"Good lord!" Ben Nevis ejaculated.

"Ay, he'd been using my cap as a basket to carry eggs to his cubs. Did you ever hear the like of that before?"

"No, I never did. Of course when Hugh Cameron of Kilwhillie and I went out to India—you remember, Bertie, when Hugh and I went out to India after my boy Hector's Colonel got worried about that woman he was getting mixed up with in Tallulaghabad?"

"I do indeed," said Bottley.

"Well, we saw some pretty extraordinary things then. I mean to say I saw a fellow put a mango-stone—you know what a mango is, MacLennan?"

"I don't believe I do, Ben Nevis."

"Well, it's a kind of a cross between a large plum and a small pumpkin, if you know what I mean. Well, this mango wallah planted the stone and about ten minutes later it had grown into a great bush. I always remember it, Bertie, because it's about the only time I ever heard Hugh Cameron make a joke. He said 'what a pity we can't take this fellow home to teach the Forestry Commission how to grow trees.' Oh yes, the older I grow the more I realise the truth of what my chaplain, old Mr Fletcher, said when some duffer was arguing that the monster didn't exist. 'There are more things in heaven and on earth, Antonio, than are dreamed by your philosophers.' I thought that was very good. It comes in old Shakespeare's play *Macbeth*."

"Yet you're not believing I saw this flying saucer, Ben Nevis," Kenneth MacLennan pointed out.

"By Jove, you've rather got me there. I say, he's rather got me there, hasn't he, Bertie? Well, I believe you saw this flying teacup or saucer or whatever it was, MacLennan. But I don't believe it hit the monster. I will not believe that."

"But the monster hasn't been seen since," Bottley reminded the Chieftain.

"It's lain up like this before. After all I've only seen it twelve times in the last fifteen years or so. That fellah What's His Name may be right. It's probably mating. The spring's the time for that."

"Not for stags, Ben Nevis," the stalker put in.

"By Jove, if the monster started rutting next October that would put the cat among the pigeons, what? But I hope this fellah What's His Name doesn't go putting ideas into the heads of these islanders that the monster is going to pay them a visit. I didn't like what he said about the possibility of the remaining monster going to search for a mate in the Minch. I took strong exception to that. These islanders would steal anything. They're quite capable of stealing our monster."

In spite of his firm declaration of confidence in the monster's survival Ben Nevis was worried by his inability to shake Kenneth MacLennan's account of the flying saucer. He could no longer comfort himself with the explanation that Bertie Bottley's head stalker had mistaken the sun for a flying saucer, and therefore he had to face up to the depressing possibility of the monster's death. Hector Hamish Mackay's belief in the existence of two monsters was no consolation when accompanied by the theory that the bereaved survivor, widow or widower, would go gallivanting off to the Atlantic Ocean in search of a mate. The Chieftain decided to look in at Tummie House on his way back to Glenbogle; he felt that an argument with Colonel Lindsay-Wolseley would restore his spirits.

"We'll call at Tummie on our way home, Johnnie," he told his driver. "And don't drive too fast up that ghastly road to the house."

Johnnie Macpherson looked at the Chieftain compassionately.

"You're getting pretty old, right enough, Ben Nevis," he observed.

"Getting old? What do you mean, Johnnie? If you're as active as I am when you're seventy, you'll do well."

"You're getting nervous, Ben Nevis," Johnnie Macpherson explained imperturbably.

"Nervous? I never heard such a peprosterous statement in my life. Just because they've kept me off the Roads Committee for over thirty years our roads in Inverness-shire are the worst in the Highlands."

"They're worse in Ross-shire and in Sutherland, too, what roads there are," Johnnie Macpherson argued. "And this is a pretty good road we're on now."

"That's because it didn't come out of the rates. It was a Government grant. But because it's a good road there's no reason to go scorching along it at forty miles an hour. If the monster saw us he'd think we were another flying saucer. I made the greatest mistake in my life, Johnnie, when I let you persuade me to get rid of the old Daimler and buy this beastly new stream-lined contraption. One of these days I shall bump my head so hard when I'm getting into it that I'll get really angry."

"You're always so impatient, Ben Nevis."

"So would you be impatient if you were as big as me and had to squeeze in and out like a cork in a bottle."

Presently they came to the turning off to Tummie and after a winding climb safely reached the gates of Tummie House, a cosy Victorian residence nestling among trees with a fine view of the country on both sides of the loch.

"Well, this is a pleasure, Ben Nevis," said Mrs Lindsay-Wolseley, her round jolly face beaming.

"I thought Wolseley would like to hear about a talk I've just had with Bertie Bottley's head stalker."

The Colonel came in at that moment.

"So you've been talking to MacLennan, Ben Nevis? I must say I am surprised to find a solid chap like MacLennan spreading such a fairy tale."

"Fairy tale?" Mac 'ic Eachainn gasped, incapable for the moment of further speech.

"I must say I'm often reminded up here of India in the old days. You used to hear the same sort of fantastic story going round on the Frontier."

"Are you seriously trying to tell me, Wolseley, that you doubt MacLennan's story?"

"I certainly do."

"In other words that he invented it?"

"I don't think it was deliberate invention. I think he saw something and that a lively imagination did the rest."

"Look here, Lindsay-Wolseley. You and I have known each other quite a few years now, and we've occasionally had our little differences—I won't go into them now—but for you to sit there and tell me that MacLennan has been pulling my leg is really a bit too much."

Mrs Lindsay-Wolseley began to laugh; she was one of those happy wives who enjoy masculine absurdity, and she did not feel that her husband needed from her a display of prickly defensive conjugality.

"I didn't say MacLennan was pulling your leg, Ben Nevis," the Colonel insisted. "I said that MacLennan was deceived by his own lively imagination. You and I had it out the other day about imagination when you fancied that clutch of otters I've been watching for a month was the monster."

"And you mean to tell me MacLennan thought that the animal he saw attacked by a flying saucer was an otter? If that's what's happened to his eyesight, the sooner Bertie Bottley gets another stalker the better. He'll find himself being dragged about all over Cloy to stalk an earwig which MacLennan fancied was a royal. And what about this flying saucer? I suppose you'll tell me that was a midge which got in his eye?"

"I understood from that interview with you in the *Daily Tale* that you yourself didn't accept the flying saucer. I thought you believed the sun had got into his eye," the Colonel said.

"That was before I'd had an opportunity of going into the matter with MacLennan. The only thing I don't believe is that this infernal flying thing hit the monster."

"Oh, I agree with you there, Ben Nevis," the Colonel chuckled.

"Alec, Alec," Mrs Lindsay-Wolseley murmured.

"Let him go on, Mrs Wolseley," the Chieftain said loftily. "I'm merely sorry for him. Some people can disbelieve anything. Look at poor old Chamberlain, he didn't believe that Hitler was out for our blood. You'd have thought a fellow would hesitate before he told a fellow who'd seen the monster twelve times that it was an optical delusion. Look here, Lindsay-Wolseley, suppose I told you that those otters you've been goggling at were an optical delusion. You'd have a right to feel pretty annoyed, wouldn't you?"

"There's a difference between an otter and a prehistoric monster, Ben Nevis."

"Yes, there's a difference of anything up to eighty or ninety feet of solid flesh, which makes it much easier to have an optical delusion about an otter than about the monster.

In fact, you may have seen the monster yourself without realising it."

"Ninety feet of solid flesh?" the Colonel queried.

"You may have seen the monster's humps and thought they were a clutch of otters."

"It's usually the other way round," the Colonel commented drily.

"It's hopeless to argue with Lindsay-Wolseley when he's in one of these moods," Ben Nevis declared, turning to the Colonel's wife. "For him black's white and there's an end to it."

"Well, let's leave the monster out of it," said the Colonel. "You haven't seen a flying saucer yet, have you?"

"I don't want to see one," Ben Nevis replied.

"But you believe that people have seen them?"

"I do now since my crack with MacLennan and Bertie Bottley this afternoon."

"And what do you think is the explanation of them?"

"I think it's probably some Communist plot to stir up trouble. I think these Bolshies of ours are trying to pretend that their friends the Russians have got a secret weapon if you know what I mean. You're Convener of the Police Committee on the Council, Lindsay-Wolseley. I think you ought to put your bloodhounds on the trail, what? Not that I think they'll discover anything. Not one of your observant county police has managed to see the monster yet. And then you expect them to catch salmon-poachers and deer stealers and Communists letting off flying saucers. It would be laughable if we weren't always having to fork out money for the police which ought to be spent on roads."

"Well, if Hector Hamish Mackay is correct—good writer that chap, it's a pity he never came out to India—well, as I was saying, if his theory is correct we shall be hearing of the monster in the Islands presently. Is that why you voted against a lobster-pool for Little Todday?"

"What's a lobster-pool got to do with the monster?"

"It would make a good nesting-place, wouldn't it?"

"Alec, Alec, don't be so naughty," Mrs Lindsay-Wolseley put in. "Don't pay any attention to him, Ben Nevis."

"My dear Mrs Wolseley, if I'd paid attention to Lindsay-Wolseley all these years I wouldn't have driven those hikers out of Glenbogle; I wouldn't have rescued that boot of ours from that fellow Waggett; and we'd still have that beetroot-headed ninny Constable MacGillivray mooning about in my country."

"Sergeant MacGillivray," said the Colonel sharply. "He was promoted."

"He's no longer mooning round at Kenspeckle, thank goodness," said Ben Nevis.

"You lost a good man when Sergeant MacGillivray went to Snorvig."

"That's your opinion, Wolseley. You only saw Mac-Gillivray in his police-station, filling up forms and all that sort of time-wasting fiddle-faddle. You didn't see him puffing up Glenbogle on that idiotic bicycle of his. So he's gone to Snorvig, has he?"

"Where he is much happier than he was at Kenspeckle."

"Well, as he never had the gumption to see the monster in Loch Ness he's not likely to see it in the Toddays," the Chieftain guffawed, as he supposed, sarcastically.

There is no doubt that in spite of the apparent confidence of that last remark Donald MacDonald, Twenty-third of Ben Nevis, was worried about the monster's future. If Hector Hamish Mackay was right in believing that there were two monsters and if Kenneth MacLennan was right in believing that one of them had been destroyed by a flying saucer, the possibility of the survivor's quitting the scene of its bereavement could not be ruled out.

"By Jove, what a duffer I am!" the Chieftain bellowed suddenly as the car turned out of the narrow winding road up to Tummie to reach the main road beside the loch. The loudness of the sudden bellow caused even the cool-headed, calm-handed Johnnie Macpherson to swerve slightly.

"Ach, I wish you wouldn't be giving a great shout like that, Ben Nevis, after sitting so quiet. I might have put the car into the loch and started another big nonsense in the papers."

"I'm always warning you, Johnnie, not to drive so fast in this wretched new drainpipe of a car I was badgered into buying."

"It sounds louder when you shout in this car than it used to in the old Daimler right enough, Ben Nevis."

"Well, I suddenly remembered something."

"I never heard any man's memory going off with a bang

like yours will," grumbled Johnnie Macpherson, who was still feeling ruffled by the swerve.

"I suddenly remembered about my ancestor Hector MacDonald, the First of Ben Nevis. You know how he was pursued by two water-horses from sunrise to sunset all over Glenbogle and the country round and how he killed them both at sunset with a claymore he found stuck in a granite boulder."

"Och, ay, Ben Nevis," Johnnie Macpherson replied with a touch of impatience. "And about the fairy woman who appeared and handed him over all the land inside the line along which the *eich uisge* chased him. Och, it's a *sgeulachd* you'll be hearing from any of them at a *céilidh*."

"Well, what does the story prove?"

"I wouldn't be knowing, Ben Nevis."

"It proves that once upon a time there were water-horses living in Loch Hoch or Loch Hoo—Loch Hoo more probably, and you mark my words, Johnnie, if the monster leaves Loch Ness it's much more likely to go to Loch Hoo than out to the Islands."

"My goodness, I'd like to see the Minister's face if he met it on the Strathdiddle road," said Johnnie Macpherson with a chuckle.

The Chieftain guffawed with relish. The Reverend Alexander Munro, the Minister of the United Free Church of Strathdiddle and Strathdun, was not a favourite of his.

"I'm afraid that won't happen, Johnnie; I don't expect the monster to go overland to Loch Hoo. No, my notion is that there may be a subterranean passage between Loch Hoch or Loch Hoo and Loch Ness. I must tell Major MacIsaac to warn all my people up there not to get scared if they see the monster."

And as soon as the Chieftain reached Glenbogle Castle he told Toker, his butler, to telephone for the Chamberlain to come and see him.

"I'm expecting to hear that the monster has been seen in Loch Hoo, Toker."

"Indeed, sir? That will certainly be stirring news for the B.B.C."

"I'm not going to have any of this wireless nonsense up here, Toker."

"I was referring to Mr Stuart Hibberd's announcement of it in the Six o'clock News, sir."

"You know I never listen to this wireless nonsense. I can't stand all this mouthing about in a box with everybody sitting round gaping like a lot of ninnies."

The butler withdrew to summon Major Norman MacIsaac, whose air of gentle melancholy and strong resemblance to the White Knight were in marked contrast to the boisterous energy of the Chieftain he served.

"Ah, there you are, MacIsaac. I've been going very carefully into this flying saucer business, and it looks to me as if the monster has almost certainly left Loch Ness."

The Chamberlain blinked.

"And I feel as certain as one can feel about anything while this Bolshie Government of ours is still in power that we shall soon be hearing of its being seen in Loch Hoo."

This time Major MacIsaac seemed to jib like an old dapple-grey horse at some strange object in its path.

"But why in Loch Hoo, Ben Nevis?"

"Because there's a subterranean passage between Loch Hoo and Loch Ness."

"But Loch Hoo is at least a thousand feet higher than Loch Ness."

"Well, what of it? I suppose a subterranean passage can go uphill, can't it?"

"But how could the water remain in Loch Hoo if there's a sort of great drain-pipe running down from it into Loch Ness?"

"The answer to that is that it does. You get more argumentative every year, MacIsaac. I suppose it comes from people always asking you to do some repairs the Estate can't afford. But I wish you wouldn't always argue with me. Especially when there's nothing to argue about. Anyway, never mind how the water stays in Loch Hoo. This fellow Epstein has upset all our old-fashioned notions about gravity. What I've asked you to come round and see me about is warning the people up in Strathdiddle. And in Strathdun too, because there's an off chance that the monster may go to Loch Hoch. I don't want any humbug from the Minister. If the people see the monster on a Sunday let them see it on a Sunday. I will not have the Reverend Mr Munro laying off about it in the pulpit. But that's by the way. The point is I don't want to hear a lot of old wives' tales about sheep being carried off and chickens and children and all that sort of thing. Make it clear that the monster is not carn . . .

well, you know what I mean. It grazes like a cow on weeds
under water."

"I wish cows would graze on weeds above water," the
Chamberlain sighed gently. "If we could persuade cows to
graze on ragwort and bracken the Highlands would be
rich."

"There you go, arguing again. The point is whatever the
monster eats it isn't carn . . . well, you know what I
mean."

"Don't you think, Ben Nevis, it would be better to wait
until somebody reports that the monster has been seen in
Loch Hoo?"

"No, I don't, MacIsaac. You know it has always been
my policy to take my people into my confidence. Look at
that hiker business. As soon as I told them I wanted nobody
to give refreshments to hikers nobody did except a few of
these Bolshies you get everywhere to-day. Thank God, the
old clan spirit is not dead in my country. Even Lindsay-
Wolseley recognises that, though he has some dunder-
headed idea that the monster is an otter. Even his wife had
to pull him up over that this afternoon."

"Are we to expect flying saucers in Glenbogle?" the
Chamberlain enquired gently.

"I suppose you want to argue now that we ought to have
a lightning-conductor on the Raven's Tower. I will not
spoil it with one of these beastly modern contraptions."

"I wasn't thinking about lightning-conductors, Ben
Nevis. I was merely asking you a question."

"Just for the pleasure of hearing me say 'I don't know,'
I suppose?"

The Chieftain rang the bell.

"Major MacIsaac will take a dram, Toker."

And when the decanter of Glenbogle's Pride was brought
the Chieftain poured a hefty dram for himself and for his
Chamberlain.

"Slahnjervaw, MacIsaac," he said before he drained the
glass. "And slahnjervaw to the monster."

"*Slàinte mhór*," Major MacIsaac echoed.

"It's an extraordinary thing, you know, when you come
to think about it, that after eight hundred years a water-
horse should come back to Glenbogle. History repeats itself,
they say. Well, there you are."

"I hope it won't chase you round the country from

sunrise to sunset," said the Chamberlain, venturing upon a mild joke after that hefty dram.

The Chieftain guffawed genially.

"No, they're not carn . . . what the devil is that word, MacIsaac?"

"Carnivorous."

"No, no, they're not carnivorous nowadays. Carnivorous, carnivorous," Mac 'ic Eachainn murmured as he poured himself out another hefty dram.

Chapter 3

WAGGETT IS SCEPTICAL

ABOUT a month after Ben Nevis had established to his own satisfaction the probability of the monster's having quitted the dangerous area of Loch Ness for the comparatively protected water of Loch Hoo, Paul Waggett was sitting in his den at Snorvig House, reading the letters which his wife had just brought back from the post office after the arrival of the *Island Queen*. The war, with all the responsibilities it had brought him as commander of the Home Guard Company of the islands of Great and Little Todday, had aged him slightly. However, he liked to think that every grey hair on his head was a veteran of active service and that none of them was a dull product of the humdrum war of attrition conducted by time against middle-age. If there certainly were a few more grey hairs the pink of his complexion had been preserved by the moist westerly air, and if his name had been, to him unaccountably, forgotten in the awards of the Order of the British Empire, his face and head were now a noble representation of its ribbon. His devotion to exercise and dislike of lolling about reading in a chair had preserved his figure. His light-grey eyes were still able to light up under the influence of curiosity, greed, cocksureness and sporting concentration. He was in fact at fifty-eight to all intents the same Paul Waggett who had decided thirteen years ago to abandon chartered accountancy in London for the life of a Highland sportsman.

Mrs Waggett, who was ten years younger than her husband, had also worn well. How far the help of peroxide had been called upon to preserve the fair fluffiness of her hair we need not enquire. The roses of her youthful complexion had been pot-pourri for so long now that the only change noticeable since the great days of 1940 was in the appearance on her small nose of one or two little purplish veins like the streaks upon a chaffinch's egg.

Paddy, the outsize Irish setter, had gone on to the canine Valhalla soon after the wreck of the *Cabinet Minister*, and his place had been taken by a Golden Labrador retriever called Monty in honour of the military commander in

whom Paul Waggett believed he could discern the closest
mental kinship to himself of any general of the Second
World War.

"Most extraordinary," he used to murmur reverently,
his sharp slightly upturned nose seeming to sniff out a
mystery of transcendental tactics. "Monty always does
exactly what I think to myself I would do if I were in his
place. Most extraordinary!"

And when the golden tail of the retriever thumped the
floor to acknowledge the mention of his name Paul Waggett
would fancy that Field-Marshal Montgomery himself was
acknowledging the endorsement of his tactics by an unknown master.

On this fine afternoon at the end of April Paul Waggett
was inclined to feel a faint sentimental regret for the great
days of war. His post was lacking in interest, and the prospect of not being able to shoot a bird for nearly four months
did not please him. He recognized the necessity of a close
season during the time of breeding, but he could not
help wishing that birds would stagger the business. If he
had read *Locksley Hall* he would have wished that the
wanton lapwing would get himself another crest in autumn
when grouse and snipe and woodcock were available for
killing, so that he would be able to kill plovers in the
spring.

"Of course, the war was a heavy strain on me, Dolly,"
he said to his wife, "but I can't help feeling it was a mistake
to disband the Home Guard. I should have been perfectly
willing to carry on here."

"Yes, dear, I'm sure you would," Mrs Waggett agreed.
"But I rather doubt if you would have had proper support
from the people. Look when you tried to start badminton
in the Snorvig hall. Nobody turned up after the first few
evenings."

"And the children were allowed to use the shuttlecocks
for toy boats," Waggett added on a note of disillusioned
reminiscence. "Oh, I know the people here have no idea of
the importance of games apart from progressive whist.
Still, if the Home Guard hadn't been disbanded I should
have been able to set an example."

"You always do that, Paul."

"I try to in my own humble way," her husband sighed,
the expression of complacency on his countenance not quite

B

in keeping with the modesty of the statement. "But don't worry, old lady. It's only just over three months to the Twelfth, isn't it, Monty?"

The dog confirmed with an assenting tail his master's calculation.

"And since Norman Macleod left Watasett for a school on the mainland there have definitely been more grouse. Definitely."

"I hear Catriona Campbell is going to have another baby."

This was the sister of Norman Macleod and wife of the schoolmaster at Garryboo, the crofting township for which Roderick MacRurie had secured a pier at the last Council meeting.

"It's all that people seem to think about nowadays," Waggett observed severely. "The chicks are very late," he added. "Hadn't the Biffer got back from Kiltod when the boat came in?"

The chicks were Muriel and Elsie, the twin daughters of the house, who since their demobilisation from the Waafs had been at home and from time to time the subject of parental debates about their matrimonial future. Their father, who admired in their blondine fluffiness what he had once admired in their mother, had been surprised that neither of them had won the heart and hand of an officer in the R.A.F. His inability to understand the young men of to-day became one of his favourite remarks.

"You know what a chatterbox Archie· MacRurie is," Mrs Waggett reminded her husband. "And the chicks themselves intended to pay quite a round of visits on Little Todday."

"I hope the chicks will bring back some eggs."

This was a family joke at which Mrs Waggett tittered dutifully; she had hardly finished when the door of the den opened with such an unwonted burst that Monty leapt to his feet and started to bark wildly.

"Lie down, sir. Lie down at once," his master snapped, all the old crisp force of military authority crackling again in his voice.

The golden labrador was so much abashed that he turned to lie down with eyes averted from his master's displeasure and in doing so knocked over the small table that held the two or three dull letters of the post.

"Chicks, chicks," their mother reproached them. "You know Daddo doesn't like us to rush into his den."

"Daddo! Mumsy!" the two young women exclaimed. "A monster came up in the sea off Pillay this afternoon!"

"With a head like a hornless bull," cried Muriel, who was dressed in smoky-blue tweed.

"And it snarled at him," added Elsie, who was also dressed in smoky-blue tweed.

The twin sisters were if possible even more alike now in their mid-twenties than they had been as little girls, and when they wore similar clothes they were indistinguishable.

"Rubbish!" their father exclaimed. "Didn't I tell you when that idiotic story came out in the *Daily Tale* some weeks ago that it was nothing but a press stunt."

"But this wasn't in the paper, Daddo," Muriel pointed out. "It was Kenny Macroon who saw it. He was setting lobster-pots round the Gobha."

Paul Waggett frowned. That dark rock between the tiny isle of Pillay and Little Todday had wrecked the *Cabinet Minister* and had therefore been responsible for the deplorable behaviour of the islanders over the ship's cargo of whisky. He thoroughly disapproved of the Gobha and was in no mood to tolerate its reappearance in the news as the haunt of a monster.

"The sooner Joseph Macroon gets that idle young rascal of his into a decent job the better," he observed censoriously. "Even if lobsters are fetching a fantastic price it's demoralizing for a young man to spend his day messing about for an hour or two every day with lobster-pots and loafing away the rest of his time."

"But, Daddo," Muriel insisted, "I'm sure Kenny thought he saw a monster. We were at the post office in Kiltod when he arrived with the news and his eyes were starting out of his head."

"You can take it from me, Muriel, that his father put him up to it. Big Roderick was saying to me only the other day he was sure Joseph would be putting it round that the Loch Ness Monster had come out to the Islands just to pay out the Inverness County Council for turning down his lobster-pool. Hornless bull, did you say?"

"Oh, but much bigger than any ordinary bull," Elsie replied.

"There's a perfectly simple explanation," her father

said. "As indeed there always is for everything," he added loftily. "If Kenny Macroon saw anything, which I doubt, he saw a Polled Angus which had been drowned crossing the ford from Mid Uist to Pendicula. The Department of Agriculture sent a Polled Angus bull to Nobost last year. You may remember when they sent one here and I gave them a lesson by importing a Hereford at my own expense because I consider the Polled Angus is a ridiculous animal for the Islands."

"But Kenny said the head of this monster was much, much bigger than a bull's," Muriel insisted.

"Of course," her father commented, tossing his nose scornfully. "We all know that a drowned animal swells up."

"But it snarled at Kenny," said Elsie.

"Gases," Paul Waggett declared in the tone of Goethe replying to one of Eckermann's more foolish questions.

"Oh, yes, and I forgot," Muriel put in, "it had a mane."

Paul Waggett regarded his daughter compassionately.

"There is such a thing as sea-weed, chick," he reminded her with a kindly smile. "Well, did you bring back Mumsy any eggs?"

The twins looked at one another in consternation. "We left the basket in the post office at Kiltod," one of them gasped.

Paul Waggett shook his head sadly.

"It's an extraordinary thing that you were both able to look after a barrage balloon in the war and now you don't seem able to look after a basket of eggs."

"Well, everybody was frightfully excited, Daddo," Muriel urged in excuse.

"There was a certain amount of excitement during the war as I remember," her father observed. "That wouldn't have been accepted as an excuse for letting your barrage balloon float away from Birmingham."

"It couldn't have done that unless we'd cut it loose," Muriel pointed out.

Paul Waggett knitted his brows in what he believed was an expression of disillusioned paternity.

"You never used to argue with me like this once upon a time," he murmured, and bending over he sought from Monty's golden coat the warmth of responsive uncritical admiration he had once never failed to find in his little daughters. "Did they, old pal?" he asked with a sigh. The dog sighed a profoundly sympathetic response, rejoicing in his master's pats.

Up in their own room, the three gable windows of which looked out over the roofs of Snorvig across the Coolish to the green island of Little Todday, the twins discussed what they decided was the pre-war attitude of their father to life in general and the monster sighted by Kenny Macroon in particular.

"You know, Elsie, it's a most frightful thing to say, but I think Daddo is getting old."

"Well, of course he *is* fifty-eight."

The twins shook their fluffy heads.

"You don't think he is going gaga, do you?" Muriel asked apprehensively.

"No, I don't think he is actually going gaga," said Muriel in a brave attempt to be optimistic. "But I think he's got into a rut."

"And Mumsy too," her sister added.

"Yes, they're both in it," Muriel agreed. "I mean to say, it was stupid of us to leave the eggs over in Kiltod, but Daddo did talk rot about barrage balloons."

The twins gazed at one another, like two boys who have just cracked a plate-glass window with a catapult: never had either of them in her most intimate self-censoring ventured to whisper such a word about her father's opinions, let alone utter it aloud. Both were sharply aware of the impiety and in a spasm of remorse tried to re-establish their father on that pedestal where they had worshipped him all their lives as an infallible being, and no doubt would have continued to do so if the Second World War had not cast its dark shadow upon domestic life.

"Perhaps it really was a dead bull that Kenny saw," Elsie suggested.

"Yes, perhaps it was," her twin concurred.

"And Daddo does know a good deal about bulls," Elsie went on, "even if he doesn't know very much about balloons."

"But of course he never had a chance to see a barrage balloon in action because he was indispensable here," Muriel said in reproach of her own impatience over her father's ignorance.

Downstairs in the den Paul Waggett, without touching the tragic heights of King Lear on the subject of undutiful daughters, was impressing his wife with the shock it had been to his paternal affection when Muriel had almost accused him of not understanding the principles underlying the duty of its crew toward a barrage balloon.

"I was quite staggered for a moment, Dolly."

"I'm sure you were, dear," she murmured soothingly.

"Of course it's all this growth of Communism. Even the chicks have come under its poisonous influence."

"Paul, you don't really think that, do you?" his wife exclaimed.

"I'm afraid I do, Dolly," he sighed. "It's the same kind of spirit in the chicks as made a lot of silly young people go and vote against Churchill at the election."

Suddenly his face was rapt with self-esteem, his light-grey eyes were twinkling.

Mrs Waggett knew the signal: her husband was going to make a joke. She waited for it, her whole mind concentrated upon not missing the point when it came. She had managed to do that once or twice even when she had been warned of a joke's approach, and Paul never forgot to remind her of these failures.

"Yes, I'm afraid, Dolly, our chicks are Rhode Island Reds," he said, the words bubbling in his mouth with amusement at his own wit.

It cost Mrs Waggett something of an effort to laugh as heartily as was expected of her. She could not see anything funny in comparing the twins to hens. And why Rhode Island Reds? If Paul must compare them to hens, why not Light Sussex, the effect of whose plumage was much more like the colour of their hair? However, she laughed away as earnestly as a studio audience at a comic turn on the radio, and Paul was luckily so much amused by his own joke that he did not notice anything at all forced about her laughter.

"Still, it's nothing to joke about," he said, becoming abruptly serious. "It's what keeps me from letting them go and stay as paying guests with your sister Gladys at Norwood, which from another point of view might be a good thing."

"You mean they don't meet enough young men in the Islands?" the mother asked.

For one mad exquisite moment a vision of them all moving from the Outer Isles to one of the Outer Suburbs of

London glowed in Mrs Waggett's imagination, but she did not venture to tell this bright dream to her husband.

"Of course, Tom Gorringe himself is quite sound."

"And so is Gladys," Mrs Waggett insisted eagerly. "Don't you remember you thought they wouldn't give her a military permit to come here because she used to attend meetings of the British Union of Fascists before the war? And I can't imagine anybody less Communist than Tom and Gladys."

Paul Waggett smiled indulgently.

"If we send the chicks to Norwood to give them a chance to meet some young men, they can't spend all their time with Tom and Gladys," he pointed out. "No, I'm afraid they'll have to put up with the old folks at home. Yes, I'm afraid so, old lady," he wound up, and on his countenance was an expression of impregnable self-sufficiency which might have annoyed some people but to his wife was reassuring. "Well, I think I'll take a stroll along to the hotel and hear what they're saying there about this nonsensical tale from Little Todday."

It was not Paul Waggett's habit to frequent the bar of the Snorvig Hotel when it was full of customers. He preferred a cosy chat with Roderick MacRurie in his own snug parlour when the bar was closed. However, he felt it was his duty to lose no time in casting doubt upon the story which his daughters had brought back from Kiltod.

"Good evening, Archie," he said to a crofter, something under sixty years old, with a nose and chin on him like a lobster's claw and a fierce red complexion. This was the Biffer whose little boat the *Kittiwake* was a feature of the rocky coast of Great Todday. Archie MacRurie was talking to a brawny fisherman, whose nickname, the origin of which had never been discovered, was Drooby. Neither Drooby nor the Biffer looked elated by the entrance of Paul Waggett, but the good manners of the Outer Hebrides made them greet him cordially enough.

"I suppose you've all been laughing at this nonsensical story that's been going round Little Todday?"

"What story would that be, Mr Waggett?" asked Drooby cautiously.

"Surely Archie has told you about young Kenny Macroon's encounter with a sea monster?"

"Ay, it was a pretty queer kind of an encounter too," said the Biffer quickly.

"And him in the *Morning Star* with one of the plugs choked and not able to move at all. It was after putting a great fear on him."

"Ach, it would do that right enough," said Drooby, drawing heavily on his tightly packed pipe. "The *Morning Star* is no kind of a craft at all in which to meet even a sailfish."

"Ay, one of them puggers was nearly after upsetting me once in the *Kittiwake*. Ay, they're puggers right enough."

"Well, perhaps the monster that Kenny Macroon thought he saw was one of these basking sharks, or sailfish as you call them."

"I never heard tell of a sailfish with a head on her like yon bull the Department sent to Snorvig a year or so before the war."

"Well, I suppose it is possible that young Macroon did see a drowned cow or even possibly a drowned bull," Waggett conceded. "Yes, I suppose it is just possible."

"Why would a cow be wanting to drown herself at all?" put in Angus MacCormac, a big crofter from Garryboo, with a heavy white moustache.

"I'm not suggesting the cow committed suicide," Waggett snapped impatiently. "It may have fallen over a cliff in one of the islands north."

Angus MacCormac gathered his moustache with a rugged hand and blew through it incredulously.

"I never heard tell of a cow who was after jumping off a cliff into the sea," he declared. "Sheep, yes, because sheep are so daring when the hunger is on them and the grass in a crack of the cliff is so green. Ach, not at all. It's no kind of a cow Kenny Iosaiph would be seeing."

"You don't seriously believe that it *was* a monster?" Waggett asked, almost irritably.

By now the rest of those standing at the bar were listening to the argument, and a murmur of agreement had hailed Angus MacCormac's disbelief in the cow theory.

"Does nobody mind when the *each uisge* was seen in Loch Skinny?" one of the company asked.

"Oh, please, don't let us revive that old story," protested Waggett. "The only Yak Ooshker ever seen in Loch Skinny was poaching my salmon."

"Oh, well, well, Mr Wackett," said Sammy MacCodrum, another Garryboo crofter, a little man with a high voice and a huge nose, "if you were effer seeing a salmon in Loch Skinny you were seeing something much more difficult to see there than a *each uisge*."

Now if there was one thing that really did annoy Paul Waggett it was for anybody to hint that the Skinny, the fishing of which was rented to him by the Department of Agriculture, was not a renowned if diminutive haunt of salmon.

"If everybody from Garryboo or Knockdown didn't poach, there would always be plenty of salmon in the Skinny. And they are not poached by Yak Ooshkers, let me add."

Big Roderick, the landlord, had been listening attentively to this conversation without saying a word. He was in fact making up his mind whether to segregate the monster as it were on Little Todday and disown it for Great Todday or whether, Joseph Macroon being as fly as he all too well knew him to be, it would be wiser to form an alliance and exploit the monster as an attraction to the visitors of both islands. He had not been too pleased when a film company had turned the two Toddays into one island and on top of that used the Island of Barra to supply their scenery. From what he had heard tourists had been thronging to Barra under the impression that the *Cabinet Minister* was wrecked there, when as everybody knew except these ignorant London folk it was never wrecked there at all. However, he did not think it would be tactful to mention the film in front of Mr Waggett, who had never been able to understand why his efforts to help the revenue had been regarded as a subject for laughter all over the world, by what they had been writing in the newspapers.

"I believe we would be wise to wait a while," he declared as he measured a dram for Paul Waggett and offered him the bottle of fizzy lemonade with which he liked to dilute his whisky. Waggett seldom took a dram in public and the spectacle of him drinking whisky and fizzy lemonade with apparent enjoyment could still shed an awe-struck silence over the bar of the Snorvig Hotel.

"Wait for what?" Waggett asked, putting down his glass.

"Ach, chust wait," said Big Roderick. "We would be
B *

looking pretty foolish if Kenny Iosaiph was seeing a monster right enough and we were not believing him and then we were after seeing this huge great Verb Sap ourself."

"Verb Sap?" Waggett exclaimed.

"Ay, that's the name they were giving this crayture in the *Daily Tale*," Roderick told him.

"But, my dear Roderick," Waggett protested, "Verb Sap means—well, it's short for something. I don't exactly remember what, but it's the same as 'Amen' or 'Enough said.'"

"Ay, ay, well, we won't be saying any more at all about this Verb Sap chust now. We'll chust wait," said Roderick firmly.

And round the bar of Snorvig Hotel the conversation reverted to the prospect of a dry spell for the peat-cutting which might soon be starting.

When he reached his den Paul Waggett looked for a dictionary which he knew he had somewhere; he found it at last supporting an occasional table, one of the legs of which had been broken when he had trodden on Monty's tail and the table had been knocked over by the dog suddenly roused from sleep.

"Yes, of course," he muttered to himself. Then he lifted the receiver.

"Wackett wants you on the telephone," Roderick Mac-Rurie's bar-boy informed him.

"Hullo! Is that you, Roderick? I remembered on my way up to the House that verb sap is short for verbum sapienti."

The hotel-keeper put his hand over the mouthpiece and turned to his wife.

"Och, the man's trying to say something to me in Gaelic and nobody can ever be understanding what he's trying to say. *Glé mhath, glé mhath*, Mr Wackett. You're getting on fine with the Gaelic," Roderick said with a faintly insincere enthusiasm when he addressed himself to the mouthpiece.

"Verbum sapienti is Latin not Gaelic," the instructor snapped. "It has nothing whatever to do with mythical monsters. In fact it means literally 'a word to the wise.'"

"*A Chruitheir*, what a man," Roderick grumbled to his wife. "There's nothing wise in him. Pulling me away from the bar like that to blow about the Latin and the Grik that's at him."

Chapter 4

THE TODDAY MONSTER

ANY suspicion in Roderick MacRurie's mind that his fellow councillor had staged the appearance of a monster off Little Todday in order to pay him out for his success in obtaining a pier for Garryboo at the expense of the lobster-pool for Kiltod would have been dispelled if he could have crossed the Coolish that evening and joined the company that thronged Joseph Macroon's shop to hear Kenny tell and re-tell the story of his adventure. It would have been perfectly clear that whatever it was that Kenny had seen, he was convinced that he had seen a strange monster such as nobody on Little Todday had ever seen before. Kenny himself was now a tall and lively young man of twenty-two with merry eyes, who as his father's only son was debarred from exploring the world as he would have liked to do. Joseph had the good sense not to insist on his son's being kept too close to the grindstone and he encouraged his activity over lobsters. Indeed, if the County Council had not turned down the scheme for a lobster-pool, he had intended to buy a larger boat, for the old *Morning Star* was by now growing decrepit.

After Peggy Ealasaid became Mrs Alfred Odd and went to live in Nottingham when the war was over, Joseph's youngest daughter Kate Anne looked after the post office. When she married Michael Macdonald, a son of Alan Macdonald who had one of the best crofts on the island, Kate Anne and her husband stayed on in Kiltod with Joseph. Kate Anne was small, with her father's shrewd light-blue eyes and quick movements, and he was inclined to discern in his grandson Iosaiph Og a miniature of himself which gratified him. Peggy like her mother before her had started off with two daughters—Lucy called after her husband's mother and Catherine called after her own mother.

Mrs Odd herself was away in Nottingham at the moment and not expected back just yet. She had carried out her intention of retiring to Little Todday for half the year and had bought the little house near the croft of Duncan Bàn

Macroon on the door of which was painted *Bow Bells*, though it was more generally known as Mistress Odd's House, or in Gaelic, *Tigh Mhistress Ott*.

The only noticeable addition to the buildings of Todaigh Beag since the adventures of the island in wartime was the new school at Kiltod of which Andrew Chisholm, the headmaster, generally known as the *Sgoileir Dubh* or Dark Scholar, and Joseph Macroon were equally proud, though Father James Macalister, the parish priest, always called it the Bad Egg and warned the *Sgoileir Dubh* that one day Waggett would be poaching it in revenge for the barnacle geese and plover shot by the people of Little Todday without regard to his rights as the shooting tenant of the Department of Agriculture. The licence to sell beer for consumption off the premises was not interpreted quite so strictly according to the letter of the law as it would have been if Sergeant MacGillivray had been happening to pay one of his visits to the island; but Sergeant MacGillivray was not the man to proceed suddenly anywhere and when he intended to visit Little Todday he always communicated his intention beforehand to Joseph Macroon, and therefore nobody this evening was worrying about the letter of the law. Indeed, it may be claimed that nobody on Little Todday had worried at all about the letter of the law since the seal-woman bore seven sons to that exiled son of Clan Donald and thus populated the island with Macroons in the dim past. In the dark days of the whisky drought Joseph Macroon, exasperated by his fellow councillors' obstinate opposition to a new school for Kiltod, had contemplated installing and equipping an illicit still, and the Excise may be grateful that the drought was relieved because if Joseph Macroon had decided to get busy with the black pot the source of the spirit in circulation would never have been discovered.

The thronged shop of Joseph Macroon was a cheerful sight on this fine evening at the end of April. Kenny Macroon was sitting on the counter and telling his tale afresh to everybody who came in to hear it. Old Bean Sheumais Mhiceil, the senior matriarch of the Macroons and now not far from ninety, had been sitting on a sack of potatoes in a corner for the last two hours and must have heard Kenny's story three dozen times already—but the slightest hint by her great-granddaughter Flora about going home to bed was waved away impatiently by a knotted old hand.

"*Isd thu! Bith sàmhach! Nach isd thu, a Fhlorag!* I want to be hearing about the monaster. Ach, it's me that wishes it was twenty years gone back and himself could be hearing Coinneach telling about the monaster. He would chust have been in his ellimans. There was neffer a man so liking it of a good story whateffer as your big grandfather Seumas, God rest his soul."

It is a tribute to Kenny Macroon's absolute sincerity that in spite of the temptation over many a repetition of his tale to exaggerate the size of the monster he did not add a foot to its stature. He insisted in spite of several attempts to make him compare the head he had seen emerge from the water to a horse that it was much more like that of a bull, except of course for the mane which he agreed was more equine than bovine. He was equally firm over the noise that the monster had made. It was not a groan or a sigh or a roar or a hoot or a bark or a gurgle or a hiss or even a growl: it was a snarl. It resembled the noise made by an unfriendly dog as it retreats when one stoops to pick up a stone to fling at it, but it was naturally a good deal louder than the snarl of the ordinary collie. He should estimate the size of the head that suddenly appeared out of the water as three times that of an ordinary bull, but he admitted that it gave him a terrible fright and that it may have appeared larger than in fact it was. He had been blowing through the choked plug at the time and was thankful he was not standing up, for if he had been he was sure he should have toppled back overboard.

"And no horns, *a bhalaich*?" the rich bass of Father James Macalister suddenly asked from the door of the shop where he had arrived in time to hear Kenny's account.

"No horns, Father."

"*Taing do Dhia,*" the priest devoutly bombilated. "I was afraid it was Satan himself who was taking a look at us on Todaidh Beag."

Nobody on Little Todday was ever perfectly sure whether Father James was laughing, and one or two in the audience crossed themselves in gratitude to Almighty God for having been spared a visit from the Tempter.

"And it really snarled at you, *a Choinnich*?" the priest asked.

"Yes, Father."

"Ah, well, well, I believe when the Excisemen blew up the *Cabinet Minister* and put all that good whisky in Davy Jones's locker, Davy Jones himself was warning you to keep off the grass."

"*A Dhia*, what's Maighstir Seumas after saying?" Jocky Stewart, a little sandy-haired crofter, turned to ask of Hugh Macroon whose shrewd eyes twinkled in that bald domed head of his.

"Och, he's just talking the way he always will be," said Hugh in that slow voice of his which lent an air of wisdom to his lightest remark.

But later on that evening, when Kenny Macroon had been examined and cross-examined by Father Macalister in his own cosy room at the Chapel House, the parish priest had to recognise that Kenny had seen something genuinely unusual in the water round the dark rock called the Gobha.

"And you're sure it wasn't a big seal, *a bhalaich*?"

"I've seen plenty seals, Father, but I never saw a seal like this, big or small."

"And it didn't look at you?"

"No, Father, thank God. It was down before I saw the face on it."

The priest exhaled a gusty sigh; he was puzzled.

Next day, taking advantage of the fine weather, the Biffer went off to set some pots on the other side of Ard Snor, the headland which shelters Snorvig from the fierce north-west. That evening he held the attention of the company round the bar in the Snorvig Hotel without having recourse to any of the club-bore tricks of the ancient mariner to make guests listen to him.

"I'd rounded Ard Snor on the way home and I was keeping in close to the land for a shot at a *sgarbh*, the way they'll always be sitting on Sgeir Geal in the afternoon and just as the *Kittiwake* was passing Uamh na Snaoiseanaich* my heart was after nearly dropping out of my mouth I was so scared. Ah, boys, you never saw the like of what I was seeing. A great head was staring at me out of the cave the size of a sack of barley with two eyes as big as pancakes. And the teeth on the mouth of it! *A Thighearna*, I never saw the like of such teeth on a hayrake. I was feeling all chewed up

* The Cave of the Snuff-taker, so called because every few minutes or so the sea would break inside with the effect of a great sneeze.

inside of me just to be looking at teeth like that. I tell you, boys, I just put the tiller hard to port and swung the *Kittiwake* away from the shore and prayed to the Lord to let me get away before I was swallowed up like Jonah. Boys, the sweat was pouring down me and when I got home Ealasaid was asking me where was I being because my nose was still red, but the rest of me was as white as a chalk."

"Was the crayture after making a noise when you came upon it in Uamh na Snaoiseanaich, Airchie?" somebody asked.

"Ay, I was forgetting about that. Noise, do you say? It was the queerest noise a man would be hearing at all. If you could be thinking of a cow that would be barking at you like a dog or a dog that would be bellowing at you like a cow and put the two noises in the foghorn of the *Island Queen*, you'd be having a sort of an idea what kind of a noise this crayture was after making when it was seeing me and the *Kittiwake*."

"Look at that now," said Big Roderick cheerfully. "My friend Mr Mackay was right enough when he said we'd be having one of these Verb Saps from Loch Ness out in the Islands. When we were talking yesterday I had it in my mind that Joseph Macroon had put young Kenny up to it, but not at all. Oh, well, well, they'll be feeling pretty annoyed in Inverness when they hear about the Todday Monster."

"You don't think they'll try and pay us out by doing nothing about the Garryboo pier?" asked Murdo MacCodrum, who as the only lorry owner in Garryboo was looking forward to a profitable monopoly.

"Ach, they would not do a dirty trick on me like that," the councillor protested. "You can't be playing quick and loose with a pier."

At this moment Andrew Thomson, the bank-agent, a swarthy man, so extremely shy as to seem disagreeable to those who did not know him, came into the bar. The ordeal of asking for his dram every evening still made him gulp so much that one might have supposed he was drinking it before the glass was on the counter.

"Good evening, everybody," he scowled in an effort to be affable.

"You'll have heard about the monster, Mr Thomson?" somebody asked.

"Imphm," the banker muttered.

And then overcome by the notion of having to express an opinion upon the phenomenon he swallowed his dram, turned on his heels, and walked out of the bar in a dusky blush.

"I wonder what will he be saying about it to the *Obaig Chimes*," somebody speculated, for it was generally believed in Snorvig that the occasional items of news about Great and Little Todday communicated to the *Obaig Chimes* emanated from Andrew Thomson. In fact it was Mrs Thomson who supplied news of great events in the two islands like sales of work and progressive whist drives.

"Ach, we've something much too high for the *Obaig Chimes*," Roderick MacRurie declared. "I believe I'll send a telegraph to that fellow in Glasgow who was here last summer and wrote a big piece about the road to the isles in the *Daily Tale*. He enjoyed himself fine at the hotel. What was his name? Ian . . . Ian . . . Ian Carmichael. Ay, that's it . . . Ian Carmichael."

Big Roderick did not add that his brother Donald, the postmaster of Snorvig, had let him know of a telegram sent off by Joseph Macroon to the same Ian Carmichael this very morning. It would not do for the people of Todaidh Mór to think that Todaidh Beag was responsible for interesting the press.

"We've had a follow-up to that telegram yesterday from Little Todday, Mr Donaldson," said Ian Carmichael to the Editor of the *Scottish Daily Tale*, and as he said this he could not resist glancing at the strip of blue sky just visible above the ravine of high grimy Glasgow buildings in which the offices of the newspaper were situated. "Look at this."

James Donaldson read the two telegrams on his big desk:

Advise investigation of huge strange creature seen by Kenneth Macroon yesterday in water near Gobha rock on which steamship Cabinet Minister was wrecked during war Little Todday believes forecast of Daily Tale that Loch Ness Monster would take refuge from flying saucepans is all correct and that monster has duly arrived in good order

Joseph Macroon
Merchant
Kiltod
Little Todday
Outer Isles
by Obaig

This afternoon enormous verb sap monster was seen looking out of cave below Ard Snor on Great Todday by Archie MacRurie crofter fisherman highly reliable and respected member of community verb sap in question showed signs of very terrible ferocity but Archie MacRurie was able to escape in his boat and tell the tale of the Lord's great mercy to him we have reports that a verb sap was seen between Pillay and Little Todday previous day which is now believed true in Snorvig suggest immediate investigation of this strange occurrence happy to reserve rooms for you in hotel on notification of your possible time of arrival

Roderick MacRurie
Snorvig Hotel
Great Todday
Outer Isles

"What on earth's he mean by a verb sap?" the Editor asked.

"I couldn't make out at first, Mr Donaldson," chuckled Carmichael, a fresh-complexioned, rather good-looking young man. "Then I turned back to our files for March and I think our friend Roderick hasn't quite understood what Hector Hamish Mackay meant by verb sap."

"It's a silly out-of-date expression anyway," said the Editor severely. "I don't know why the sub didn't take it out. I suppose you think you are ear-marked for this investigation?"

"Well, I know the people there, Mr Donaldson. I mean to say I could get busy right away, and this second telegram from Snorvig does look as if something strange had been seen. And I thought as I handled the flying saucer business in March you'd like to keep everything in one key."

"Losh, I wish sometimes I were a young reporter again," said the Editor, and this time it was his eye that was turned in the direction of the strip of blue sky above the ravine.

While young Ian Carmichael, with a light heart, was westward bound the monster was seen for the third time.

During the war the Little Todday platoon of the Home Guard had made a surprise landing on Garryboo in gas-masks and acutely frightened Morag and Annag, the two eldest daughters of Bean Shomhairle, the wife of Samuel MacCodrum. Morag and Annag were now away in service on the mainland, and it was the duty of Chrissie and Lizzie, their younger sisters, to carry up any flotsam or jetsam marked down by their father in the course of beachcombing operations, for the building of the pier for Garryboo had not yet started, and the low rocky promontory of Ardvanish, a mile away from the few houses of the township clustered together below the road round the island, was a lonely enough spot, seldom visited except by beachcombers at low tide. After school on the afternoon following the Biffer's adventure by Uamh na Snaoiseanaich, the Cave of the Snuff-taker, Chrissie and Lizzie MacCodrum were sent off to bring back a ship's grating which their father had left on Ardvanish that morning. They dallied for a while to weave the first daisy-chain of the year from the flowers with which the fine weather already starred the green machair land between the township and the sea, the only stretch of such grass in Great Todday, where the soil was almost all rocky moorland, although its sister island was entirely machair land.

"*A Thighearna*, Lizzie, we'll be late for tea," said her sister, and the two little girls started to run towards the sea.

Suddenly Chrissie stopped and with something between a gasp and a scream clutched Lizzie's arm.

"What is it at all?" she quavered.

There was no gasp from Lizzie; a wild shriek pierced the quiet afternoon air, and a moment later she was running back to Garryboo as fast as she could, followed by her sister.

Ten minutes later, breathless and half-sobbing, they burst into their mother's kitchen. Bean Shomhairle was spreading jam on slices of bread under the hopeful eyes of her two youngest children, both boys, and the irruption of Chrissie and Lizzie nearly made her cut herself.

In a stream of indignant Gaelic she threatened her daughters with the severest belting they had ever experienced unless they could explain what they meant by their behaviour.

"A huge animal was coming out of the sea on Tràigh Bhuidhe," said Chrissie.

"Bigger than an elephant," said Lizzie.

"What do you know about elephants, you silly girl?" her mother demanded. "You never saw such a thing in your life."

"Mr Campbell showed us a picture of an elephant in school, with tusks sticking out in front like huge teeth."

At this moment the father of the household came in to hear of his daughters' adventure.

"Right enough the Biffer saw teeth on the monster in Uamh na Snaoiseanaich," said Sammy MacCodrum. "They put him in mind of a hayrake they were so long and so fierce. How pick was this crayture on the tràigh?"

"We only saw its head coming out of the sea," said Chrissie. "We were running away as fast as we could."

"We were afraid it would come after us," Lizzie explained.

"Its mouth was wide open," said Chrissie, "and we could see its teeth. Och, they were terrible!" She shuddered at the memory.

"Get on with your tea," their father told his daughters. "I'm going down to the tràigh to see what I can see and later I'll take you both in to Snorvig in the lorry."

"Are you daft, a Shomhairle," his wife ejaculated.

"Ach, I want the Biffer to hear the story from themselves, wife. They'll be thinking in Snorvig that we're just seeing the monster in Garryboo to make them feel so small."

There was no sign of the monster when Sammy Mac-Codrum reached Tràigh Bhuidhe or Vooey as it was usually printed in maps and guidebooks, but the achievement of his daughters filled him with such elation that he picked up the ship's grating on the promontory and carried it all the way back to the croft himself.

In spite of his wife's protests Sammy persisted with his plan of taking the two little girls into Snorvig, and although they were both sick most of the way home on the lorry after all the lemonade they drank and all the cakes they ate Chrissie and Lizzie considered that evening to be the finest they had yet spent. It may be added that the Biffer, far from resenting the appearance of the monster at Garryboo, was delighted to have the size of its teeth confirmed by independent eye-witnesses.

Next day Ian Carmichael reached the Islands and it was not long before the *Daily Tale* was able to publish the story.

HAS MONSTER DESERTED LOCH NESS?

STRANGE CREATURE ASTOUNDS ISLANDERS

AMAZING STORY

'The people of the two remote islands of Great and Little Todday are again making headlines in the news, and by an amazing coincidence the dark rock called the Gobha (pronounced Gowa and meaning blacksmith) on which the S.S. *Cabinet Minister* with a cargo of whisky was wrecked in March 1943 is the scene of the first appearance of the monster whose advent has literally convulsed the Outer Hebrides from the Butt of Lewis to Barra Head.

Last Monday week Kenneth Macroon, the son of Mr Joseph Macroon, the postmaster and principal merchant of Kiltod who represents Little Todday on the Inverness County Council, was setting his lobster-pots round the Gobha. This black rock rises from a submerged reef some two hundred yards from the dark cliffs on the eastern face of the tiny island of Pillay which lies about a mile off the north of Little Todday. It was a calm cloudless morning and while Kenneth Macroon was engaged in adjusting the machinery of his little motor-boat, the *Morning Star*, he heard a curious noise which he describes as like the "snarling of an unfriendly dog." Looking up he saw what seemed to be the back of an immense bull with a mane disappearing below the water. When young Macroon came back to Kiltod with his amazing story he was sharply questioned by Father James Macalister, whose Gaelic broadcasts have from time to time given so much pleasure to listeners on Scottish Regional, whether what he had seen might not have been the head of an unusually large seal, but young Macroon claims to have seen enough seals to know that this strange head which snarled at him was three or four times as large as any seal.

Interviewed by a special representative of the *Daily Tale* Mr Kenneth Macroon said:

"In spite of the mane which was clearly visible I would prefer to compare the back of the head I saw to that of a hornless bull about three times as big as the head of an ordinary bull. But I was so frightened that I would not care to be too sure. It may have been more than three times as big."

"But not less."

"Definitely not less," Mr Kenneth Macroon declared.

"And you heard this strange creature snarl before it dived."

"That is the nearest description I can give of the noise it made."

The day after the monster appeared to Mr Kenneth Macroon it was seen in even more dramatic circumstances by Mr Archie MacRurie on the coast of Great Todday. Mr MacRurie had also been taking advantage of the clement weather to set his lobster-pots and when he was returning to Snorvig, the harbour and the chief town of the two Toddays, he passed with his boat, the *Kittiwake*, close under the headland of Ard Snor which shelters Snorvig from the north-west, and as he passed what is called the Cave of the Snuff-taker, on account of the effect of a mighty sneeze produced by waves breaking inside at certain stages of the tide, Mr MacRurie was amazed to see an immense head staring at him from the cave.

"Did this alarm you, Mr MacRurie?" our representative asked.

"Wouldn't you be frightened if you saw a head as big as a sack of barley with two eyes like pancakes staring at you from a cave, and wouldn't you be fit to drop down dead with fright if you saw this head had a mouthful of teeth like a hayrake and was making a noise like a fog-horn?"

"Did you notice the mane which Kenneth Macroon saw?"

"I couldn't see the back of the creature's head and I wasn't going to hang around for that."

"You steered for Snorvig?"

"I did indeed, and glad I was to get safely into the harbour."

Perhaps the most amazing encounter was on the following afternoon when Christina and Elizabeth Mac-Codrum, the two daughters of Mr Samuel MacCodrum, a crofter of Garryboo, which is a small village some five miles north of Snorvig, actually saw the monster emerging from the sea on the sandy beach called Traigh Vooey.

Our representative called at Garryboo School where Mr George Campbell, the headmaster, kindly allowed our representative to interrupt the little girls' studies by interviewing them.

"And I believe you both saw these teeth, Christina and Elizabeth?"

"Yes, we did. They were terrible and we were so frightened that we ran all the way home."

Our representative tried to obtain a more detailed description of the teeth, but the little girls had evidently been too much shaken by their amazing experience to be able to say more than that these teeth were as big as elephants' tusks and that the head of the monster itself was as big as an elephant's.

There is no doubt whatever that the Todday Monster has already been seen by four credible eye-witnesses in circumstances which are at least as convincing and in some respects are even more convincing than those which have attended the many appearances of the Loch Ness Monster at intervals during the last fifteen years.

The question which will certainly be widely debated is whether the Todday Monster is the Loch Ness Monster itself, a survivor of two Loch Ness monsters, or a new monster altogether which has appeared for the first time.

Mr Hector Hamish Mackay, who has always maintained that there were two monsters in Loch Ness, expressed his satisfaction at the news from the Islands.

"This bears out my theory," he told the *Daily Tale*. "What we have to ascertain now is whether the Todday Monster is male or female. There is, however, another possibility. Both the Loch Ness monsters disturbed by the flying saucers may have gone to seek sanctuary among the Outer Isles. We are not yet in a position to say that the monster seen off Little Todday is identical with the one seen in the cave of Great Todday. But whether the dead body of one monster is now lying on the fathomless bottom of Loch Ness or whether both managed to escape, what does seem certain is that there is no longer a monster in Loch Ness."'

Chapter 5

BEN NEVIS AND THE EDITOR

ON the day that Ian Carmichael's story of the Todday
Monster appeared in the *Daily Tale* the Lady of Ben
Nevis was sitting in the chintzy privacy of her own room in
Glenbogle Castle which was still known as the Yellow
Drawing-Room, though it had not been either yellow or a
drawing-room for nearly forty years. The post had just
arrived and Mrs MacDonald's tranquil and majestic shape
loomed above the annual report of the Kenspeckle Branch
of the Women's Rural Institute, of which she was the
President, like one of Glenbogle's guardian bens above a
lochan. She was just saying to herself how satisfactory the
attendance at the winter ceilidhs had been when she heard
from some part of the castle a sound like the agonized roar
of a love-tormented stag in October. A few moments later
Mac 'ic Eachainn burst into the room, his countenance
aflame, his beaked nose aglow.

"Trixie! Trixie!" he shouted. "Look at this abominable
rag! Read what these scoundrels say! I've never been so
absolutely furious in my life! I've told Johnnie to bring the
car round at once! I'm going to Glasgow to horsewhip the
editor of this beastly rag! I'll ... I'll ... I'll ..." speech
failed him.

He spread the morning's issue of the *Daily Tale* on his
wife's table, obliterating with its noisome pages the annual
report of the Kenspeckle Branch of the W.R.I.

"Read it, Trixie, read it," he gasped, flinging himself
down into one of Mrs MacDonald's chintz-covered arm-
chairs. "No longer a monster in Loch Ness! Good lord,
we'll be told next that Lochiel has gone to spend a week-end
with Molotov and MacCailein Mór's flying the red flag
over Inveraray. As a matter of fact, I wouldn't be so surprised if a Campbell did fly the red flag." He guffawed
bitterly.

"Don't work yourself up, Donald," his wife boomed as
gently as the soft diapason of an organ in some glimmering
cathedral at evensong. "Let me read what the paper
says."

"You'll never read such foul and filthy dunderheaded damnable nonsense . . . you'll . . ."

"I certainly shan't if you keep interrupting me," the Lady of Ben Nevis put in severely.

The Chieftain, breathing heavily, refrained from saying anything more while his wife perused the account of the monster seen in the Islands.

"Well, you know I never attach undue importance to what the papers say," Mrs MacDonald commented when she had read the offending article. "And I thought you yourself believed the monster might go to Loch Hoo."

"What I said was that if the monster had been driven out of Loch Ness by this flying brute it was more likely to take refuge in Loch Hoo or Loch Hoch than go gallivanting off to the Islands. I don't accept the fact that the monster *has* been driven out of Loch Ness. This fellow Hector Hamish Mackay is nothing but a miserable mushy writing nincompoop."

"Nobody *has* seen the monster since that curious story told by Hubert Bottley's head stalker."

"Well, practically nobody saw it all through the war. I think it lay up. It's probably lying up again. And I don't blame the creature. I should jolly well lie up if one of these flying saucers came skating across the top of my head. What I object to is this peprósterous idea that the monster has gone to the Islands. I tell you what, Trixie, if any more of this drivelling fat-headedness goes on I shall get Tom Rawstorne to take me out to the Islands in the *Banshee* and investigate for myself, and if I find that these Islanders have somehow lured our monster out there I'll jolly well get it back to Loch Ness somehow. Mind you, I don't believe it is our monster. I don't believe our monster could have curled itself up inside one of these finicking little caves you find beside the sea. If it was in Prince Charlie's cave on Ben Booey there might be something in this pettifogging story."

Toker came in at this moment to say that Macpherson had brought the car round, and that Mrs Parsall wanted to know if Ben Nevis would take a picnic lunch with him.

"Donald, you aren't seriously thinking of going to Glasgow?" his wife protested.

"I jolly well am, Trixie. I'm determined to get to the bottom of this outrageous yarn, and if the editor or whatever he's called of this vile rag tries any of his Clydeside

Bolshie impudence with me I shall give him the soundest thrashing he's ever had in his life. Tell Mrs Parsall to put up a picnic lunch, Toker, and don't forget a bottle of Glenbogle's Pride."

"Certainly not, Ben Nevis."

The butler withdrew.

"Donald, there are times when I think you're just seven instead of being just seventy," his wife sighed profoundly. "All I can hope is that the long drive will cool you down sufficiently not to cause a scandal in Glasgow."

"It never cools me down when I drive through Glencoe," the MacDonald Chieftain declared. "You know my blood always boils when I drive through Glencoe."

An hour or so later Ben Nevis halted the car outside the King's House where the Campbells gathered on that February night.

"We'll eat our lunch outside, Johnnie," he proclaimed. "I won't soil my brogues by crossing the threshold of such an accursed house."

When lunch was eaten, Mac 'ic Eachainn gave Johnnie Macpherson a dram and poured out one for himself.

"This is where those infernal Campbells gathered on that appalling night, Johnnie."

"I believe they did, Ben Nevis."

"Gathered like a lot of beastly vultures. Down with Campbell of Glenlyon, down with that brute Dalrymple, down with Breadalbane . . . wait a moment, there's one more to down."

He poured out another dram.

"Down with Dutch William!" He emptied his glass. "I feel better now, Johnnie. You know the way that contraption in front of a car sometimes boils."

"Not the radiator of this car, Ben Nevis," Johnnie Macpherson said indignantly.

"Well, practically all the way up the glen I was boiling like one of these contraptions, but I feel cooler now. Hector, the Thirteenth of Ben Nevis, had married a daughter of MacDonald of Glencoe about fifty years before this abominable massacre and so you can understand my boiling over, Johnnie."

"Ay, it was a bad business right enough, Ben Nevis."

"Well, we must be getting on to Glasgow," said the Chieftain. "I don't think you'd better have another dram,

Johnnie, or you'll be tearing through Tyndrum at forty miles an hour."

In fact Johnnie Macpherson left Tyndrum behind him at fifty-five miles an hour, but the cockles of Mac 'ic Eachainn's heart had been warmed by Glenbogle's Pride, and his triumph over the ghosts of dead Campbells made him feel so benign that he fancied Johnnie was driving rather more slowly than usual and told him he could add five miles to the speed; it was not until they reached Loch Lomondside that he said, "Steady now, Johnnie."

The janitor of the *Daily Tale* offices was used to kilted visitors and, being a strong Conservative, was inclined to regard them all with disapproval as Scottish Nationalists anxious to disturb the even tenor of Caledonia's life. When this kilted visitor demanded an immediate interview with the Editor he asked if he had an appointment.

"Certainly not, I want to see the Editor."

"Who shall I say?"

"Ben Nevis," the Chieftain roared.

"Ben Nevis?" the janitor repeated in bewilderment.

"MacDonald of Ben Nevis, you ninny," the Chieftain roared again.

For a moment the janitor was under the impression that one of the trams in Buchanan Street had crashed through the doors of the *Daily Tale's* offices.

"I'll ask if Mr Donaldson will see you, sir," the janitor said, almost obsequiously.

"Donaldson? Is this fellow's name Donaldson?"

"The Editor is Mr James Donaldson."

"Good lord, a clansman! Extraordinary behaviour for one of my fellow clansmen!" Ben Nevis ejaculated.

A minute later the Chieftain was in the lift under the escort of a small page-boy who as an embryo Nationalist looked up at him with stern approval.

"Are you a Scottish Nationalist, mister?" he asked in a high Glasgow voice.

"Am I what?" the Chieftain gasped.

"A Scottish Nationalist? Ma father is."

"Who the devil is your father?"

"Och, he's the Secretary of the Gorbals Branch of the League for Scottish Independence. He wears the kilt to meetings the same as you do. His name's MacDonald. Hector MacDonald. I'm Donald MacDonald masel'."

It took a good deal to deprive Ben Nevis of the power of speech, but that page-boy of his own clan, three feet ten inches tall, achieved what Lochiel had never managed to achieve, nor Simon Lovat before him, at many a session of the Inverness County Council. In fact it was a temporarily subdued Ben Nevis that was shown into James Donaldson's editorial office.

"This is a great honour, Ben Nevis," said the Editor, offering his hand. "I hope you weren't kept waiting too long."

"How do you do, Mr Donaldson? I've come about this article, as I think you call them, in this morning's *Daily Tale*."

"Do sit down, Ben Nevis. I wonder if I might have the privilege of offering you a little refreshment? I'm afraid it's not the famous Glenbogle's Pride, but it's a decent malt whisky."

"Oh, thanks very much ... perhaps, a small dram."

Ben Nevis found that it was indeed an excellent malt whisky and he began to wonder if this editor chap, who after all was a MacDonald even if he used this vile English variant of it for his name, might not be a more reasonable kind of fellow than he had been supposing.

"You were interested by the news from the Islands in our morning's issue? Young Ian Carmichael whom I sent out to look into the strange business is a bright lad and you can rely on his report."

"What I took exception to was that disgusting statement at the end by this writing fellow."

"Old Hector Hamish Mackay? Ah, well, you know, he's a great enthusiast."

"That doesn't entitle him to say in this cock-a-whoop way that the Monster has left Loch Ness for the Islands."

"Don't worry, Ben Nevis, our man will test that hypothesis."

"I hope he'll make it clear that it was just a hytop ... just a piece of dunder-headed theorizing and nothing more. As soon as I read that peprosterous speculation I got into my car and drove straight to Glasgow."

"You've had a long drive. May I give you the other half of that dram?"

The Chieftain surrendered to the invitation and this time he drank the Editor's health.

"Slahnjervaw, Mr Donaldson. I wonder why you call

yourself Donaldson. I mean to say it's a queer sort of place, Glasgow, but after all it isn't England."

"I used to be on at my old dad about that," said the Editor. "But I'll be frank and admit that I've stuck to it because there are more MacDonalds than Donaldsons in Glasgow."

Ben Nevis remembered his diminutive namesake in the lift.

"Yes, I see what you mean."

"Don't you think it would be helpful if I sent Hector Hamish Mackay out to the Toddays to try and clear up the mystery?"

"As long as he doesn't insist on pretending that this jumped up jackanapes in the Toddays is the Loch Ness Monster. I warn you, Mr Donaldson, that if he does I shall go to Snorvig myself and deport him. I don't suppose you ever heard of my expedition to Great Todday to rescue a left-footed boot which these islanders had stolen from my Home Guard Company."

"I never did," said the Editor. "I wish we could have covered such a remarkable expedition."

"Well, as a matter of fact it happened just when Hitler invaded Russia and you were probably jolly busy emptying whitewash over the Russians, what?"

"I hope that if you do decide to lead another expedition to the Islands you'll give us the tip beforehand. There ought to be a splendid story in it. Will you go over in the *Island Queen*?"

"Good Lord, no, my friend Tom Rawstorne will lend me his yacht the *Banshee*. If these rascally islanders go on arguing that this monster of theirs is the Loch Ness Monster I must do something about it. I must prove that they're wrong. And if this writing fellow Mackay tries to argue with me I shall deport him. I suppose he's entered into some kind of beastly alliance with that fellow Wig . . . Wog . . . Waggett. Yes, that's his name."

"This telegram we had this morning may interest you, Ben Nevis," said the Editor, pushing a piece of paper across the table.

Paul Waggett owner Snorvig House interviewed last night quote consider monster delusion of mass suggestion and attempt emulate Inverness exploitation of equally imaginary monster for gullible

tourists unquote urge important secure investigation Hector Hamish
Mackay soonest possible personally convinced Todday people have
seen something outside ordinary experience

Carmichael

The countenance of Ben Nevis was darkened by an angry flush.

"Loch Ness Monster imaginary," he exclaimed in stupefaction. "Imaginary? I don't know what the world's coming to. I really don't. This fellow Waggett was the prime mover in that boot business. He's completely unscrupulous. Oh, I see this expedition of mine is going to be absolutely necessary."

"And when do you propose to set out?"

"I shall wait till June, and if the Monster has not been seen before then I shall choose a fine spell and go into the whole matter personally."

"I believe you don't accept the flying saucer as a fact?"

"I didn't when that reporter fellow of yours came and saw me in Glenbogle. However, after going into it with Kenneth MacLennan I decided that some kind of a something did go whizzing down the loch, but I refuse to believe that the Monster was hit."

"You think that the Todday monster has no connection with the Loch Ness Monster?"

"I hope not, because if it should turn out to be our monster I shall have to discover some way of getting it back to Loch Ness. You must remember I've seen our monster twelve times. I shall know at a glance whether this Todday monster is ours or not. Meanwhile, I do hope that you'll not encourage people to think that the Loch Ness Monster was killed by this flying brute or that it has been frightened away from Loch Ness."

"Are you returning to Glenbogle at once?" the Editor asked.

"I intended to drive back after dinner," the Chieftain told him.

"I wonder if you'd give me the very great pleasure of dining with me at a rather good new restaurant we have in Glasgow?" the Editor asked.

"That's very kind of you, Mr Donaldson."

"I thought with your permission I would like to publish the substance of our talk and I'd like you to vet it before we go to press. Perhaps you'll be kind enough to call in for me about half-past six and we could go on to dinner. I do think it's important that the *Daily Tale* should be able to present an authoritative point of view like yours."

"You mustn't breathe a word about this expedition of mine."

"Of course not."

"This'll be the third expedition of a MacDonald of Ben Nevis to Todday. Yes, an ancestor of mine went over once and hanged the MacRurie of the time in his own chimney. Yes, by Jove, he did. Smoked him like a ham and delivered the result to King James IV in Holyrood, poor chap."

"Well, well, I daresay he deserved it."

"I didn't mean this scoundrelly MacRurie. I was thinking of King James IV. Flodden and all that, if you know what I mean."

"The Flowers of the Forest?"

The Chieftain sighed deeply.

"The Flowers of the Forest. Exactly."

The Editor replenished his glass.

"Slahnjer," the Chieftain woofed.

"Slahnje," the Editor echoed.

At half-past six Ben Nevis returned to the offices of the *Daily Tale* where the Editor invited him to approve the following:

FAMOUS HIGHLAND CHIEFTAIN VISITS GLASGOW

'To-day everybody on the staff of the *Scottish Daily Tale* was walking more jauntily after a visit from no less a Highland personality than Donald MacDonald, Twenty-third of Ben Nevis, who drove specially from Glenbogle Castle to discuss with the Editor of the *Scottish Daily Tale* the right approach to the amazing problem set by the monster whose appearance in the sea around Great and Little Todday was exclusively announced in the *Scottish Daily Tale* yesterday, and caused a profound sensation throughout the country.

Ben Nevis believes that Mr Hector Hamish Mackay is premature in suggesting that the monster already seen by four witnesses may be the Loch Ness Monster or its mate. He does not reject Mr Mackay's theory that there may be two Loch Ness Monsters, but he does not consider that theory to be an established fact, and he is unwilling to admit on the evidence available at present that the Loch Ness Monster or its supposed mate was killed by a flying saucer. At first he was inclined to disbelieve in the phenomenon of a flying saucer, but after discussing the matter with Mr Kenneth MacLennan, the original witness of the amazing incident, he is now firmly convinced that it happened exactly as Mr MacLennan described it. He maintains, however, that the monster was not actually hit but succeeded in diving to safety, and that its failure to appear since is due to the natural resentment it felt at the intrusion upon its peaceful domain of this flying saucer. He confidently expects at any time to hear of the re-emergence of the Loch Ness Monster from its temporary retirement and refuses to consider for a moment the theory that one monster was killed and that the survivor is now searching for a mate on the western seaboard. He shrewdly points out that we know nothing of the breeding season or habits of these monsters, nor even whether they are viviparous or oviparous . . .'

"What's that?" the Chieftain interposed to ask. "Vipiferous or opiferous?"

The Editor explained.

"Well, I think you'd better use shorter words. I'm sure some of your readers won't know what on earth you're talking about."

"I believe you're right," James Donaldson agreed and amended the sentence.

'. . . whether the young are born alive or hatched from eggs. He does not pour cold water on Mr Mackay's speculation that the monsters may, like eels, go far out to sea to reproduce themselves, but he doubts if in the state of our present knowledge we have the right to put forward theories in which what he scathingly calls "these scientific know-alls" would be delighted to pick holes.

When asked whether he considered the Todday Monster was of the same species of monster as the hoary denizen of Loch Ness, Ben Nevis replied that he was prepared to wait until he had seen the Todday Monster before committing himself to an opinion. When he was informed that Mr Paul Waggett of Snorvig House had

expressed his disbelief in the Todday Monster the Mac-
Donald Chieftain replied tersely that some people could
disbelieve anything. When further informed that Mr
Waggett did not believe in the Loch Ness Monster Ben
Nevis retorted that such an attitude made any opinion
expressed by Mr Waggett about the Todday Monster
utterly valueless.

The *Scottish Daily Tale* desires to take this opportunity
of congratulating a famous Highland Chieftain upon the
robust health with which he carries his seventy years and
of wishing him many more years of such health. Figures
like Ben Nevis grow more rare all the time, and after the
inspiring visit we received from this Chieftain of high
degree and ancient lineage the *Scottish Daily Tale* echoes
with enthusiasm the motto of this branch of mighty Clan
Donald, "Ben Nevis Gu Brath—Ben Nevis for Ever."

In *Happy Days Among the Heather* by Hector Hamish
Mackay we read:

"In the year 1546 a party of marauding Macintoshes
were surprised by the MacDonalds of Ben Nevis led by
Mac 'ic Eachainn in person and every single one of them
killed. Some years later Clan Chattan took its revenge
for this defeat by descending on Strath Diddle, when the
young men were raiding the Cameron country to the
south, and baking thirty-two old and infirm MacDonalds
in an oven. For this Hector the ninth of Ben Nevis exacted
a terrible penalty from Clan Chattan when, marching
through a stormy December night in the year 1549, he
caught the Macintoshes unawares on a Sunday morning
and burned forty-five of them in church. While the unfortunate victims of Hector's vengeance were burning,
Hector's piper Angus MacQuat improvised a tune and
played it to drown their shrieks. This tune, called *Mac 'ic
Eachainn's Return to Glenbogle*, is still played by a MacQuat
whenever MacDonald of Ben Nevis returns after spending
even a single night away from his Castle."

"Will your piper be waiting for your return from
Glasgow?" the Chieftain was asked.

"Certainly," he replied. "Angus will be there."'

The prophecy made by Ben Nevis was fulfilled. When
at 4 a.m. Johnnie Macpherson drove up to the front door
of Glenbogle Castle Angus MacQuat, who had been dozing

in the Great Hall among the antlers and Lochaber axes, woke as if at the touch of an unseen hand warning him that the Chieftain was come home. He hastily inflated the bag of his pipe and by the time Ben Nevis had extracted himself from the car and come surging through the front door Angus was marching up and down the Great Hall in full blast.

Ben Nevis beamed at him patriarchally, and when the wind had been emptied from the bag he poured out three hefty drams of Glenbogle's Pride, one for Johnnie Macpherson, one for his piper and one for himself.

"Well, I enjoyed myself in Glasgow," said Mac 'ic Eachainn, now safely returned. "Extraordinary thing, the boy who took me up in the lift was called Donald MacDonald."

"Och, there's hundreds of Donald MacDonalds in Glasgow, Ben Nevis," Johnnie Macpherson assured him a little impatiently.

"Are there, Johnnie? Well, Glasgow isn't really such a queer place as I thought it was." The Chieftain yawned widely. "Good night to you both."

On his way to his own room Ben Nevis put his head round the door of his wife's room.

"Yes, I'm awake, Donald. I heard the pipes. Well?"

"Very decent fellow, this editor of the *Daily Tale*. Donaldson, his name is. A fellow clansman. I've told him to come and stay with us any time he feels like it. Extraordinary things newspapers. I've just been reading what they call an interview with me which you'll all be reading to-morrow. I don't know how they do it. And the boy in the lift, about the size of a shrimp, told me his name was Donald MacDonald. Oh, yes, and we damned all Campbells on our way through Glencoe and then damned them again on our way back. It was quite eerie in the moonlight. I shouldn't have been a bit surprised to see a lot of ghosts covered with blood."

"Really, Donald!"

"This clansman James Donaldson is keen as mustard on the Monster. I was very pleased with his attitude and he understands absolutely why I object to the notion that the Monster has left Loch Ness. So I shall drive in to Inverness to-morrow and try to get rid of what we used to call alarm and despondency in the war."

Chapter 6

MRS ODD ARRIVES

THE account of the Todday Monster in the English editions of the *Daily Tale* was merely a brief paragraph, for the paper shortage meant rationing of news and naturally the women of England were more interested in the love-affair of a divorced film-star than in a Hebridean monster. Nevertheless, brief though that paragraph was, it acted on Mrs Odd like a galvanic shock.

The old lady had just finished washing up after breakfast and was sitting in the little parlour at the back of the shop in Nottingham. Her son, the ex-sergeant-major, was serving customers across the counter with the packets of gaspers for which they craved. Her daughter-in-law Peggy was upstairs with both hands for housework and one eye for Lucy, aged three, and Catherine, aged two, who were capable jointly or indeed separately of extraordinary destructiveness.

"Well, if anybody had of told me I was going to be grandma to a couple of walking buzz-bombs," the old lady had exclaimed when the crash was louder than usual, "well, you was always one for blowing round the house with a tin trumpet, Fred, but you was a dome of silence beside these two terrors you've landed on Nottingham. Goose Fair? Goose Fair's the crip in dear old St Paul's beside what it's like in our house. Not that I mind. I like to hear children enjoying themselves, I do."

Mrs Odd was now seventy-five, but with her fresh complexion, snow white hair and lively step she did not look a day older than when she attended her son's wedding on Little Todday, and her bright eyes were reading the newspaper without glasses.

"Good land alive," she ejaculated, and jumping up from the leather-covered armchair, which became Ma's chair after Pa had relinquished it over fifteen years earlier, she was behind the counter just as Fred was handing a packet of gaspers to a customer.

"Fred, the Loch Ness Monster has arrived on Little Todday and I'm off back to-night so as I can catch the

Island Queen to-morrow morning. You read your *Daily Tale* this morning, Mr Quidling?" she asked the customer.

"Not yet, no, Mrs Odd," the customer replied gloomily. "I don't get a chance to see it till after my tea, and I only see it then if the Missus doesn't want it."

"I couldn't be bothered to tell that old spoilsport about the monster," Mrs Odd said to her son when Mr Quidling had left the shop. "Still, I suppose it preyed on his mind when people started in calling him Quisling during the war, though, goodness me, you'd think anybody 'ud only be too glad to give people a chance of a bit of fun at such a time. Still, what's the good in talking? Some people is only happy when they're miserable. Yes, I reckon I'll get the connection from St Pancras and give Captain MacKechnie a surprise to-morrow morning. I'll send a telegram to young Kenny so as he can meet me when I get to Snorvig. He can come back for his father later. You know the way your par-in-lore always hangs around while they're sorting the post. And I'll send a telegram to Duncan Bang to meet me at Kiltod with his pony and trap and drive me to Bow Bells. I wonder if Duncan has seen the monster yet."

I reckon you'd better get off as soon as you can, Ma," her son advised. "Otherwise you'll be seeing a monster in the Trent. You was going anyway in another fortnight."

It was a calm sparkling morning when Captain Donald MacKechnie, the skipper of the *Island Queen*, who from the bridge was eyeing the arrival of passengers from the train, heard a loud "ship ahoy!" and looked down to see Mrs Odd beaming up at him.

A minute later they were shaking hands cordially.

"Ah, well, well, Mistress Ott, it's glad I am to be seeing yourself on such a fine morning," the Skipper declared in his high voice. "*Fàilte d'on duthaich.* Welcome to the country. Will you be taking a wee dram chust to settle the smell of the train?"

"At half-past six in the morning?" Mrs Odd exclaimed. "What a nerve! But I'll have one with you after my lunch. Well, they say all the nice girls love a sailor, and I'm not surprised, I'm not. Now, I'm not going to interrupt you with your tiddley-bits. I know you won't be fit for a good old chin-wag till you're well out on the briny and nothing to bump into before Great Todday."

"It's yourself that's a ferry wise woman, Mistress Ott,"

Captain MacKechnie assured her. "And how's the Sarchant and Peigi Ealasaid?"

"Both in the pink and hoping for a little corporal next autumn."

"Is that so? Ah, ferry coot, ferry coot. And the two wee curlies?"

"Oh, a proper pair of terrors. What a set out we had only the day before yesterday when young Luce edged young Kitty on to try and drink some of that black-currant vitamings out of a tin and Kitty got the juice all over her face. Peggy thought she'd cut herself and started in to holler for Fred to fetch a doctor, and of course it wasn't blood at all, it was just black-currant juice. But look here, don't start me off chattering when you've got to get them all aboard the *Margate Belle*."

"The market pell?" Captain MacKechnie echoed in a puzzled voice.

"Yes, the good old *Margate Belle*. Oh dear, what times I've had in her in the sweet long ago. Packed like sardines and all enjoying ourselves. Well, tootle-oo till after lunch."

When the *Island Queen* had nothing between her and America except Great and Little Todday, and the Atlantic, a silvery-blue expanse, was breathing as gently as a sleeping nymph, Mrs Odd joined Captain MacKechnie in his cabin.

"I'm afraid I haven't a drop of Minnie left," he told her.

Minnie was the endearing diminutive by which the whisky saved from the wreck of the *Cabinet Minister* had been known.

"Drunk it all, eh? I should say so!"

"Ay, and there were still gallons of that peautiful stuff when the excisemen sent it all to the pottom of the sea. Ay, Governments are queer craytures, right enough. What would a fish be making of such peautiful whisky? There's no fish alive that isn't a teetotaller, Mistress Ott."

"What a shocking waste, eh?"

"You've said the ferry words. Chust a shocking waste. Still, you won't find this too bad at all."

He took the cork out of a bottle and poured the golden liquid into a glass.

"Here, I don't want to roll ashore at Snorvig like a barrel," Mrs Odd protested.

"You won't be rolling at all on any whisky they give us to-day. *Slàinte mhath!* And I'm ferry proud to be offering you a welcome to the land of pens and clens and heroes. Ay, *tìr nam beann, nan gleann, nan gaisgeach.*"

"And now what about this monster?" Mrs Odd asked. "Have you seen it?"

"No, no," said Captain MacKechnie cautiously. "But I believe it will have been seen right enough. Kenny Macroon, Airchie MacRurie—that's the Biffer—and Sammy MacCodrum's two little curls. Ach, it would be a pold man who would be saying like Mr Wackett that the monster is chust a nothing at all."

"Waggett doesn't believe anybody sore a monster? Oh dear, oh dear, what a dismal Jimmy that feller is. Good land alive, anybody would think with all this austerity, and which I say means eating horse instead of good old roast beef, well, really anybody would think it was time we had somethink to cheer us up. Well, as soon as I read that bit in the *Daily Tale* about the Loch Ness Monster being seen in Little Todday and Great Todday I was off like a bullet out of a gun. I mean to say, I don't want to miss seeing this monster. Certainly not. Oh dear, what a pity they can't get it down to dear old London. What a drore it would be in the Zoo. Well, look at that Giant Pandar all the kids went so potty over."

Captain MacKechnie looked puzzled.

"You know," Mrs Odd said. "That animal as looked like a teddy-bear dressed up for a pierrot."

"Pierrot?" echoed the Skipper. He felt he should be familiar with anything that had to do with piers, but he was baffled.

"You know what a pierrot is. Those fellers with white faces and black pongpongs you'll hear singing on the pier, and on the beach too."

"Is it oyster-catchers you're meaning, Mistress Ott?"

It was her turn to look puzzled.

"Well, I daresay they do catch oysters when there's an R in the month. And whelks and winkles when there isn't if it comes to that."

"Ach, you'll have another dram, Mistress Ott," the Skipper pressed.

"No, thanks, one's enough, or I'll be seeing monsters with pink spots. And I think I'll go and have a bit of a lay down now. I was arguing the point all night with the train."

Mrs Odd retired to a corner of the saloon and drowsed

gently until the *Island Queen* warned Snorvig with a series of long hoots that she was arriving.

The first person she met as she stepped ashore from the gang-board was Paul Waggett dressed in the suit of light blue tweed latticed with dark blue which with the passage of years had lost that bright Putney to Mortlake look.

"Hullo, Mr Waggett, how are you? What lovely weather the monster has brought with him, hasn't he? Well, I haven't wasted much time in getting here. It's a real excitement, isn't it?"

Paul Waggett stiffened.

"More excitement than real, I'm afraid, Mrs Odd," he said, his nose expressing a superior scepticism, his lips trying to soften that superiority with a compassionate smile for weaker minds than his own.

"Oh, go on with you," she laughed, digging him in the ribs. "Don't be such an unbelieving Chinee."

Any protest Waggett may have been on the point of making was quashed by the arrival of Joseph Macroon.

"Welcome back, Mistress Odd. How are they all in Nottingham?"

"Oh, everything in the garden's lovely in Nottingham. So the monster's come to Todday."

"Ay, ay, the crayture reported here all correct. Kenny will tell you about it when you're crossing to Kiltod. The daisies are looking beautiful on Little Todday."

While the *Morning Star* was chugging across the Coolish, as the stretch of water separating the two islands was called, Kenny Macroon gave Mrs Odd a full account of the monster's various appearances. Since Chrissie and Lizzie MacCodrum had seen it coming out of the sea by Tràigh Vooey claims to have seen it had been put in from the banks of Loch Skinny and Loch Bob, but the general feeling was that both appearances were due to the jealousy of the people of Knockdown and Bobanish and indeed of the whole east side of Great Todday at the attention which the appearance of the monster had secured for the west side of Great Todday and for Little Todday. In fact jealousy was growing. A Nobost man had brought news of the monster's having been sighted off Mid Uist and Mr Carmichael, the *Daily Tale* representative, had chartered Drooby's *Flying Fish* to investigate that story, which everybody in both Toddays was sure was devoid of the least foundation.

"We'll be hearing from Peigi Bheag in a minute that the monster has been seen by the Coddy in Barra."

Peigi Bheag was Joseph Macroon's third daughter and was now married to Neil MacNeil, one of the Barra schoolmasters. The Coddy exercised in Barra the same kind of influence as Roderick MacRurie in Great Todday or Kenny's father in Little Todday, and it may be added that both Roderick and Joseph recognised in the Coddy a foeman worthy of their steel. If the Coddy made up his mind to evacuate the monster to Barra it would be by no means an easy job to prevent him. He had already, according to general belief, persuaded the 'fillums' to deprive the Toddays of the *Cabinet Minister* and substitute for them the coast of Barra. Indeed, he had somehow managed to appear in the film of *Whisky Galore* himself in the act of pouring out whisky from a pig at the *réiteach*, and though Big Roderick and Joseph Macroon had both appeared by name neither had been invited to appear in person.

"Well, we must keep a sharp look-out on Little Todday," Mrs Odd declared. "I know I shall and that's one sure thing. Ah, there's Duncan Bang. I wonder he hasn't seen the monster yet."

Duncan Bàn Macroon was a Gaelic poet who when he inherited a croft from his grandmother had abandoned the University and the career intended for him as a schoolmaster. It was he who had found for Mrs Odd the cottage. Here he was on the pier at Kiltod, a man already in his forties but seeming always young with his glowing countenance and tumbled fair hair and eyes of kingfisher-blue.

"Ah, well, well, Mistress Odd, it's glad we are to have you back with us in the Isles of the Blest," he said warmly, and soon he with Mrs Odd and her luggage were jogging in the trap on the only metalled road in the island, which ran from Kiltod to Tràigh Swish, a long beach of white sand facing the Atlantic. After a couple of miles they turned off to take the track that led across the rolling green machair to Duncan's own house called the House of the Bard, and a couple of hundred yards beyond Tigh nam Bàrd to a thatched cottage with thick white walls and small deep-set windows. This was Bow Bells.

The cottage was sheltered from the fury of the west by mounds of close-cropped grass starred with daisies and primroses, and above the sweet silence in which Bow Bells was set could be heard the long sigh of the ocean on this tranquil afternoon, a sigh that could sink to a whisper or rise to a moan and from a moan to a roar when the wind blew.

"Come in, Duncan, I've got something for you," Mrs Odd told him.

It was a bottle of whisky.

"I oughtn't to encourage you," she told him. "But I like encouraging people."

"*A Dhia*, you oughtn't to be spending your money on me, the terrible price that whisky is in these degenerate days. But you're quite right, Mistress Odd. There's nothing I like better than encouraging people whether it's whisky or piping or poetry. You'll just take a wee dram with me right off the reel."

"But I had a whopper with Captain MacKechnie in his cabin. I can't have another so soon."

"Yes, and you can now," the poet insisted. "Old friends don't meet again every day."

So Mrs Odd and Duncan Bàn pledged one another.

"And here's jolly good luck to the monster," she added. "Funny you not having seen it yet. I mean to say when you think of all those fairies you've seen, most of them no bigger than wurzits, you'd have thought you was bound to see the monster."

"Ah, well, he may not be so far away at all just now. Meanwhile, Florag Yocky will be coming along and I'll be away back home."

Presently Florag, a fifteen-year-old daughter of Jocky Stewart, arrived to give Mrs Odd a hand with her unpacking. She was a plump apple-cheeked girl who devoted a couple of hours every morning to Mrs Odd when she was at Bow Bells and the rest of the day to work on her father's croft.

"Well, isn't it grand to be back on the island, Flo!" the old lady exclaimed. "My goodness, you've widened out since last October, haven't you? You'll be as big a woman as your mother yet."

Florag's mother, Bean Yocky, was the largest of several large women on the island, and her daughter pulled a face at the prospect.

"Don't you be looking down your nose at a bit of ombompong, Flo. Ombompong is much better for a girl than being all skin and grief. Well, it stands to reason. No man wants to cuddle a living skelington or a rasher of wind."

"I wouldn't like to be so big as my mother," Florag protested.

"Well, I daresay she is a bit too much Jumbo's only rival," Mrs Odd admitted. "But that's because she's tall with it. You take more after your dad. How is he?"

"He's quite all right."

"How many cows has he got now?"

"Four cows, two heifers and six stirks."

"Good land alive. Buffalo Bill the Second! Look, I've brought you this."

Mrs Odd presented Florag with a printed cotton frock.

"If it's too small for you give it to your sister Annie and I'll get you another one."

However, fortunately for Florag's anxiety about her figure, the frock was not too small.

"It's lovely," Florag breathed reverently. "It's really lovely, Mistress Odd."

"Yes, if the monster catches sight of you in that frock you'll get the best view of him anybody's had yet."

"*A Mhuire, Mhuire*, don't be saying such a thing, Mistress Odd," Florag gasped.

"Wouldn't you like to get a good view of this mysterious creature?"

"Indeed, no, I'd be falling down dead with fright, I'm sure."

"Oh, well, if we all thought alike it would be a dull world," said Mrs Odd. "Now, there's nothing would give me more pleasure than to look out of the window at this very moment and see the monster rolling in through the garden gate."

As she spoke there was a loud rap on the door and Florag screamed.

"*A Mhuire Mhathair*, it's coming to attack us."

But it was Father James Macalister come to greet Mrs Odd.

"Duncan was telling me you'd just arrived. Well, well, *ceud mìle fàilte*," he said sonorously.

"Well, whatever it is, the same to you, Father James. Florag thought you was the monster."

"Ay, and she'll be sure I am next Sunday if she and the rest of the choir don't sing more in tune." He shook his head

c*

reproachfully. "Oh, great sticks, it was really terrible. Do you know what cacophony is, *a Fhlorag*?"

"No, Father," she mumbled.

"Well, you'll know what it is next Sunday if you do it again. And how's Peigi Ealasaid and my old friend the Sergeant-major?"

"Both in the best of pink," Mrs Odd told him. "And the two kids too. We're expecting another in September. And which means I'll have to get back earlier this year."

"All the same, it's great news. Is Peggy giving them plenty of Gaelic?"

"Oh, she lays into them in Garlic all right when they're naughty, and that means most of the time."

"Good shooting! The naughtier they are the better I'll be pleased."

"All I hope is I'll get a peep at the monster before I go back to Nottingham."

"Ah, well, I hope you will. But you know it's a strange business right enough. The Biffer was over yesterday morning telling me what he saw in that cave, and if he saw it, and he's a good man is Airchie, it's something none of us have ever seen before."

That evening in spite of anything Florag could say to dissuade her Mrs Odd went for a walk by herself along Tràigh Swish.

To her immense disappointment she saw nothing that the moonlight could charm into the shape of a monster. There was only the shimmering expanse of the Atlantic and the run of the sea lacing the white sand and the call of the whimbrel to welcome the merry month of May.

A month passed without anybody on either of the Toddays even imagining that he or she had seen the monster. Ian Carmichael went back to Glasgow after investigating one or two claims from other islands that it had been seen. The Editor of the *Scottish Daily Tale* decided that the story from which he had hoped so much had petered out like all too many another, and cancelled the arrangement for Hector Hamish Mackay to visit the two Toddays. Even the weather proved that it had flattered only to deceive and during the second week of that disillusioning month turned to a cold drench of rain followed by a chill wind from the east that blew for ten days and threatened to ruin the grazing.

It was, in the words of Mrs Odd, really chronic, and the only cheerful person on the two islands was Paul Waggett, who stopped all he met to let them hear him congratulate himself on his own acumen in having refused from the first to accept the appearance of the monster as a fact.

At home he lost no opportunity of reminding his twin daughters how lucky were to have such a judicious father and thus had been prevented from indulging in the credulity of the many.

"Boys," said the Biffer one evening in the Snorvig bar, "I never came so near to hitting a man as I came to hitting Wackett this afternoon. Do you know what the clown was after asking me?" A sympathetic murmur of interrogation was heard. "He was asking me as chicky as you like if I wass after seeing any more otters in Uamh na Snaoiseanaich. Me who has taken more otters than any man in Todaidh Mór!"

"*Seadh, seadh!*" the company agreed.

"'The Lord forgive you,' Mr Wackett, I wass saying. 'The Lord forgive you,' just like that, 'if you're after thinking it was an otter I was seeing,' and I was minded to say 'And if you think yon crayture was an otter you'll be thinking Sahtan is the minister,' ay, and I would have said it if I wasn't thinking with the evil that's in him he would be running to the Reverend Angus and telling him I wass after saying he was no better than Sahtan. And I wouldn't like to be hurting the feelings of the wee man, I wouldn't that. *A Chruitheir*, the clown will be asking next if it was a cock-lobster or a hen-lobster I was seeing in Uamh na Snaois-eanaich. Well, well, well, well!"

The Biffer called for a dram, and stood for ten minutes in moody and silent reflection upon the enormity of Paul Waggett's insinuation.

"*Mac an diabhuil*," he muttered at last, and then he walked out of the bar without even bidding the company good-night.

"Ah, poor Airchie," said somebody. "He took it very bad that Wackett would be saying it was an otter he was seeing."

"He'd petter not be saying to me that it wass an otter Chrissie and Lizzie were seeing on Tràigh Vooey," said Sammy MacCodrum fiercely. "He'd have plenty enough to say if the Home Cart was telling him that Hitler wass chust an otter."

"*Bhitheadh gu dearbh*," the company murmured in approval.

Over on the mainland the spirits of Ben Nevis rose steadily under the absence of any more news of a monster in the Islands. Indeed, they became boisterous when a rumour reached Glenbogle that one of the monks at Fort Augustus had sighted the monster in Loch Ness apparently as lively as ever. However, the rumour proved baseless. No monk at Fort Augustus had caught a glimpse of the monster since those two novices who had reported the appearance of its forked tail. Nor was the story believed of a tinker who declared that as he was trudging behind his cart between Drumnadrochit and Inverness just after dark a huge head had come out of the loch and drenched him with water. It was generally believed that he had fallen into the loch and invented the story to quieten his wife who was known everywhere as a relentless scold with a tongue as long as the monster itself.

However, as the weeks went by without any news of the monster even the high spirits of Ben Nevis began to flag. He enjoyed a brief exhilaration when word came from the clachan of Ballyhoo that old Ailean Ruadh, now close on ninety, had seen a strange dark object in Loch Hoo. Alas, when he reached the old man's little black house in which he lived alone he found that he had merely expressed a wish that he could be seeing something in the waters of Loch Hoo because he was sure that if he did, himself, and that was Ben Nevis, would be bringing him a bottle of whisky, the taste of which he had not savoured for "munss *agus* munss *agus* munss," so hard was it for him with the "room-atiss" that was on him to get Lloyd George's pension for himself and a dram in Kenspeckle at the same time.

Ben Nevis was shocked by the old man's invalid state and gave orders that a bottle of Glenbogle's Pride was to be sent to him once a month to fortify the brief time that was obviously all that was left to him in this world.

In Inverness itself pessimism deepened steadily. There was now a growing body of defeatist opinion to argue that the monster really had been killed by a flying saucer, and the fact that the catastrophe had occurred in the month of March meant that the problem of the monster's fate could be written off as an attraction for the summer season. It was small consolation to be able to feel more certain than ever that the monster must have been real because it had not been seen since its collision with the flying saucer. As for the Todday Monster, people in Inverness just smiled contemptuously and recalled that for the last fifteen years monsters had been appearing at intervals all over the world but had all vanished as soon as their appearance had been reported. The only permanent feature in the world of monsters had been the Loch Ness Monster and except during the war nobody could remember nearly three months passing without seeing at least one of its humps. Not even a hump had been signalled since that flying saucer had gone whizzing down the loch on its destructive mission.

"Och, it's like driving a funeral to be driving Ben Nevis beside the loch these days," grumbled Johnnie Macpherson. "And there's no arguing with the man. It's always 'you're driving too fast, Johnnie,' and me crawling along at ten miles an hour for him to think every dirty little bit of an old log he sees may be the monster and squeezing himself out of the car just to squeeze himself in again and tell me it's only a bit of wood and then grunting and grumbling to himself because he hasn't got the old Daimler any more. It's just getting on my nerves altogether, and the wind as cold as if it was winter."

And then, when the only monsters left in the world all seemed to have retired behind the Iron Curtain, the east wind died away, leaving a blue sky behind it, to welcome June, and the Todday Monster appeared again on the unimpeachable testimony of Mrs Odd.

Chapter 7

MRS ODD AND THE MONSTER

"MANY and fair are the long white beaches that stretch beside the western shores of the islands at the edge of the mighty Atlantic, but none is fairer than lovely Tràigh Swish of Little Todday. Philologists differ about the origin of the name. So let us fly backwards out of the prosaic present upon 'the viewless wings of poesy' and accept the derivation from Suis, a Norse princess of long ago who, legend relates, flung herself into the ocean from that grey rock which marks the southern boundary of the strand. Alas, her love for a young bard of Todaidh Beag, as Little Todday is called in the old sweet speech of the Gael, was foredoomed."

Little did Hector Hamish Mackay think when he wrote those words in *Faerie Lands Forlorn*, which none need hesitate to call the romantic vade cum mecum of everybody privileged to explore the Outer Isles, little did he think that one day that grey rock, or rather to be more precise, that small grey headland, after a placid existence for hundreds of years ever since a Norse princess chose it as a medium for suicide, would again inspire his eloquence.

The topographer himself, whose pages in the words of an enthusiastic reviewer are "literally scented with the breath of the moorland and hold in their magical descriptions the sound of the sea as in a shell," was a small man in a kilt with slightly shrivelled but well-weathered knees, a prim Edinburgh accent, and spectacles.

Disappointed by the cancellation of his assignment to the Todday Monster by the editor of the *Scottish Daily Tale*, he had found that east wind that May more than usually trying, and when at the beginning of June the weather forecast of the B.B.C. announced a spell of fine weather along the western seaboard of Scotland the topographer was seized with an impulse to take the road to the isles without bothering about getting his expenses guaranteed by the *Daily Tale*. It was probably nothing more remarkable than a mild attack of wanderlust, but in a new and revised edition of *Faerie Lands Forlorn* Mr Mackay has speculated whether that sudden impulse to go west may not have had a supernatural prompting; it must be admitted that the coincidence of his arrival at Snorvig when he did was most remarkable, even if we can find a prosaic explanation for the voice that seemed to whisper in his ear "Go at once to Kiltod" in the fact that every room in the Snorvig Hotel was taken by the members of the Land Court, who were in session to decide disputes about the removal of neighbours' landmarks and the trespasses of cows and hens.

Certainly Hector Hamish Mackay did go to Kiltod as soon as Joseph Macroon had put the mailbags and the stores in the *Morning Star* and without doubt he did decide, after a delicious high tea in which a lobster with a larger and juicier claw than Edinburgh ever dreamed of played a noble part, to walk across the island to Tràigh Swish. We may attribute that walk to the prompting of a voice that whispered in his ear the place we should visit or, if we insist on the humdrum, to the prompting of the topographer's own digestion.

Mr Mackay avoided the metalled road and followed the winding grassy tracks across the undulating machair dotted with grazing cows and stirks, gilded with buttercups and powdered with eyebright and daisies. From time to time Mr Mackay would plant in the turf his stout cromag cut from a hazel and indulge in a kind of pole-jump, his glasses flashing in the eye of the westering sun as he leapt triumphantly from one knoll to another. Mr Mackay reached the edge of rolling dunes that backed the length of the long white beach between Carraig an Ròin and Ard Swish. He debated whether he should walk north, where the sand was firm by the edge of the tide which had begun to flow about half an hour ago, towards the grey rock shaped like an immense seal which legend related was the petrified shape of the seal-woman from whom the Macroons sprang, or whether he should turn southward to Ard Swish. He chose the latter direction and was within forty yards of the narrow natural arch which led through Ard Swish to a small cave beyond called Tràigh Veck (Bheag) when suddenly from the arch appeared a plump rosy-faced old woman with snow-white hair.

"The monster, the monster," she was crying. "Come on, Rob Roy, or whatever you call yourself. It's the monster."

Mr Mackay ran up the beach in a diagonal as fast as he could on sand that grew softer as he neared the headland, the end of which was never unwashed by the sea even at the lowest ebb of a spring tide.

Mrs Odd, for of course it was she, had turned back under the natural arch and a moment or two later Mr Mackay found her standing in the further entrance of the arch gazing out to sea.

"You weren't nippy enough," she said. "It was here when I came hollering through to tell you to hurry."

"I did run as fast as I could," Mr Mackay panted. "But what was it you saw?"

"What was it I sore? I saw the monster as near as you're standing to me now," she declared.

"You did? Please tell me all about it. My name is Mackay—Hector Hamish Mackay."

"Hi! Hi! Hi! Mr Mackay, take me with you when you fly, back to the Isle of Skye," she hummed. "Here, are you the feller as wrote that book Duncan Bang gave me the loan of to read? I remember your name because I remember it looked like a sneeze in the middle, and Duncan said it was the same as James. 'Well,' I said, 'poor old James must have had a shocking bad cold in the head when he wrote his name like that.' Yes, and you spelt 'fairy' wrong, and which did surprise me because I thought people as wrote books had to know how to spell."

"Spenser spelt it the way I do."

"Then Spencer ought to have known better. I lay Marks wouldn't have spelt it that way or his name wouldn't have been Marks. Yes, but never mind about the alphabit, it's the monster I want to talk about."

"So do I," said Mr Mackay fervidly.

"Well, sit down and I'll tell you all about it. I'm Mrs Odd. Mistress Odd they call me here, and which I'm bound to say I like."

"We still use the prefix in Edinburgh."

"In Eddingborough, do you? I'll have to pop in and have a look at Eddingborough one of these days. Yes, my boy Fred married the fourth of Joseph Macroon's Peggies. We all live in Nottingham. But every summer I come to Little Todday and where I have a cottage near Duncan Bang. My goodness, won't Duncan be hopping mad when he hears I've seen the monster and he hasn't."

"I know Duncan Bàn Macroon well. It's high time a volume of his poetry was published. He's a real bard."

"Well, to get on with my story. As soon as I read about the monster in the *Daily Tale* wild horses couldn't have kept me in Nottingham, and up I came to Little Todday. There's hardly a day passed since I came up but what I've gone for a peep at the sea, and the weather has been chronic until now, but the monster wasn't having any, and that feller Waggett was sniffing about there being no such a thing as the monster. An invention, he called it. 'Well,' I said, 'Mr Waggett, so was arioplanes an invention, but that doesn't say there's no such a thing as an arioplane as you'd soon have found out if you'd been in dear old London when there was a war on. Oh, I've no patience with that nosey-parkering Know All. And fancy calling that great yellow dog of his 'Monty'. What a liberty! Just for the pleasure of ordering him about and swanking he's a Commandering-Chief himself. I only wish the monster could have got his teeth into him the same as he nearly did into me."

"His teeth?"

"I never saw such teeth on any animal. Well, I said to myself, 'shall I walk up the beach or down the beach this afternoon?' And I picked a dandelion and blew its fluff off the same as we used to blow them when we was kids for he loves me and he loves me not when anybody was potty on some soppy boy. And the last bit of fluff said 'down the beach.' So I took my umbreller, and which I always do, wet or fine, because you never know what you want to poke at when you're out for a toddle. And a good job it was I did take my umbreller, for if I hadn't of I reckon the monster would have been worrying me instead of worrying the beach like a dog worries a rat."

"But where was this creature and what was it like?" Mr Mackay asked.

"I'm telling you, I was walking down the beach to what they call Ard Swish and when I come to the arch, and which is more of a tunnel really, I thought I'd have a look see on the other side as the tide was out. So I walked through thinking to myself how strong it smelt of bloaters, and when I come out on the other side I saw a brute as big as an elephant cloring up the sand with its teeth and I said 'Oo-er!' and whipped open my umbreller, and which I always do if one of Buffalo Bill's cows come prancing about too close for comfort. And the monster let out a noise something between a bark and a moo and a groan and went plunging down the beach into the water, and I came running back through the arch and saw you and hollered out but you was too slow and when you got here the monster had dived and where it is now, well, that's anybody's guess."

"Do you think it could have been an exceptionally large seal?" Mr Mackay asked.

"Don't be silly, my dear man. I know what seals look like. Good land alive, when I've been out lobstering with Kenny I've seen any number of seals bobbing up out of the water all round us and all of 'em looking the spitting image of my butcher in Nottingham. Name of Dumpleton. Well, poor old Dumpleton wouldn't win a prize for his face at a beauty competition, but he doesn't wear his teeth outside. And what teeth! Like a row of pickaxes. Well, I'm not easily scared, but when I sore it cloring up the sand . . . well, you can see for yourself what a mess it's made of the beach."

And sure enough when Mr Mackay looked at the sand it was scored and striated in every direction, and not a footmark anywhere to suggest that a human being had been elaborating a hoax.

"Could you give me some idea of the shape of this strange creature, Mistress Odd?" Mr Mackay asked.

"It was no shape at all, only just a whopper, but mark you when I came out of the arch and saw this large animal cloring up the beach I was properly scared, and I daresay if I hadn't of opened my umbreller it would have clawed me up the same as the beach. One thing I noticed, the brute's head was covered with hair."

"Like a horse's mane?" Mr Mackay asked quickly.

"No, more like Jo-Jo."

"I beg your pardon?"

"Jo-Jo, the dog-faced man from Siberia."

"I'm afraid I still don't quite follow. Not a Communist?"

"Communist, no. They wasn't invented then. One of Barnum's Freaks."

"Ah, I never saw them, I'm afraid. You may remember, Mistress Odd, that young Kenny Macroon compared the back of the head of the creature he saw to a hornless bull."

"That's right, it was all bunched up like a bull and a

kind of yellowish-brown colour on top. But Kenny only saw the brute's back. He never saw those shocking teeth."

"Yes, of course, the teeth. And it was the teeth which impressed Archie MacRurie and MacCodrum's two little girls."

"Well, small wonder. Look at the beach. That was done by these teeth. I tell you they was like pickaxes."

"Most interesting, most interesting," Mr Mackay murmured to himself. "Oh dear, oh dear, if only that sand hadn't been so soft."

He gazed across the empty ocean.

"It looks as if I will have to abandon my theory," he said at last. "No, I don't think this mysterious creature can be the Loch Ness Monster."

Five days later the readers of the *Scottish Daily Tale* were invited by the Editor to study carefully the article contributed by Mr Hector Hamish Mackay and try to win £250 offered by the *Daily Tale* for the first properly authenticated photograph of the monster whose existence had been reported from various islands in the Outer Hebrides, and more particularly from Great and Little Todday. The article in question will still be fresh in the public memory, but no apology is offered for taking advantage of Mr Hector Hamish Mackay's generous permission to reproduce it here:

'Edinburgh had been ravaged for nearly a fortnight by a ruthless and persistent east wind and even I than whom our noble capital knows no more devoted citizen was beginning to weary of such an unkind May. I mention this because I do not want to exclude a natural explanation for the sudden impulse to leave Edinburgh and revisit the Western Isles. Nevertheless, as will presently transpire, I cannot but regard it as something more fatefully* pregnant than a mere coincidence, for if I had not made up my mind to board the good ship *Island Queen* just when I did I should have missed almost the greatest thrill of a life that has been granted more than a modicum of thrills. Do we not all too often dismiss the "divinity that shapes our ends" as coincidence? I trow we do.

Nor did what I must with all reverence call the guiding

* An overzealous sub-editor changed "fatefully" to "fatally" in the original article.

hand of Providence relax its grasp upon my shoulder when I reached the picturesque little port of Snorvig in Great Todday, for I was unable to enjoy the lavish cheer of mine host and old friend Roderick MacRurie owing to the demands made upon the spatial accommodation of the Snorvig Hotel by the "most potent, grave and reverend signiors" of the Land Court. As a result I begged shelter of another old friend Joseph Macroon at his hospitable house in Kiltod, the diminutive port of Little Todday, two miles away across the strait that divides the two islands. From here after a sumptuous tea I set out across the rolling machair, which for the benefit of those unfamiliar with the tongue our first parents spoke in Eden, means the grassy land found all along the west of the Outer Isles. I was all agog to see again the three-mile long beach of Tràigh Swish on whose glittering white sands the breakers of the mighty Atlantic murmur or roar according to Neptune's mood.

I might have turned in either direction. The guiding hand of Providence turned my steps in a southerly direction toward the granite headland known as Ard Swish which is pierced by a natural arch some ten yards long which leads to a small sandy cove beyond known as Tràigh Veck, or more correctly Bheag.

As I drew near I was hailed by a female form and bidden to make all haste. Alas, in spite of my efforts I arrived just too late to see the Todday Monster which only a minute or two before had been savagely tearing up the beach with its huge teeth.

But I was able to see the scars this creature of the primeval deep had made and I was able to note that there was not a single footprint upon that beach, proving conclusively that Mrs Lucy Odd had not ventured beyond the opening of the arch from which she had seen the monster. Mrs Odd is the mother of ex-Sergeant-major Alfred Odd, who when occupied with the business of Mars during the war in training the stalwart men of the two Toddays to resist invasion was smiled upon by Venus, or in other words wooed and won Peggy Macroon, one of Mr Joseph Macroon's lovely daughters.

A word about Mrs Lucy Odd. She is a Londoner born and bred, and for a woman some years past the allotted span of a truly remarkable vigour and alertness. Her

courage may be realised when instead of fainting or flee-
ing when she surprised the monster upon the beach of
Tràigh Veck she opened her umbrella and drove it back
into the sea. Mrs Odd's encounter with the monster confirms the existence of its unusual teeth which had already
been noted by Mr Archie MacRurie of Snorvig and by
little Cairistiona and Ealasaid MacCodrum of Garryboo.
Mr Kenneth Macroon, it may be recalled, only saw the
monster's yellowish-brown back.

I have never had the slightest doubt about the accuracy
of the previous stories, but I confess that until I saw with
my own eyes the condition of the sand in Tràigh Veck
I had been inclined to suppose that the teeth of the
monster may not have been quite so large as it now
appears certain they are. In venturing that opinion I
allowed my judgment to be influenced by prejudice and
freely admit it. I had put forward a suggestion, based on
my belief in the existence of a male and female Loch Ness
Monster, that if one of them had been killed by the flying
saucer the survivor would probably seek another mate
for itself on our western seaboard. Therefore, let me be
frank, I was anxious to identify the Todday Monster
with what we know about the Loch Ness Monster. That
theory is no longer tenable. The Todday Monster is as
large as an elephant, according to Mrs Odd, but it
definitely lacks the length of body we have learned to
associate with the Loch Ness Monster. I discard as fanci-
ful and even absurd the theory that the Loch Ness
Monster in the manner of certain lizards disencumbered
itself of its tail when it met the flying saucer.

I shall remind such theorists that not a single one of
the authenticated descriptions of the Loch Ness Monster
makes any mention of these enormous teeth which are
the outstanding feature of the Todday Monster. The
story that it had been seen crossing the road by Drumnadrochit with a sheep in its mouth was almost immediately
discredited. Everything we know about the Loch Ness
Monster indicates that it is—I still hope I do not have to
say "was"—a placid and even amiable vegetarian. The
grief felt in Inverness when the news was published of its
possible slaughter by a flying saucer expressed the genuine
affection which the Loch Ness Monster had roused all
over the North.

Furthermore, another characteristic of the Loch Ness Monster is—or was—its mane. Those who have seen the Todday Monster are unanimous in declaring that it does not possess a mane, and though Mr Kenneth Macroon who saw the back of the Todday Monster was at first under the impression that he saw a mane he is convinced that this mane was in fact a long streamer of sea-weed the yellowish brown tint of which led him to suppose that it formed part of a capillary growth on the monster's neck.

There were a few theorists who maintained the possibility of the Loch Ness Monster's mane having been burnt off by the flying saucer. I find it easier to believe that the monster which had been observed at close quarters by five people in Great and Little Todday has revealed the existence of a great mammal or saurian hitherto unknown to science. We are only at the beginning of what should be a period of intensive observation throughout the length of our western seaboard. The new monster has probably been sighted in several other islands besides Great and Little Todday, and there is no reason why we should not presently hear from Lewis or Harris or Barra, not to mention the Inner Isles, of as close an encounter with it as was enjoyed by Mrs Odd on Little Todday.

I am myself determined to devote the whole of this summer to searching for the monster, for I cannot believe that the guiding hand of Providence directed me to Tràigh Swish at that moment merely to leave my curiosity baulked.

In conclusion, I should like to express to the people of Inverness-shire my sincere hope that the Loch Ness Monster or its mate will soon be seen again rushing across the silvery water in sportive zest. At any rate, wherever the Loch Ness Monster may be at the present moment the people of Inverness-shire can feel completely confident that it has not emigrated to the West.

And yet one more word. While admittedly the Todday Monster's teeth must make the most ardent naturalist pause and reflect before he decides that it is as harmless as the Loch Ness Monster, I think the fact of its retreat before Mrs Odd's expanded umbrella may well be an indication that it is a shy, even a timorous creature in spite of its teeth, and that, given the requisite prudence,

"I always keep well, Maclean, but Kilwhillie has had what they call a chill on the liver."

"Tut-tut. I'm sorry to be hearing that. Nasty things livers."

"Beastly!" the Chieftain woofed. "Well, you've seen in the *Daily Tale* that this writing fellow Mackay has given up his idiotic notion about our monster having gone to the Islands?"

"I did indeed, Ben Nevis. But they're not at all pleased about it in Inverness."

"Do you mean to say they wanted our monster to go gallivanting off to the Islands? That's that Bolshie Councillor Macaulay from Lewis, I suppose. I always say I have a great respect for Lewismen, but once a Lewisman gets an idea into his head nothing will knock it out, nothing. I'm glad he's the only Lewisman we have on the Inverness-shire Council. I'm told nobody dares say a word in Dingwall at the Ross-shire meetings for fear of upsetting them all in Stornoway."

"No, no, Ben Nevis, it wasn't that anybody here wanted the Loch Ness Monster to go to the Islands. The trouble is Obaig."

"You don't mean to say Dunstaffnage is saying he's seen our monster in Loch Etive?"

"No, no, no, Ben Nevis, the Captain of Dunstaffnage hasn't said a word about the monster. No, it's the hotels."

"Hotels?"

"Yes, the hotels here think that the *Daily Tale* was put up to offer this £250 reward by the Obaig people. They reckon this monster in the Islands will be a big attraction to the Americans."

"What do Americans want with £250? They're rolling in dollars."

"Ach, it's not the money, Ben Nevis. It's the advertisement. They're reckoning in Obaig that, whatever the weather, they'll have the best season ever."

"Well, of course I had a feeling that the Argyll people would cash in on this. I was saying so to Kilwhillie. You're a Maclean."

"I'm a Maclean right enough."

"Well, I don't have to tell you that you simply cannot trust a Campbell. I never thought about this hotel business. My idea was they might try and say our monster had gone to Loch Fyne or Loch Awe, and in that case I was prepared to take strong measures. But this sneaking hotel business is just the way the Campbells would go to work. However, I'll stop their little game."

"And how will you be doing that?" Maclean asked.

And for answer Ben Nevis indulged in a gesture in which few had seen him indulge. He put a finger to his great eagle's beak and winked slowly at the dapper porter of the Porridge Hotel.

Chapter 8

LOVE AT FIRST SIGHT

MR SYDNEY PREW, the Secretary of the National Union of Hikers, sat in his office at 702 Gower Street and, his lips tightly pursed, looked at what he called the mountain of correspondence on his desk.

"I've never known so many enquiries about camping sites for so early in June, Miss Wriggleston."

Mr Prew's amanuensis, a thin woman in her mid-forties, sighed sympathetically. She had not yet abandoned hope of luring Mr Prew into matrimony, though she had been luring away now for over ten years and all her friends assured her that he was a confirmed old maid.

"It's this monster they've been seeing in the Hebrides, Mr Prew."

"Yes, yes, I'm sure it is," he agreed. "Dear me, it's about twelve years since I was in the Highlands, and I've never been to the Islands at all. I'd like to go before I retire from active service."

"Retire, Mr Prew?" Miss Wriggleston echoed apprehensively.

"Well, in another three years when I shall be sixty I think it will be my duty to resign and give way to a younger pair of knees."

Mr Prew tittered to himself at this affectionate little allusion to the hiker's costume.

"Not that I shall give up hiking of course," he added quickly. "No indeed. To paraphrase that grand song of Harry Lauder's, I intend to hike right on to the end of the road."

The shrivelled little man with the eyes of a kindly old maid gazed out of the grimy window of the Gower Street office at the June sky above Bloomsbury. Could Miss Wriggleston but have known it, he had divested himself of his trousers in fancy and was pulling on the old shorts to feel once more the light summer breeze playing round his spidery legs.

"I think I shall suggest to the Acting President that I

will take my vacation in a week or two's time, instead of
waiting until August as usual."

"I wish I could take mine then," Miss Wriggleston said.

"Yes, well, I'm afraid the office cannot spare both of us
simultaneously."

He did not think that his amanuensis had seriously intended to sigh for the unattainable in the shape of a hiking
duet with himself, but it was just as well to make its utter
unattainableness perfectly clear. He turned back to the
mountain of letters.

"Nobody loves young people more than I do, but I do
think they are getting rather lazy," he commented after
reading through another half dozen. "One can understand
enquiries about how to get to Great Todday, but I do not
think it necessary to ask whether it is better to go from
Euston or King's Cross to Glasgow and certainly not to ask
us to send them a selection of trains."

Just then there was a knock on the door, and a young
man in his mid-twenties came into the office, a large but
lanky young man with dark wavy hair, a good-looking,
indeed a handsome young man in a slightly farouche way.

"Oh, good morning," he said, scowling with shyness.
"I'm sorry to bother you but I was told you might be able
to help me."

"Quite, quite. We're always glad to do that. You're a
member of the N.U.H. of course?"

"I beg your pardon?"

"The National Union of Hikers."

"Well, I'm not actually, but I'd like to be. It was Lord
Buntingdon who advised me to come and see you."

"Ah, Lord Buntingdon, our revered President."

"Yes, he very kindly asked me down to Ouse Hall to
study his tortoises. It's the most wonderful collection of
tortoises in the world."

"I know, I know," said Mr Prew crisply. "Though, alas,
I'm not"—he played for a moment with the word "testudin-
ologist" but rejected it—"I'm not a tortoise man myself.
May I have your name?"

"Brownsworth. W. W. Brownsworth."

"Might we have the prefix in full? Miss Wriggleston,
will you be good enough?"

"William Waterlow Brownsworth, 22 Wilberforce Gar-
dens, S.W. 7."

"The annual subscription is five shillings," said Miss Wriggleston brightly when she had entered those details. "You'd like a badge, of course?"

"Oh, thank you very much."

She took from a drawer the green badge with the device of two crossed staffs in white above the motto—*Hike On, Hike Ever.*

"That will be another half a crown."

Brownsworth forked out.

"Let me shake hands to welcome the latest member of our great Union, and a friend of Lord Buntingdon," said Mr Prew.

Brownsworth gulped.

"I don't think I can exactly call him a friend. I mean to say when I wrote to ask him if I could visit his tortoises he very kindly asked me to come down to Ouse Hall and when I told him that I was a keen member of the Society of Palaeontological Research and wanted to go into the question of this mysterious creature reported from the Hebrides he advised me to consult you about accommodation and all that sort of thing. He said you knew every corner of Britain."

"Oh, that's too generous of Lord Buntingdon. Wonderful man, isn't he? Almost the last great Liberal we have left. Dear me, I fear that such peers as Lord Buntingdon will ere long themselves pass into the domain of palaeontology."

"I spent a fortnight last year investigating the Loch Ness Monster in the hope of being able to link it up with a plesiosaurus, an ichthyosaurus, or indeed with any of the megalosaurs."

"Quite, quite. Most interesting, I imagine."

"I wasn't satisfied by the evidence," said Brownsworth. "To be frank, I'm not convinced that the Loch Ness Monster exists. The evidence for the existence of this strange creature on the western seaboard of Scotland looks on paper much more solid."

"I wouldn't know," said Mr Prew, who found in the catchphrase of the moment an elixir of youth.

"So I thought I would go and investigate for myself on this island, Great Todday, and what I was wondering about is accommodation."

Mr Prew shook his head.

"I'm afraid a good many people are wondering about that. There is an hotel at Snorvig, the port of Great Todday, and one Joseph Macroon can board and lodge three or four visitors on Little Todday. Some of the crofters on both islands offer accommodation in the season to visitors who do not ask for the amenities of a fashionable seaside resort. However, I have been satisfied that for the rest of the summer there is no possibility of accommodating any more visitors."

"I see," said the young palaeontologist in a depressed voice. Then he brightened. "But couldn't I camp out?"

"My dear sir, of course you can camp out," Mr Prew replied with enthusiasm. "And I fancy I may venture to presume that Lord Buntingdon sent you to me because with that extraordinary sagacity of his he expected that if you wanted to spend any time in Great or Little Todday you would only be able to carry out such a project if you were prepared to camp out."

"And Mr Prew has forgotten more about camping out than most people ever knew," Miss Wriggleston interposed.

"I'm afraid Miss Wriggleston's enthusiasm makes for exaggeration," said Mr Prew modestly. "But I suppose I have studied the art of camping out more intensively than most people. Where haven't I camped out? The Gobi Desert, the Kalahari Desert, the island of Tiburon in the Californian Gulf, on the slopes of Cotopaxi, in Patagonia, among the hairy Ainus in northern Japan, and perhaps most often of all in that wild no man's land where Burma marches with China."

"I say I do envy you, Mr Prew," the young palaeontologist gulped in admiration.

"Oh, I mustn't give you the idea that I have actually visited those places in the flesh. No, no. I'm afraid I must wait until my ship comes home before I manage to do that." And then, feeling that his phraseology was becoming a little old-fashioned, he suddenly leant across his desk, and pointing at his visitor and allowing his kindly old maid's eyes to glitter with a demoniac knowledgeableness he ejaculated:

"Sez you!"

Brownsworth was sure that he was meant to laugh at this point, but he was not perfectly sure and so instead he twisted his mouth into a clumsy smile.

"But don't be downhearted," said Mr Prew, who did not realise that his visitor was smiling. "I do know a great deal from practical experience about camping out in the Highlands, and I don't think the technique for camping out in the Islands will vary greatly. In any case, I shall soon know, for I am planning to visit Great and Little Todday myself before June is over. I beg your pardon, Miss Wriggleston?"

"I didn't say anything, Mr Prew."

This was true. Miss Wriggleston had only released an involuntary sigh.

"By the way, I ought to warn you my information is that Great Todday is a Protestant island, whereas Little Todday is Roman Catholic."

"That doesn't worry me one way or the other," said Brownsworth, whose study of primeval life had discouraged the spirit of sectarianism."

"Quite, quite. But I thought you should know, though of course the N.U.H. is all embracing. Indeed, we have quite a few Communists. Oh yes, rather. We will not have nudists, though. The Nudist Ramblers' Association has been trying to muscle in for years now, but we have always firmly rejected their repeated applications to be affiliated. Mind you, I've nothing against nudists myself. Not at all. But you see, a lot of hotels all over the country use our green signboards with N.U.H. on them, and you just can't run the risk of Nudist Ramblers trying to obtain accommodation and of course inevitably being refused. The next thing would be that some of our jolly young people would arrive rather lightly clad as they often are, and the proprietor thinking they were more nudists would refuse them accommodation. Well, now, if you're going to camp out on either of the Toddays this is what you'll want."

Ten minutes later Brownsworth was on his way to the store recommended by Mr Prew for the provision of a camping outfit.

"And I do hope you'll win the £250 prize offered by the *Daily Tale*," Mr Prew had assured him before they parted.

"I'm only interested in the palaeontological side of this business," the young scientist had replied.

"And you will let Lord Buntingdon know that we looked after you in Gower Street. I won't say good-bye. Just au revoir, because I think we shall be meeting again."

"A very good type," the Secretary of the N.U.H. observed to his amanuensis. "I do like to see hiking pinned on to a definite object. That's true democracy."

Muriel Waggett and her mother were on the pier at Snorvig on the day that Brownsworth came down the gangway from the *Island Queen* with that look which hikers under the weight of their camping equipment share with John Bunyan's Christian under the weight of his sins.

"Another of these trippers hoping to win that money," said Mrs Waggett.

A minute later Brownsworth had unbuckled himself from his load and, head erect, was standing beside it on the pier to look round him. In that moment Muriel Waggett, who as a Waaf had regarded with frigid indifference over months some of the bushiest moustaches in the Royal Air Force, fell in love.

"Poor young men," said Mrs Waggett, "I'm afraid they're all going to be very disappointed."

Muriel would have liked to stand up for this handsome stranger's chance, but the cunning which Cupid injects in female hearts with the virus of love warned her to be cautious.

"I couldn't care less," she said severely.

That night when Paul Waggett tuned in to the Brains Trust, which always gave him a much relished opportunity to expose human fallibility at a post-mortem in which he was the intellectual coroner, a listener from Peckham Rye asked the Brains Trust if it believed in love at first sight. A laddered bluestocking from the London School of Economics having knocked out a hopefully romantic Tory M.P. in the last round, the Question Master summed up in the style of the Delphic Oracle and left Peckham Rye as uncertain of what the Brains Trust believed about love at first sight as once upon a time Athens was about the strategy to be adopted against Sparta.

"I couldn't understand what the Brains Trust believed about love at first sight," Muriel Waggett said when her father had switched off and the intellectual inquest began.

"Well, I think it's all hooey," Elsie commented.

"I don't know what *you* know about it," Muriel snapped.

"I know as much as you do anyway," her twin snapped back.

The effort to preserve her self-control which this challenge cost Muriel may be imagined.

"What does Daddo think?" she muttered.

"Daddo thinks it's nothing but imagination," he declared loftily. "And we've all had a lesson about the effect of that over this imaginary monster. I suppose there was the usual mob of trippers from the *Island Queen*. Well, nobody was more anxious than I was to stop Hitler, nobody, but I sometimes wonder if we haven't fallen out of the frying-pan into the fire, as the saying goes. You remember what a fuss the Toddayites kicked up when I tried to make arrangements about the scorched earth policy? And who would have had to bear the brunt of such a policy? I should. Scorched earth would have ruined my shooting on the Toddays for years. Well, the Germans did *not* manage to occupy Todday and so as luck would have it the local opposition to the scorched earth policy didn't matter so much as it might have. You know, Mumsy, if I had my way now I would apply the scorched earth policy to all those trippers who are swarming over the island to look for this imaginary monster."

"Oh, Paul, you wouldn't really burn down all the houses?" his wife exclaimed.

"No, no, no, of course not," he said impatiently. "What I mean is that the Toddayites ought to refuse to supply them with anything. Anything," he repeated in a dream of thwarted ferocity. "But, of course, they think first of their pockets. They have an opportunity of overcharging these trippers for eggs and milk and butter and everything else, and they can't resist it. Do you know I drove right round the island this morning and couldn't get an egg anywhere?"

"But our hens are still laying quite well, Daddo," one of the chicks put in.

"We can never have too many eggs in waterglass," said their father. "And this is the time to get them. The same with butter."

"Butter in waterglass?" Mrs. Waggett exclaimed.

"Of course not, Dolly. I mean the same scarcity of butter," he said in a voice that tried to express an infinite sufferance of human stupidity. "I couldn't get so much as half a pound of butter. I actually found three of these hikers fishing in Loch Skinny and when I told them that the fishing was strictly preserved, do you know what one of them said? 'I

D

always heard the Scotch were mean.' I made what I thought was rather a neat retort. 'Well,' I said, 'I happen to be an Englishman and I've always heard that an Englishman's home was his castle.'"

"You must have made him feel rather small," said Mrs Waggett with conjugal flattery. "What did he say to that?"

"Most insolent. He turned round to his fellow poachers and said 'Look what lives in an aquarium.'"

"How disgusting, Paul."

"Oh, I paid no attention. All I said was, 'Well, you've been warned.' And then I found three more of these trippers fishing in Loch Sleeport and when I told them fishing was strictly forbidden one of them said he hadn't fought with the Eighth Army in Africa to be stopped fishing at home. If only Monty wasn't so friendly with everybody I should have been tempted to set him at these poachers, and let them know they were back in the Eighth Army. And then Sergeant MacGillivray wasn't very helpful. He said he was afraid he hadn't time to go round the island stopping poachers because he was kept so busy stopping the kids in Snorvig from pulling the pegs out of these tents. 'Well, Sergeant,' I said, 'I think my trout more important than these trippers' tents.' It obviously made no impression on him at all. I think the world's going mad."

"There's some music on the cinema organ for half an hour in the Light Programme," Mrs Waggett reminded him soothingly after consulting the *Radio Times*.

"Oh, that's good," her husband said, and soon he was sitting back listening, all problems insular and mundane banished by the music drawn by St Cecilia up aloft from the silver organ-pipes of Paradise.

That night Muriel was lying awake, wondering whether the member of the Brains Trust who had said that love at first sight implied an immediate mutual attraction between two people was right. The good-looking hiker had not seemed to notice her, but after all, if he had fallen in love with her at first sight he would not have wanted people on the pier to know he had. Had not she herself pretended not to have noticed him when Mumsy had said she was afraid so many people were going to be disappointed?

"I saw rather an attractive hiker talking to Archie MacRurie while I was waiting for the post," Elsie murmured through the darkness.

Muriel's heart began to thump. She and her twin could not each have seen an attractive hiker; they must have seen the same one.

"Oh, what was he like?" she asked, making the bed creak to conceal any quavers in her voice.

"Tall with dark wavy hair and a sort of intense look," her twin replied.

"He sounds rather like Bungo Jones," said Muriel.

"Not a bit like Bungo Jones," Elsie snapped back. Squadron-Leader Bungo Jones had been for several months the main topic of Elsie's letters from Lancashire during the war to her twin in the Midlands.

"He had dark wavy hair, hadn't he?" Muriel reminded her twin.

"So what?" Elsie snapped again.

"Oh, all right," Muriel grumbled. "But if you've no objection I want to get to sleep."

"I'm not stopping you," said Elsie.

With a simultaneous movement the twins turned over and lay back to back in their two beds.

Elsie was soon asleep, but Muriel stayed awake for a long time, wondering how she could manage to meet the handsome stranger before Elsie managed to meet him, and how after she had succeeded in meeting him she could conceal from Elsie the fact that she had met him. How her heart would have leapt could she have known that, while she lay sleepless in the big bedroom she shared with Elsie at Snorvig House, out on Ard Snor the handsome stranger himself, equally sleepless, was wondering to himself who was the fair fluffy-haired girl he had seen on the pier. It would have given another kind of a leap if she had known that he was under the impression that he had seen her for the second time when she was coming out of the post-office.

It might put an undue strain upon romantic licence to suggest that it was the thought of a fair fluffy-haired girl he fancied he had encountered twice that was depriving Bill Brownsworth of sleep. It was not. This insomnia was induced by trying to sleep on a waterpoof sheet spread upon the hard ground of Ard Snor beneath a tent so low that if he sat up his head touched the canvas. Obedient to Mr Prew's instructions to excavate a small depression for his shoulder-blade he had unfortunately disturbed a metropolis of ants and after holding out against the agitated population for twenty minutes he had had to pitch his tent at a safe distance from the little brutes. This time he decided to dispense with any earthy receptacle for his shoulder-blades and they were not long in letting him know that they resented such neglect of their comfort. Unable to sleep he put out his hand for his matches in order to light the lantern which Mr Prew had impressed on him as a vital accessory to camping out; but where he thought his matches were there was a large slug; he grasped that instead, and yelled with horror. If there were any other campers in the vicinity they might have been forgiven for supposing that the Todday Monster had found a victim.

Brownsworth was annoyed with himself when he found what had caused him to yell like that. He felt, and rightly, that it was humiliating for a palaeontologist bent upon solving the riddle of a primeval monster to be frightened by a slug. He could not quite bring himself to overcome his guilt complex by picking the disgusting gasteropod up in his fingers and ejecting it from his tent. So he emptied a two-ounce tin of tobacco into his pouch, coaxed the slug into the tin with a twig from a dwarf sallow, and flung it forth. Then he snuggled down into his sleeping bag and started to read Commander Gould on sea serpents. Suddenly over the top of the volume appeared a yellow, green and purple monstrosity diabolically arched with a face like a drunken navvy and a threadlike pink forked tail waving above it. Bill Brownsworth, hurling the book away, leapt up so violently that he brought the tent down on top of himself, and after a free for all in which he burnt his cheek on the lantern, got some toothpaste in his eye and upset the pail of water he had fetched from a lochan a quarter of a mile away for his morning toilet he found himself further from sleep than ever.

Bill Brownsworth was a palaeontologist, not an entomologist, and he may be excused for not immediately recognising the caterpillar of the puss-moth for what it was, but that does not excuse a palaeontologist who has deliberately pitched his tent as near as the lie of the land allowed to the sea-cave in which Archie MacRurie had seen the monster for surrendering to the terror which the caterpillar hoped it was inspiring in the enemy who had interrupted its meal on sallow leaves.

The dawn was dove-grey in the sky above Ben Stickla and Ben Bustival before Bill Brownsworth at last fell asleep in his tent, and the sun was high before he woke to a cloudless morning. The discomforts and discomfitures of the night were forgotten in the placid beauty of the scene. The green carpet of Little Todday was spread out on the other side of the pale blue water of the Coolish. The smoke of Snorvig was sapphirine above the dark-tiled roofs. The sands of Garryboo, the only yellow sands in miles of white beaches up the western seaboard of the Outer Isles, may never have seemed so yellow as now they seemed against the azure of the Atlantic. Ben Bustival and Ben Stickla rose dark against the morning sunlight and though neither reached 1500 feet they seemed as majestic as the mighty bens of the mainland.

Bill Brownsworth strolled down the headland to stand above Uamh na Snaoiseanaich—the Snuff-taker's Cave—from which even on so tranquil a morning he could still hear from time to time the sound of a gentle sneeze. His palaeontological self-respect was restored, and the man who had yelled at the touch of a slug and leapt at the sight of a puss-moth caterpillar peered down now into the water at the base of Ard Snor ready to defy the teeth of any monstrous survival, palaeozoic, mesozoic or cainozoic.

Presently Brownsworth set out with his pail to secure water for his toilet from the lochan further up the headland. He was glad to see no other tent was in sight and made up his mind to take advantage of the good weather by chartering Archie MacRurie's boat and examining the Snuff-taker's Cave from the sea.

Bill Brownsworth's toilet did not worry him, but the cooking of his breakfast did. In spite of the apparently windless air the flame of the spirit lamp seemed to want to burn everywhere except under the little kettle where it ought to be burning, and then long before there was a sign of boiling the flame expired. He lighted another methylated cube and when that was exhausted the water in the kettle was still only luke-warm. He had been so intent on his preparations for a cup of tea that he had not noticed the approach of a young woman with fair fluffy hair in smoky-blue tweed.

"Won't it boil?" he heard a pleasant sympathetic voice ask.

"Oh, hello," he said and to his great surprise he did

not feel in the least shy. "No, the methylated spirit doesn't seem to last long enough."

"Let me try," she offered.

And with that curious command over the inanimate which women possess, the kettle was boiling away merrily in a minute or two.

"Extraordinary," Bill Brownsworth ejaculated.

"Not so much tea," Muriel Waggett said quickly. "Let me make it."

"Thanks awfully. I say, didn't I see you on the pier yesterday when the boat arrived?" he asked.

She nodded.

"I was with my mother."

"And then I saw you again in the post-office."

Muriel made a lightning-like decision.

"Yes, you did."

Of course, he would have to know sooner or later that she had a twin sister, but if she were clever it might be too late for Elsie to do anything about it.

"I say, I've only got one cup," said Bill Brownsworth.

"I don't mind," Muriel assured him tenderly.

"I say, what's your name?"

"Muriel. Muriel Waggett. What's yours?"

"Bill. Bill Brownsworth."

And as they sipped tea in turns from Bill's only cup both of them thought that it was the most delicious cup of tea either of them had ever drunk, and since both of them hated condensed milk such enjoyment should have convinced even a laddered bluestocking in the Brains Trust that there *was* such a thing as love at first sight.

Chapter 9

CABLE, TELEPHONE AND POST

ON the morning of the day when Bill Brownsworth and
Muriel Waggett established the existence of the phenomenon known as love at first sight, Ben Nevis received a
telegram from America, waving which like a flag he rushed
off in a state of high excitement to find his wife.

"Trixie! Trixie!" he bellowed. "Trixie, where on earth
are you? Trixie!"

In the Great Hall Toker informed him, with a hint of
reproachfulness in his tone, that Mrs MacDonald had
driven into Fort William.

"What the deuce has she gone to Fort William for?" the
Chieftain asked.

"Mrs MacDonald is meeting Miss Mary and Miss
Catriona, sir."

"Oh, I forgot. Of course. They were coming back from
London last night, weren't they?"

"They were, sir."

Cheated of his pleasure in announcing the news in the
cablegram to his wife the Chieftain announced it to his
butler; he had to tell somebody.

"Mr and Mrs Royde are sailing almost at once from
New York and hope to be at Knocknacolly in about a
fortnight, Toker."

"We must hope that the spell of clement weather which
we are enjoying will still be with us when they arrive, sir."

Chester Royde was the young American financier who
had bought the forest and lodge of Knocknacolly some
years previously from Hugh Cameron of Kilwhillie, and he
and his wife Carrie, a Canadian Macdonald before she
married Chester, had managed to spend a few weeks almost
every year in the house they had built on the site of the old
lodge. They never arrived usually until the beginning of
August.

"Yes, poor souls, they have had it rather wet once or
twice. The interesting thing is that Mr and Mrs Royde have
been hearing about this monster in the islands over in
America and Mr Royde wants to charter a yacht to go and
dig this brute out of its lair. Get me Mr Rawstorne on the

telephone. And don't go away while I'm talking through it in case I want you for the machinery."

Nothing could have revealed to Toker more clearly the tremendous excitement of Mac 'ic Eachainn than his intention to make use of an instrument he abominated.

"Hullo . . . hullo . . . hullo! Is that you, Tom? This is Donald Ben Nevis speaking. You knew that, did you? How on earth . . . well, if I don't shout into the beastly thing I can't hear what anybody says. Yes, I can hear you all right . . . I never suggested you were deaf . . . well, don't let's start an argument on this beastly contraption . . . look here, Tom, you know you said you thought you might be able to take the *Banshee* over to the islands later in June . . . I know it wasn't certain . . . well, look here, Chester and Carrie Royde have just heard about this monster and they're sailing right away. Royde wants to charter a yacht to hunt this monster and I thought it was a deal right up your street . . . of course he'll pay for it . . . well, you don't want to soak him if you know what I mean, because although he's as rich as Croesus he hates being soaked . . . well, charge him the top price you'd charge anybody else . . . you'd better cable him direct . . . and do it right away, Tom . . . he'll probably be cabling some confounded agent or other . . . you know what Americans are . . . they call it hustling. I don't know why they can't call it bustling, the same as we do . . . How are you keeping, Tom? . . . good . . . well, we don't want a long conversation on this beastly contraption. You'll cable Royde at once, won't you?"

"Do I ring this idiotic bell now or just put it back on the stand?" Ben Nevis asked his butler.

Toker stepped forward to relieve his master of the receiver.

"I can't think why the telephone was ever invented," Ben Nevis declared.

"It can be an extremely convenient method of rapid communication, sir."

"Yes, I suppose it is," the Chieftain admitted grudgingly. "Now tell Johnnie to bring the car round at once. I want to go to Kilwhillie."

"The car will hardly be back from Fort William just yet, sir."

"Oh lord, I wish trains wouldn't arrive from London just when I want the car. Well, I'd better go in the lorry."

But the lorry turned out to be away on some estate job in Strathdun.

"I suppose I shall have to telephone again. Kilwhillie won't like it, of course. He hates the beastly thing as much as I do. And don't go away, Toker, in case the machinery goes wrong."

"Kilwhillie is quite an adept with the telephone these days, sir. He has rung me up himself on more than one occasion."

"Go ahead then."

"Ben Nevis would like the Laird to speak to him . . . Oh, this is Toker speaking, sir . . . Ben Nevis wishes to speak with you."

The butler handed over the receiver.

"Hullo! Hullo! . . . is that you, Hugh? . . . how are you? . . . and the liver is all right again? . . . I was coming over to see you but Trixie has taken the car to Fort William to meet the two girls on their way back from that horrible place London . . . look here, I've had a cable from Chester and Carrie Royde to say they're coming over almost at once because Chester wants to charter Tom Rawstorne's *Banshee* and have a go at this monster out in the islands . . . we've simply got to kill this blundering tale that's going round about our monster having gone off to the islands . . . and I'll do it if I have to tow this island brute back behind the *Banshee* . . . what's that? . . . you've had a cable from America too? . . . from Yu-Yu? . . . she'll love a good hunt for this island monster . . . oh, she's not coming herself? . . . Deirdre and her husband . . . I never remember his name . . . oh, yes, Wilbur Carboy . . . well, that'll be splendid . . . of course they can come with us . . . I'm sure little Deirdre's as keen as mustard . . . she saw our monster once, you remember . . . we'll put them up at Glenbogle if you're fussing about these preparations for Walter Dutton's birthday . . . but you've got nearly four months to get ready for that . . . nonsense, Hugh, of course you must come on this expedition . . . I never can understand your objection to the sea . . . I'm never seasick . . . yes, well, we can't argue about our insides on this beastly telephone . . . it always pings at me when I start arguing on it . . . I'll come over and see you to-morrow, Hugh."

Ben Nevis hung up the receiver and shook his head at his butler.

D *

"Can you understand why some people are always sea-sick, Toker?"

"I believe, sir, it's a matter of the constitution. Some gentlemen and many ladies are allergic to the motion of the sea, and Mr Rawstorne's yacht has the reputation of being what in nautical parlance is called a lively craft."

"Did you say allergic just now?"

"I did, sir."

"Allergic?"

"Allergic, sir."

"Where do you get hold of these extraordinary words, Toker?"

"I pick them up, sir, in the course of my reading."

"I don't pick up words in that way. They seem to stick to you like burrs."

"I often delve in the dictionary, sir, in my spare time."

"Allergic," the Chieftain repeated to himself. "Do you think they'd know that word in Inverness?"

"I think it extremely possible, sir."

"Do you think if I asked those nincompoops on the Roads Committee why they're so allergic to a road up Glenbogle they'd know what I was talking about?"

"I feel sure some of them would, sir."

"A-L-U-R-G-I-C?"

"A-double-L-E-R-G-I-C, sir."

I suppose you're certain it is allérgic and not állergic?"

"I have never heard the latter pronunciation, sir."

At that moment Toker caught sight of the car returning from Fort William.

"The car, sir," he said and hurried to the front door followed by the Chieftain.

"Ah, here you are at last. I was getting rather allergic to waiting for you. Ha-ha-ha!" He guffawed with boisterous glee over his new word. "Enjoy yourselves in that horrible place London?"

The two hefty daughters of Mac 'ic Eachainn extracted themselves from the car to greet their father.

"Chester and Carrie Royde are coming over almost at once. So are Deirdre and her husband—I never can remember his name. We've got Tom Rawstorne's *Banshee* and we're going to rout out this Todday monster."

"Oh, good-oh," said Mary MacDonald gruffly; Catriona grunted endorsement.

The Chieftain's plan to pursue the Todday monster to its lair was threatened by the apparent ubiquity of the quarry. Where was its lair? Or indeed had it a lair at all?

Hector Hamish Mackay used to say afterwards that without the help of Bill Brownsworth he believes his reason would have given way under the strain of trying to keep in touch with what was generally known as the Todday monster, though as is made clear by the selection below of letters from the correspondence of the *Scottish Daily Tale*, not all of which were published in its columns and some of which were addressed personally to Mr Mackay himself, many of these correspondents much resented the monster's affiliation to Todday and blamed Mr Mackay for it.

Sir,

I do not know why you persist in writing of the "Todday" Monster. Are you aware that it has been seen on no less than seven occasions on both the west and east coasts of Lewis—in Loch Seaforth and Loch Erisort on the east and in Loch Roag and Uig Bay on the west. A Bernera woman, who was gathering crotal close to where the bridge linking Bernera with Lewis should have been built years ago, looked up from her creel to see the monster glaring at her, round the corner of a high rock. Hearing its teeth champing the woman fainted and but for the fact that the tide was ebbing at the time she might easily have been drowned.

Yours, etc.,
Leodshasach

Sir,

I sometimes ask myself if there is anything that the people of Lewis will not claim for themselves as we in Harris know too well to our cost. If the monster is to bear the prefix of any island we in Harris would much prefer it to be called the Todday Monster than the Lewis Monster. But why not the Long Island Monster?

Incidentally, you will be interested to know that the Long Island Monster has been seen twice by the schoolchildren of Scarp in the water of the strait which separates Scarp from Hushinish. I will remind you that the each uisge or water-horse has been a recurring phenomenon through the centuries in the natural fauna of the beautiful Island of Harris, whereas no authentic example of one having been seen on the Island of Lewis is recorded.

Yours, etc.,
Indignant Harrisman

Sir,
   Why the Long Island Monster? It has been seen at eleven different points on both the east and west coasts of Skye from Sleat to Trotternish.

Yours, etc.,
Sgiathanach

Dear Mr Mackay,
   I am at present staying in the beautiful island of Harris in connection with my researches into the problem whether the late Sir James Barrie was in fact a changeling himself and therefore whether the story of Mary Rose may not have been partly autobiographical. Naturally in the course of my researches I have had to spend many hours in solitary meditation upon the small island in one of the Harris lochs which all are agreed inspired Barrie to write his masterpiece.

   You spoke in your article of the guiding hand of Providence. On June 11th—numerologists will recognize the significance of the date—June=6, 1+1=2, 6+2=8, the number of Fate—I had myself put ashore on the island by the gillie who makes himself responsible for my transport. I looked at the time on my watch when I stepped ashore and noted that it was exactly six minutes past eleven. 1+1=2, 2+6=8, the number of Fate again. I had arranged to remain on the island until 4 p.m., having brought with me some sandwiches, at which hour my gillie, Angus Macleod, was to call for me. You, Mr Mackay, who are a man of imagination, will understand the mysterious drowsiness which is apt to overtake anybody in tune with the infinite who finds himself under the spell of the magical west of which nobody has written with more appropriate eloquence than yourself. To such a drowsiness I succumbed on June 11th and fell fast asleep. Suddenly I awoke with a feeling that something was watching me, and to my amazement I saw beyond a knoll covered with bell-heather an arched neck about ten feet long surmounted by the head of a large horse with eyes that reminded me of a crocodile. I lay without moving a muscle and almost holding my breath, for I must admit that I have never felt more frightened in my life. Presently the neck of the monster began to develop a kind of upward corkscrew motion and opened its mouth wide. Supposing that it was about to attack me I uttered a cry of terror which apparently alarmed the monster, for with a rapid downward corkscrew motion the neck and head vanished.

I am ashamed to say that my fears got the better of my scientific curiosity and instead of trying to see what happened to the monster, I lay where I was without moving.

It has occurred to me since that the monster may have been yawning when it opened its mouth, for I perceived no sign of those long teeth which have figured in other accounts and the monster I saw approximated much more nearly to the descriptions of those who have seen the Loch Ness Monster. Consequently I have asked myself whether your original hypothesis that one of the Loch Ness Monsters had left Loch Ness to seek another mate after the death of the original mate may not be the true explanation of the phenomenon. I ask myself further whether the condition of the beach on Little Todday may not have been caused by this corkscrew motion of the monster's neck rather than by its teeth. Perhaps you will consider this tentative suggestion of mine and let me know what you think of it?

Finally, may I say that when after the monster's departure I looked at my watch the time was seven minutes past two which, allowing for a minute for the withdrawal of the monster after I shouted, would make the time when I saw it first six minutes past two. $6+2=8$, the number of Fate yet again. From then until four minutes past four when Angus Macleod came for me in the boat ($4+4=8!$) nothing unusual happened. I cannot help being glad that no monster visited the island while the late Sir James Barrie was, as I believe, recapturing from its atmosphere his own memories of fairyland before he was brought to Thrums as a changeling.

It would have been almost impossible for the great dramatist to avoid mentioning the monster in Mary Rose, in which case some of the more materially minded members of the audience might have come away from the Haymarket Theatre with the impression that Mary Rose herself had been swallowed up by a monster instead of being carried off by the fairies.

I have written to you at some length about my extraordinary experience on "the island that likes to be visited" because I revere you as a writer whose life has been dedicated to damming the dark and turbid flood of materialism which threatens to sweep away all that is most sacred in the life of our country.

If you have time to give me the benefit of your observations upon my experience will you be good enough to write to me c/o Mr Tom Cameron, Tarbert Hotel, Isle of Harris.

Yours faithfully with
my sincerest homage,

Wilfred Cartwright

author of Why I am a Psychometrist, The Secret of Numbers, On the Threshold of the Beyond, The Illusion of Time, *etc., etc.*

P.S. *It occurs to me that my experience as a psychometrist might be of use in determining the whereabouts of the Todday Monster, could I be brought in contact with some spot which shows physical evidence of the monster's attentions. I regret to say that when I walked round the island after my alarming experience on June 11th I could find no visible sign by the disturbance of the vegetation of the passage of a great body, and so I was unable to employ my psychometrical gifts to any advantage. The absence of any visible sign of the monster's having landed on the island suggests to me that the long neck and horse's head I saw may have been extruded directly from the water. The place I fell asleep was within a dozen yards of the loch and if one allows a length of twenty feet for the whole neck it could easily have been seen by me. If those who estimate the total length of the Loch Ness Monster at round about eighty feet are right it could surely rear itself twenty feet from the water with consummate ease.*

Nobost Hotel,
Mid Uist,
June 9

Sir,
    Last Sunday morning while I was walking along the path on the north side of Loch Stew to note what prospect there was of an early run of sea-trout I saw the back of what looked like a large yellowish-brown hornless bull emerge from the water and almost instantly submerge, having presumably scented my proximity. I saw nothing of any mane, but I did see what appeared to be large tufts of hair sticking out on either side of its head.

Yours, etc.,

Henry Hotblack
Lt.-Col. (retd.)

Free Presbyterian Manse,
Gibberdale,
East Uist

Sir,

We were disagreeably surprised in East Uist to read Colonel Hotblack's letter in your issue of yesterday. Nobody in East Uist would venture to profane the Lord's Day by thirsting after fish on the Sabbath.

During the war we had occasion to protest more than once against aeroplanes using the East Uist aerodrome on the Sabbath, and now that the war is over we resent strongly the notion that monsters can rouse worldly thoughts on the day which the Lord our God has set aside for His service.

We know that our neighbours on Mid Uist do not see eye to eye to us in this matter of Sabbath observance, but we hope that they will pay regard to our feelings in East Uist and do all that they can to prevent visitors like Colonel Hotblack from encouraging idle sight-seers to offend the Lord by staring at fish or at monsters on the Sabbath.

Yours etc.,

(Revd.) *John MacCodrum*

To *Hector Hamish Mackay.*

How much have you been paid by those well-known robbers, Joseph Macroon and Roderick MacRurie, to pretend that this monster is their personal property? You cannot be ignorant that this monster has visited every island in turn and though you pretend to be such an authority on the islands and have written a lot of in-accurate nonsense about them in books that I wouldn't dirty my fingers to open you are nothing better than a tout for interested parties.

Fair Play

Sir,

We in Inverness are surprised that you should lend your columns to the wild speculations of Mr Hector Hamish Mackay, and we are astonished that Mr Mackay, who in the past has enjoyed our hospitality in no mean fashion, should turn round and bite the hands that fed him by lending himself to the exploitation of a chimera.

Yours etc.,

Disgusted Invernessian

Sir,

We in Obaig take strong exception to the attack on Mr Hector Hamish Mackay made by your anonymous correspondent who signs himself 'Disgusted Invernessian.' We recognise the devotion with which Mr Mackay is trying to establish the identity of the Islands Monster. 'Disgusted Invernessian' would do more to assist the spread of knowledge if he refrained from abuse of a Scottish writer to whose slogan 'See the Highlands and the Islands First' in his brilliant series of broadcasts last year we Gaels owe an immense debt of gratitude. 'Disgusted Invernessian's' annoyance at the loss of the Loch Ness Monster through 'enemy action' should not lead him into intemperate abuse. We sympathise with the chagrin of the 'Capital of the North,' but that will not keep the 'Capital of the West' from doing all it can do to welcome the great influx of visitors who are now thronging to Obaig and after they have enjoyed the famous hospitality of the 'Capital of the West' speeding them on their way to the Isles of Enchantment.

Yours etc.,
Obaig Gu Brath

Sir,

We should be glad to know by what right 'Obaig Gu Brath' claims the title of Capital of the West for Obaig. The Capital of the West is and always will be Fort William.

We are, Sir,
Your obedient Servants,
Donald MacDonald of Ben Nevis
Hugh Cameron of Kilwhillie

"Oh dear, oh dear," Mr Mackay sighed to Bill Brownsworth as he looked at the letters scattered over the table in the parlour at Joseph Macroon's house. "And here's a letter from my editor":

Dear Mr Mackay,

I feel that when you have looked through this correspondence you will probably want to follow the track of the 'monster' right up the Long Island. I think too it would be as well if you visited Skye also. It will not do for the Scottish Daily Tale to give the least impression of prejudice in favour of any particular island, especially of the islands with so comparatively small a population as Great and Little Todday. I suggest that it might be better if you didn't visit Inverness or the neighbourhood just at present. The feeling is rather strong, especially in Glen Urquhart where, I'm sorry to say, many people have cancelled their orders for the Daily Tale *because they think we have taken up a hostile attitude to the Loch Ness Monster. I am sure that if you can get some really good stories from Lewis any suspicion of bias will vanish, and it will go a long way to offset the effect of that letter from the Wee Free Minister in East Uist.*

I expect you'll be able to leave the Toddays in the hands of a reliable man who could telephone to us in case of emergency.

Please get up round all the Long Island as soon as possible. Carmichael has gone to Inverness.

Yours sincerely,

James Donaldson

P.S. *We had a great laugh yesterday, when our wee Marjorie announced that she had seen a Teddy Monster in Vincent Square. The creature in question was the Lord Provost in his robes!*

"I don't understand why the Inverness-shire people should be annoyed with me," said the topographer. "Surely I made it quite plain that I had abandoned my theory that the Loch Ness Monster has gone to the islands? People cannot read their papers intelligently. However, magna est veritas et prevalebit," he concluded solemnly. "Will you hold the fort while I'm away, Brownsworth?"

The young palaeontologist had no hesitation in agreeing, not the least cogent of his reasons for doing so being the chance it gave him of occupying Mr Mackay's room in Kiltod. He and the topographer had met when the Biffer asked Brownsworth if he would mind Mr Mackay's company in the *Kittiwake* while they took advantage of the fine weather to explore the Snuff-taker's Cave. Bill Brownsworth would have much preferred to enjoy Muriel Waggett's company in the *Kittiwake*, but she had exclaimed in alarm at the prospect of the gossip it would cause in Snorvig if she were to be seen out alone with a stranger to the island.

"You see, Father's position here must be remembered. In a way he's really the equivalent of the Laird and I mustn't give the people a chance to gossip."

Muriel did not add that if she went out in the *Kittiwake* with Bill her twin sister would undoubtedly hear about it and would resent having been omitted from the invitation. She had not yet told Bill Brownsworth that she had a sister and had warned him not to greet her even if he saw her alone in Snorvig. She had taken this precaution in case he should meet Elsie and, imagining Elsie to be herself, give the game away.

In fact Bill Brownsworth did meet Elsie once or twice and with the audacity that love at first sight inspires he had tried to convey to her without other people's noticing it how glad he was to see her, and he had much admired the way his love was able to receive the quick signals of affection without turning a single fair hair.

"I saw that rather good-looking hiker in Snorvig," Elsie would say, for Elsie was pleasurably aware of attracting his dark fervid glances. "Couldn't we get Daddo to ask him up to the house?"

"You know what he feels about trippers," Muriel had always replied. She was determined not to run any risk of changing the focus of love at first sight.

In the end after three stolen meetings on Ard Snor Muriel had told Bill that she thought it would be better if he went over to Little Todday and camped out there.

"But I shan't see you then, Muriel," he exclaimed in dismay.

"I'll find an excuse to come over and we'll be able to go for a long walk together," she promised.

"But why can't I go to your father and say we want to be engaged?"

"Oh, no, Bill, no. He's awfully conventional and if you went to him dressed in shorts and said you wanted to marry me he'd never understand that you wouldn't be dressed like that all the time."

"Surely I could make it clear, that I'm only dressed like this because I'm investigating this monster?"

"Yes, but he doesn't believe in the monster. You couldn't say anything that would annoy him more. You couldn't, really."

"Well, we can't go on for ever being afraid to tell your father. It's like the Brownings in Wimpole Street."

"But you never suggested an elopement, Bill. That would be rather marvellous, wouldn't it?"

"I don't see any point at all in an elopement," Bill Brownsworth demurred. "That would upset my people. And if I get this Readership in Palaeontology at Norwich University next autumn, which I've every hope of doing, we can be married."

"Darling, how marvellous!"

"And if I can only identify this monster I'm bound to get that Readership. I mean to say, if it turns out to be a survival my name will be . . . well, it'll be world-famous."

"But even if you did find the monster it would be better to meet Daddo for the first time in some other connection. He hates being wrong. I thought I'd get my friend Rosemary Smith to ask me down to stay with her in London and then I could write and say I'd met you in her house, and Mr Smith is a company director whom Daddo used to know."

"Well, of course, we don't want to upset your father, I see that," said Bill. "And you think I ought to go over and camp out on Little Todday?"

"Oh, I do, darling. I really do."

"As a matter of fact Hector Hamish Mackay strongly advised me to make a thorough exploration both of Pillay and of Poppay, and of course there's that beach in Little Todday. Try Swish it's called."

"I know. I'm sure you'll be wise to go over there."

Bill Brownsworth was not so sure that he had done well to choose the machair for a camping-site when on his first night he was woken, from a nightmare that the candidate he feared most as a competitor for the Readership at Norwich was trying to smother him in a silo, to find that he was being fanned by a blast of hot air smelling of damp grass. As he sat up with a start he heard a loud snort and a moment later he was sitting up under the stars, his tent having been whisked off him. Fortunately the stirk disembarrassed itself of the canvas before it went thudding off, but he did not at all enjoy the job of pitching his tent again to the accompaniment of a thunderous tattoo of hooves all round him in a kind of infernal rodeo.

However, if Bill's night was disturbed he enjoyed sitting at a table again for breakfast with Mr Mackay in Kiltod, and when the topographer left him in charge of any news about the monster with the chance of sleeping once more in a bed Bill Brownsworth was glad that he had surrendered to Muriel's discretion.

Visitors who enjoyed Joseph Macroon's board spoke with less enthusiasm of his beds; Bill Brownsworth thought he had never slept in so comfortable a bed in his life. Those fresh from urban luxury used to wonder sometimes if board did not include with those high teas soaring to the zenith on lobsters and cream the bed to which they retired later.

"I don't know why Mr Mackay told me his bed was so hard," Bill Brownsworth said to his host, who was wearing that red knitted woollen cap, which, when he was busy among the lumber heaped up in the great shed at the back of his house, made him look so much like a troll.

"Was he after telling you the bed was hard?"

"Yes, I can't think why. I found it extraordinarily comfortable," said Bill with enthusiasm.

"I'm sure you would. Will you be wanting the *Morning Star* to-day?"

"I thought I'd like to land on Pillay if it's possible and have a look round."

"Ay, I believe you'll be able to land quite O.K."

"Did you see that report about the monster being sighted in Barra?"

"Ay, in Northbay," said Joseph. "That's where the Coddy lives. He'll be putting his net out and trying to keep it there. But I believe the monster'll be one too many even for the Coddy."

Chapter 10

THE PILLAY MANIFESTATION

THE small island of Pillay extends to something over three hundred acres. It rises up from the sea along its western face in a series of rocky terraces at first and then by steep grassy braes to the summit, which consists of a level plateau of rough herbage and heather dotted with numerous small lochans. On the east the cliff falls sheer to the sea for about three hundred feet in a magnificent sweep of black basaltic columns whitened by the droppings of innumerable seabirds. The northward side is equally sheer but not so high, and all along the southern end the shore is strewn with huge fragments of basalt from which it is an arduous climb to reach the braes above. The only landing-place is below a small hook-shaped headland running north-west from the coast of the island below which a ledge of rock provides a rough quay. However, the little bay formed by the headland faces due west and only after a spell of calm weather such as the islands were experiencing this June did the heavy groundswell allow a boat to get alongside the rocky ledge. The origin of the name Pillay is in dispute. Some Gaelic topographers say it means 'the island of the winnowing,' others argue for a purely Norse derivation from a word cognate with pillow, but the majority agree that it means 'the island of the return' because so many people had tried to land there and failed.

The grazing was good, and one or two of the crofters of Little Todday had sheep on Pillay, but the difficulty of performing the various operations that sheep require through the year, coupled with the heavy losses over the cliffs, did not tempt their neighbours to envy them.

Unsuitable though the island was for sheep, Pillay offered an ideal breeding-place to the grey Atlantic seals, the young of which are born on land early in October and have to be taught to take to water in the lochans before they descend to the wild November seas.

The Macroons, owing to their legendary descent from a seal-woman, had never persecuted the breeding seals either on Pillay or Poppay, its sister isle off the south of Little

Todday. It can be imagined how much they resented the theory put forward in some papers that the Todday Monster was nothing more than an outsize grey seal.

There were no seals ashore on Pillay on this lovely June day when Kenny Macroon took Bill Brownsworth across in the *Morning Star* to land him safely in the little bay called Fearvig. Yet even on such a placid day there was enough groundswell to make it impossible for Kenny to leave his boat, and he went off to look at his lobster-pots round the Gobha while Brownsworth poked around on shore.

Brownsworth found when he had scrambled over the rocks to the head of Fearvig that the sand uncovered by the tide was ploughed in every direction similarly to the way Mackay had described the state of the beach beyond Ard Swish where Mrs Odd had seen the monster and that the dry sand above high water showed marks which appeared to be the movement of a huge body across it. He was so excited by this discovery that he lifted up his voice and uttered several resounding "hurrahs!" From the other side of the headland which was not more than fifty feet high his shouts were answered by a noise between a bark, a bellow and a whistle.

In a fever of excitement Brownsworth scrambled up to the top of the headland not without difficulty, but to his intense mortification when he was able to look down at the other side he could see nothing except the black boulders and shattered columns of basalt along the base of the dark cliffs, and nowhere in the ocean so much as a speck.

He remained for an hour on the watch, but he heard nothing and saw nothing. Then he scrambled down again into Fearvig to re-examine the condition of the sand. The longer he looked at it the more difficult was it to escape from the conviction that these striations were made by the huge teeth of some great animal unknown to zoology. He decided when Kenny took him back to Kiltod to go and call on Mrs Odd. She might have some clue which she had failed to pass on to Hector Mackay.

"Do you still think the noise you heard was more like a snarl than anything else?" he asked Kenny Macroon when the latter was pointing out the place where he had seen the monster's back submerge.

"Just the very same," Kenny insisted.

"You didn't hear anything like a whistle?"

Kenny shook his head.

Brownsworth had made up his mind not to say anything about the state of the beach in Fearvig or about the noise he had heard on the other side of the headland, for he did not want inquisitive people to land on Pillay.

"I think I'll go and camp out on Pillay," he announced.

"You could never be doing that," Kenny told him.

"Why not?"

"Every why. You might be there for months before anybody could take you off, and there are *bòcain*. No so many *bòcain* as there are on Poppay, but plenty *bòcain* right enough."

"Bokun?" Brownsworth echoed.

"Ghosts."

"I don't believe in ghosts," said Brownsworth severely.

Kenny shrugged his shoulders. He was not going to argue with this poor ignorant Sasunnach about the existence of ghosts because his pride would not allow him to run the risk of being laughed at.

"But of course I couldn't afford to be cut off on Pillay," Brownsworth admitted.

"If landing there wasn't so difficult we would have put the whisky there."

"Whisky? Oh, the whisky from the *Cabinet Minister*?"

"Ay," said Kenny. "We did try and make the Excise Officers think we'd hidden a lot of the stuff there, but they were too cunning." He spat overboard. "Ach, it would have done the Excise a lot of good to be cut off on Pillay for a few months. They'd have been pretty tired of eating sheep and nothing else. It would have been a good lesson for them right enough." He spat overboard again.

That afternoon Bill Brownsworth walked across the island to call on Mrs Odd. Normally he would have been much too shy to introduce himself to a stranger, but his palaeontological enthusiasm had been so pumped up by the evidence of the monster's propinquity he had found on Pillay that he would have introduced himself to a Duchess at a Charity Bazaar if she had been in recent contact with the monster.

"Good afternoon," said Mrs Odd cordially. "I suppose you've come about the monster?"

"Well, yes, I have as a matter of fact."

"Don't look so frightened. I'm no monster myself. And I'm getting used to questions by now. 'Here,' I said to one of these walking catechisms, 'What do you think I am, a Sunday School?' But come on in. What paper are you from?"

"I'm not from any paper, Mrs Odd. I'm a palaeontologist."

"A what? You'll sprain your jore, if you start in trying to swallow the dictionary all at one go. Would you like a cup of tea?"

"That's very kind of you."

"Oh, I'm always glad for the excuse of a cup of tea. My son Fred always says he never knew any teetotaller so fond of an occasional drink of something else so long as it wasn't coffee. Oh, I can't abide coffee. Nutshells and water is what I call coffee. Would you like a dram before you have your tea? Did you hear that? I am getting Scotchified, aren't I? But I'm a true Cockney myself. Yes, born within sound of Bow bells. Where do you come from?"

"South Kensington."

"Where the Natural History Museum is, eh? Oh dear, how I used to love going there when I was a kid. We used to like stroking the whales. Well, they was the only thing anyone could stroke, because I suppose they couldn't afford to put glass over such whoppers, could they? So we got the smell as well. And it was a smell. Like damp linoleum. But us kiddies liked it."

By now Bill Brownsworth was seated in an armchair and the old lady was watching the kettle.

"I'm a friend of Mr Hector Hamish Mackay," he told her. "He was going to bring me round to call on you, but he has had to go up to Lewis and Harris, and probably Skye."

"Oh, he was bound to go sky-rocketing with a name like that. Hi! Hi! Mr Mackay, take me with you when you fly, back to the Isle of Skye," Mrs Odd warbled. "But you take it from me, young man, he won't find the monster anywhere but in the Toddays."

"As a palaeontologist . . ."

"There you go again. And what's in the pail when it's at home?"

"I am studying extinct animals and so naturally I am tremendously interested in this mysterious creature which has been seen here."

"Exstinct? It's no more exstinct than you and me are.

If you'd have seen it prancing about Try Veck as lively as a penny toy on the pavement you'd have soon seen how exstinct it was."

"Yes, but it appears to be a survival, and if the fact of a survival could be established and identified palaeontological research . . ."

"Look here, young man, don't you try and say that word till you've drunk up your tea, or it'll be returning on you."

"Mrs Odd . . . by the way my name's Brownsworth . . . I believe the noise you heard this creature emit was something between a bark and a bellow?"

"And a yawn."

"Not a whistle?"

"No, there wasn't no whistle. What makes you ask that? I've been asked a lot of funny noises, but that's a new one on me."

"Well, I wonder . . ." Bill Brownsworth hesitated.

"Go on."

"I wonder if you can keep a secret?"

"Me keep a secret? What, I'm the grave's only rival with a good secret, I am."

Brownsworth decided to be frank, and told Mrs Odd about his experience on Pillay that morning.

"But you'll understand why I want to keep quiet about it for the moment because I do not want everybody to go exploring on Pillay and perhaps frightening the creature away."

"Besides getting two hundred and fifty golden soverings from the *Daily Tale*."

"No, this is not a matter of money, Mrs Odd. This is science."

"Yes, of course. That's what the doctors tell you. But they don't forget to send in the bill, do they? Or they didn't until this National Health come in and people could get ill for nothing. But get back to this here whistle you heard. What kind of a whistle was it? A sort of a guard's whistle or a look round and let's see your face, Gladys, you've got pretty legs whistle or . . . well, I mean to say, whistle? That can mean anything, can't it?"

"It came at the end of this noise between a bark and a bay and a bellow."

"It's a proper one-man band, this monster, isn't it? No,

I never heard no whistle myself, but poor old Sneezer was puffing so hard when he came through the arch he'd have drowned any whistle with his wheezing."

"Sneezer? Did you say sneezer?"

"Hector Tishoo Mackay. Though there's no hectoring about him. Oh, I like the man, I do. But if I had cocoanut knees like what he has I'd keep out of kilts. No, don't look at yours. They haven't got knobs on like Sneezer's. But really, you know, men are funny. First they aren't happy till they're old enough to leave off knickerbockers and get into trousers and then they aren't happy till they've got out of trousers back into knickerbockers again. And women! If a girl's got legs like a couple of bolsters depend upon it she won't be happy till she can show them off in these shorts as they call them."

"Couldn't you give me some idea of the teeth?" Bill Brownsworth interposed earnestly.

"Teeth? Oh, the monster's teeth. I'd forgotten about the monster for a moment, thinking about these young dreams in shorts. Well, as I've said, they was more like pickaxes than teeth. It takes a lot to scare Lucy Odd, but I don't mind telling you I was properly scared and no mistake when it started in champing at me with these unnatural grinders. If you'll take my advice, and which of course you won't, you'll watch your step before you go mouching around Pillay on your lonesome. You don't want for Sneezer to come back and find nothing of you left excepting a plate of Irish stew and half a mince-pie."

Bill Brownsworth thanked Mrs Odd for her solicitude and then in another burst of frankness suddenly confided in her that he had become engaged since he arrived in Todday.

"You have?" she exclaimed. "Not to one of these female Robinson Crusoes in a tent?"

"No, she lives in Great Todday."

"There must be something in the air in these islands. My Fred came here in the war to teach the Home Guard how to make an Aunt Sally of that blaring Hitler, and he turned me into a granny instead."

"He married one of Joseph Macroon's daughters, didn't he?"

"That's right. A lovely girl if ever there was. If you pick yourself another Peggy, never mind about this reward for the monster, you'll go back to dear old London a richer man than what you came."

Bill Brownsworth was on the verge of revealing to Mrs Odd whom he had picked when there was a knock at the door and the rich voice of Father Macalister was heard asking if anybody was at home.

"Hick into the stye, Father James," Mrs Odd called out. "That's the Garlic for 'come in,'" she told the young palaeontologist.

"Hullo, hullo," the sonorous bass reverberated. "Have you seen Duncan anywhere, Mistress Odd?"

"I sore him this morning."

"Was he in good order?"

"He couldn't be better."

"Good shooting. I've just had a telegram from the B.B.C. to say they're sending over to make some recordings of us all at home and I want to see Duncan about it."

"This is . . . and now I've forgotten your name," Mrs Odd said to her visitor.

"Brownsworth."

"That's right. I could only think of Ha'porth, and I knew it wasn't that."

"Welcome to Tìr nan Òg, Mr Brownsworth," Father Macalister said. "You'll be here to meet the monster, I suppose. *Am bheil Gàidhlig agaibh?*"

Brownsworth looked bewildered.

"He's asking you if you can parlyview Garlic?" Mrs Odd explained.

"No, I'm afraid I can't."

Father Macalister sighed deeply.

"Ah, well, well. And what will you say if you do meet the monster, for depend upon it, my boy, the monster won't understand a word of this new-fangled language called English."

"Mr Brownsworth is a pail . . . well, he's a pail of something, but he'll have to tell you what's in the pail himself."

"A palaeontologist," Brownsworth elucidated.

The priest nodded gravely.

"And a very respectable beautiful thing to be," he declared sonorously. "Ay, ay. But you mustn't laugh at our monster, Mr Brownsworth. You must let Mr Waggett do that."

"I haven't met Mr Waggett yet," the young man gulped.

"Have you not? Oh, well, you've missed a treat. You really have. Ay, ay, he'll tell you more about us than we know about ourselves. Well, well, I must be going. Tingaloori, Mrs Odd."

"Tingaloori, Father."

"Is that Gaelic for 'goodbye'?" Bill Brownsworth asked. The priest threw his head back in a mighty gust of laughter.

"Oh, that's a beauty. No, no, Mr Brownsworth. It's just a little word of my own."

"Isn't it Garlic at all?" Mrs Odd exclaimed. "Well, aren't you the giddy limit, Father James. And me telling everyone in Nottingham it's how you say 'so long' in Garlic."

Brownsworth said that he too must be getting back to Kiltod.

"Roll right along with me, my boy," the priest urged.

And so sympathetic did Bill Brownsworth find his company that to him he did tell the story of his experience on Pillay as they walked across the machair together.

"There's something pretty strange in these waters," the priest said with conviction. "What do you think yourself?"

"I'm completely baffled at present," Brownsworth replied. "If only I could catch a glimpse of this creature. According to the descriptions of it I've been given it doesn't conform to any reconstruction we have made so far from the fossilised remains of any creature discovered in the course of excavations. I suppose Kenny Macroon is right in advising me not to camp out on Pillay?"

"He's dead right, Mr Brownsworth. Now Poppay is different."

"But the creature hasn't been seen on Poppay."

"Not yet, but while there's life there's hope."

"Mr Mackay has gone up to Lewis to investigate reports from there."

"Poor old Hector Hamish," said the priest. "Ay, ay, the Leodhasaich will chew him up if he doesn't admit that the monster is their exclusive property. And he daren't go near Inverness for a while."

"I investigated the stories of the Loch Ness Monster last year," Brownsworth told his companion. "And I couldn't find anything like the evidence I've found for the creature here, quite apart from my own extraordinary experience on Pillay."

"Could you not? Ah, well, if you take my advice you'll leave the Loch Ness Monster alone. Poor old Hector Hamish is in sad disgrace for suggesting it might have left Loch Ness for the Isles of the Blest."

"He was rather worried about some of the letters he received."

"Ay, ay, I'm sure he will have been."

"Don't you think I ought to wire him to come back? I mean to say he might be rather annoyed with me if I didn't let him know what happened this morning."

"You'd be doing him a kind action, Mr Brownsworth. Besides, he ought to be here when the B.B.C. invade us. I'm sure they're hoping to be able to broadcast the noise of the monster. And listeners to Scottish Regional will be thinking they've tuned in to the Third Programme by mistake."

So when he got back to Kiltod Brownsworth telegraphed to Stornoway:

Almost met our friend this morning strongly urge you return Kiltod soonest possible

Brownsworth

Three or four days later Paul Waggett received by mistake the *Daily Tale* instead of his own paper. This did happen sometimes and when it did he was always in ruffled spirits, for as he used to say, "How can I keep in touch with the international situation unless I have my own paper?"

On this occasion his annoyance was fed by the following headlines:

EXPERT ON TRACK OF MONSTER

AMAZING ADVENTURE OF YOUNG SCIENTIST

'William Waterlow Brownsworth, who is considered one of the most promising of our younger palaeontologists (palaeontology is the study of extinct creatures), has had an amazing experience on the small island of Pillay lying off the north-west corner of Little Todday. Taking advantage of the recent spell of calm settled weather in the west of Scotland Mr Brownsworth undertook what is regarded as the dangerous task of landing upon Pillay. His boatman having put him ashore went off to look at his lobster-pots, and Mr Brownsworth with characteristic enthusiasm set about the task of making a meticulous examination of the beach in the little bay of Fearvig which affords the only possible landing-place in Pillay. To his amazement he discovered that the sand below high-water mark had been gashed and ploughed in the same way as the beach on Little Todday seen by Hector Hamish Mackay and Mrs Odd, of whose experience the *Daily Tale* was able to give that exclusive account which caused a world-wide sensation.

Mr Brownsworth further discovered in the soft sand above high-water mark clear signs of an immense creature having dragged its great bulk across it.

HARROWING BELLOW

In the natural exultation of his discovery the young palaeontologist emitted what he calls a "whoop of triumph." No sooner had the echoes died away among the forbidding cliffs of Pillay than from the other side of the low narrow headland which protects the little bay from the north-west Mr Brownsworth heard his whoop answered by what he describes as a "harrowing bellow" such as might be emitted by a bull the size of a mammoth, but partaking also of the baying of a gigantic hound and ending in a sort of whistle. Pressed to be more precise about the whistling Mr Brownsworth said that it resembled at first the noise of an infuriated or terrified horse but was definitely a whistle and not a shriek.

Without hesitating Mr Brownsworth ran toward the headland and desperately scaled it in order to obtain if possible a sight of the creature which had uttered this nerve-shattering roar. However, when at last the young palaeontologist achieved the summit it was too late for the reward which his courage deserved. There was no living creature in sight.

Asked if he was not frightened by the noise Mr Brownsworth replied modestly:

"I was really too excited by the prospect of seeing the monster to have time to think about being frightened."

The amazing adventure of Mr Brownsworth on Pillay will undoubtedly stimulate still further the already intense interest which has been aroused all over the world by this mysterious visitant to the Western Isles. The *Daily Tale's* offer of £250 to the first person successful in obtaining a photograph of this creature is still open, and we take this opportunity of reminding readers that while the fact of the monster's appearance having been recorded first from Great and Little Todday has led to its becoming generally known as the Todday Monster, numerous authentic reports from the rest of the Long Island and Skye indicate that its presence is not confined to the Toddays.

Mr Hector Hamish Mackay, who has been gathering evidence of the monster's visits to other islands besides the Toddays, wished to repeat and stress his conviction that the Todday Monster is an entirely different creature from the Loch Ness Monster, and that he no longer attaches any importance at all to what he calls his "too hasty speculation" that the Loch Ness Monster or its possible mate, angered by the flying saucer's aggression, had deserted Loch Ness.

The *Scottish Daily Tale* associates itself with this expression of opinion from Mr Hector Hamish Mackay, and pending the re-appearance of the Loch Ness Monster, has empowered its special representative to investigate any report which may suggest that the Loch Ness Monster escaped injury. Meanwhile, the *Scottish Daily Tale* ventures to express its profound sympathy with the people of Inverness-shire in the ordeal of anxiety through which they have been passing since the flying saucer was seen in March and the painful story of its encounter with the Loch Ness Monster was first reported in the columns of the *Scottish Daily Tale*.'

"Poppycock!" Paul Waggett snapped. "Complete and utter poppycock! Where are the chicks?"

"What, dear?" his wife asked, anxiously disentangling her mind from the pull-over she was knitting, and the impression that something had gone wrong with their fowls.

"There's a disgraceful story in this horrible rag which they've sent up from the post-office instead of my own paper."

"Oh dear, how careless of them."

At that moment Muriel came into the room to hear with a shiver of apprehension her father say:

"One of these disgusting trippers called Brownsworth has apparently been writing up this stunt for the Press."

"Brownsworth?" she murmured unhappily.

"William Waterloo—no, Waterlow Brownsworth," her father repeated.

"What has he done?"

"He's been telling some cock-and-bull story to the *Daily Tale* about seeing the footprints of this imaginary monster on Pillay and hearing it roar. I suppose he's staying on Little Todday. I shall go over to-morrow morning and warn him that the Pillay shooting belongs to me. It's one of the best places for barnacle geese anywhere in winter. Anywhere!"

"I'm sure it is," said Mrs Waggett soothingly. But you never can get there in the winter, can you, dear?"

"That's no reason, Dolly, why I should allow these trippers to go tramping all over Pillay as if it were Hampstead Heath. It's bad enough having to let the Little Todday crofters put sheep on it."

"I don't suppose he knew he was trespassing, Daddo," Muriel put in.

"Then the sooner he does know the better," Paul Waggett replied. "He'll be under no illusions about shooting rights when I have talked to him. Calls himself a . . ." he turned back to the newspaper.

"A palaeontologist?" Muriel asked.

"How did you get hold of that word?" her father asked sharply.

"Oh, I heard somebody—it must have been the Minister —say something about there being a palaeontologist on Little Todday. I meant to ask you what it meant, Daddo."

This was a deliberate and skilful diversion by Muriel. Her father smiled with superior knowledge.

"Palaeontology is the study of extinct creatures," he explained, after another glance at the paper. "So presumably a palaeontologist is somebody who studies extinct creatures."

"Thank you, Daddo. I did so wonder what it meant."

"And thanks to Daddo now you know," said Daddo benignly.

"All the same," thought Muriel, "I'll have to see Bill somehow and warn him not to argue with Daddo if he does meet him. This makes it quite impossible for Bill to ask

Daddo about our engagement yet. How lucky Elsie didn't hear me come out with 'palaeontologist' like that. She wouldn't have believed I'd heard it from the Reverend Angus."

Over in Kiltod Hector Hamish Mackay read the account of Bill Brownsworth's adventure with considerable satisfaction. The Editor had handled the whole business with great tact, and the people of Inverness should surely recognise that the last thing he had wanted was to offend them over the Loch Ness Monster. The stories he had heard all the way up the Long Island had none of them possessed anything like the circumstantial detail of the stories in Great and Little Todday, but the *Daily Tale* had not suggested the slightest prejudice on his part and he might surely expect that the abusive letters he had been receiving would now cease.

"You did perfectly right to fetch me back, Brownsworth," he assured Bill. "And I think the story has been really well handled."

"I've never seen my name in print before," the young man said. "It's a curious sensation. Rather like leaving the door of a bathroom unlocked and having somebody fling it wide open. I wonder what my people will say."

"I would imagine they'd be delighted to find how keenly you are pursuing your researches."

"Oh, I expect it will be all right," said Bill a little doubtfully. "But my father's rather a retiring sort of chap. He was awfully annoyed when one of our maids blew up the geyser and there was a paragraph about it in the *Kensington Courant*. He said that kind of thing was an intrusion upon the English idea of family life."

"An unknown monster is hardly on a par with a geyser," Mr Mackay suggested.

"No, of course it isn't. If only we could establish what it is I shouldn't mind."

"Dum spiro spero, as our friends the Romans used to say. I am confident that you and I are going to establish what this creature is. My head is buzzing with plans. What a triumph if we could put this B.B.C. unit in touch with it. It would be a landmark in broadcasting. By the way, you're holding to your plan of camping out in Tràigh Veck?"

"Absolutely."

"Courageous. Very courageous, I think. But where

E

should we be to-day if scientists had not been prepared to take risks? 'Light, give me more light,' as Goethe said before he died. Still, you always have an avenue of escape through the arch to Tràigh Swish."

"Oh, rather," Bill Brownsworth agreed.

Chapter 11

WAGGETT ON THE WARPATH

WHEN Paul Waggett sent along to enquire if the Biffer
would be crossing to Kiltod next morning word came
back that he was taking Dr Maclaren over and that no
doubt the Doctor would be glad to give him a lift.

"That means I can only take one chick with me,"
Waggett ruled. "Quis?"

"Ego," the twins cried in one voice.

Their father ruled that it was a dead heat. "I shall have
to toss for it." He tossed a penny in the air, caught it on
the back of one hand as he simultaneously clapped it down
with his other hand, and with the smile of a juggler who
had displayed a dexterity beyond the emulation of anybody
in the audience he asked who was going to call.

"I will," said Muriel.

"Muriel will call," said her father in the tone of a Daniel
come to judgment.

"Heads," Muriel quavered.

But when the paternal hand was lifted it was tails.

"Hard cheese," said Elsie, accepting her victory like the
good sportsgirl she was.

Muriel's tradition of accepting defeat in the same spirit
was hardly proof against the bitterness of her disappointment.

"Weren't you going to bike over to see Mrs Beaton at
Bobanish to-morrow morning?" she reminded her twin.

"Oh, that'll keep," said Elsie ruthlessly.

"But why can't we both go?" Muriel pressed.

"You know I don't like being under an obligation to
Dr Maclaren," her father replied. "That's why I'm not
taking Monty. He's going to be disappointed too, poor old
boy."

Muriel was afraid to make an appeal to Elsie's better
nature and persuade her to surrender her place in the
Kittiwake, for she would at once become suspicious of such
anxiety to go over to Kiltod. She consoled herself with the
thought that if her father intended to warn Bill about the
shooting on Pillay he would probably want to see him alone.

Oh dear, why hadn't she called 'tails' instead of calling 'heads'? She felt sure that if she went down to the pier Dr Maclaren would invite her to come aboard, but that would annoy Daddo who had such a thing about knowing how to accept defeat with a smile. He was always trying to teach the people here to be sporting, and when the Garryboo tug-of-war team had walked off the field last August at the Todday Games because, they said, Daddo had favoured the Snorvig team, he had been thoroughly upset. No, she must not go down to the pier, and anyway, if she did go over to Kiltod she probably would not have a chance to warn Bill not to argue with Daddo either about the shooting on Pillay or the monster. Surely Bill would realise that he must be tactful for the sake of their future happiness, but oh, why hadn't she called 'tails'?

"Well, Waggett," said jovial Dr Maclaren next morning, "going over to see that nobody on Little Todday poaches the monster?"

Waggett gave a tired smile. He always found Dr Maclaren's boisterous facetiousness wearisome. "I don't think that there's any danger of that," he said.

"I wouldn't put it past our friend Airchie," said the Doctor, looking down at the crofter who was blowing away at a choked plug.

"Nor would I if the monster really existed," said Waggett.

The Biffer's spit overboard was not intended as a contemptuous gesture; in the agitation Waggett's scepticism caused him he had managed to ingurgitate a mouthful of petrol from the choked plug.

"Really existed?" he exclaimed indignantly, "was it an otter that young chap from down in England somewhere was hearing on Pillay?"

"No, it was probably a seal."

"I'll talk to you about that when we're clear of the pier," said the Biffer.

The Doctor rubbed his hands in pleasurable anticipation, and when the *Kittiwake* was requiring no more attention from her owner than a light hand on the tiller he returned to Waggett's seal.

"So you think it was a seal, eh?" he asked.

"Of course. It was obviously a seal that Kenny Macroon saw. It was obviously a seal that Sammy MacCodrum's

girls saw. It was probably a seal that Mrs Odd saw, if she
saw anything at all."

"And was it a seal I was seeing in Uamh na Snaoiseanaich?" the Biffer demanded.

"I've told you already, Archie. I think you saw a large
otter."

The *Kittiwake* herself seemed shocked by such a suggestion, and the engine began to splutter indignantly.

"Mr Wackett, if I wass to be telling you that yon great
yellow dog of yours wass a canary bird would you be thinking I wass wise?"

"No, I certainly shouldn't."

"Well, then, and I don't think you're so very wise if you
think that a great beast with teeth on him like a hayrake is
an otter. Man, I'm telling you the cave was full of the
crayture."

"You have your opinion, Archie. I have mine," said
Waggett with gracious obstinacy.

"Och, I think you're being a bit hasty in your opinions,
Waggett, I don't believe our friend Airchie could mistake
an otter for the kind of beast he saw."

"Well, what is it, Doctor?"

"That's what we're all anxious to learn."

"And I'm very, very much afraid you'll have to go on
being anxious," said Paul Waggett, with kindly and conde-
scending sympathy. "Yes, I'm afraid it's just another case
of auto-suggestion."

"Like your road blocks to stop German tanks on Great
Todday," the Doctor said with a grin.

"I don't accept that comparison. It's not a patriotic duty
to imagine this ridiculous monster, and the country's no
longer in a state of emergency."

Elsie feared that tempers were rising and, brave girl, she
drew her father's fire upon herself.

"Wouldn't it be fun, Daddo, if the monster suddenly
came up beside us in the Coolish?"

"So as to attract a few more of these trippers, I suppose,"
he said distastefully. "That isn't my notion of fun."

"And it wouldn't be my notion of a fun at all," said the
Biffer. "She might be clawing the gunwale from the *Kittiwake* herself with those teeth. Och, it would be a pure
disaster if the crayture was to come up beside us."

By tacit consent the conversation was allowed to drift

away from the monster to less controversial topics and in due course the *Kittiwake* was brought alongside of the steps in the tiny harbour of Kiltod.

"*A Dhia*," Joseph Macroon had muttered to Hector Hamish Mackay. "Here's Waggett, what's he come over to plague us about now?"

"I'll go and speak to him," said Mr Mackay. Joseph Macroon sighed with relief.

"Ay, if you can steer him away I'll be much obliged to you, Mr Mackay. I've a lot of work this morning, and I must be getting the trap for the Doctor. Kenny's away to his pots."

The topographer greeted Waggett cordially on the quay while Doctor Maclaren went on to Joseph's house.

"Mr Waggett, I believe. My name is Mackay. I had intended to call upon you, but I was summoned to the other side of the Long Island. Stirring times here, eh, Mr Waggett?"

"I'm afraid I don't appreciate so much stir, Mr Mackay. You may be aware that I have the shooting and fishing rights over both Great and Little Todday."

"Yes, yes, I know that."

"And owing to the popular agitation in the Press about this imaginary monster both islands are infested with trippers."

"Oh, hardly infested," the topographer objected. "I agree there may be a few more visitors than usual, but that's all to the good from the point of view of the people here."

"Not from the point of view of my grouse and salmon," said Waggett sternly.

"Why, yes. I know there are a couple of brace of old grouse who were brought here from Ireland by Sir Robert Smith-Cockin when he owned the two islands, but salmon? I've never heard of a salmon in any of the streams of Great Todday. Never. Why, a salmon would cause as much excitement as the monster."

Paul Waggett stiffened.

"I consider that remark quite uncalled for, Mr Mackay. In fact, I take the very strongest exception to it," he said.

"My dear sir, if I may venture to say so, you are taking my little pleasantry too seriously altogether, but at the risk of causing you still further offence I must remind you of the

old Gaelic proverb which says of a stupid man that his
brains are like MacRuaridh's salmon. In other words, that
his brains are non-existent."

"I am not in the habit of paying attention to Gaelic
proverbs," said Paul Waggett. "I regard Gaelic proverbs
as old wives' tales. All superstition is to me equally objectionable, and I think a man like you should be ashamed to
encourage this nonsense about an imaginary monster for
the sake of what is obviously a Press stunt."

"The sincere pursuit of truth can never be a Press stunt,
Mr Waggett," the topographer insisted.

"That is where I'm afraid you and I must agree to
differ," said Waggett loftily. "Verbum sapienti. However,
the reason why I have come over to Kiltod this morning is
to interview this so-called . . . this so-called scientist who
was trespassing on Pillay recently. I believe you are in
touch with him."

"I have been in touch with Mr Brownsworth, certainly.
An enthusiastic and most courageous searcher after the
truth."

"Where is he to be found?"

"He is now camping on Tràigh Veck, which was the
scene of Mrs Odd's encounter with this strange creature."

At this moment Waggett caught sight of the trap waiting
to take Dr Maclaren on his rounds. He did not like to be
under an obligation to the Doctor, but the walk to the other
side of the island was long enough to make a lift for some of
the way attractive on this sunny morning. Besides, Joseph
Macroon charged quite enough for the trap at the ratepayers' expense to give one of them a certain satisfaction in
letting Joseph know that full value was being obtained from
his bill.

Joseph himself was not too well pleased at Waggett's
getting a free ride, but at any rate it would take him out of
the way and that was something.

"Room for two little ones?" Waggett asked.

Doctor Maclaren beckoned Elsie and him into the trap.

"I'll be turning off some time before Tràigh Swish," he
warned them.

"Beggars can't be choosers," said Waggett with a
gracious smile.

Bill Brownsworth had pitched his tent where the blown
sand, bound by marram grass and silverweed, had remained

in a cosy hollow of the dunes about twenty yards inland
from Tràigh Veck, and therefore he was out of sight of the
beach when Paul Waggett and Elsie emerged upon it from
the arch under Ard Swish.

"Nobody here," said Waggett petulantly.

"He may have gone for a walk," Elsie suggested.

"There's no sign of any encampment. Curious ideas of
truth that man Mackay has."

Bill Brownsworth was reading an absorbing account of
the discovery of a large clutch of fossilised dinosaurs' eggs
in Central Asia when he heard voices and, jumping up a
moment later, was on the point of shouting 'Muriel!' when
he saw the stern figure of Muriel's father just behind her.

"Oh, good morning," the stern figure, to whom Bill
Brownsworth had hoped to be introduced as a prospective
son-in-law in happy circumstances, said with cold hauteur.

"Good morning, sir," he replied.

Paul Waggett was gratified at being called 'sir.' Even
when he commanded the Todday Home Guard it was only
Sergeant-major Odd who ever called him 'sir,' the others
had had the greatest difficulty even in addressing him as
'Captain Waggett' rather than 'Mr Waggett.' He was
indeed so much gratified by this young man's obvious
respect for him that he smiled a lofty smile. This was just as
well because Bill Brownsworth himself at that moment had
not been able to check giving Elsie a lover's quick smile.

"I understand that you recently landed on Pillay, Mr
Brownsworth."

"Yes, I did, sir."

This second 'sir' acted upon Paul Waggett's heart like
borax upon hard water.

"Well, I don't want to be unduly severe," he said, "and
of course you may not have realised that the shooting on
Pillay is leased to me by the Department of Agriculture."

"I had no intention of shooting anything, sir."

"Quite. Quite. I appreciate that, but as a matter of
principle I like people to ask my permission before they
land on Pillay."

"I'm sorry, sir. I hadn't realised I was trespassing. In
fact I understood from young Macroon that it was very
rarely possible for anybody to land on Pillay."

"That may be so, but the principle remains. In autumn
Pillay is a wonderful place for barnacle geese, and I do not

want them to be disturbed by indiscriminate shooting. I had a very unpleasant experience two or three years ago over my barnacle geese."

"I'm sorry to hear that, sir."

"Yes, the people here happened to get hold of a lot of whisky, and having soaked some barley in it they proceeded to scatter this doctored barley all over the feeding-ground of the geese on Little Todday. What was the result? The unfortunate birds were all staggering about in a state of intoxication and the people here were able to knock as many as they wanted on the head. The most unsporting thing I ever heard of in my life. So naturally I'm anxious to do all I can to protect these unfortunate geese and give them a refuge on Pillay."

"I fully appreciate that, sir. But there are no geese on Pillay at this season of the year, and I should be very glad to have your formal permission to land again on Pillay if the opportunity occurs."

Suddenly Paul Waggett thought of a really good joke.

"On this wildgoose chase after an imaginary monster, eh?" he asked, gurgling with amusement at his own humour.

Bill Brownsworth remembered Muriel's warning; taking advantage of the preoccupation of what he hoped was his future father-in-law with his own joke he flashed an ardent glance at Elsie and covered its fire with a blink.

"I am far from suggesting, sir, that the creature I heard on Pillay has yet been positively identified as a primeval survival."

"You suggested that in the *Daily Tale*," the sceptic reminded him sternly.

"I only told Mr Hector Hamish Mackay about my experience. Apart from him the only other person I told was the parish-priest here—Father Macalister."

"Father Macalister?" Waggett echoed, with a slow head-shake of disapproval. "I'm afraid Father Macalister can always be relied upon to make the most of anything. Are you a Roman Catholic?"

"Oh, no."

"Well, you know what Roman Catholics are. They revel in superstition. I think you can take it from me that what you heard was a seal."

"And the marks in the sand?"

E*

"Razor-fish. Perfectly simple explanation. By the way, don't let Joseph Macroon persuade you that razor-fish are edible. He persuaded me once when I was a newcomer to the islands, and I never had such indigestion in my life. I don't think a bicycle tyre would have given me such indigestion."

"I shall remember your advice, sir."

"I'm always anxious to help strangers. The people here take a lot of knowing. But I suppose I understand them as well as any Englishman *can* hope to understand them."

"I suppose you speak Gaelic, sir?"

"Oh, I don't pretend to be a Gaelic scholar. But I get along in it. The trouble is the people are so awfully stupid about their own language. Or it may be, of course, that they don't want other people to speak it, and so deliberately pretend they can't understand their own language when somebody talks to them in it. Well, I'm glad to have met you, Mr Brownsworth. When you're over in Snorvig Mrs Waggett and I will be glad to see you at Snorvig House."

"I'm afraid I haven't got any proper clothes for calling, sir."

"Come just as you are," said Paul Waggett kindly. "We lead the simple life here. Some rather good shooting and some rather particularly good fishing," he added dreamily. "Yes, yes, call in just as you are. This is my daughter."

Bill Brownsworth clasped Elsie's hand with such warmth and let it go with such reluctance that Elsie felt sure that the deference which this handsome young man had shown to her father must have been inspired by his interest in herself, and when her father was in the arch she turned to look back. How right she had been! The handsome young man was kissing his hand to her. Elsie looked quickly to see if Daddo was safely ahead. And then she kissed her own hand in response. 'Bungo Jones,' she thought scornfully as she hurried on through the arch. Oh, well, poor Muriel shouldn't have called 'heads.' If she had called 'tails' she might have met this young man. "I wonder when he'll come and call. If I only knew I'd manage to get Muriel to be out," she said to herself.

Bill Brownsworth went back to his sandy hollow, but the account of the large clutch of fossilised dinosaurs' eggs seemed less important than it had been before the visit of Muriel and her father to Tràigh Veck. How lovingly Muriel must be thinking of him at this moment! How proud she must be feeling of the good impression he had obviously made on her father! She had worried about introducing him in shorts as a suitor for her hand. That was nothing to worry over now.

Indeed, Bill Brownsworth had reason to feel optimistic. That afternoon the shooting tenant of the Department of Agriculture expressed to his wife his gratified astonishment at finding their trespasser upon Pillay so comparatively unobjectionable.

"I've invited him to call at Snorvig House, Dolly," he informed her.

"That will be very nice, dear."

"I found him quite reasonable as soon as I explained that the noise he heard was made by a seal and that the marks on the beach were razor-fish. Obviously this fellow Mackay has used him as a tool in order to keep this Press stunt going for his own advantage. He was rather shy about calling in shorts, but I put him at his ease about that. I told him we were leading the simple life here and that he need not feel embarrassment."

"How kind of you, Paul!"

"We older folk have to face up to our responsibilities towards the younger generation," he said weightily. "I've never forgotten that with the chicks."

"I know, dear. You've been an elder brother to them as well as a wonderful Daddo."

Just then Muriel came in with the tea things.

"I've been telling Mumsy about our expedition to Little Todday. This young man Brownsworth seems quite a gentleman. I was pleasantly surprised. In fact, I've invited him to come over and call on us."

"Careful, Muriel darling," her mother interposed anxiously. The thrill her father's announcement gave her had caused Muriel to make an unwonted clatter with the cups and saucers.

"He's not at all pig-headed about this imaginary monster, I'm glad to say. But he's been encouraged by this fellow Mackay, and also, of course, by Father Macalister. I hope he isn't trying to proselytize him. He's quite incorrigible. He actually tried to proselytize me once."

"Paul, you never told me that," his wife exclaimed in horror.

"Yes, I was only trying to be pleasant and put him at his ease. I said 'Ah, well, Father Macalister, we all work in the same vineyard.' And then he gave one of those affected sighs of his and said 'Very true, Colonel . . .' you remember that maddening habit he had of calling me Colonel when I was commanding the Todday Home Guard. 'Very true, Colonel, but we planted it.'"

"What an extraordinary thing to say!"

"Proselytizing."

"And what did you reply?"

"I can't remember exactly what I said, but he saw it was no use trying to proselytize me. I'm told that the B.B.C. have asked him to arrange a ceilidh for them. They're sending a recording unit. And who do you think they've asked to get together people here?"

"Mr Morrison?"

"As a matter of fact they did ask him, and he, without referring to me, suggested Alec Mackinnon, who is going to do it."

While her mother and father were lamenting the folly of the B.B.C. in entrusting their recording unit to the guidance of the Minister and the Headmaster of Snorvig School, Muriel was wondering how she could bring the conversation back from the B.B.C. to Bill Brownsworth.

"Perhaps the B.B.C. want to give listeners the latest news about the monster," she said.

"The B.B.C. are very stupid," her father observed contemptuously, "and as you know I've written several times to tell them how to improve their programmes, but I don't think even the B.B.C. would be so stupid as to broadcast a lot of nonsense about an imaginary monster, even in this Third Programme of theirs. Well, if that young man comes to call on us to say Father Macalister has asked him to gabble a lot of rubbish into the microphone he won't be asked to call again."

"I'm sure he won't do that, Daddo."

And as she expressed this conviction Muriel told herself that somehow she must see Bill and warn him how much the course of true love would be smoothed if he could give her father an assurance that nobody should ever persuade him to come to the microphone and talk about the monster.

"No, that's what Elsie said," her father informed her. "Where is Elsie?"

Muriel had no desire at that moment to know where Elsie was.

"I told her I was taking in the tea things," she replied with a touch of irritation. "Must I go and shout all over the house for her?"

Fortune which had been so unkind to Muriel over the toss made up for her malice next day. Elsie had set off on her bicycle to Bobanish to pay that visit to Mrs Beaton, the wife of the schoolmaster, when word came over from Kiltod that Mrs Hugh Macroon had a White Leghorn cockerel from her noted strain of layers.

"Oh, Paul, what a pity you didn't call in to see Mrs Macroon," the henwife exclaimed.

"I could hardly know that she had a cockerel for you without being advised beforehand, could I, Dolly?" he asked with courtly patience.

"No, dear, of course not. But I did so want one of Mrs Macroon's Leghorns. They're the best layers in either of the islands."

"Well, Muriel didn't come with me yesterday. Why doesn't she go over in the *Morning Star*? It'll be coming back to meet the boat."

Thus it fell out to Muriel's delight that she was able to cross to Little Todday without arousing any possible suspicion of her willingness to undertake the transport of the Leghorn cockerel.

"Oh, I didn't mean for you to come all the way over from Snorvig," said Mrs Hugh Macroon, a prim dapper little woman of something over fifty with hair already grey. "Not at all. I was just anxious to know if Mrs Waggett was still wanting the cockerel. Hugh would have brought it over for her, which is it? Muriel or Elsie? *A Mhuire Mhuire*, you're both so like to the other there's no telling."

"This is Muriel. Elsie came over yesterday with my father."

"Now you won't want to be carrying a live cockerel all the way back to Kiltod. Hugh will bring it to Joseph Macroon's. He's going in to meet the *Island Queen*."

"That's awfully kind of him, Bean Uisdean. *Moran taing*."

"Look at that now. And isn't it you that's getting on well with the Gaelic?"

"Being away all through the war didn't help my Gaelic much," Muriel said.

"Och, that terrible war! But God was very good to me to bring back Michael safe from North Africa and Anthony without a torpedo in four years. Wasn't it just wonderful? And he's doing fine too. Yes, yes. Second mate in the *Highland Maid*, and off to South America last week. You'll take a cup o' tay."

After a pleasant gossip over a cup of tea with Mrs Hugh Macroon Muriel announced her intention of taking a walk along Tràigh Swish.

"Perhaps I'll see the monster, Bean Uisdean."

"Indeed, and I hope you won't. Mistress Odd was telling me about it, and I was really shivering. Poor soul, she might have been eaten alive, and I believe she would have been right enough except she had her umbrella. God was very good to her. So do you be careful, Muriel *eudail*."

Muriel did feel rather apprehensive as she walked through the arch under Ard Swish to Tràigh Veck, and her heart gave a jump when she saw Bill on all fours beside the edge of the tide, for she had a sudden fear that he had been wounded by the monster in a savage encounter.

"Bill! Bill! Are you hurt?" she cried.

To her relief he rose unscathed.

"What are you doing, Bill darling?"

"I was examining the effect of razor-fish on the sand. I didn't like to contradict your father yesterday, but I think he's wrong. The marks I saw were quite different from these."

"Oh, Bill," she said when his arms were round her, "you were wonderful yesterday. I was so proud of you. I knew how much you must love me when you didn't argue with Daddo about the monster."

"Well, I remembered your warning. He was awfully kind to me."

"I know. He liked you awfully. Oh, Bill, I'm so happy. And fancy his inviting you to our house. All the same you won't be in too much of a hurry to tell him we want to be married in shorts?"

"I'm not proposing to be married in shorts," said Bill, who must have been infected with the facetiousness of his sweetheart's father.

"Don't be silly. You know what I mean. But oh, Bill,

darling Bill, I can't tell you how happy I am. And what do you think of Elsie?"

"Who's Elsie?"

"My sister."

"Your . . . your sister?" Bill gasped. "You never told me you had a sister."

"I know. It was naughty of me, but I was afraid she would be jealous. It would be too frightful if she fell in love with you. And you never can tell with twins. But as it is everything has worked out splendidly."

"Yes, oh yes," Bill mumbled doubtfully. He was thinking of that kiss which Elsie had blown him in response to the kisses he had blown to her.

"You'll come and call on us very soon? And if you handle Daddo as tactfully as you did yesterday, he'll probably ask you to dinner. Well, perhaps not to dinner. He's rather conventional. He might think coming to dinner in shorts wouldn't do. But anyway he's sure to ask you to come again, and then perhaps again, and then you can go to London and if you get this appointment at Norwich I'll get Rosemary Smith to ask you to dinner, and I'll write to Daddo and say you've proposed to me, and of course you'll write to him and he won't be prejudiced against you as he might have been if he didn't know you. He was terribly prejudiced against you after he read that account of your adventure on Pillay in the *Daily Tale*. But you handled him quite marvellously yesterday. When will you come and call? To-morrow?"

"I don't think I'll be able to come to-morrow," Bill said.

"The next day?" she pressed.

"I don't think I'll be able to manage the next day either. But of course I will come."

"Bill, why do you keep looking at me in such a strange way?" Muriel asked.

"I didn't mean to look at you in a strange way. It's the glare from this white sand probably."

"But you seem so cold."

"Do I? I suppose it was going along on my hands and knees to examine these razor-fish marks."

"I meant cold in manner," Muriel explained reproachfully.

"You're imagining things," said Bill, putting his arm round her.

"Kiss me," she murmured. And after he had kissed her she said, "Bill, why do you keep looking over my shoulder at the arch?"

"Oh, I suppose I've got in the habit of keeping an eye open all the time. It's the monster. I'm on the look-out all the time."

"You weren't thinking of Elsie, were you?" Muriel asked with that horrible clarity of perception which jealousy promotes.

"Why on earth should I be thinking of Elsie? I didn't know she existed until you told me just now. I mean to say, of course I realised she existed as soon as I saw her, but I didn't know her name was Elsie until you told me just now. I like the name Muriel much better."

"Do you, Bill? I'm glad."

"Much better," he repeated fervidly.

"I'm awfully glad I didn't tell you I had a twin sister," said Muriel firmly. "You might have liked her better than me."

"How could I possibly do that?"

"And I'm awfully glad I didn't tell Elsie about you. She's much more jealous than I am."

"Is she?" said Bill, his heart sinking.

"And she might not have been able to resist telling Daddo about you and me on the way back. I think she rather liked you herself."

"Do you? What makes you think that?" Bill asked apprehensively.

"Oh, just a twin's instinct."

"I see," he gulped miserably.

"Well, you don't mind, do you?"

"No, of course not. I'm in love with you, aren't I?"

"You are so strange to-day, Bill."

"Well, as a matter of fact I'm rather worried. I may have to go back to London sooner than I expected."

"Bill!"

"I may have to consult some books. I can't afford to make any mistake about this monster."

"But you can't go back to London without coming to see us first."

"Can't I? No, no, of course I can't. Oh, I expect it'll be all right."

But on her way back to Kiltod with the Leghorn cockerel

Muriel was worried. The luck which had given her an opportunity to come over to Little Todday and see Bill did not seem to have been so bountiful as she had supposed it was.

On reaching the pier at Snorvig Muriel found everybody in a high state of excitement. Murdoch MacCodrum had just arrived in the Garryboo lorry with the news that Jemima Ross, the assistant at George Campbell's School, had been chased for two hundred yards along Tràigh Vooey by the monster, which was as large as two elephants and moved as fast as his own lorry.

Chapter 12

PAUL WAGGETT, K.C.

WHEN George Campbell, the headmaster of Garryboo
School, married Catriona Macleod, his mother, as she
had threatened she would, left the Schoolhouse and went to
live with her sister in Glasgow. Here, still unreconciled, the
old lady had died a year ago. It had been Mrs Campbell's
plan that George should marry Jemima Ross, his assistant
teacher, over whom she felt she had established in advance
the influence which she believed a mother should always
have over her son's wife. Jemima Ross, in spite of her disappointment, did not apply for a transfer when her headmaster married, and though George Campbell himself
would have been glad to lose her he had not the heart to
make her position unpleasant.

So Jemima Ross stayed on, still lodging where she had
lodged for the last six years with Mrs Angus MacCormac.
She was a carroty wisp of a woman now close upon thirty,
the daughter of a Black Isle man who had married a Skye
woman and settled in Skye. The general opinion of Jemima
Ross in Garryboo was that she was inquisitive and, like so
many inquisitive people, a gossip; she had a significantly
long thin nose. She was a good disciplinarian, though the
parents of her pupils considered that she used the strap to
excess; she was at the same time a good teacher, so good
indeed that George Campbell, who was as conscientious a
man as there was in the two islands, would, apart from his
natural kindness, not have felt justified in trying to get her
transferred.

When school was over that June day Miss Ross had gone
down to Ardvanish Point to gather for herself some carrageen or sea-moss, which, when cooked with milk, makes a
pudding resembling cornflour with a faint flavour of iodine.
While bending over to gather the sea-moss from the rocks
she had heard what she described as a noise like somebody
beating a carpet accompanied by a snarling bark. She had
looked up and to her horror she had seen a huge animal
galloping towards her along Tràigh Vooey. She had
dropped the carrageen in a panic, hurried as fast as she

could along the flat slippery rocks of Ardvanish Point, fearful of falling and being seized by the monster, until she reached the safety of the grass, and had run all the way back to Garryboo to collapse in Mrs Angus MacCormac's kitchen from exhaustion and fright.

These were the hard facts of Miss Jemima Ross's alarming experience. The story that the monster chased her for two hundred yards along Tràigh Vooey, tearing out pieces of her skirt with its teeth, must be regarded as an exaggeration of what occurred, and it is a tribute to Mr Mackay's zeal for the truth, the whole truth and nothing but the truth, that in the account of Miss Ross's adventure which he sent to the *Daily Tale* he did not try to pander to the public's appetite for sensationalism.

"What we can now consider an established fact," he said to Bill Brownsworth, "is that this mysterious creature is capable of moving with speed upon dry land. I confess that I should not care to find it gaining on me rapidly half way along Tràigh Swish. Even you, Brownsworth, with youth and long legs in your favour, might feel a little nervous in such circumstances, eh?"

"I certainly might," Bill agreed.

"There's one thing. This latest appearance of the Todday Monster makes it imperative for you to remain here," said Mr Mackay. "You can't afford to run away from what may be a scientific discovery of supreme importance. You'd never be able to look knowledge in the face again."

"Yes, I think I ought to stay," Bill assented.

"You think?" Mr Mackay exclaimed. "You *know* you ought to stay."

That evening Bill Brownsworth wrote to his friend Dick Spinnage. They had been at the same prep. school together; they had been at St James's School together; they had been at London University together; they had been together on active service in the latter part of the war. To write to Dick Spinnage was to address his *alter ego.*

June 16   *c/o Post Office, Kiltod,*
                                        Little Todday,
                                              Outer Hebrides,

Dear Dick,

  Since I wrote to you about my secret engagement to Muriel Waggett a most awkward thing has happened. Her father came to see me about trespassing on this small island where he rents the shooting, and as a matter of fact we got on very well together, which made me feel quite bucked. With him was what I thought was Muriel and of course every time I could do so without her father seeing me I tried to show her how pleased I was to see her. At the end of the interview he said 'This is my daughter' and of course I thought he was introducing me to Muriel. And when he had disappeared under a natural arch which joins the little beach above which I'm camping to a much larger beach beyond, I kissed my hand to what I thought was Muriel and she kissed her hand back to me. And it wasn't Muriel at all!! It was her twin sister Elsie. Muriel herself came to see me next day and I only just managed not to let her know I'd made this ghastly mistake. Her father had asked me to go and call on the family in Snorvig and naturally Muriel was very keen I should call as soon as possible, the idea being that I should rather suck up to the old gentleman and then that we should meet in the autumn in London and she would write and say I'd proposed to her and all would be quite O.K. Well, after this ghastly mistake I didn't see how I could possibly go and call. It really has put me in a frightful position. Even you, Dick, who's had much more to do with girls than I have would find it pretty frightful. So I told Muriel that I might have to go back to London at once to consult some books, and that seemed to strike rather a low note. Anyway, this 'monster' has been seen again and what is more it has been seen moving at a rapid pace along a beach on Great Todday. I can't go away when I may be on the verge of identifying this creature. You know how keen I am to get this Readership at Norwich. Do give me your advice. Muriel says that her sister is very jealous and I think Muriel is inclined to be jealous herself. I always thought twins saw eye to eye about everything, but I realise that if one made love to twins simultaneously it could cause very unpleasant complications. If I tell Muriel that in a way it's her fault because she never told me that she had a twin sister I shall be quite justified, but you know how unreasonable girls are and she'll be watching her sister and me all the time like a hawk. And then there's Elsie to consider. It occurs to me now that I may have several times given her looks—you know what I mean—when I've met her in Snorvig— thinking all the time it was Muriel. You know I'm not conceited about girls, but I think she was attracted. She must have been to kiss her hand like that. You've no idea how much alike they are— identical really. I sweat when I think that it might have been Elsie who came to see me and that I might have found myself engaged to her quite easily. Another complication is that Mr Waggett does not believe in the existence of this 'monster' and if I'm to keep in with him I can't make the monster an excuse for not calling. I mean if I say I'm always on the look-out for it and don't like to leave my post of observation, he'll be prejudiced against me over Muriel.

The only way out of this ghastly muddle is for you to help me. Do you think you could possibly get a fortnight's leave from your firm now and come up here? One's always reading about friends who fall in love with the same girl. It's possible, isn't it, that you might fall in love with Elsie Waggett? At any rate even if you didn't fall in love with her you could give her the impression that you had and I could say to Muriel something like 'I'm glad Dick Spinnage didn't meet you before I did or I shouldn't have had much chance.' However, the important thing is that you must, if you possibly can, come up here. We can discuss the plan of action when you get here.

Bring your camera. You might easily have the luck to get a snap of this animal, in which case £250 would be rather pleasant.

Wire me as soon as you get this. What worries me is that Elsie may tell Muriel about my having kissed my hand to her and then of course Muriel will get suspicious and ask me why I didn't tell her I had made this mistake.

You won't have to camp out. I've arranged with a very nice chap called Duncan Macroon to give you a bed in his house. So you won't have to wear shorts, which will apparently make a good impression on Mr Waggett.

I'm sorry to inflict this huge letter on you, Dick, but I really am in a spot and I know you're the only person who can get me out of it.

Yours aye,

Bill

"Will nothing stop this fellow Mackay?" Paul Waggett demanded, flourishing a copy of the *Daily Tale* outside the post-office in Snorvig so violently that Monty, under the impression that he was being urged to attack something, rushed at Simon MacRurie's middle-aged collie which was lying peaceably in the sun outside his shop. Monadh retreated yelping within to be pursued by Monty round the customers' legs. There was a stream of excited Gaelic which became more excited when Monty's master pursued Monty in turn and after bumping into half-a-dozen cailleachs at last managed to seize the golden retriever by the collar.

"That dog of yours is too savage altogether, Mr Waggett," said Simon MacRurie severely.

Simon was the leading merchant in Snorvig and an elder

of the church with a great idea of his own importance in the eyes of God and of his fellow-men.

"He wouldn't hurt a child," Waggett snapped irritably.

"You want to keep him on a lead," the merchant insisted.

"I have him under perfect control. But I was upset by this disgraceful story about Miss Ross in the *Daily Tale*."

"Ah, poor soul," said Mrs Angus MacCormac who was shopping. "And wasn't she almost dead in our kitchen chair. Oh, dear dear. I was really sorry for the poor soul, she was that scared. '*Och, a Bhean Aonghais,*' she says to me, 'I'm nearly killed dead by the monaster. Run? You were never seeing anything run so fast in all your life.' Indeed, yes, that's just what she was saying, and '*m'eudail,* Miss Ross dear,' I was saying to her, 'don't be frightened, for the Lord has kept you safe and brought you back to us and I'm sure there's nobody in Garryboo so pleased as me to be seeing you when you are in our choir.' Ach, poor soul, she was away down to Ardvanish just to be getting herself some carrageen for a wee pudding, and if she had not been hearing that terrible thump-thump on the Tràigh it's herself would have been just nothing better than a pudding in another minute."

"Nothing but complete hysteria," said Waggett loftily. "I don't believe a word of it."

And before Mrs Angus MacCormac could reply he had stalked out of the shop, the dignity of his exit being slightly marred by Monty's looking round to growl at Monadh and having to be dragged after his master.

"Oh, well, well, they're queer right enough these Engelish peoples," Mrs MacCormac observed. "Just stick the noses of them up into the air and believe nothing at all."

The paragraph in the *Scottish Daily Tale* which had roused Paul Waggett's indignation was as follows:

MONSTER PURSUES TODDAY SCHOOLTEACHER

AMAZING ESCAPE

'On Wednesday last Miss Jemima Ross, the much respected assistant teacher at Garryboo School in Great Todday, took advantage of this glorious June weather to gather carrageen from the rocks below Ardvanish Point which juts out into the sea at the north end of Tràigh Vooey and affords a precarious shelter to the fishermen of Garryboo pending the erection of a pier on which it is understood work will begin this summer under the enlightened auspices of the Inverness-shire County Council. Carrageen or sea-moss is a sea-weed which when dried and cooked with milk provides a succulent dish reminiscent of a cornflour pudding.

Miss Ross was engaged upon her task which necessitated stooping and therefore she was unaware of the danger lurking in the vicinity, upon those yellow sands unto which she in her innocence had come. Suddenly the schoolteacher, her mind preoccupied with visions of the pudding she was going to make, heard behind her what she describes as a dull thud repeated at intervals and accompanied by a kind of snarling bark. She looked up, curious to know what could cause such an unwonted sound upon those tranquil sands, when to her horror and amazement she saw advancing along them at a rapid pace a huge monster which she estimates as larger than an elephant according to her recollection of the elephant she saw on a visit she once paid to the Edinburgh Zoo.

"Did you observe any teeth, Miss Ross?" we asked.

"I was too frightened to observe anything except the size of this monster and the way it was galloping towards me as fast as a man running."

Miss Ross dropped her basket of carrageen and somehow managed to reach the grassy land at the head of Ardvanish Point which itself is covered with flat slippery rocks. Without looking back she ran up the slight incline all the way to Garryboo to reach the house of Mr and Mrs Angus MacCormac with whom she has resided ever since she was first appointed to Garryboo School six years ago.

It will be remembered that Tràigh Vooey was where Christina and Elizabeth MacCodrum encountered the monster, and Miss Ross's experience confirms that of her young pupils on whose story some strangely incredulous people have ventured to cast doubt. We hope that this latest appearance of the Todday Monster has taught such sceptics a lesson.

One wonders, a little anxiously, what was the object of the mysterious visitant from the deep in approaching

Miss Ross at such speed. Can it be that, like the sea-monster from which Perseus rescued Andromeda in the days of yore, the Todday Monster is also carnivorous?

Meanwhile, the excitement is intense and those ardent young adventurers who have flocked to Great and Little Todday in the hope of winning the prize of £250 offered by the *Scottish Daily Tale* for the first authenticated photograph of the monster are more ardent than ever. An element of danger has been definitely added to the explorer's task, and who responds more quickly to danger than the youth of Britain? In the classic words of Field-Marshal Montgomery on the eve of Alamein, the *Scottish Daily Tale* wishes those adventurers "Good Hunting!""

"There's only one thing I can do about this, Dolly," her husband announced, "I must see Jemima Ross myself and make her admit that she got into a panic about nothing."

"Do you think . . . of course, you know best, dear . . . but you know what the people here are like. They don't really want anybody to disprove the existence of the monster."

"Of course they don't. That's all the more reason for trying to get at the truth of this matter. I'm not going to encourage people to imagine monsters just because they're able to charge these trippers more for their board and lodging."

So after tea Paul Waggett with Monty set off in his car to Garryboo. He called first at the Schoolhouse to let George Campbell know that he intended to interview Miss Ross.

"Why, it's Mr Waggett," exclaimed Catriona Campbell, to whose skirts was clinging a small boy of two and a half with eyes as bright and as dark a brown as her own. "Say 'how d'ye do,' Iain," she bade him. Whereupon Iain tried to turn his mother's skirts into a cave in which he could hide from this intruder.

"He's awful shy, Mr Waggett. You'll just have to excuse him. *Och, Iain, na bith gòrach.*"

But Iain, called after his grandfather Iain Macleod up at Knockdown, was determined to be foolish. Indeed, if the visitor had been the monster itself he could hardly have displayed a more apprehensive agitation. Then the visitor smiled, and that finished Iain off; he began to howl.

"Och, Iain, you really make me feel ashamed of you. Please go into the sitting-room, Mr Waggett, and I'll fetch George."

She showed him into the flimsy sitting-room which, though hardly ten years old, looked as prematurely aged as all the rest of the buildings erected in the Islands since 1920.

George Campbell would always be shy, but he was a much less shy George than in the days when his old Gorgon of a mother ruled the Schoolhouse of Garryboo. He was over forty now, but he looked younger than he did in the days when he was Sergeant in command of the Garryboo section of the Home Guard.

"Will you take a little something to refresh you after your drive, Mr Waggett?"

"No, thank you, Mr Campbell. I never drink anything when I'm driving. I'm the only careful driver in Todday, but I'm bound to have an accident one day because all the lorry-drivers here are so reckless and I wouldn't like anybody to be able to say that I'd had even one dram. I've come up to talk to you about this latest disgraceful stunt in the *Daily Tale*. You must be feeling very annoyed at such rubbish being printed about Garryboo?"

"Och, I think we've all rather enjoyed it, Mr Waggett."

"Enjoyed it?"

"We were beginning to feel in Todaidh Mór that they were keeping the monster shut up on Todaidh Beag."

"I should have thought you'd have been only too glad to think that such nonsense was confined to Little Todday. One expects Father Macalister to encourage this kind of credulity. After all, where would Roman Catholics be without their credulity? But I think Great Todday should try to set an example."

"You wouldn't say surely that this monster was entirely imagination, would you, Mr Waggett?"

"Entirely. Do you remember what difficulty I had when the war was on to convince the people here that Hitler might invade us?"

"Yes, it was pretty difficult."

"And yet now they're ready to believe in a real impossibility like this monster. Don't you consider that perverse and pig-headed?"

"I wouldn't call it that, Mr Waggett. Here in Garryboo

we have had pretty definite evidence that some kind of a strange creature is round about these waters."

"Evidence? You're an M.A. of Glasgow University, aren't you?"

"I am."

"Extraordinary! I never expected to hear an M.A. of Glasgow University tell me he believed in the existence of a prehistoric monster."

"I'm not prepared to say that this creature is prehistoric, Mr Waggett. We just don't know what it is, but I think we can feel quite sure that it is something nobody here has seen before."

Paul Waggett sighed.

"I'm disappointed by your attitude, Mr Campbell. I came to Garryboo this afternoon in the hope of trying to convince Miss Ross that this creature she is supposed to have seen galloping towards her on Tràigh Vooey was either a seal or an hallucination, but what chance have I got of doing that if her own headmaster encourages her hysterical behaviour?"

George Campbell might have added that he was well aware of his subordinate's weaknesses, but he was far too loyal to do that.

"Have you any objection to my examining her about this alleged monster?" Waggett asked. "All sorts of outrageous stories about the incident are now circulating in Snorvig. One of my daughters came in to tea to tell us that old Ben Yacken William was going round telling everybody that this imaginary monster had bitten off the top half of Miss Ross's skirt. I think she was making vulgar jokes about the—er—result, but of course I don't encourage my daughters to report that sort of thing."

"Ah, well, Mr Waggett, Bean Eachainn Uilleim is famous for being a bit of a wag . . ." George Campbell broke off with a blush . . . "I mean a bit of a comic."

"Personally I never find vulgarity comic. But to come back to what I was saying. Have you any objection to my interviewing Miss Ross?"

"It has really nothing to do with me, Mr Waggett."

"Well, you know what my attitude always was in the Home Guard. Never listen to any complaints over the head of a man's commanding officer. So I wanted to approach Miss Ross through the proper channels."

Soon after this the stickler for military etiquette called at the MacCormac house, where Angus blew at him through his big moustache while his wife went to fetch down Miss Ross from her room.

"You'll take a cup of tea, Mr Wackett, please," he was urged when he and the teacher had been shown into the parlour.

"No, thank you."

"You'll take a dram, maybe?" the big crofter asked, cupping his moustache.

"Thank you, no, Angus. I never touch anything alcoholic when I'm driving my car."

Angus and his wife withdrew and left their lodger with her visitor.

"Please sit down, Miss Ross," Paul Waggett urged.

The thin carroty young woman with the pointed nose sat down in an armchair covered with green velvet; so did Waggett. They sat for a moment in silence under the stony gaze of an enlarged photograph of Angus MacCormac's grandfather, whose beard was to his grandson's big moustache as a haystack to a haycock.

"I thought I would like to ask what exactly you did see on Tràigh Vooey, Miss Ross?"

"Quite so, Mr Waggett. Yes, I'm sure I understand. Will you be wanting to write something in the papers about it?" the schoolteacher asked, with a hint of hunger, for she had already developed an appetite for publicity on the strength of her appearance in the columns of the *Daily Tale*.

"I do not write for the papers," said Waggett coldly. "I am merely anxious to arrive at the truth of this business."

"Oh, it's just what they say in the paper. I was terrified. I was picking carrageen . . ."

"Yes, I know what you were doing, Miss Ross. I want to hear from your own lips what exactly you saw."

"I saw this huge creature galloping at me and I was so frightened . . ."

"Yes, I know what you did, Miss Ross," Waggett interposed. "I want to know what exactly you saw."

"I've told you."

"Huge creature may mean anything . . . a rhinoceros or a hippopotamus or an elephant . . ."

"It was more like an elephant."

"Have you ever seen a hippopotamus?"

"No, I never have, Mr Waggett."

"Then how do you know it was more like an elephant? Had this monster got a trunk?"

"I didn't mean it looked like an elephant. I meant it was as big as an elephant."

"Did you see its legs?"

"I didn't have time. I was too frightened."

"But you say it was galloping. How do you know it was galloping if you didn't see its legs?"

"It was going up and down."

"Like the motion of a seal when it is disturbed and makes for the water."

"It was much bigger than a seal."

"I said like the motion of a seal."

"And much quicker than a seal."

Waggett smiled with weary patience.

"I am not trying to suggest that you were suffering from an hallucination, Miss Ross," he said kindly. "I accept the fact that you did see something, but could you go into the witness box and declare on oath that what you saw was not a seal?"

"I never thought it was a seal."

"I daresay not, but it was a long way from you, wasn't it?"

"Indeed, thank goodness it was, Mr Waggett."

"So I suggest that you saw this big seal slithering along down to the water and with your mind full of the monster you thought it was larger than it really was."

Miss Ross was not going to sacrifice her heroine status as easily as that.

"I'm not accustomed to imagining things, Mr Waggett," she said, her thin lips closing tightly on this statement.

"We can all be wrong, Miss Ross. I've been wrong myself once or twice," he added generously.

"I did not imagine anything I didn't see," Miss Ross repeated obstinately. "If I'd been given to imagining I would have been imagining these teeth, but I didn't see those big teeth the others have seen."

"Or thought they saw," Waggett corrected.

"I don't care to be always criticising other people," said Miss Ross.

Waggett would have liked to tell her that this was her

reputation all over Great Todday, but he refrained on the principle of *noblesse oblige*.

"Well, I see you're determined to believe that you saw the monster."

"I'm determined to believe my own eyes, yes, Mr Waggett."

"And so I'm afraid there's nothing more for me to say, Miss Ross," he replied with dignity.

The only satisfaction Paul Waggett derived from his visit to Garryboo was his ability to be able to say to his wife that night just before he put out the light:

"I sometimes regret, Dolly, I didn't take up the Law instead of Chartered Accountancy."

"Do you, dear?"

"I think I should have made an extraordinarily good cross-examiner."

"I'm sure you would, Paul."

"Oh, well," he decided philosophically, "I suppose if I had been a leading barrister I should still be grinding away down in the Law Courts instead of leading the simple life here, though if this nonsense about an imaginary monster continues much longer we might as well go and live in one of these holiday camps. However, the papers will get tired of this monster soon. They even got tired of the war towards the end."

On this remark Waggett put out the light and prepared himself to recede from the petty irritations of the moment into a self-satisfied sleep.

"What are you doing, Dolly?" he asked presently with a touch of irritation.

"I was feeling for my biscuit, Paul. I'm sorry I disturbed you," she said with conjugal humility.

"I hope you haven't been reading this nonsense in the papers about night starvation," he asked severely.

"What's that, dear?"

"Another of these Press stunts," he told her.

On the other side of the Minch the account of Miss Ross's adventure, which had so much annoyed Paul Waggett, filled Ben Nevis with renewed zest for the expedition he was planning.

"This is certainly not our monster, MacIsaac," he told his Chamberlain. "Not that I ever thought it was. Our

monster has never chased women and children anywhere on
Loch Ness side. You can't name a single instance of that,
MacIsaac. That's what infuriates me. Our monster wouldn't
hurt a fly and yet it's being forced to lie up because of these
vile flying saucers whizzing about all over the place. No, I
never thought for a moment our monster had gone to the
islands. All the same, with so many nincompoops and
dunderheads cluttering up the countryside since this Bolshie
Government . . ." a sudden thought darkened the Chieftain's brow . . . "let them try to nationalise our monster.
Mind you, MacIsaac, they're quite capable of it. But let
them try. I think they'll find they've bitten off more than
they can chew at the Scottish Office. Where was I? Oh yes,
I was going to say now that this island monster is definitely
proved not to be the Loch Ness Monster I think you ought
to warn my people in Strathdiddle and Strathdun to be on
the alert. Ha-ha! Do you remember when those War Office
bigwigs, all wig and no brain, told us that the Home Guard
always had to be in a state of suspicious alertness?"

"I do indeed, Ben Nevis."

"Well, that's what I want my people in Strathdiddle and
Strathdun to be in case our monster is lying up in that
tunnel between Loch Hoo and Loch Ness. And don't let
them think it's going to copy the habits of this Todday
monster and start chasing women and children and what
not. Well, I'm bound to say I am a little relieved that it's
not our monster. I was beginning to think I'd bitten off more
than I could chew, if you know what I mean, when I said
if I found these Islanders had stolen our monster I'd bring
it back to Loch Ness myself. It might have been rather a
job, and as you know, when I say I'll do a thing I always do
it. Mind you, MacIsaac, I don't blame this Todday monster for chasing these Islanders. If they had their way they'd
double the rates, building them piers and lobster-pools and
bridges and I don't know what not."

"Yes, they're rather grasping," his Chamberlain agreed.

"Rather grasping? If you'd heard that fellow Roderick
MacRurie screwing a pier out of us at the last Council
meeting for some one-eyed township called Garryboo.
Garryboo? Why, that's where this Todday monster has
been chasing this schoolteacher. I suppose if Chester Royde
and I make a big game show out of our expedition we
should have all these blood-sport ninnies on our track. The

head of this Todday monster would look jolly well in the Great Hall with half a dozen Lochaber axes on each side of it. Still, I suppose it wouldn't do. They'd be saying we were as bad as flying saucers."

"No, I don't think it would do, Ben Nevis."

"Well, the Knocknacolly party will be here in less than a week now. Perfect weather which looks like lasting. It's going to be a splendid expedition. I simply cannot understand why people go and commit suicide. It's extraordinary, isn't it? I'll tell you what I will do, MacIsaac. I'll ask Bertie Bottley to let me have Kenneth MacLennan for a week. He'll be able to say definitely that this Todday monster is not the Loch Ness Monster he saw attacked by that beastly flying saucer. That will stop all argument once and for all. People think I'm prejudiced for some reason or other. By Jove, I've got it," the Chieftain suddenly bellowed. "What a duffer I am!"

His Chamberlain waited as on so many other previous occasions he had waited for the announcement of some plan which it would require all his tact to dissuade the Chieftain from trying to carry out.

"We'll try and frighten this Todday monster away from the two Toddays. Then it'll probably go north and we shan't hear any more of this Campbell jiggery-pokery about Obaig being the capital of the West. Of course, we don't want it to go too far north or else those Mackenzies and Macraes will be cashing in on it and they're almost as bad as the Campbells."

"Yes, I see your point of view, Ben Nevis, but may I utter a word of warning?"

"Oh, of course you'll have to do that, MacIsaac. You've been croaking away at me like a raven for over twenty-five years. I ought to be used to it by now. Well, croak away."

"It occurred to me that you couldn't be sure the monster or whatever it is . . ."

"Monster or whatever it is? What else could it be? Look here, MacIsaac, for goodness sake, don't you start being a Doubting Thomas. All right, go on."

"I was going to say you couldn't be sure the monster would go north if you succeeded in frightening it away from Todday, Ben Nevis. It might go south. It might go to Tiree or even to Mull, and nothing would suit the people of Obaig better than that."

"Yes, I see what you mean," said the Chieftain in a tone which from any other lips than his would be described as pensive. "Oh, well, whatever we decide to do, it's going to be a jolly expedition. How poor old Murdoch would have loved it!"

The Chieftain's second son, Lieut.-Commander Murdoch MacDonald, had been killed in the last few months of the war.

"Yes, yes, a sad thought," said the Chamberlain. "And it's a pity Young Ben Nevis can't be with us."

"Oh, well, Hector and Pel . . . he and Penelope are enjoying themselves in Kenya. She's a great girl, MacIsaac. I couldn't have wished for a better daughter-in-law, but I only wish he'd picked a different name. I'm always saying Pelenope instead of Penelope. Well, I think we'd better have a dram and drink slahnjervaw to the Todday monster. I was a bit allergic to it at first if you know what I mean—ha-ha!—but I'm getting quite fond of it now that it's been discovered by this fellow Mackay to be carnivorous and therefore definitely not even a distant relation of our dear old Loch Ness Monster. Hullo, here's Toker with the whisky. How did you know I was going to ring for the decanter, Toker? Wonderful chap, Toker," he said to his Chamberlain when the butler had retired. "Always seems to know what I want just at the very moment I want it."

While Ben Nevis was looking forward with the liveliest anticipation to the cruise of the *Banshee* when his friends arrived from America, at the headquarters of the B.B.C. in Queen Margaret's Drive, Glasgow, some of the moving spirits of Scottish Regional were hardly less excited by the prospect of their visit to Great and Little Todday.

"It would be wonderful," said Francis Urquhart, who was to be in charge of the outside broadcasting equipment, "if we could get a broadcast of this monster."

"Ay, it would be great. It really would," agreed Duncan MacColl, to whom was entrusted the task of co-ordinating all Gaelic activity on the air.

"The only thing that worries me," said Francis Urquhart, "is whether we can land the equipment on Little Todday."

"I rather doubt it, Frank. But of course I don't want to butt in on the technical side. In fact, I've already written to Father Macalister to ask if he can manage the *cèilidh* in the Snorvig Hall. He's just as popular in Great Todday as he is in his own parish. The snag is that we want to record a *luadh*."

"A what?"

"A *luadh* or waulking is a gathering to shrink the tweed, and it's done by about a dozen women who sit on either side of a long table and shrink the tweed to the accompaniment of waulking songs. Of course, it's not actually done any more in the Toddays as it was once upon a time, but the Little Todday women, thanks to Father James himself, have kept up the traditional singing. The question is whether the Little Todday women will agree to come over to Snorvig."

"Why wouldn't they?"

"It's always tricky to arrange a combined operation between the islands. Local feeling, you know. However, I hope Father James will exercise his influence. I don't really think you'll ever get the equipment across to Kiltod. That's why I was so pleased to read about this Garryboo appearance again. If we could only get a recording of those noises. You'd enjoy doing the O.B. wouldn't you, Frank, if the monster was galloping along the beach."

"I'd enjoy it fine," said Francis Urquhart. "I don't know how much the engineers would enjoy it?"

"They'd be quite safe inside the waggon. It would be a terrific thrill for listeners."

At this moment the Director came in.

"London has just been through to suggest that Howard Marshall should come up on the chance of our being able to establish contact with the Todday monster."

"What?" exclaimed Francis Urquhart. "Why don't they send Wilfred Pickles up as well and Richard Dimbleby and the whole bl . . ."

"Now don't get excited, Urquhart," the Director interrupted. "I'm going to ask if we get a good recording whether they won't take it on Home and Light . . . they might take it on Third as well. After all, it has a great scientific interest."

"But what does London want to interfere for at all? The damned monster didn't bob up in the Thames. Och, I've nothing against Howard Marshall, but I think a monster in the Hebrides is entirely a matter for Scottish Regional."

"Well, I had put that point of view to them."

F

"Point of view!" Francis Urquhart scoffed. "When did London ever understand our point of view up here?"

"Now, don't worry, Urquhart. I shall suggest how very unlikely it is that we shall have the luck to be on the spot at the same time as this mysterious creature and that the main preoccupation of the unit will be recording the local atmosphere—talks with old men, and the economic position, and of course a ceilidh. Well, obviously you and Mac-Coll will have to look after all that, and if—a very large 'if' too—if this mysterious creature does materialize, why, then, you'll be perfectly able to handle the emergency. I think it will be all right."

The Director withdrew on this optimistic note.

"Just because we won't take their cricket broadcasts," Francis Urquhart commented bitterly. "I'm sure that's the reason they want to send Howard Marshall up here. It's nothing whatever to do with the Todday monster. It's just a trick to make us take their cricket broadcasts on Scottish Regional. If I were Director I'd say 'we'll take your cricket broadcasts if you'll take Duncan MacColl's Gaelic quarter of an hour.' That would bring in a few letters from listeners to the Light Programme."

Meanwhile, over in Little Todday, Bill Brownsworth was waiting anxiously for a reply from Dick Spinnage. Something much worse had happened to him than he had foreseen when he sent that S.O.S. to his friend.

Chapter 13

A SLIGHT MISUNDERSTANDING

ALTHOUGH Bill Brownsworth would have preferred not to go near Great Todday until he had the support of his friend Dick Spinnage, he had allowed himself to be persuaded by Hector Hamish Mackay to accompany him on his second visit to Miss Ross at Garryboo.

"I want you to watch her very carefully, Brownsworth, and tell me quite frankly if you think she is an hysterical subject."

"But I don't know anything about female hysteria," he protested.

"In the prehistoric Eden you fancy there would have been no hysteria?"

"I shouldn't care to commit myself to so general a statement as that," the young palaeontologist said.

"No, but you could observe Miss Ross closely while she is answering my questions and let me have your impressions of her reliability as a witness."

"But you've talked to her yourself and you were satisfied of her reliability when you gave her story to the *Daily Tale*."

"Yes, but I've just had this rather peculiar letter from Mr Waggett which I feel I cannot ignore without running the risk of his writing over my head to James Donaldson, and you know what editors are."

"Well, I don't really," said Bill Brownsworth, who was disinclined to admit his knowledge of anything that would take him over to Great Todday without Dick Spinnage.

"Editors are extremely sensitive people."

"Are they?" Bill Brownsworth asked in surprise. Had he been driven into expressing an opinion about editors he would have been likely to venture a comparison between their hides and those of the megalosaurians with which he was more familiar.

The topographer gave him the letter he had received from Paul Waggett:

Snorvig House,
Great Todday,
June 20th

Dear Mr Mackay,

I read with astonishment what I assume was your report to the Scottish Daily Tale on the subject of the alleged 'monster' to Miss Jemima Ross, the assistant teacher at Garryboo School.

As soon as I had read this report I made it my business to interview Miss Ross and obtain from her an admission that what she had seen was nothing more unusual than a large grey Atlantic seal slithering down from Traigh Vooey into the water. I do not wish to suggest either that Miss Ross deliberately exaggerated the occurrence or that you allowed your pen to exaggerate it. At the same time, in the interest of truth, I shall feel it my duty to notify the Editor of the Scottish Daily Tale of the true facts of what happened and if he fails to publish my communication I shall notify the rest of the Scottish Press of what I consider his deliberate intention to work up a sensation with the object of obtaining publicity for his paper.

I do not wish to be unfair to you, and therefore I take this opportunity of warning you that Miss Ross has the reputation of being a gossip of which you may not have been aware when you encouraged her to talk so freely about this imaginary monster. Verbum sapienti.

Yours faithfully,
Paul Waggett

"Of course, I don't know how far our friend Waggett has involved himself in the risk of a slander action by accusing Miss Ross of being a gossip," the topographer observed, "but I'm afraid Donaldson won't consider that. He will be entirely concerned with his own position in regard to other editors, and if Miss Ross has admitted that it was a seal, he and I will both be in an extremely awkward position. So, quite apart from the value of your opinion about Miss Ross's emotional condition, it is really essential for me to have a third person present when I interrogate her, for my professional reputation is at stake, Brownsworth."

So with a prayer to fortune that they would not meet any of the Waggett family Bill Brownsworth had accompanied Hector Hamish Mackay to Garryboo.

From the point of view of the latter the expedition had been a complete success because not only had Miss Ross denied indignantly any admission to Paul Waggett that the creature she saw was a seal but George Campbell had testified warmly in favour of her accuracy as an observer of nature.

"Very satisfactory. Very satisfactory indeed," the topographer had declared when they landed again at Kiltod, and inasmuch as Bill Brownsworth had not caught sight of any of the Waggett family he had been able to echo Mr Mackay's enthusiasm with sincerity. Indeed, he had been sufficiently impressed by Miss Ross's account of her adventure when not being antagonised by Waggett's forensic ambitions to be anxious to get back as soon as possible to Tràigh Veck in the hope of enjoying a similar adventure himself.

"I'd like you to see the letter I propose to send to Waggett."

So Bill Brownsworth had waited for the counter-attack.

"I think that will put him in his place," said Hector Hamish Mackay:

> *c/o Mr Joseph Macroon,*
> *Kiltod,*
> *Little Todday,*
> *June 21st*

Dear Mr Waggett,

I received your letter and at once charged myself with the duty of re-examining Miss Jemima Ross. I am satisfied that you were mistaken in supposing her to have admitted that the creature she saw was a grey Atlantic seal.

I was discreet enough not to mention to Miss Ross that you had accused her of being a gossip because I would not wish to involve anybody in an action for slander, particularly somebody who is as ardently concerned as I am to ascertain the truth.

I may mention that I was accompanied by Mr William Brownsworth, a rising young palaeontologist, who, like myself, was completely satisfied by the bona fides of Miss Ross and was unable to detect in her the slightest tendency toward hyperbolism.

> *Yours faithfully,*
> *Hector Hamish Mackay*

"I say, would you mind very much leaving out that last bit about me?" Bill Brownsworth asked anxiously.

"But why? I want to impress this fellow Waggett with the fact that I am not playing a lone hand in this matter."

"Yes, I know, but I've got rather a special reason for not

wanting you to mention me to Mr Waggett in connection with this creature."

"Come, come, Brownsworth, creature is hardly the word for poor little Miss Ross, who surely deserves your chivalrous support."

"I mean in connection with the monster. I told you he came to warn me about trespassing on Pillay, and well, . . . I can't explain yet exactly why I don't want you to mention me in connection with this creature . . . with this monster, but it is rather important for me that you don't. And anyway, if he thinks what I heard on Pillay was the noise of a seal he won't pay any attention to my opinion."

"As you will, Brownsworth," said the topographer, the east wind of Edinburgh giving a bite to his agreement. "But I take it you have no objection to my quoting you to my Editor?"

"Oh, none at all."

Bill Brownsworth reached his camp in the sandy hollow above Tràigh Veck on that warm afternoon, still without any word from Dick Spinnage, and decided to take off his shirt and have a nap. He awoke with that sense of danger in the vicinity which is so usual an alarm clock to men of action in adventure stories.

"The monster" was his first thought, and he hastily pulled on his shoes in case he had to clamber over rocks. Then he sprang up just as Muriel (or was it Elsie?), just as Elsie (or was it Muriel?) emerged from the arch.

"Hullo, darling!" he exclaimed with all the ardour he could infuse into what was so often a nonchalant greeting, and while congratulating himself on the presence of mind which had saved him from saying 'Muriel', cursing himself within the same instant for the lack of it which had not saved him from saying 'darling.'

Then, with what those at a safe distance from such a desperate situation as Bill Brownsworth's may censure as a stupid gesture, he held out his arms. Bill himself argued that if the apparition in a flowered cotton frock he had never seen before melted into his arms he could assume that it was Muriel. The apparition duly melted, but as the apparition's lips met his he was assailed by a horrible doubt whether they were not in fact the lips of Elsie. After all, if Muriel had fallen in love with him at first sight her twin sister might have fallen in love with him with equal celerity, which would account for what otherwise might have seemed too easy a surrender.

"All well at home?" Bill asked in the hope that whichever girl it was would mention the other in reply.

"Father's still on the warpath," Muriel or Elsie replied.

"On the warpath?" Bill echoed with a frown of apprehension.

"Against the monster."

"Yes, of course. I was afraid at first you meant me."

"Oh, no, he's taken quite a fancy to you. But you know that."

A dead end. Either of the sisters might have told him this; in fact, Muriel already had. He tried a bolder approach.

"How's your sister?"

"She came over to Kiltod with me."

Bill Brownsworth hoped that whichever girl it was would attribute the beads of sweat upon his forehead to the normal sudatory effect of the sun.

"She may be coming along here," he suggested gloomily.

"Oh, no. Don't worry. She's having tea with old Mrs Odd."

"But won't she be wondering where you are?"

"Not a bit. I told her I was going to see Mrs Hugh Macroon."

Another dead end! Muriel had been to see Mrs Hugh Macroon the last time she visited Tràigh Veck. It must be Muriel after all. Oh, yes, of course it was Muriel. He was letting himself get into a stew about nothing.

"I've written to ask my greatest friend, Dick Spinnage, to come and stay with me," said Bill Brownsworth. "Wouldn't it be wonderful if he fell in love with your sister and she fell in love with him? We could have a double wedding."

"A double wedding," she murmured softly, with a sweet emotion.

"Dick and I have been friends ever since our prep. school. The other chaps nicknamed us Bill and Coo, though Dick was also called Turnip Tops, and at St James's he was called Topsy."

"And didn't you have a nickname?"

"No, I was always Bill."

"Bill. I'm glad. I love the name Bill."

Bill Brownsworth was again a prey to doubt. He had a sudden macabre suspicion that she did not know until this moment that his name was Bill. Oh, he was worrying himself needlessly. He mustn't start fancying horrors. Muriel was often saying how much she liked the name Bill.

Then he felt beads of sweat glistening upon his forehead beyond even the power of a tropical sun to precipitate. If this was not Muriel he had practically proposed to her sister. What mad impulse had lured him into talking about a double wedding? If this was Elsie she must now be supposing that Dick Spinnage had been invited here to fall in love with Muriel. If this was Elsie she must be supposing that she was to be his own bride at this double wedding.

"It's frightfully hot," he gulped, mopping his forehead.

"Is your friend Dick Spinnage good-looking?" she asked.

"Oh, awfully good-looking. He's rather like Ivor Novello."

"I say!"

"You think your sister will like him?"

"I'm jolly sure she will. But he might not fall in love with her, might he?"

"I'm positive he will. Our tastes are identical. That's why I'm so keen for him to come up here."

"When's he coming?"

"I don't know exactly. I was hoping for a telegram this morning."

"Perhaps he'll be on the *Island Queen* when she arrives this afternoon. I'll tell you what Muriel says about him when we meet again."

Bill Brownsworth had a momentary impression that somebody had caught him a sharp crack on the head with a hammer.

"Muriel?" he repeated in a hollow voice.

"That's my sister's name."

"Oh, is it? I thought it was Elsie."

"Did you think I was Muriel?"

"No, of course not. I just got the names the wrong way round."

When Elsie had departed to pick up her sister and go back to meet the *Island Queen* Bill Brownsworth could have kicked himself the full length of Tràigh Swish for not having given a bold affirmative to that question. The words he ought to have said flowed now that she was no longer able to hear them.

"Yes, I did think you were Muriel. Otherwise I shouldn't

have asked you to kiss me. It is only right to tell you that Muriel and I are engaged. We fell in love with one another at first sight. She wished our engagement to be kept a secret at present because she didn't know how your father would take it. When he came to speak to me about trespassing on Pillay I thought it was Muriel who came with him."

That was what he ought to have said, and although he might have made a lifelong enemy of his future sister-in-law by saying it that would have been better than the deplorable position in which he had left himself out of sheer cowardice. It had been bad enough when he had mistaken Elsie for Muriel the first time, but it was nothing to the situation he had brought about by talking about a double wedding. It was the sort of thing one might say in a bad dream, but not in reality. What else could Elsie imagine but that he had been making her a proposal of marriage? He recalled with a heavy heart the tone of her voice when she had murmured 'a double wedding' with all too evident a pleasure at the prospect. The tone of her voice tolled in his ears with the solemn melancholy of a passing-bell.

The only crumb of comfort he could extract from this disastrous meeting was Elsie's awe when he had said that Dick Spinnage was rather like Ivor Novello. Obviously if he had not made such a mess of things she would have been quite prepared to fall for Dick. And he had not exaggerated. If Dick were a composer and a dramatist and a singer and an actor and his profile were enhanced by the meretricious glamour of the footlights he would be rather like Ivor Novello.

But what was the good of all these comparisons between Dick and Ivor Novello? Dick had failed him; Dick had not even written; his appeal had been coldly ignored by his best friend. For the rest of that afternoon Bill Brownsworth gave himself up to self-recrimination. It was so easy to explain the misunderstanding to Elsie when Elsie was not there, and then from being worried about what Elsie would say and do he began to be even more worried about what Muriel would say and do. In his anxiety about Elsie he had forgotten the explanation he would owe to Muriel. Muriel would say, and she would have a right to say it, that if he was capable of mixing her up with her twin sister he could hardly be as much in love with her as he pretended to be. Muriel would not believe that her outward resemblance to

F*

Elsie could deceive one who truly loved her. She was bound
to resent the slight upon her personality.

Then he fell back upon a day dream. Dick had arrived
and had made an immediate impression upon Elsie.

"I'm sorry for poor Bill, Elsie, but I love you, and all's
fair in love and war. You love me. I will tell Bill what has
happened, and when he knows that you love his best friend
I feel somehow that Bill will turn to Muriel, and that
Muriel will console him. You and she are superficially very
much alike, but I love you and I do not love Muriel. I know
Bill. He will face up to facts. The one thing he would not
be able to stand would be for you to give yourself to him
when all the while you were in love with me. That would
be a mortal blow to poor old Bill, and he would be bound
to find out the truth. He analyses everything. Science is his
God. We should never be able to keep the truth from him.
So let me tell Bill to-night that fate has brought you and
me together and that bitterly sorry as I am to step between
him and the girl he loves, I cannot live a lie."

Bill Brownsworth was in the middle of this vicarious
eloquence when he heard his name shouted from the arch,
and saw Kenny Macroon.

"I've brought along a friend of yours, Mr Brownsworth,
who came by the boat."

Bill's heart leapt with joy. He jumped up and ran to greet
his longed-for friend, but as he reached the arch he heard·
a prim voice say,

"Eureka."

And it was not Dick Spinnage. It was Mr Sydney Prew,
the Secretary of the National Union of Hikers, bowed down
beneath a weight of camping equipment, the dark hairs
between the top of his stockings·and the bottom of his
shorts fluttering in the light June breeze.

"Yes, here I am," said Mr Prew. "And full of plans to
contact the monster. Yes, some of the jolly young people
here and I have already discussed the possibility of forming
non-stop monster patrols. Lord Buntingdon is intensely
interested and desired to be remembered to you. He of
course, loyal as ever to the Testudinaceae, does not conceal
his hope that the monster may prove to be a great turtle
hitherto unknown to testudinaceous experts. And this is
your camp? Delightful. You'll not object to my teaming up
with you to-night? I want to hear of your adventures round

a roaring camp-fire. And don't think I'm going to upset your commissariat. Oh, no. An old timer like myself doesn't do that. I hope you like ' Spam '? I always say there's nothing like ' Spam ' for giving a spice to life."

Bill Brownsworth was dimly aware of the grin on Kenny Macroon's face as in a daze he led Mr Prew to the sandy hollow above Tràigh Veck.

Chapter 14

THE POPPAY MANIFESTATION

THE small isle of Poppay lies rather nearer to the south coast of Little Todday than Pillay to the north coast. Moreover, unless a south-westerly gale is blowing hard Poppay can be reached without difficulty, there being a well-protected small bay facing north-east with a wide shelf of rock by which a boat may be moored on a clean bottom and lie snug enough in any weather and at any state of the tide. Bàgh nam Marbh or the Bay of the Dead is so called because in the old days Poppay was the burial-place of the Macroons. The body was put aboard from Tràigh nam Marbh, the Strand of the Dead, at the south-east end of Little Todday and ferried across to its last resting-place. The old burial-ground lay above the sands of Bàgh nam Marbh at the bottom of a long brae sloping up to the cliffs which fall sheer to the sea in columns of dark basalt along the northern and western faces of Poppay. The grass grows rank in the old burial-ground, and in one corner of it are the crumbling walls of a little ancient church, in another a cock-eyed Celtic cross. If tombstones ever marked where the dead slept none of them remains to-day. Yet this old burial-ground, disused for nearly two centuries, preserves an almost eerie solemnity, so that the visitor who sits in the lush grass beside a small burn that winds down the brae, the banks of which when it reaches the level of the burial-ground are bright in the month of June with golden flags, is apt to look over his shoulder from time to time, under the impression that he is being watched by an invisible presence. He is not surprised to be told that Poppay is the resort of *bòcain* whose haunting influence extends to Tràigh nam Marbh on Little Todday, a strand along which no native of the Islands likes to walk without a companion in the flesh.

Beyond the burn the rocky southerly horn of Bàgh nam Marbh rises more steeply to a terrace of sparse greenery which gives access to a large cave called Uamh nan Cnàmh, the Cave of the Bones, in which according to legend a Macroon chief with a strong sense of conjugal duty had starved his wife to death for having gazed, as he imagined amorously, at the eldest son of the MacRurie Chief of the time.

The origin of the name Poppay is in dispute, but most philologists now accept it as a variant of Pabbay—the Priest's Island. There is, however, a small but noisy minority which prefers to seek for the etymology of the name in *pìdb* —Pipe Island—from a fancied resemblance to a piper of an isolated basaltic fragment rising from the sea just off the point of the northerly horn of Bàgh nam Marbh. Certainly this rock is still known as *Am Piobair*, but, as Mr John Lorne Campbell of Canna has observed sternly, "there is no excuse for flouting every canon of etymology in order to gratify a taste for the facile picturesque. Poppay is clearly a piece of debased eighteenth-century topography for Pabbay, and indeed, on a rare map of Todaidh Mór and Todaidh Beag in my possession dated 1780, I find Pobbay. After the deliberate efforts of the S.P.C.K., financed from London, to extirpate Gaelic and Latin from the Islands and Wester Inverness through the latter half of the eighteenth century, it is a matter for grateful surprise that corrupt nomenclature like Poppay is not more frequent."

The mind of Joseph Macroon was not disturbed by etymological problems as he sat in the prow of the *Morning Star* on the anniversary of the famous invasion of the Toddays by Major Donald MacDonald of Ben Nevis and C Company of the 8th Battalion of the Inverness-shire Home Guard to recover a left-footed boot which he considered had been stolen from him by Captain Paul Waggett of G Company. It was just such another tranquil and sunny June morning again. The reason for Joseph Macroon's visit to Poppay was to extract from what was left of his share of the whisky saved from the wreck of the *Cabinet Minister* a bottle of Stalker's Joy, in order to present it to Mr Hector Hamish Mackay whose loyal championship of Little and Great Todday against the jealous attempts by other islands to claim their monster he felt merited a gesture of appreciation.

Joseph Macroon was esteemed as hard a man at a bargain as anybody in the Long Island, but when he gave he gave generously, and in giving Mr Mackay a bottle of Stalker's Joy he was giving him a bottle of the brand that was his own special favourite.

In choosing Poppay as the repository for his'liquid treasure Joseph was actuated by the desire to protect it as much against the people of Little Todday as against the Excise. Poppay was no place at all for a nocturnal excursion on account of its ghostly population, and if anybody had visited his hiding-place during the daytime Joseph could not have failed to hear of such a raid.

Kenny Macroon knew that his father had concealed the whisky in Uamh nan Cnàmh, but even he had never ventured to linger long enough in that haunted cave to discover exactly where, and on this morning he remained in the *Morning Star* moored to the rocky shelf in Bàgh nam Marbh, while his father went off through the rank grass of the burial-ground a foot or two above the sandy beach toward the steep rocky slope that led up to the Cave of the Bones, the terrace in front of which was some thirty feet above the sea.

As Kenny watched his father's red knitted cap going up the slope he thought to himself that the *bodach* was still pretty lively. If this was the reflection that occurred to him when his father was on the way up it occurred to him much more forcibly when he saw his father coming down.

"*A Dhia*," Kenny muttered to himself. "I never saw the old man move so fast since he heard the shooting and thought the Germans had landed on Tràigh nam Marbh. *A Dhia*, he is running like a pony with a cleg biting him."

Kenny watched his father's red cap bobbing above the rank grass of the burial-ground, and when he hailed him to find out what was the matter as his father reached the corner of the beach near the landing-place, for answer he snatched his red knitted cap from his head, fell on his knees, crossed himself and said three Hail Marys, followed by a Paternoster and three more Hail Marys.

"Och, he will be making an Act of Contrition now. *Dé rud, athair?*"

Joseph waved his hand for his son not to interrupt his devotions. When they were finished he came along the shelf and got back into the boat.

"Are you after seeing a *bòcan*?" Kenny asked.

"I'm after seeing a fearful terrible thing, *a Choinnich*. Ah, well, God forgive me that I would even be wondering if the Biffer wasn't seeing so much as he said he was after seeing. Ay, ay, God forgive me. Teeth? *A Dhia na Gràs*, it was a terrible thing right enough. I was just bending over to get a bottle of Stalker's Joy for Mr Mackay when I was after hearing . . . snarl were you saying? . . . not at all . . . it was more of a roar with a whistle on the end of it from the far back of the cave and then I saw it looking at me." Joseph crossed himself again. "And the eyes of it!" He shuddered. "But the teeth were the worst."

"Like pickaxes Mistress Odd said they were," Kenny reminded him.

"Och, pickaxes," Joseph scoffed. "A pickaxe wouldn't be seeming much bigger than a toothpick besides such huge great weapons. Och, well, it will cost me a new statue for St Tod for getting me away from those teeth. I've been meaning to get one for him ever since the roof of the Chapel leaked on to his mitre and turned the face of him as green as grass. 'Poor old St Tod,' Maighstir Seumas was for ever saying with a quick look at me and me knowing what he was wanting would be looking the other way. Ay, ay, I'll tell Father James to order a new statue right away and I'll pay for it, carriage and all. *A Dhia*, it's me that's glad I'm not a Protestant this day, or there would be a few more bones in Uamh nan Cnàmh right enough, for it was St Tod himself who pulled me out of the business, and the holy man will have the best statue my money can buy for him. There won't be a better statue in Morar or Moidart, no, nor in Mid Uist or Barra."

"Did you get the whisky?"

"How would I be getting the whisky?" Joseph demanded indignantly. "Is it whisky I would be thinking of when I was staring into two eyes you wouldn't see the like of in Hell itself." He crossed himself again. "Ay, ay, poor Airchie, it was just as well he was in the *Kittiwake*, for he'd never have come out of Uamh na Snaoiseanaich alive, and not a saint for the poor soul to call on to help him."

During the journey back to Kiltod Joseph Macroon sat in the bows of the *Morning Star*, shaking his head from time to time in grave reflection on God's mercy to him as a Catholic.

"Did you hear about wee Jonathan Munro in school, *athair*?" his son asked.

"What was that?"

Jonathan Munro was the only young Protestant in the Kiltod School.

"Why, when Miss MacDonald was taking the infants

Michael Anthony Macroon held up his hand and said Jonathan Munro had made a big swear. 'Och,' says Miss MacDonald, 'what was that at all?' 'Please, miss, Jonathan Munro was saying that God is a Protestant.'"

"Ay, ay, look at that now," said Joseph sombrely; in his present mood of chastened gratitude for his safety he did not think the story at all funny.

When Kenny stopped the engine of the *Morning Star* to come quietly alongside the stone steps down from the quay of Kiltod's diminutive harbour, his father said in tones that left his son in no doubt that he expected him to pay attention.

"You'll not be saying a word to anybody about Poppay, Kenny. Not a word, mind you, not a word. I'll be seeing Father James myself just now."

Joseph Macroon walked along to the Chapel House where the parish priest who was saying his office laid down the breviary and motioned his visitor to the armchair on the other side of the fireplace.

"I've been thinking, Father James, that it looks pretty bad for St Tod to have that kind of a green face on him, and Little Todday so full of towrists."

"Ay, ay, it looks pretty bad right enough, *a Iosaiph*," replied the priest, pondering his leading parishioner's remark the way a chess-player will consider the gambit offered him by his opponent."

"So, I've been saying to myself, *a Mhaighstir Sheumais*, wouldn't it be a good idea now if there was to be a new statue."

"Oh, a glorious beautiful idea it would be, right enough," Father James agreed. "But if you're suggesting a whip round to subscribe for a new statue, Joseph, you'll be waiting till the contributions have been collected for my coal."

"It's not a collection I would be making at all," said Joseph Macroon, with a touch of self-righteousness in the tone of his reply. "And if it's your coal for the year that you're thinking about, Father, you needn't be thinking at all because the puffer will be here early next month and your coal is on order all correct. No, no, Father, I was thinking I would be offering the Chapel a new statue of St Tod and paying for it myself, carriage as well."

"Good shooting!" the priest approved sonorously.

"That was a nice wee statue of St Anthony the Sgoileir

Dubh was after giving when the new school was built, but
a patron saint oughtn't to be squeezed into nothing at all
like that, and so I'd like St Tod to be able to hold his own
with Our Lady, Star of the Sea, on the other side of the
Chapel. And that means just twice as big as he is now."
Joseph hummed to himself for a moment or two. "It'll cost
me the price of a new engine second-hand for the *Morning
Star*, but if we get that lobster-pool maybe I'll buy a new
boat next year."

"And will I put the order for St Tod in hand, Joseph?"

"You'll do that, Father, please, right away."

"Would you say it was too early in the day, Joseph, for
a sensation?" the priest asked.

"It would be too early on most days, Father, but I
believe I'd take a sensation to-day. I believe it's what I need
to restore the balance."

The priest rose and went to a cupboard in the corner
from which he produced a bottle of Stag's Breath and a
couple of dram glasses.

"*Slainte mhór*, Father," said Joseph, draining the glass.

"*Slainte mhath, a Iosaiph*," the priest responded. "And I
hope St Tod will give you your lobster-pool."

"Och, it's not to be getting something out of the man
I'm giving the statue to the Chapel."

"Is it not, Joseph?"

"No, no, Father, it's for a favour received."

And Joseph Macroon went on to tell Father Macalister
the story of his alarming experience on Poppay.

"You'll be telling Mr Waggett that story you've just been
telling me, Joseph."

"Indeed, and I'll be doing no such thing, Father. And
it's just because I don't want a soul except yourself to know
what happened to me in Uamh nan Cnàmh that I'm after
telling you."

"Ay, but you haven't told me the whole story, Joseph,"
said the priest. "You haven't told me about the Minnie you
have hidden in Uamh nan Cnàmh."

Joseph was on the verge of crossing himself, so slight was
seeming to him at that moment the difference between
Father James Macalister and the Devil himself.

"Ah, well, well, you know too much and that's the truth,
a Mhaigstir Sheumais. Ay, there may be a little Minnie left
right enough," Joseph admitted, and then added hastily,

"but it's little enough, more's the pity, and there will be none left at all if these towrists and visitors go looking for the monster and find the Minnie."

"Ay, ay, you'll do well to move it, Joseph. How many bottles have you?"

"Och, there might be half-a-dozen or perhaps a full dozen."

"Or a couple of dozen and half-a-dozen more. You'd better be moving it pretty quickly, Joseph."

"I wouldn't go into Uamh nan Cnàmh and see those eyes looking at me and those terrible teeth for all the whisky in the country. But that's not to say I'm wanting these towrists to clear me out. Och, I don't know what to do about it at all, at all."

The priest leant back in his chair and looked up to the ceiling for inspiration.

"This is what you'll do. Joseph," he announced at last in a voice an oracle would have envied. "You'll tell Mr Mackay just how things are . . ."

"Och, if I tell him I'll be in the papers right away."

"You'll tell Mr Mackay and young Brownsworth and you'll ask them to get your Minnie away if the coast's clear and what you'll do with it after that is your own business except that you'll be giving me two bottles of King's Own if there's any of it left."

"There's no King's Own, Father. I never saw another bottle of it after my daughters broke a dozen bottles on me when they thought the Excise was after it. *Obh bh'obh*, what a terrible day that was!"

"Well, well, you'll be giving me a couple of bottles of whatever you have. And you'll be giving Mr Mackay a couple of bottles."

"Wasn't I going to fetch a bottle of Stalker's Joy for him when the monster nearly had me in his jaws?"

"And if young Brownsworth gets a photograph of the monster and wins £250 you'll be telling him that we want a new stove in the sacristy and that's the way he can show his gratitude for a favour received."

"I'll do that, Father."

"Ay, and you won't be putting into his head, Joseph, that you're expecting anything for yourself out of that £250."

"Would I ever do a thing like that?"

"No, no, I couldn't imagine your doing such a thing. That's just why I was telling you that you wouldn't be doing it, because I know you wouldn't like St Tod to be under an obligation to a Protestant."

"Certainly not, Father James. That would be taking the gilt off the gingerbread for his goodness to me altogether."

"It certainly would. And now there's something else you can do. The B.B.C. have let me know that they won't be able to give their broadcast from Little Todday and they want me to arrange a *luadh* in Snorvig. I'll be telling the *cailleachan* in Church on Sunday from the altar that they'll be going over to Snorvig and when you open the shop after Mass you'll not be listening to any nonsense about the people of Snorvig sitting back to criticise them. I've spoken to the Dot and they'll all go in the *St Dot*."

The Dot was the name under which Donald Macroon, a small swarthy taciturn man, was generally known, and his sizable fishing-boat, the *St Tod*, was always called the *St Dot* by Father Macalister.

"Alec Mackinnon is arranging for the performers from Great Todday and we'll just have Duncan Bàn from here with Andrew Chisholm and Michael Gillies for some piping and old Michael Stewart for a *port a beul*."

"I'll do what you say, Father," said Joseph Macroon.

"By all the holy crows, and you certainly will, Joseph, or you'll find me much less inclined than St Tod to get you out of a predicament."

"What a man," Joseph Macroon reflected as he walked over to his shop from the Chapel House. "Ay, ay, he got back at me right enough for not letting him have a bottle of the real Mackay that time he had nothing but altar wine for a dram last month and the wind in the east. But how did he know I had any Minnie left in Uamh nan Cnàmh? It would be the Devil who was wanting a long spoon if he was taking brose with Maighstir Seumais. What a man, what a man! Och, if I save the Minnie from those towrists it's three bottles of Stalker's Joy I'll be giving him."

Hector Hamish Mackay and Bill Brownsworth were impressed by Joseph Macroon's adventure on Poppay. To his relief the topographer was as much against giving the news to the papers as he was himself while a bottle of Minnie remained in the Cave of the Bones.

"What we have to guard against now," said Mr Mackay,

"is the possibility of idle trippers landing on Poppay and disturbing the monster."

"They can't be getting there except by boat," said Joseph. "I'll be seeing the Biffer and Drooby and I'm sure they'll never be putting a towrist alone on Poppay from Todaidh Mór."

"What about Mr Waggett?" Bill Brownsworth asked. "Doesn't he have the shooting on Poppay?"

"Ay, he goes there missing more snipe than he hits in the autumn, but there's nothing for him to shoot at just now, *taing do Dhia*."

"Yes, but there was nothing for him to shoot at on Pillay," Brownsworth pointed out. "But he wasn't at all pleased that I had landed there. And then he's very much against the idea that the monster really exists. He may want to go to Poppay and contradict Mr Macroon's story."

"There's no contradiction in it," said Joseph indignantly. "You can't be contradicting the nose on a man's face. Ach, but what's the sense in bothering about Waggett? If it isn't in the papers he'll know nothing about Poppay. There's just one little thing, though, and if you can both help me here I'll be much obliged. You'll be going to have a look at the cave?"

"We certainly will," said Mr Mackay.

"If you find when you get there that the monster isn't at home, will you give a call to Kenny and you'll be able to get the whisky safe aboard the *Morning Star* between the three of you."

"Whisky?" Mr Mackay echoed.

"Ay, ay, was I not telling you about the whisky? Yes, I have a few bottles I've been keeping. Yes, in Uamh nan Cnàmh, and I wouldn't like the monster to get at them with those huge teeth of his."

When Hector Hamish Mackay and Bill Brownsworth landed upon Poppay that afternoon and looked across at the Cave of the Bones their hearts were beating at the prospect of a scientific triumph to which the element of danger in that prospect gave an accelerated tempo. As they made their way through the rank grass of the ancient burial-ground, Mr Mackay related to Bill Brownsworth the legend of the bones, and though this penalty of love was inclined to disturb the thoughts of one whose amorous glances had involved him in getting engaged to two sisters at once, the possibility of meeting the monster face to face banished all worry and Bill Brownsworth strode on, hearing academic voices prophesying fame. He was so preoccupied with that Readership at Norwich University that he strode into a thicket of particularly vicious nettles which attacked his knees with alacrity.

"Look out, nettles!" he warned his companion.

"So I see," said Mr Mackay, who, though he deplored the myopia which compelled him to wear glasses with the kilt, never allowed vanity to get the better of caution.

When they reached the rocky slope up to the terrace in front of the cave they relieved the anxious strain upon their minds by hushing one another when the steps of either disturbed a loose pebble and sent it clattering down.

"Look," Bill Brownsworth whispered when they stood upon the sparse vegetation of the terrace. He pointed to a track further along to the right of the cave.

They moved across on tip-toe to find clear evidence of a track beyond the slope leading directly down into the sea below the south-easterly horn of Bàgh nan Marbh.

Mr Sydney Prew, whose company by the way they had had some difficulty in shaking off when they went aboard the *Morning Star*, would have paid his tribute to contemporary youth by ejaculating 'Smashing!' Hector Hamish Mackay chose a word with a larger dignity.

"Stupendous!" he breathed in awe.

Bill Brownsworth, like stout Cortez on a peak in Darien, said nothing, but his brown eyes burned.

"Well," Mr Mackay whispered, "it's no longer a case of 'excelsior' but of 'interior.'"

"Every time," Bill Brownsworth agreed.

"Yes, indeed it is," Mr Mackay whispered again. "Do you think one of us ought to stay outside with the camera?"

Brownsworth shook his head.

"I think we both ought to go in," he insisted. "It may not come out. In fact, it probably won't.

"Yes, yes, there's always that probability," Mr Mackay agreed.

"And in that case," Brownsworth suggested, "it would be better if we both saw it. If I count the upper teeth will you count the lower ones? I attach great importance to these teeth from a palaeontological standpoint."

"Oh, I fully appreciate the importance of these teeth,

Brownsworth. Well, interior, eh? Kenny Macroon looks so snug down there in his boat, doesn't he?"

"Hush," Brownsworth whispered, and began to move toward the entrance of the cave.

"Just a moment," Mr Mackay murmured. "If the creature charges, mind you I don't believe for a moment it will charge, but if it does I imagine we had better retreat by the same route as we came up."

"It'll probably go down to the sea by the track it obviously always uses."

"Yes, exactly," Mr Mackay whispered.

"But if by luck it does charge straight ahead," said Brownsworth, "I shall cut quickly to the left and try to get a snapshot of it as it pursues you down the slope."

"Yes, I appreciate your strategy," Mr Mackay said. "Yes, that ought to make a very effective picture, if the monster doesn't move too quickly and spoil it. Well, in we go, eh? Hush, what was that?" he put a hand on Brownsworth's arm.

"I didn't hear anything."

"I thought I heard a sort of rumbling noise. Yes, there it is again."

"Borborhygmus," Brownsworth whispered.

"What kind of animal is that?" Mr Mackay asked nervously.

"Rumbling in the guts. My guts were rumbling."

"Of course, of course. My mind was running on something else. Yes, yes, the Greeks had a name for it, eh? Well, in we go."

And this time they really did go into the cave. It was empty.

"Dash it, what a disappointment!" Mr Mackay exclaimed, in tones more appropriate to enthusiastic relief than to yearning regret.

"However, it's an ill wind that blows nobody any good, Joseph Macroon will get his whisky.'

Following the directions they had been given they penetrated to the further end of the cave where there was a narrow passage terminating in a smaller secondary cave. Here, under a heap of straw, lay seven cases stamped EXPORT ONLY. Besides these there were twelve bottles of whisky buried in a patch of loose soil by the entrance of the cave.

"I say," Mr Mackay exclaimed, "Friend Joseph doesn't mind asking favours from his friends. I hope he'll decide that the labourer is worthy of his hire."

Poor Bill Brownsworth was too much disappointed by their failure to find the monster at home to worry about the transportation of the contraband whisky to the *Morning Star*, and not having been on Little Todday when the *Cabinet Minister* was wrecked he did not realise the risk he ran of appearing as a criminal in the eyes of the man whose son-in-law he hoped to be.

The conveyance of the whisky to the *Morning Star* proved a less arduous task than it threatened to be because Kenny Macroon, who had a less expansive sense than his father of what one could ask others to do for one, insisted on bearing the chief shape of the burden.

"I didn't know the old man had managed to hide all that lot," he said. "Isn't it he that's smart? And him girning for ever because Peigi Ealasaid and Kate Anne broke all those bottles on him when they thought the Exciseman was coming to Kiltod. Ah, well, *tha è cho carach ris a mhadaidh ruaidh gu dearbh*. It's only Father James who can take the eyes out of him, and how he's thinking we will be getting all these cases to his store without anybody seeing I don't know at all."

But Kenny was soon to find out, for as soon as they reached Kiltod with the *Morning Star*'s cargo he was told to take it round to Bàgh Mhic Ròin on the north coast of Little Todday where he was to wait until his father arrived in the grey dusk of the Hebridean summer midnight to take it back in his trap to the big shed at the back of his shop.

"Ay, ay," said Joseph with a sigh of satisfaction when the whisky was safely housed and hidden behind the junk of years, "they can put me in the papers now when they've a mind to."

However, when he informed Mr Mackay accordingly next morning at breakfast, his guest asked him to preserve the strictest secrecy for the present about all the monster's movements on Poppay.

"I understand you, Mr Mackay, you can trust me to keep my mouth shut," and by a process of reasoning that was peculiar to Joseph Macroon he was able to suppose that any obligation was now entirely on the side of his guest. However, to do him justice he did give Hector Hamish

Mackay two bottles, not of Stalker's Joy but of Thistle Cream, which was nearly as good.

"You see, Mr Brownsworth and I do want to be the first in the field."

"Ay, first in the field," said Joseph. "That's always the best place, without a doubt. And the gilt stays on the gingerbread all correct."

Hector Hamish Mackay had good reason to warn Joseph Macroon against telling everybody about the monster's presence on Poppay. The Secretary of the N.U.H. had lost no time in organising the hiker's patrols he had mentioned to Bill Brownsworth the previous evening, and while Joseph's whisky was being transported from the Cave of the Bones to the *Morning Star* Mr Prew had taken advantage of the Biffer's arrival at Kiltod to get a passage back with him to Snorvig. In the course of the afternoon he arranged for a non-stop patrol along Tràigh Vooey, which was considered the most likely place for the monster to reappear, and much to Bill Brownsworth's relief he found a note in his tent when he got back to Tràigh Veck that evening after an optimistic meal with Hector Hamish Mackay to say that Mr Prew would be camping himself near Garryboo for the present with a very jolly trio of young men from the Ealing Branch of the N.U.H. He found a second note which, when he read it first, gave him a momentary feeling that he had gone off his head:

Snorvig House,
Great Todday,
June 22nd

Dear Mr Brownsworth,
Mrs Waggett and I will be glad to see you at tea-time to-morrow. I understand that you are a friend of Mr Spinnage, who is staying with us, and who arrived by the boat last night from Obaig.
Yours sincerely,
Paul Waggett

Chapter 15

MOLES

AFTER his stevedore's labour in transporting Joseph Macroon's whisky from the Cave of the Bones Bill Brownsworth should have slept soundly to the soft music of the tranquil ocean upon that night. The shock of the news in Waggett's letter was so severe that sleep did not come to him until the small hours and Mr Mackay had not finished his breakfast when he arrived at Joseph Macroon's.

"The most amazing thing has happened," he told Mr Mackay.

"You've seen the monster at Tràigh Veck?" the topographer asked eagerly.

"No, no, something much more extraordinary than that. You remember I invited a friend to come and stay with me here?"

"Yes, and you were wondering why you hadn't heard from him."

"Well, he's here!"

"Is that so very extraordinary?"

"Yes, because he's staying with Mr Waggett. I found a note from Mr Waggett when I got back last night asking me to go over to tea with them this afternoon without a word from Dick Spinnage to explain this extraordinary business. I'm absolutely staggered."

All sorts of fantastic theories had been chasing one another through Bill Brownsworth's brain during the moth-grey Hebridean night, but in the clear light of morning all seemed equally far-fetched and he would have been ashamed to repeat them to Mr Mackay. He had contemplated taking Mr Mackay into his confidence and asking his advice about his difficult position, but when he saw this prim lifelong bachelor by the clear light of morning he shrank from consulting him about a problem so dependent for its solution on a belief in love at first sight.

"Well, you'll find out the explanation when you go to tea in Snorvig this afternoon. I'm glad Mr Prew has betaken himself and his unpleasant impedimenta to Great Todday, though it will be extremely annoying if he and his officious patrols succeed in establishing contact with the monster. You say Mr Waggett is prejudiced against hikers?"

"Very."

"A pity," Mr Mackay commented drily. "He and Mr Prew seem to have the same kind of boy-scout mind, judging by the stories I heard of him when he commanded the Home Guard here. By the way, the B.B.C. have written to ask if I will say a few words about the monster next week at the *luadh* and *céilidh* which is to be broadcast from the Snorvig Hall. A little plan is simmering at the back of my head, Brownsworth. Of course, it may not materialise, but if it did it would give listeners one of the greatest thrills the microphone has ever given to them. But I see you're not interested," Mr Mackay concluded with a touch of pettishness. The thought of Mr Prew seemed to bring out the old maid in himself.

"I'm so sorry," said Bill Brownsworth hastily. "My mind had gone back for a moment to this extraordinary business about my friend Spinnage. What is your plan?"

"Why, it occurred to me that, if you could be stationed on Poppay and if by a happy turn of fate you could establish the presence of the monster there at the moment when the broadcast begins, it would be a superb dramatic effect if you could reach the Hall when I am actually talking about the monster and announce what you had just seen on Poppay."

"Wouldn't Mr Waggett be rather annoyed about my trespassing on Poppay?" Brownsworth demurred.

"Really, really, my dear boy," said Mr Mackay irritably, "you call yourself a palaeontologist and now with an opportunity to put palaeontology on the map you're prepared to sacrifice that opportunity to the petty self-importance of an English shooting-tenant. After all, if the monster doesn't appear nobody need be any the wiser about your vigil, and if it does appear I hardly think Mr Waggett's shooting rights, for which, by the way, I'm told he pays only £40 a year to the Department, will matter a great deal. It's a thousand pities that we cannot land the broadcasting equipment on Poppay and give listeners a chance to hear the monster for themselves, but that's impossible. As it is, listeners will hear me make the dramatic announcement and you'll be able to say a few words yourself into the microphone."

"Oh, no, I couldn't possibly do that," Brownsworth gasped.

"And why not?"

"Well, when I feel embarrassed I get a curious constriction of my throat which makes a kind of gulping noise and that would sound very loud on the microphone—like when somebody pours out a drink in a wireless play. I mean to say, even if an announcer's throat tickles and he gives a little cough, he always begs the pardon of listeners."

"In that case I'll just have to tell the story myself and when the broadcast is over I'll telephone through to the *Daily Tale* the full account of what you saw on Poppay."

"Perhaps the monster won't be there," Brownsworth suggested, with a regrettable note of hopefulness in his voice from a young man whose god was science. "After all, it wasn't there yesterday afternoon."

"We'll take a chance, Brownsworth, and meanwhile we'll keep away from Poppay. Perhaps it's just as well that this antipathetic Prew creature is working up these patrols. The more activity there is along Tràigh Vooey and Tràigh Swish the more likely the monster is to appreciate the peace and seclusion of Poppay. That beach down from Uamh nan Cnàmh to the sea, eh? It's like the opening of Beethoven's Fifth Symphony. Fate knocking at the door. I had the same feeling I had in Edinburgh last month when I suddenly made up my mind to take the road to the isles. I haven't the second-sight myself, but I'm always on the edge of it. I have intimations. You know what I'm trying to say?"

"Oh, rather," Brownsworth assured him. He had not the least idea what Mr Mackay was trying to say, but since reading that note from Paul Waggett the foundations of the scientific approach to life had been so severely shaken that for the nonce he was willing to truckle even to superstition.

After all, it was no more absurd to suppose that the monster might be on Poppay when the broadcast started than to suppose that Dick Spinnage would be staying with the Waggetts at this moment. Indeed, it was much less improbable, and on his way across the Coolish to Snorvig that afternoon Bill Brownsworth began to wonder if conceivably there might not be some more reliable evidence for the phenomena known as flying saucers than he had taken the trouble to examine.

To his relief when the *Morning Star* reached Snorvig, Bill Brownsworth saw Dick Spinnage waiting for him on the pier. At any rate, he would not have had to spend an agonised hour or so hoping for a chance to find out why he was staying with the Waggetts.

"Dick!" he exclaimed, and though he tried to keep reproachfulness out of his voice he could not quite manage it. There came back to him from the past a moment at his prep. school when Dick had had a secret with a boy called Twining whom he hated and when for a week he and Dick had been cutting one another under the emotional strain of threatened friendship.

"Bill!"

There was no trace of apology in Dick's greeting. He stood there in a Donegal tweed suit as apparently sure of his audience's welcome as Ivor Novello himself could always be.

"Why on earth didn't you let me know you were coming to stay with the Waggetts?" Bill asked.

"I did."

"I never had your letter."

"I wrote you by return. And then I wrote again."

"I didn't get that letter either."

In case the failure of Dick Spinnage's two letters to reach his friend should seem to cast a reflection upon the post-office at Snorvig or the postal service of Scotland, here is the text of them as they came back to Dick Spinnage a year later from the New Hebrides by way of Sydney, N.S.W. Nobody at the sorting office for W.C. 2 knew that there were islands off the coast of Scotland called the Outer Hebrides, and as Dick had omitted to add Scotland to the address his letters had been sent to the Pacific.

Blundell, Blundell, Pickthorn and Blundell,
Chartered Accountants,
15, Crumple Inn, W.C. 2
Wednesday

Charles W. Blundell, F.I.C.A.,
Edward R. Pickthorn, F.I.C.A.,
Walter C. Blundell, F.I.C.A.

Dear Bill,
Nothing would suit me better. Old Charles Blundell knows your future father-in-law well. In fact, he was a partner in this firm until

he sold out about five years before the war and went up to live in the Hebrides. He's writing to Waggett. I'll be with you in about a week. I think I can handle this business for you all right, though I'm not going to commit myself to falling in love at first sight with the fair Elsie!

Yours aye,
Dick

And the second letter from the same address was:

Dear Bill,
Your future father-in-law has telegraphed inviting me to stay with him. I'm arriving by Thursday's boat from a place called Obaig. I'll look out for you when I get to this island. It's an extraordinary coincidence that things should play into our hands like this.

Yours aye,
Dick

"I thought I'd gone mad when I got Mr Waggett's note to say you were staying with them," said Bill after his friend had explained what had happened. "What do you think of my girl?"

"A very nice little girl indeed, Bill. But you certainly said it when you said they were alike. If I'm going to make the running with Elsie I'll have to get them to pin a label on with their names, or I'll be making the running with your girl."

"I don't think that would matter."

"Bill!" his friend exclaimed.

"I mean if you could make a mistake like that it would salve Muriel's pride over Elsie. But do you like Elsie?" Bill asked anxiously.

"Oh, she's quite attractive. But her father isn't so hot. Not that I'm suggesting Elsie is hot," he added quickly.

"Of course you've had more experience with girls than I have," Bill reminded his friend.

"I suppose I have," Dick agreed.

"Oh, much more. I mean to say you wouldn't be so likely to fall in love with a girl at first sight as I should."

"You know," said Dick a moment or two later, as they were nearing the gateway to Snorvig House, "I believe it mightn't be a bad idea if I did try to make love to your girl. She'd get annoyed."

"Yes, I suppose she would," Bill agreed a little doubt-fully. He had a tremendous respect for his friend's sway over the hearts of girls.

"Of course she would," said Dick. "And then I'd say 'Good lord, I thought it was your sister.' I wouldn't do this till just before I was going away because even if I began to have a soft spot for Elsie I really couldn't face our late partner at Blundell's as a father-in-law. And then when I was apologising to your girl I'd tell her you'd made the same mistake over Elsie and how badly you felt about it."

"I believe you've hit on it, Dick," said Bill. "Of course, if you *could* fall in love with Elsie I'd be tremendously bucked because it would be so grand to have you as my brother-in-law."

"I wouldn't be your brother-in-law. I'd be Muriel's. And you wouldn't be mine. You'd be Elsie's."

"Well, it's more or less the same thing," said Bill. "I mean to say we could go off on our holidays together. In fact, we might share a house."

"Too risky, Bill," said Dick, who was a good deal stronger on neontology than his friend.

"Still, if you could fall in love with Elsie," Bill said as they reached the gateway of Snorvig House, "I do think your other plan will put things right."

Paul Waggett was happy with two young men in front of whom he could show off as a country gentleman and he enjoyed the opportunity it gave him of demonstrating to his wife and daughters the amount of deference he was able to secure from those who really knew what a sportsman was.

"Come along, Brownsworth. I'm glad you were able to get over this afternoon. You haven't met Mrs Waggett. Dolly, this is Mr Brownsworth. You've met this daughter, but you haven't met my other daughter, Muriel."

Bill Brownsworth was grateful to a state of affairs which allowed him to treat both sisters as strangers and indeed, if the uncomplicated existence of this family leading the simple life was not to be tangled up, demanded that he should. He was so much afraid of letting Muriel or Elsie fancy that he was paying more attention to her twin than to herself that he was unable to give himself an opportunity of searching for any distinctive marks on either twin that would secure him in future against confusing one with the other.

"Of course, it's a great pity you chose June for your visit, Spinnage. We *might* get a salmon in Loch Skinny and we *might* get a good run of sea-trout in Loch Sleeport, but it's a bit early. I suppose Charlie Blundell is becoming just as much of a stickler as his old dad was about holidays. That was really the reason why I sold out. I said to myself 'what's the use of slaving on just for the sake of making a little more money?' I had enough to buy Snorvig House and, though I say it, I wouldn't exchange my shooting and fishing here for any in Scotland or England. I wouldn't really. Grouse, cock, plover, snipe, geese, salmon, sea-trout, what more does anybody want? I don't miss the pheasants and partridges. I mean to say, every year I used to be one of a syndicate for a pheasant and partridge shoot somewhere in the Home Counties, but, I'll be quite frank with you, Spinnage, I didn't really enjoy shooting with a syndicate. I found the gamekeepers thought about nothing but squeezing every tip they could out of the members. It was too commercial for me altogether. I sometimes wish I had a small forest here—but I don't care for stalking so much as all that. I was offered an eight-head forest last year in Wester Inverness, but I said 'no.'"

Mrs Waggett and his daughters looked up at this revelation; it was the first they had heard of such an offer. They did not know it had been made to all the readers of *The Field*, an odd copy of which Daddo had picked up in the smoking-room of one of the Obaig hotels.

"Have you done much stalking, sir?" Dick Spinnage asked.

"No, no. I don't really care for it. You ought to have come up for the Twelfth; oughtn't he, Monty, old boy."

The golden retriever thumped the floor with his tail.

"Wonderful mouth," said Monty's master dreamily. "Of course, I trained him myself. I never lose a bird. Unless I make a boss shot of course," he added, smiling broadly at such a magnificent joke against himself. "But I'm a fairly good shot," he added modestly. "I think any gun who can count on eleven brace of snipe out of twelve in the rough going we sometimes get here can call himself a fairly good shot. I had a wonderful Irish setter who died three years ago. He outgrew his strength, poor old Paddy. The people here were frightened of him. I used to say to the children 'if you don't run away he won't run after you.'

But you can't teach these Islanders anything. They've been boxed up here for hundreds of years, and they think they know everything. It would be funny if it wasn't sometimes so pathetic. When I was in command of the Home Guard Company here I tried to explain to them the importance of the blackout. And what do you think they used to argue? They actually used to argue that because the harbour lights were showing all the way up the Long Island there was no point in bothering about chinks in their windows. I used to try and explain the principle of the thing. Quite useless. They just don't believe in principles. You've heard about that whisky ship? I can't tell you what a responsibility it was for me. All they could see was that there was a cargo of whisky and therefore it must be theirs. They regard law and order as their natural enemies. Of course, they used to be pirates in days gone by, but what I say is they've never stopped being pirates. Still, if you want to enjoy the pleasure of living far from the maddening crowd you have to take the rough with the smooth, and of course an Englishman is always at a disadvantage. Clannishness. That's the trouble. Look what's happened here over this imaginary monster. Why do you suppose everybody here is determined to believe it exists? Clannishness. Why do you suppose the people in Inverness get so annoyed if anybody ventures to doubt if the Loch Ness Monster exists? Clannishness. The whole of Scotland is ridden with clannishness. I wonder what would happen to England if all the Smiths suddenly started getting clannish. Fellows like Hector Hamish Mackay flatter this clannishness in order to sell their books. He gives the people here an entirely false sense of their own importance. You've noticed that, of course," he said turning to Bill Brownsworth, whose desire to propitiate what he hoped was his future father-in-law would not drive him into criticism of a man who had shown him so much kindness and hospitality.

"No, sir, I can't say I have noticed that,' he said, looking quickly to see if Muriel was showing signs of agitation at what bordered upon a contradiction. He did notice an apprehensive look in her eyes, but he noticed something that was to him much more important; he noticed that just behind the lobe of her left ear she had a small beige-coloured mole. It was an exquisite oasis in a desert of similarity.

"Have you read any of Mackay's books?" Paul Waggett
asked.

"I've read the one about these islands, sir."

"Well, you must have noticed the way he flatters the
people here. You'd think to read *Faerie Lands Forlorn* that
the people here were all poets. There's no poetry in them.
I arranged a poetry reading for them soon after I came to
live here, and I read them some of Rudyard Kipling's best
known poems and some of Adam Lindsay Gordon's—oh,
yes, and Macaulay's poem about the Armada, and *The
Charge of the Light Brigade*, and they sat there like a lot of
dummies. They just sat like a lot of dummies. Mr Morrison
the minister who was quite young then and had only just
come to Snorvig was in the chair and he had to flatter them
when he was proposing a vote of thanks to me. Yes, he
actually complimented the audience on the close attention
with which they had tried to follow what for most of them
was a foreign tongue in poetry, and they applauded the
minister's remarks much more loudly than they applauded
my reading. It wasn't that which annoyed me. Not at all.
What did annoy me was his suggestion that there was something clever in not being able to understand English poetry.
However, it was worse in the Kiltod Hall because Father
Macalister deliberately sighed all the time I was reading,
and then he made a speech in Gaelic and though I couldn't
follow absolutely all he said it was evidently intended to
be funny."

Mrs Waggett shook her head sadly.

"I must say Father Macalister does behave very strangely
sometimes for a clergyman," she sighed.

"But he's not a clergyman, Dolly," her husband con-
tradicted. "He's a priest. Priests are not allowed to marry.
So they have no sense of responsibility. Every man ought
to marry."

"I do agree with you there, Mr Waggett," said Bill
Brownsworth fervidly.

"I consider celibacy *most* unhealthy," Paul Waggett
declared, his nose tilting upward as if the very word had an
unpleasant smell. "Are you engaged, Brownsworth?" he
asked.

Brownsworth was saved from replying by swallowing
some tea the wrong way, and by the time he had recovered
from coughing his host was holding forth on the iniquities

G

of what he called a gang of hikers who were camping out on the machair above Tràigh Vooey.

"I warned the fellow who was apparently in charge—a most objectionable type—that I had the shooting rights and could not allow any camping where he was, and what do you think he had the impudence to reply? 'I have sought and obtained permission from the Garryboo crofters to camp here.' I was quite staggered for a moment. And then he produced his card. Sydney Prew, National Union of Hikers. One of these Communist agitators, no doubt. I suppose he thinks he'll curry favour here by supporting this idiotic imaginary monster."

"I don't think he's a Communist, sir," Bill gulped. "The National Union of Hikers is the same kind of organisation as the Cyclists Touring Club."

"I distrust any organisation which doesn't respect shooting and fishing rights," Waggett declared. "I've notified Sergeant MacGillivray that this gang of hikers is swarming all over Garryboo signalling to one another like a lot of boy scouts, but of course it's a waste of time. Sergeant Mac-Gillivray's only idea is to keep the peace."

"Well, that is what the police are for, isn't it, sir?" said Dick Spinnage.

"But you mustn't misunderstand what I said about boy scouts," Waggett went on, deciding to ignore his guest's interjection. "Oh, no, I'm a keen supporter of the scout movement. In fact, I tried to start a troop here, but the only thing they cared about was blowing their whistles all day long for about a week and nearly driving my old Irish setter mad and then it all petered out and I saw their sisters wearing the MacRurie tartan scarves with which I'd presented them. So I gave it up."

When Bill Brownsworth said it was time for him to be getting back to Kiltod and Dick Spinnage volunteered to walk down to the pier with him their host had been talking for twenty minutes about the Normandy landings in which both of them had taken part. Dick Spinnage had made one effort to check the flow of information by mentioning this fact, but it only made their host more eloquent, for, as he said, they would appreciate all the more the problems by which Montgomery was faced and the curious way in which his solution of them had always coincided with his own.

"Why don't you two girls walk as far as the pier with us?" Dick suggested.

Bill, as always, was dazzled by his friend's assurance, especially when Daddo said graciously:

"Run along, chicks, a breath of air will do you good."

Then Dick became even more dazzling.

"Why don't we charter this chap—the Biffer or Buffer or whatever he's called—and have a picnic supper over the water? I'll bring them safely back, sir."

"What does Mumsy say?" Daddo asked.

"I think it would be very nice for them, Paul."

So that was that.

"Why do you keep looking at my hair, Bill?" Muriel asked as they walked down to the pier. "Is it untidy?"

"I was looking at that mole behind your ear."

"Behind my left ear?"

"Yes."

"Elsie has one too, just in the same place."

That exquisite oasis in a desert of similarity was nothing but a mirage after all. How fortunate he had not notified Dick of it as a landmark!

"Oh, Bill, isn't it wonderful to be together like this?" she sighed.

"Absolutely marvellous."

"And do you know, I believe Elsie is rather more than a little interested in Dick."

"Do you really think so?"

"I do really," she said seriously.

"That would be marvellous."

"Wouldn't it?"

"Oh, absolutely."

"I wonder if Dick's interested in her."

"I think he is definitely," Bill affirmed.

"Of course he is very attractive."

"I'm jolly glad you didn't meet him before you met me."

"Don't be silly."

"Well, he might have fallen in love with you."

"Wouldn't Elsie be jealous if he had?" she murmured.

"You think she would?" Bill asked anxiously.

"Imagine what I should feel if I thought you were attracted by Elsie."

"Well, I couldn't be, could I?"

"You know, I did have one horrid moment when I thought you had been rather attracted by her. She talked about you an awful lot that night when you met her on Tràigh Veck."

"I don't know why."

"I think she was very attracted by you," Muriel said, her blue eyes open wide.

"But not since Dick came," Bill urged quickly.

"No, I think she's more interested in Dick now."

"That's what I mean. You might be attracted by Dick if he made love to you."

"But, Bill, your best friend would never do such a thing. It would be frightfully dishonourable," Muriel exclaimed in obvious revolt against such unromantic behaviour.

"Oh, yes, absolutely the end," he agreed.

"Why, I'd as soon imagine your making love to Elsie."

"That's what I mean. It's unthinkable."

"All the same I wouldn't trust Elsie," said Muriel, frowning to herself.

"I say, you oughtn't to say things like that about your sister," he protested.

Muriel was silent.

"You don't know Elsie," she said presently.

In the first exhilaration of seeing how well Dick was making the running with Elsie Bill had been tempted to confide in Muriel the absurd mistake he had made in confusing her with her sister, but Muriel's obvious belief that Elsie considered all fair in love and war deterred him. If he had made the mistake only once he felt that he could have carried it off. '*Do you know, the first time I saw Elsie, I actually blew her a kiss, thinking it was you. Ridiculous, wasn't it?*' Muriel might not have liked it, but, after all, in common fairness she would have had to admit that it was ridiculous. But it was the second time. '*Do you know, the second time I saw Elsie I actually called her "darling," and talked about a double wedding? Ridiculous, wasn't it?*'

"A penny for your thoughts, Bill," Muriel said suddenly.

"My thoughts?" Bill ejaculated with a startled expression. "Oh, my thoughts? I really don't know. Not worth a penny anyway."

"I wondered if you were thinking about me."

"Muriel! As if I'd say my thoughts about you weren't worth a penny!"

"You were looking so worried, Bill. Is anything worrying you?"

"No, I was just wondering where we'd have supper."

"Oh, on Tràigh Veck, of course."

"You don't think that's too far?" Bill demurred. He would have preferred any background to that of the natural arch for this picnic.

"We could hire Joseph Macroon's trap, couldn't we?" she suggested.

Later he was grateful to Muriel's happy suggestion, for Dick drove with Elsie beside him, and so Bill, sitting with Muriel at the back, was able to discover that Elsie had a very small coffee-coloured mole under her right ear.

"Don't move, darling," he said to Muriel as he looked round behind her neck.

"What is it, Bill?" she asked nervously.

"Nothing much," he said, flipping away an imaginary something with his finger. "Only a ladybird."

"You did give me a fright."

"I thought it was another mole."

"No, I haven't got a mole there. Elsie has, though."

"Has she?" said Bill, in a tone which he hoped conveyed the utter indifference he would like Muriel to think he felt about her sister's moles.

"Yes, Mumsy used to say that when we were tiny tots Elsie's other mole was the only way she could be sure which was which."

"Really?" said Bill. "That was rather ingenious of your mother. Haven't you got moles anywhere else?"

"Bill!" Muriel exclaimed. "Aren't you dreadful?"

He blushed, for he was naturally an old-fashioned young man and his passion for palaeontology had preserved his old-fashioned notions.

"I say, I'm awfully sorry. One gets in the habit of asking questions like that when one's identifying fossilised remains."

Muriel laughed.

"What's the joke at the back?" Dick Spinnage turned round to ask.

"Bill's been comparing Elsie and me to fossilised remains," Muriel told him.

"I like that!" Elsie expostulated without a trace of indignation because she was wondering if Muriel was feeling frightfully jealous of the way she herself had obviously made such a completely contrary impression upon Dick.

The picnic on Tràigh Veck was a complete success, and the scenic effects, combined with superlative lighting, made Dick Spinnage look more like Ivor Novello than ever, so that when after supper he suggested taking Elsie for a stroll along Tràigh Swish, Bill felt buoyantly sure that his friend would be bewitched by the magical atmosphere into making love to Elsie and possibly even into proposing to her.

"Well, you may say what you like, darling," he murmured to Muriel, "but I'm jolly glad I had the luck to meet you before Dick arrived. I wouldn't have had a chance."

"But, Bill, I fell in love with you at first sight."

"Yes, but you might have fallen in love with Dick at first sight, and if you had Elsie wouldn't have had a chance."

"Oh, Bill, I do love you," she sighed rapturously.

Bill may not have had much experience of women, but by falling in love with a twin he had discovered a great deal about them in a very short time.

"If Dick does propose to Elsie," he said, when kisses required an interval of words, "I shall tell your father before I leave that I want to marry you. I meant to talk about my prospects in an indirect way this afternoon, but your father didn't give me a good opportunity."

"Poor old Daddo, he doesn't often get a chance of holding forth except to Mumsy and us and he did enjoy himself. I'm afraid when Elsie and I get married he's going to feel rather lost up here. Of course, Mumsy is longing to go and live near Aunt Gladys in Norwood. Still, que voulez-vous? Daughters must get married some day."

"Oh, rather," Bill agreed, "every time. But I wish your father wasn't so prejudiced against this mysterious creature or monster. I mean to say if I do succeed in identifying it he'll be so annoyed to find he's wrong. However, don't let's look on the gloomy side. Things have gone so much better for us than we could have dreamed of only a day or two ago."

"What's the time, Bill?" Muriel asked. "We mustn't be too late."

"Half-past kissing time. Time to kiss again," said Bill. "I had a nurse who always used to say that when I asked her the time. I used to get furious with her. Now it seems a pretty sound remark."

While the girls were getting themselves adjusted for the

crossing to Snorvig, Bill had an opportunity to talk to Dick
for a minute or two.

"You didn't propose to Elsie this evening?" he asked
hopefully.

"No, I certainly didn't. Mind you, she's not a bad little
girl, and I was strongly tempted to put an arm round her,
but I thought of you, Bill, and resisted the temptation."

"Thought of me?" Bill exclaimed.

"Well, if you're serious about marrying Muriel it would
hardly do for your best friend to start making love to her
sister without serious intentions."

"I wish you would marry Elsie," Bill sighed.

"I couldn't take old Waggett as an in-law. I simply
couldn't, Bill. I never heard a man talk so much. Thank
god, he left Blundell *ad lib.* before I joined the outfit. Mind
you, I daresay he could be quite useful as a father-in-law
in the way of hurrying on that partnership. Charlie Blundell
spoke of him with real affection and said he was a great loss
to the firm. I suppose he talked out even the Income Tax
people."

"Well, if you're not going to propose to Elsie, Dick, you
must carry out this plan about Muriel. It's more important
than ever now because if Elsie has fallen badly for you
she'll be so disappointed and jealous that she may enjoy upsetting Muriel."

"I won't let you down, Bill."

"Listen, Dick. This is very important. In case you aren't
perfectly sure that it is Muriel look at the back of her right
ear."

"What?"

"If it's Muriel there won't be a very small coffee-
coloured mole."

"So what?"

"But if it's Elsie there will be. They both have much
paler moles under their left ears."

"Bill, for heaven's sake have a heart. It may be your
technique to go sniffing around the moles at the back of a
girl's ears, but, boy, believe me it isn't mine."

"I don't want to go sniffing around their moles. The
point is that if you're in the least doubt which girl it is you
can always make sure."

"I see, Muriel's got a coffee-coloured mole and Elsie
hasn't."

"No, the other way round, Dick," Bill protested. "They both have paler moles, but only Elsie has this coffee-coloured mole."

"Café noir or café au lait?"

"Compared with the others more like café noir," said Bill very seriously.

"Don't worry. I'll be safer with my own instinct than your moles," Dick assured him. "I was never in a moment's doubt this evening which was which."

"It was quite easy. One of them had a light green tweed wrap and the other a pale blue one. And anyway, Muriel was with me all the time. I don't want to fuss, but, after all, I did make the same mistake myself twice."

Dick smiled.

"I shan't, Bill. But wait a minute. Suppose when I tell Muriel I thought it was Elsie she tells Elsie? I'd be hooked myself."

"No, you wouldn't. Elsie might be annoyed, of course, but that won't matter to you."

"Oh, I expect it'll be all right. I hear the girls coming."

"Well, if you're at all doubtful, don't forget that Elsie has a coffee-coloured mole under her right ear," Bill muttered.

"What are you two whispering about?" Elsie asked.

"Bill was giving me some tips about natural history," Dick told her with a grin. "Well, it's been a grand evening, Bill. When are you coming over to Snorvig?"

"I'll probably come over the day after to-morrow," he said. "The day after to-morrow," he repeated, giving his friend a dark grimly earnest look such as the villain in an old-fashioned melodrama used to give the hero to disturb an audience of happy unsophisticated playgoers with a promise of trouble brewing for the heroine in the near future.

"All the same," he thought when he had waved the *Kittiwake* out on to the oxidised silver of the Coolish in the breathless gloaming, "all the same, it would be much simpler if Dick proposed to Elsie."

Bill turned in to Joseph Macroon's again to have a talk with Mr Mackay before he went back to his tent.

"Ah, good, I'm glad you looked in, Brownsworth. I've just had a telegram from the B.B.C. Would you care to read it?"

Delighted you will give five minute talk at ceilidh about monster stop we propose arrive with our unit on Tuesday boat stop ceilidh will start 7.45 Thursday and run till 9 stop full programme will be arranged in consultation with Father Macalister and Mr Mackinnon of Snorvig School stop we shall make recordings round Great Todday of characteristic Hebridean scenes and shall appreciate any cooperation you care to give stop understand Ben Nevis will be at Snorvig with yacht suggest possibility of recording interview with him and suggesting to Father Macalister possibility of inviting Ben Nevis to say a few words at ceilidh and should again appreciate your cooperation as experienced broadcaster Duncan MacColl

"It's a very nice telegram, I think," said Mr Mackay. "It's always pleasant to know that one's efforts are appreciated. And here's another nice telegram from the *Daily Tale*:

Carmichael accompanying Ben Nevis to Snorvig stop you should do utmost to effect his contact with subject of your interesting letter just received stop your work has been usefulest Donaldson

"I don't quite understand how Ben Nevis comes into this," said Bill Brownsworth in bewilderment.

"Oh, he's a great enthusiast for the Loch Ness Monster."

"Ben Nevis? Ben Nevis, did you say?"

"Yes, yes, Donald MacDonald of Ben Nevis. One of the last of the rare old Chieftains. A great figure." Suddenly Mr Mackay realised Bill Brownsworth's perplexity. "Oh, laddie, laddie, you didn't think Ben Nevis was the mountain? Oh dear, that's rich. Oh, I must tell Father Macalister that one. That would be a case of the mountain coming to Mahomet with a vengeance. We must have a dram of Thistle Cream on that one."

When he had set the glasses on the table and poured out the drams Mr Mackay returned to the exciting future.

"I decided to write at once to Mr Donaldson, the Editor, giving him in the strictest confidence our news about Poppay and proposing to him our plan of action. He's evidently delighted. Young Carmichael is a capital lad. You'll like him and of course he'll be able to be with you on Poppay in case the monster appears at the right moment. Oh, it's great, it's splendid. If only the monster will appear. It'll be one of the supreme moments in broadcasting. And,

G*

look here, if you're thinking about that photograph, don't worry. I'm sure if Carmichael gets one you'll be given the credit, ay, and the cash too. Really, I don't think I've ever felt quite so excited in the whole of my life. No, not even when I thought I saw Oscar Slater sitting opposite me in one of the Leith trams. But we must be as close as oysters over Poppay. We don't want that fellow Prew starting non-stop patrols there. The monster must be persuaded that it has found a quiet spot in Uamh nan Cnàmh. By Jingo, I'd like fine to go over and have a look at Poppay with you to-morrow. But we won't. We'll leave it all to Providence, and I feel certain, do you know, that Providence is not going to let us down. You're not drinking your whisky, man. Drink up; drink up. We've a great week ahead of us."

Chapter 16

THE OCEAN WAVE

TO the disappointment of Ben Nevis, Deirdre and Wilbur Carboy could not reach Scotland in time to sail with the *Banshee*, for it was felt that it would be tempting fortune too hard to postpone the expedition and risk a change in this lovely June weather.

"But I do wish you'd have one more shot to persuade Hugh to come with us," the Chieftain said to Chester Royde. The laird of Knocknacolly, in spite of having put on weight during the last decade, did not look much older than when he and Carrie came to stay at Glenbogle Castle a year or two before the second war. The double chin he had had when he was twenty-five was a rather larger double to-day, his complexion was pastier, and his pugnose was now approximating to a bulldog's nose. Nevertheless, with the heavy work of a great financial house increasingly upon his shoulders Chester Royde gave an impression of the liveliest vigour. As for Carrie Royde, with her red hair and beautiful complexion, she seemed not a day older.

The laird of Kilwhillie was adamant.

"No, I will not take part in this expedition," he declared firmly. "I dislike the sea and I am much too busy getting ready for Walter's birthday at the beginning of October when we are to have the formal ceremony of adopting him as my heir."

"Now look, Hugh," said Chester, "if you'll join in this monster chase, Carrie and I will stay over here till after your celebrations. And what's more, we'll somehow get Myrtle and Alan over. They've got this tropical bug pretty badly and are bumming around in the West Indies just now, but I'm going to make a big point of their coming over."

Myrtle was Chester Royde's sister who had married the Scottish poet, Alan MacMillan.

"Nothing will give me greater pleasure than to welcome Myrtle and Alan," said Kilwhillie. "But I will not cross the Minch."

"But, Hugh, I've got a crackerjack new gun. It's an

elephant gun and you'd be pretty sore if I bagged this island monster and you weren't there."

"I shall be pretty sore, as you put it, if you do bag it," said Kilwhillie severely. "I never heard of such an outrageous proposal. Do you mean to tell me that Donald Ben Nevis is prepared to take part in such a piece of vandalism? It's the kind of thing I should expect from General MacArthur."

When his visitors had gone Kilwhillie took the receiver from the telephone, the expression on his face that of a man who is removing a noxious reptile from his slipper.

"I wish to speak to Ben Nevis, Toker," he said when the Glenbogle butler acknowledged his ring.

"Certainly, Kilwhillie. Will you hold on, sir, please, till I can find Ben Nevis?"

A minute later Kilwhillie blinked for a moment as the receiver suddenly vibrated.

"I can hear you perfectly well, Donald," he said coldly. "Chester Royde has just been here trying to persuade me to cross the Minch with you. I will not cross the Minch . . . yes, I daresay the Minch and the Atlantic are both as smooth as a mill pond at present. I have no intention of finding out for myself what they're like. That's not what I've rung up about. . . . Chester Royde has just announced to me that he has bought a new elephant gun with which he's proposing to make an attempt to bag this monster, as he puts it. Were you aware of this disgraceful project? . . . the likelihood of his hitting it does not enter into the question . . . you did, in fact, know that this project was afoot . . . well, all I can say is that I am appalled by such a piece of vulgarity . . . yes, I did say vulgarity . . . I'm sorry if you think my language is too strong, Donald, but I don't think any language could be too strong for this disgraceful vandalism, and I must stand by what I have said. . . . What would you say if you heard that I was abetting an American millionaire in an attempt to take the life of the Loch Ness Monster? . . . *you'd* be appalled, precisely . . . if Chester Royde wants to go shooting with this elephant gun of his, let him shoot a few film-stars or members of the present Government or crooners as they're called or any other kind of public nuisance . . . I don't agree that doing your best to dissuade Royde is enough. You can make it clear to him that either you go or the elephant gun goes to the Islands, and that Chester must choose which ... I'm sorry, Donald, I'm not interested in the rest of your party. All I am concerned with is this disgraceful gun."

Kilwhillie put the receiver back.

"Is anything the matter, Donald?" the Chieftain's wife asked when she found him sitting by the telephone in a state as near to dejection as it was possible for Mac 'ic Eachainn to achieve.

"That was Hugh on the telephone. He rang me up."

"How is he?"

"I think this liver of his is still causing trouble. He suggested that Chester Royde should shoot all the members of this Bolshie Government of ours."

"Shoot them?" Mrs MacDonald boomed in amazement.

"Yes, he has a new elephant gun."

"Did you say shoot them?" Mrs MacDonald asked.

"Yes, the poor old boy's obviously rather under the weather."

"The weather could hardly be better," Mrs MacDonald commented. "The weather is no excuse for Hugh Cameron's extraordinary proposal."

"Yes, well, Chester Royde isn't likely to fall in with it," said the Chieftain.

"Indeed, I shouldn't think so. I hope Dr Macgregor knows about these extraordinary ideas of Hugh's. I'm sure he'd rule out visits from you as much too exciting for him."

"Look here, you're making a molehill out of a mountain, Trixie, you really are. I'm sorry Hugh won't come with us in the *Banshee* because I think the sea breezes would have blown away his liver and all that sort of thing. However, he won't come with us and that's the end of it."

The Roydes were dining at Glenbogle that night and when the financier and the Chieftain were sitting over their port the latter said:

"I've been thinking about this plan of yours to shoot this island monster, Chester, and I'm getting a little worried about it."

"You are?"

"Yes, I really am. You see, it might put it into somebody's head to have a shot at our monster and if they did I think you'd be blamed. There's some word when a tinker

breaks into an alms box in a church and takes the cash—
I can't remember for a moment what the word is, but that's
what people in the North would think shooting at our
monster was. Now, you wouldn't like to be accused of
encouraging what this word is that I can't remember.
That's why I hate those vile crossword puzzles they print
all over the place nowadays."

"Is it 'sacrilege' you're trying to say, Ben Nevis?"

"That's the brute, yes. Bravo, Chester. Sacrilege. Sacrilege. Well, they're very allergic to sacrilege up here if you
know what I mean."

"But I thought the Loch Ness Monster had been taken
for a ride by this flying saucer, Ben Nevis. I don't see why
we need worry any about the Loch Ness Monster."

"But nobody up here believes that our dear old monster
was killed by this flying saucer. We think it's lying low.
And though I regard these islanders as a set of robbers I
don't feel easy in my mind about shooting their monster.
Hugh Cameron feels the same."

"You're telling me," Chester exclaimed. "When I told
him about this new gun of mine and how I was hoping to
bag this island monster he looked at me as if . . . well, you
know the way Kilwhillie can look at anybody as he'd been
dead a fortnight and it was time to ring and have him taken
away. Still, I don't want to upset anybody up here. I
certainly don't. So if you think this new gun of mine had
better be left behind, that's O.K. with me."

"Very good of you, Chester. Fill up your glass. I don't
much care for port myself. Always think it tastes a bit like
stewed plums, if you know what I mean. Yes, I'm very
grateful to you for being so—er—co-operative. Wonderful
thing co-operativeness except, of course, when these Bolshies
down in Whitehall try to nationalise it. You don't mind
Kenneth MacLennan coming with us? He's the chap that
saw the outrage in Loch Ness in March and I want him as
an eyewitness to stop all this nonsensical bubble-babble
about the island monster being our monster."

"Sure, bring him along."

"And there's one more thing. The Editor of the *Scottish
Daily Tale*, who's a fellow clansman of mine, wants to have
a representative on board in case of any excitement. I
promised him he should come if you've no objection. A
very decent young chap called Carmichael. He's been

round Loch Ness trying to find evidence that our monster is still there."

"Sure, bring him along too."

"Well, then we shall be you and Carrie and me, Catriona and Mary, Bertie Bottley, this lad Carmichael and Kenneth MacLennan, and of course Toker as Chief Steward, what? Oh, yes, and I'm bringing my piper, Angus MacQuat. I asked Tom Rawstorne, but I'm glad to say he can't come, because owners can be an awful nuisance on board their own yachts. So fussy about scratches on the deck and all that sort of old-maidish stuff. We sail on Tuesday morning from Axedge, and I'm looking forward to a wonderful cruise. If we don't have any luck in the Toddays we can carry on up to Nobost, and for that matter right up the Long Island as far as Stornoway."

It was a drive of over twenty-five miles to the little port of Axedge which lay about three miles up the wooded banks of lovely Loch Dooin on the Lochaber side. Ben Nevis, with Catriona and Mary, drove with Chester and Carrie Royde in the Knocknacolly Rolls-Royce. Johnnie Macpherson took Angus MacQuat, Toker and two cases of Glenbogle's Pride in the Glenbogle car.

"I'm sorry old Hugh isn't with us, Carrie," the Chieftain said. "I knew it was going to be a glorious morning."

"It's just too bad he hates the sea so terribly," Carrie said.

"All imagination of course," the Chieftain commented scornfully.

"No, no, I'm not going to stand for that, Ben Nevis," she protested. "I've been terribly sea-sick once or twice even when crossing in the *Ruritania* and that certainly wasn't imagination."

"Extraordinary!" the Chieftain woofed. "Nobody looking at you would ever suppose you could be sea-sick. But Hugh isn't happy on board ship until he *is* sea-sick. I remember when he and I sailed to Bombay how miserable he was. I got quite worried once when a pretty girl asked him if he would judge the costumes in the fancy-dress dance. I thought for a moment he was going to throw her overboard. I did really."

The *Banshee* was a trim craft and as she lay beside the little pier at Axedge on that flawless morning in June those who would presently entrust themselves to her for the eighty-mile voyage felt as confident of her graceful sea-worthiness as if she were the mighty *Ruritania* or *Ecstatic*.

"I'd like to sail at eleven o'clock to catch the tide," Captain Gillies told his passengers with a dark glance at the Chieftain's brogues.

"We ought to be able to do that, Captain," said Chester Royde.

"Sir Hubert Bottley isn't here yet," Captain Gillies observed sternly. He had had to wait for the laird of Cloy on one or two previous occasions.

"Oh, he'll be here in good time," Ben Nevis barked genially. "In fact, there he is now."

The Bottley Bentley had just emerged from the woods at the head of the loch, and presently its plump amiable owner was greeting everybody.

"Ah, there you are, MacLennan," said Ben Nevis. "I'm glad you were able to come. I want you to tell Mr Royde that story of yours about the fox which pinched your deer-stalker."

"Say, that sounds a pretty good story," Chester Royde commented.

"One of the finest stalkers in the north," Ben Nevis observed, without embarrassing the eagle-beaked Coinneach Mór who was perfectly aware of his own skill. "I wish you had him at Knocknacolly."

"Look here, Donald," said Bottley with a grin, "we have all our work cut out to deal with black-market deer-poachers without your trying to poach my head stalker."

"I know," Ben Nevis barked. "We've got to do something about it too. There won't be a deer or salmon left unless we're allowed a free hand with these ruffians. Lindsay-Wolseley, of course, was as sticky as a blob of glue when I put up to him the idea of setting mantraps. He said mantraps were illegal. 'So's poaching' I reminded him. And then he started some dunderheaded argument about two blacks not making a white or two whites not making a black. Hopeless. The North-West Frontier must have been like a Sunday School when Wolseley was soldiering up there."

At this moment young Ian Carmichael of the *Daily Tale* came up to salute Ben Nevis and was introduced to Chester and Carrie Royde.

"Glad to have you with us on this trip, Mr Carmichael."

"I assure you your kindness is much appreciated, sir. Have you seen this morning's *Daily Tale*? I brought one with me from Fort William. There are two or three paragraphs you might care to see."

The young reporter handed Chester Royde a copy of the current issue, and he read out the following:

"'Lively interest has been roused by the news that Mr Chester Royde, Jr., of the great financial house of New York, has joined hands with MacDonald of Ben Nevis to lead an expedition in search of the Island Monster with the object of disproving once and for all its connection with the Loch Ness Monster. The famous Lochaber Chieftain attaches the greatest importance to this in view of what he scathingly calls 'the attempts of interested parties' to encourage the idea that the Loch Ness Monster has deserted the mainland for the islands. Sir Hubert Bottley of Cloy, who is accompanying the expedition himself, has lent the services of his headstalker, Mr Kenneth MacLennan. Inasmuch as it was Mr MacLennan who last March, as first reported in the *Daily Tale*, was an eyewitness of the amazing collision between the Loch Ness Monster and a flying saucer, general gratification will be felt at the news that Coinneach Mor (Big Kenneth) as he is affectionately called on Loch Ness side, will be at hand if and when the Island monster shows itself.

"A special representative of the *Scottish Daily Tale* will accompany the expedition which will sail this morning from Loch Dooin in Mr T. Rawstorne's S.Y. *Banshee*, and our readers will be kept in close touch with the latest developments of this amazing story which, without at present being able for obvious reasons to say more, are likely to prove nothing less than sensational.

"It is a matter of particular satisfaction to the *Scottish Daily Tale*, which believes that the future happiness and prosperity of the world depends upon a continuous strengthening of the bonds which link the British Commonwealth with the United States that the expedition of the *Banshee* is a joint operation.'"

"Why, I think that's very, very sweet," said Carrie, smiling at Ian Carmichael whom she suspected rightly of having written this puff preliminary. Ian Carmichael blushed. Carrie Royde's eyes were as fatal to good-looking young men as depth-charges to submarines.

Soon after the *Banshee* cast off to the strains of *Clan Donald is Here* and *Over the Sea to Skye* piped by Angus MacQuat. Ben Nevis, his countenance glowing, announced that it was time to tap the steward and Toker was bidden to bring in a bottle of Glenbogle's Pride to toast the expedition. Long gone were the days when Chester Royde drowned the noble liquid with soda and chilled it with ice, at any rate on this side of the Atlantic. What he did with highballs on the other side was, so far as Ben Nevis was concerned, wrapped in a merciful oblivion.

"Gee, this is certainly a great whisky, Ben Nevis," he declared reverently after putting down a couple of drams.

"Well, of course I'm rather prejudiced, but I don't think there's anything to touch it," said the Chieftain with a touch of complacency. "Slahnjervaw, everybody."

"I wonder what the old bean would say if we sank a dram instead of this horrible sherry," Catriona muttered to her sister.

Mary tried the experiment.

"Slahnjervaw, father," she boomed in that deep voice which both daughters had inherited from their mother.

"Slahnjer . . ." and then the Chieftain stopped. He was privately not at all displeased that one of his hefty daughters should be a chip of the old block, but in fancy he was on the mat in the yellow drawing-room at Glenbogle trying to explain to his wife why he had not immediately asserted himself as a father when Mary took a dram at eleven o'clock in the morning. Before he could decide what to say Catriona had followed her sister's example. The attention of Ben Nevis was distracted from his daughters by a signal from Toker.

"What is it?"

"Might I have a word with you, sir, for a moment in your cabin?"

"What on earth's the matter?" he asked when the butler had closed the door of the cabin.

"It's a little question of footwear, sir," Toker replied.

"Footwear?"

"Yes, sir, Captain Gillies observed that there were tacks on your brogues and, if I may be permitted a rather vulgar expression, went off the deep end about them to me. Being well aware of the peppery nature of many sea-captains, I let him—er—do the talking until he cooled down and returned to the navigation of the yacht."

"What's the matter with the tacks in my brogues?" the Chieftain barked.

"Apparently, sir, the effect of them upon the deck of a yacht is deleterious. Definitely deleterious."

"In other words, Captain Gillies is allergic to my brogues, what?"

"That would express the present condition of the Captain's mind with absolute accuracy, sir."

"I see, well, what am I to do about it?"

"I have ventured to enquire whether the yacht's stores were capable of coping with the emergency, sir, and I have succeeded in procuring a pair of what in the days of my youth we used to call sandshoes."

Toker went to a locker and produced a pair of heelless rubber-soled shoes the uppers of which were of speckled black and grey canvas.

"Good lord, Toker, I can't wear those," the Chieftain protested. "I shall look as if I were wearing a couple of flounders with that beastly dark skin on top."

"Nevertheless, sir, I venture to hope that you will humour Captain Gillies in this little matter."

"Little matter? It isn't a little matter to expect me to go bouncing about the deck like a tennis ball."

"I think, sir, if you would kindly try them on you will find them less objectionable when worn than they appear upon their own. You may have observed, sir, that Sir Hubert and Mr Royde are both in nautical attire and wearing rubber-soled buckskin shoes, and it would unquestionably relieve the Captain's solicitude for the condition of the deck if you could see your way to indulge him in this matter. There is, of course, an alternative. You could wear your buckled patent-leather evening brogues, but I thought the notion of wearing these with a tweed doublet might be distasteful."

"It certainly would be, Toker. It would be disgusting. I don't want to look like a piper at a wedding."

"Precisely, sir. And so if you will sit down I will ascertain if the pair of sandshoes I have chosen are comfortable."

"You are without exception the most persistent fellah I ever knew, Toker," said the Chieftain.

"Thank you, sir," the butler replied as he offered Ben Nevis a shoehorn. "*Nil desperandum* has always been my favourite motto. And of course *sic itur ad astra*."

"Now don't you start talking about sea-sickness."

"Excuse me, sir. I was quoting Latin. *Sic itur ad astra.* Thus do we reach the stars."

"I was always very allergic to Latin when I was at Harrow. Never could see any point in it. Mensa, a table. Mensa, O table. Whoever wants to talk to a table in any language? If I'm reduced to talking to tables I'll talk to them in English. Mensa, O table! I think Latin is a wooden-headed language."

"How do you find the shoes, sir?"

The Chieftain got up and stamped about the cabin.

"Well, they don't feel as beastly as they look. So I suppose I can stand them while we're actually at sea."

"I feel sure Captain Gillies will much appreciate your conciliatory attitude, sir."

"I suppose, my boy Murdoch would have supported the Captain, wouldn't he?"

"I think the Commander undoubtedly would have, sir."

The Chieftain sighed gustily, and blew his nose. "I wish he were with us, Toker."

"Indeed, sir, we all wish the Commander were with us."

"Well, I'd better be getting back on deck," Ben Nevis said. "Lunch is at one, isn't it?"

"Yes, sir, I thought with the appetite for which the sea is famous you would prefer lunch half-an-hour before your usual hour."

"Quite right. In fact, I'm beginning to feel quite peckish already."

"You are, sir? I wonder if you would like a cup of cold consommé now? It won't spoil your appetite for lunch, but it will remove that feeling of the watched pot which never boils."

"I think we'd all like a cup of consommé. And by the way, Toker, when you're handing round the whisky I think it would be better to pass by Miss Catriona and Miss Mary."

"I always do, sir. The young ladies were drinking sherry just now."

"They weren't. That's just it. They were drinking whisky. I was wondering what to do about it when you called me away about these shoes. Mind you, I think whisky is much

better for them than these ghastly cocktails tasting of hair
oil and methylated spirits, but I don't think their mother
would quite understand."

"It might perplex Mrs MacDonald, sir."

Conscious of having carried out his paternal duty, Ben
Nevis rejoined the others.

"I see you've put on a pair of winged sandals, Donald,"
the laird of Cloy said in that high voice so often heard from
the lips of plump men.

"They're not sandals; they're sandshoes, Bertie. Toker
managed to get hold of a pair for me. Did you say 'winged'?
What on earth are you talking about?"

"Perseus and Andromeda and all that," said Bottley.

"Who on earth are Persus and Romeda?" Ben Nevis
asked.

The laird of Cloy giggled.

"Perseus put on a pair of winged sandals to rescue
Andromeda from the sea-monster."

Ben Nevis shook his head.

"I expect it's very funny, Bertie, but it's beyond me. Do
you know what he's talking about, Chester?"

The financier shook his head.

"Of course you do, Chester," Carrie Royde put in, and
before he could reveal the full extent of his ignorance she
related the ancient story.

"This fellow Perseus seems to have been a bit of a flying
saucer, what?" said Ben Nevis when Carrie had finished.
"Do you believe that yarn, Bertie? It sounds to me a
pretty tall story. It's a pity, though, we can't get hold of a
Gorgon's head. By Jove, this Bolshie Government of ours
would be an absolute quarry before I'd finished with them.
But all we've got is Gorgonzola, what? And not much of
that."

Mac 'ic Eachainn was so pleased with this joke that he
forgave the laird of Cloy for what he had been inclined to
condemn as showing off..

After lunch Toker found an opportunity to talk to Ian
Carmichael on a subject near to his heart.

"Will you excuse me, sir, but during lunch I happened
to overhear you comment on the fact that Mr Hector
Hamish Mackay is at present on the island of Little
Todday."

"Yes, he's working there for our set up."

"I had divined as much from his recent articles in the *Daily Tale*. Will you think it presumptuous on my part to ask you to give me a chance of telling Mr Hector Hamish Mackay what his books have meant to me for many years?"

"Och, I'm sure he'll be delighted."

"You think he will? On one occasion I did write to tell him what a world of romance his book *Faerie Lands Forlorn* had revealed to me, and I received from Mr Hector Hamish Mackay a gracious acknowledgment. That note is among my most treasured possessions. I have heard him broadcast, but it has never been my good fortune to come into personal contact with him and I am, if I may use an expression which Mr Mackay himself would never use, all agog, Mr Carmichael, to tell a great writer in my own inadequate words how much I venerate his poetic eloquence. It was most painful when I heard Ben Nevis stigmatise him as a mushy nincompoop because in the first flush of excitement caused by the news of the flying saucer's attack on the Loch Ness Monster Mr Mackay ventured to speculate whether the monster's bereaved mate might not seek a refuge in the Islands. However, Mr Mackay has since then expressed his conviction that the Island Monster is, as the old Romans used to say, *suo genere*, and I have no doubt whatever that as they also used to say, Mr Mackay is now *persona grata* with Ben Nevis. Please forgive me for expressing myself at such length, but I was anxious to let you know how earnestly I was hoping to have an opportunity of offering my homage to a master of the English language."

"I'll make it my business to see that you do get this opportunity, Mr Toker," the young reporter promised with that pleasant smile which extracted so much useful information for his paper.

"Toker, sir, if you don't mind," the butler murmured gently. "I do not wish to sail under false colours. If the occasion presents itself will you just say 'this is Toker, the butler at Glenbogle Castle, who is one of your most ardent admirers.'"

"I'll do that. You can rely on me, Toker."

"I am extremely obliged, sir. In the hope of having this opportunity to let Mr Hector Hamish Mackay know of my admiration for him I have ventured to bring with me a selection of his books in which I shall be so bold as to ask him to inscribe his name. *Happy Days Among the Heather, Faerie Lands Forlorn, The Glamour of the Glens, In the Footsteps of Prince Charlie, Came Ye by Athol?, By Loch and Ben, Wandering in Wester Ross,* and last but by no means least one of his earliest books, *Land of Heart's Desire*—a gem, Mr Carmichael, a gem of purest ray serene as our great English poet Gray has it. Do you think I shall be trespassing too far on Mr Mackay's indulgence if I ask him to inscribe these eight books?"

"I'm sure he'll be pleased to sign them."

"Thank you, sir. You have taken a great weight from my mind. May I get you any refreshment?"

"No, thanks, Toker. I'm not going to touch a drop of anything till we've had a definite 'yes' or 'no' to this monster. I've a feeling that we're going to surprise the world in the next three or four days, and I want to have a clear head."

"Bravo, sir. Bravo, indeed. Self-abnegation is the cornerstone of scientific research, as Professor Honeywood says in his *Compendium of Science for Everyman*. I check my pleasure in romantic dreams by keeping in touch as far as I am able with the latest developments of science."

"Well, I hope we're going to give science a nasty poke in the eye by producing a prehistoric monster for them. Losh, it'll be the biggest scoop ever."

It was about six o'clock of a golden afternoon when the *Banshee* entered the Coolish and dropped anchor about three hundred yards from Snorvig harbour. The *Island Queen* had already arrived and was moored along the pier. Ian Carmichael went ashore at once, and presently came back to ask if Mr Mackay could pay his respects to Ben Nevis. The Chieftain looked at his sandshoes. The notion of receiving Hector Hamish Mackay in sandshoes displeased him, but he did not want to rouse the hostility of Captain Gillies by putting on his heavy brogues. The skipper of the *Banshee* had already been sniffing the air suspiciously and saying that if there was the least sign of a change in the weather he would have to weigh anchor and make for Nobost in Mid Uist. Ben Nevis believed him capable of going to Nobost merely to pay him out for the tacks in his brogues.

"I think he'd better dine with us, Carmichael, and you too of course."

"That's awfully good of you, sir. I'll go ashore right away, but I'm afraid I've only this old tweed doublet and I don't expect Mr Mackay will have glad rags."

"Glad rags?"

"Evening dress."

"Extraordinary," the Chieftain woofed.

Ian Carmichael was not sure whether his host meant the expression or the lack of evening clothes was extraordinary.

"Well, I shall expect you both at eight. Don't bother about dressing."

Ben Nevis himself put on his tartan doublet buttoned up to the neck with eagles' heads of silver and set off by a lace jabot; this allowed him to wear his buckled brogues with propriety. It was a majestic figure that received Mr Mackay and Ian Carmichael on deck that evening.

"I am really incapable of expressing in suitable words what this privilege means to me, Ben Nevis," said the topographer.

"Will you take a dram?"

"Many thanks."

"Or would you prefer one of these cocktails?"

"Indeed, I never drink cocktails."

"Quite right," the Chieftain barked approvingly. "When I was in India I used to have to drink something they called a gimlet. I made rather a good joke once. I said, 'I suppose you call this beastly mixture of gin and lime a gimlet because it's such a boring drink?' Ha-ha-ha!"

If Hector Hamish Mackay was overwhelmed by meeting Ben Nevis, Toker was not less overwhelmed by meeting Hector Hamish Mackay. Ganymede could not have served Zeus with a cup of nectar more reverently than Toker poured out a hefty dram of Glenbogle's Pride for his most esteemed author. Indeed, in his emotion he very nearly offered the whisky to Catriona and Mary instead of the sherry.

Presently the strains of *Beinn Nibheis Gu Brath*, the tune which had heralded Mac 'ic Eachainn's dinner from time immemorial, were heard and the party moved below to the saloon.

"I wonder if your piper will give me the pleasure of hearing *Iomradh Mhic 'ic Eachainn*. I remember once as a lad passing by Glenbogle Castle when your revered father was still alive and hearing his piper playing it under his window early on a fine morning in May. I have never forgotten what was for me a most thrilling experience."

Ben Nevis was gratified by this and when presently the topographer asked for *M'Eudail M'Eudail, Mac 'ic Eachainn*, Ben Nevis began to warm towards him, and soon he was in a glow when Mr Mackay said:

"Although I think that the Clanranald Macdonalds claim this melody under the name *M'Eudail M'Eudail, Mac 'ic Ailein* I have always maintained that the Ben Nevis Macdonalds have the prior claim."

"Well, we don't press the point too hard," said Ben Nevis tolerantly. "After all, it's a domestic matter if you know what I mean. Of course, if the Campbells or the Macintoshes tried to poach one of our tunes that would be different. We wouldn't stand for that. I was after your blood when you started that peprosterous idea about the Loch Ness Monster having gone to the Islands."

"That was based on my theory that there were probably a male and female monster in Loch Ness, and when the news about the flying saucer was first published I was anxious to look at the bright side because the death of the Loch Ness Monster seemed to me to strike a blow at the very roots of Highland life."

"Well, of course, I maintain that the monster took what these flying fellahs call evasive action," said the Chieftain. "I will never believe that our monster was killed."

"I think you're right, Ben Nevis. At any rate, this island monster clearly has no connection at all with the Loch Ness Monster and I have said as much in the columns of the *Daily Tale* in no uncertain fashion. I believe Mr Donaldson, our Editor, had the privilege of meeting you recently."

"And I found him a very pleasant sensible fellah," said the Chieftain.

"And an admirable editor. Now, as you know, Mr Donaldson is particularly interested in your visit to Great Todday, and he has sent our young friend Carmichael to cover what he believes may be one of the greatest stories in the history of journalism."

"It won't be much of a story if we don't see this monster," said Ben Nevis.

Mr Mackay lowered his voice.

"If I might have a word with you in private after dinner,

Ben Nevis, I have a most important communication for your ears alone."

So after dinner the conversation was resumed in the smoking-saloon while the rest of the party sat on deck, watching a glorious sunset.

"Well, perhaps now you'll put me in the picture," said Mac 'ic Eachainn after he and Mr Mackay had drunk a couple of potent drams."

"I have discovered a cave which the monster is in the habit of frequenting and though I have not actually seen the monster a young palaeontologist and myself are quite satisfied . . ."

"A young what?" Ben Nevis interjected.

"A young expert on the remains of prehistoric creatures."

"But you didn't say that at first."

"Palaeontologist."

"What an extraordinary word! Pal . . . say it again slowly syllable by syllable."

"Pal-ae-ont-ologist."

The Chieftain muttered to himself for a moment or two. Then he rang the bell.

"Oh, Toker," he said when his butler came in. "I forgot to say that if a young . . ." Ben Nevis drew his breath like a defiant stag . . . "if a young pal-ae-ont-ologist comes aboard you can show him down into the smoking-saloon."

"Very good, Ben Nevis," said the butler.

"You know what a pal, a pal-ae-ont-ologist is, Toker?"

"I believe, sir, it is the word for one who studies the fossilised remains of the prehistoric monsters that used in days of yore to roam the earth."

"Yes. Quite," said Ben Nevis in a subdued voice. "By the way what's his name, Mr Mackay?"

"Brownsworth."

"All right, Toker, that's all I wanted to say." This was not perfectly true. What Ben Nevis had wanted to say was that at last he had found a word to make Toker blink.

"Extraordinary chap, my butler," he said to Mr Mackay. "He's a walking dictionary. And by the way he's a great reader of your books. He's apparently brought a whole packet of them with him and wants you to write your name in them."

"Certainly. I shall be delighted."

"That's very kind of you. He didn't tell me, but he told

young Carmichael, who asked me if I would mind if Toker asked you. But to get back to this . . . Good lord, the name's gone already."

"Palaeontologist."

"It's no use. I shall never remember it. What's he called —Brown something."

"Brownsworth."

"You were saying?"

"Young Brownsworth and I discovered unmistakable signs that the monster resorts to a cave on the little island of Poppay known as the Cave of the Bones. Uamh nan Cnàmh."

"We've got a cave with the same name on Ben Gorm," the Chieftain exclaimed. "Macintosh bones they were, the remains of some Macintoshes who were smoked to death in it in the days of Hector the Sixth."

"I've told the story in my book *The Glamour of the Glens*. Well, as soon as I'd established the fact of the monster's frequenting this cave I decided that not a word should be said about it in the Press because I did not want all those hikers . . ."

"Hikers? Did you say hikers?"

"There are quite a few camped out on both islands, all hoping to win this £250 offered by the *Daily Tale*."

"Well, let's hope this monster is carnivorous," said Ben Nevis.

"So far not a word has leaked out about the monster using this cave on Poppay and I thought that when we had this *céilidh* broadcast from Snorvig on Thursday it would be a wonderful dramatic stroke if young Brownsworth could arrive at the *céilidh* and bring news that the monster was at that very moment in its cave. Then I thought I would announce this to listeners and tell them that Ben Nevis in person was going over at once to Poppay to establish once and for all that it was not the Loch Ness Monster and that if all went well the programme later in the evening would be interrupted for a minute or two to give listeners the latest news. And now you understand why I was so secretive at dinner. I shall tell young Carmichael, of course, because he will have to stay behind on Poppay when Brownsworth brings word to the *céilidh*. Mr Donaldson knows; you know; and I know; but nobody else knows except Joseph Macroon . . ."

"Well, if Joseph Macroon knows he'll try and put the monster on the rates. He'll probably want us to build a pool for him and a new pier."

"It was, in fact, Joseph Macroon who discovered the monster's refuge, and pretty scared he was by what he saw. And now there's one more favour I have to ask. The B.B.C. are most anxious that you should say a few words into the microphone at the *céilidh* in order to give listeners the pleasure of hearing your voice."

"What, talk on the wireless? I wouldn't know what to do."

"It's as simple as talking into a telephone," Mr Mackay urged.

"I don't call that very simple. In fact, I never knew anything more complicated."

"Well, I won't press you now, but it would give a very great deal of pleasure to thousands. And now if you'll excuse me I think I must be wending. I have to cross to Kiltod."

"You'll have a jockendorrus?"

"Well, I can't say 'no' to that old Highland custom. And you will not breathe a word to anybody about the monster's probable whereabouts?"

"I shan't say a word." The Chieftain raised his glass. "Well, slahnjervaw to the monster."

"*Slàinte mhór.*"

"And don't forget to write your name in Toker's books," Ben Nevis said. "He deserves it after knowing what a . . . well, you remember the word."

That night in the cabin he was sharing with Kenneth MacLennan Toker sat up in his bunk and played with his eight signed copies of Hector Hamish Mackay's works as a little girl plays with her dolls.

Chapter 17

THE CAVE OF THE BONES

POSSIBLY stimulated by that whacking *deoch an doruis*
which Ben Nevis gave him, possibly moved by Toker's
recognition of him as a figure in Scottish literature to be
mentioned in the same breath as Ossian, Hector Hamish
Mackay suggested taking Ian Carmichael to Poppay in
order to effect a reconnaissance of the monster's movements.

"I'll consult Joseph Macroon and if he's willing for
Kenny to take us there to-night in the *Morning Star* I think
it would be a good thing for you to see the lie of the land,
Carmichael."

The young reporter did not require either a *deoch an
doruis* or Toker's homage to support Mr Mackay's suggestion with enthusiasm, and at midnight they boarded the
Morning Star with the avowed intention of fishing for pollack,
though Joseph Macroon was taken into their confidence
and impressed once more with the need of strict secrecy, a
need which he in turn passed on to his son.

Those who have never experienced the magic of a fine
Hebridean midnight at the end of June may have difficulty
in imagining the romantic exaltation of Hector Hamish
Mackay and Ian Carmichael as the *Morning Star* chugged past
Tràigh nam Marbh to reach Bàgh nam Marbh in Poppay.
The sea was tarnished silver; a luminous glow in the western
sky had hardly faded when the eastern sky came to life in
lavender and rose; the landscape seemed to quiver like the
wings of grey moths. It was, however, the quality of the air
itself, combining the twilight of evening with the twilight of
dawn, which gave the time and the scene a peculiar magic,
and which it is beyond the power of any painter to portray
or the skill of any writer to evoke.

When the *Morning Star* came alongside the landing-place
in the Bay of the Dead, Mr Mackay and young Carmichael
stepped ashore on tiptoe not so much because they were
thinking about moving quietly to avoid disturbing the
monster but because the visible world seemed to be a
whisper which they must be chary of interrupting.

Ghost moths came dancing up from the rank herbage as they walked silently across the ancient burial-ground; a corncrake rasped.

"Losh, what was that?" Carmichael asked apprehensively.

The topographer told him.

"A queer noise for a bird to make," the young man commented.

"I'm awful fond of that noise," said Mr Mackay with a sigh. "It takes me back to the summers when I was young. The bird grows rarer every year on the mainland. But not another word. We're getting near the slope up to the cave. Try not to kick down any loose stones. When we reach the terrace in front of the cave I will approach and listen from the right of the entrance and you will approach and listen from the left. Both of us must keep out of the monster's sight if we possibly can. The way down to the sea about which I told you is on the left as we stand and if the monster does show itself I think you'd be wise to get over to the right and give it a clear road. Now then, on we go. And as quietly as possible."

In years to come Hector Hamish Mackay would declare that one of the supreme moments of his life was the moment when he cautiously put his ear round the corner of Uamh nan Cnàmh and heard from its innermost depths a brobdingnagian snore, and he would always add that the greatest temptation he had ever resisted was the temptation to lure the monster from its den that night and satisfy his curiosity once and for all.

"Indeed, I don't know how I was able to come away and leave the mystery unprobed, Carmichael," he said, when they were making their way back to the *Morning Star* across the burial-ground.

"It's all just luck, Mr Mackay. We're playing for big stakes and I'm sure Mr Donaldson would agree that they are worth it. If the monster isn't at home on Thursday evening when the ceilidh is being broadcast we can feel fairly sure of finding it later on that night and we'll get a flashlight picture. If we'd disturbed it to-night we couldn't have had a photograph and people might have said we were just inventing the whole thing as a stunt for our paper. But what a snore! Losh, I haven't heard such a snore since I shared a wee room in a cottage with a Paisley commercial when the bus ran into a snowdrift in Sutherland last winter."

"Yes, yes, I'm sure we've done the right thing," Mr Mackay agreed. "And we've certainly done the honourable thing. Young Brownsworth might have thought that I'd double-crossed him. He's kept his word and never been near Poppay since we rescued Joseph Macroon's whisky, and the temptation to a rising young palaeontologist must have been great. Well, well, if that snore is the nearest I ever get to the monster I shall always maintain that we did the right thing."

Presently they reached the landing-place.

"Och, it's myself that's glad to see you, Mr Mackay," said Kenny in a tone of relief. "I didn't like being down here alone at all, at all. I was all the time thinking I could see *bòcain* walking about."

"Ay, it's a haunted spot, Kenny. I'd have felt a bit nervous myself if I'd been alone. I certainly would. Well, the monster's in Uamh nan Cnàmh at this very moment."

"Are you after seeing it?"

"No, but we're after hearing it. It's asleep in the cave and snoring like an earthquake. But not a word of this to a living soul, Kenny. We must be patient till Thursday comes."

"It wasn't a stirk you heard snoring?" Kenny suggested. "A stirk can snore pretty loud."

"A stirk would have to be the size of three bulls to sound as loud as the noise we heard in the Cave of the Bones," Mr Mackay declared.

"Or a commercial traveller," added Carmichael. "And it couldn't have been a commercial traveller."

"It may be a bit early for the crayture to go to its bed by the time the *céilidh* will be starting," Kenny suggested.

"I'd thought of that," the topographer said. "But the B.B.C. wanted the *céilidh* to finish in time for the nine o'clock news. We must just take our chance, and I've a feeling that the monster is not going to let us down."

It was two o'clock before Hector Hamish Mackay and Ian Carmichael went to bed, and the eastern sky above the bens of Great Todday was already lavender.

Next morning they went over to see Bill Brownsworth at Tràigh Veck to let him know about the snoring in the cave.

"I felt a wee bit guilty by going over to Poppay without you, Brownsworth, but I wanted to take the opportunity of showing Carmichael the lie of the land and I knew you'd understand."

"Oh, rather," said Brownsworth.

"I've arranged for Kenny Macroon to land you and Carmichael to-morrow at half-past seven. Then you'll both reconnoitre the cave and if the monster is at home Carmichael is to hold the pass while Kenny takes you over to Snorvig as quickly as he can. If the monster comes out before the *Banshee* . . ."

"The *Banshee*?" Brownsworth echoed.

"The *Banshee* is the yacht with Ben Nevis and his party. As soon as you arrive like a messenger in a Greek play with the news, the *Banshee*, which will have steam up, will take Ben Nevis and his party, myself, Father Macalister and possibly one or two others over to Poppay and the secret of the monster will be revealed. Should the monster emerge before you get back Carmichael will secure a photograph, and I think I'm right in saying that the credit of this photograph will be given to you accompanied by the no doubt welcome cash in recognition of your co-operation."

"That's what Mr Donaldson would wish," said the young reporter.

"But that's hardly fair on Carmichael," Brownsworth objected.

"Forget it," Carmichael said. "It's all in the day's work for me."

"I wish I could persuade you to come to the microphone yourself, Brownsworth," said Mr Mackay. "Would you not try the effect?"

"But I know I should gulp," Brownsworth protested.

"I really don't think a gulp would matter. What do you say, Carmichael?"

"Och, I think a good gulp would add to the effect. It would suggest Brownsworth's excitement," Carmichael replied.

"Why don't you try the effect?" Mr Mackay urged. "Let's suppose that this beach is the hall and the natural arch the entrance. You and Carmichael have established the monster's whereabouts and Kenny Macroon has brought you over to Snorvig—by the way, I hope he won't have trouble with his engine on Thursday; that would be a disaster. Shall I show you my idea of the entrance? Mind you, Urquhart and MacColl, the two B.B.C. chaps, may not agree to this handling of the situation, but my notion would be to interrupt whoever is singing or talking at the *céilidh*. That can be settled later."

Hector Hamish Mackay· disappeared into the natural arch to prepare his entrance, and it happened a moment later that one of Jocky Stewart's cows which had been wandering came down on to Tràigh Veck pursued by Jocky's daughter Florag who, when not herding her father's cattle, helped Mrs Odd in the house.

Florag thumped the cow's stern with a stick and adjured it in angry Gaelic to get back on to the machair.

"*Suas thu, a Bhuttercup, suas, suas, a nighinn an diabhuil.*"

Through the natural arch came Hector Hamish Mackay. "Great news, great news," he cried. "The monster is . . ."

The remainder of the messenger's announcement was drowned by a piercing shriek from Florag as she ran up the sandy slope.

"*A Mhuire Mhathair*, the monster, the monster," Florag screamed. "Oh, God help me, what will I do?" And as she made this appeal she tripped over a tussock of marram and fell prone.

The effect of Hector Hamish Mackay waving his cromag and flashing his glasses in the entrance of the arch, combined with Florag's screams, excited Buttercup the cow and she began to prance round the beach, lowering her head and kicking her heels in the air, and obviously perfectly ready to jump over the moon if the moon had been there to be jumped over. Every time that Mr Mackay attempted to cross the beach and join the others the cow, which was an Ayrshire, lowered her horns and drove him hurriedly·back into the shelter of the natural arch; it was not until Brownsworth and Carmichael between. them had managed to convince Florag that the monster was not in the neighbourhood that she was persuaded to get up and exercise her authority over Buttercup.

"Well, there's not likely to be a cow in the Snorvig Hall, Brownsworth," said Mr Mackay. "So I'll try again."

He emerged from the natural arch for the second time.

"Great news, great news, the monster is in its den on the island of Poppay. That's what I should like. you to say,

Brownsworth. Then I'll go to the microphone and tell listeners that under the leadership of Ben Nevis some of us are going to beard the monster in its den, after which Francis Urquhart will inform listeners that the programme will be interrupted later on in the evening in the event of there being any news. Surely, Brownsworth, you could manage that one simple sentence? Great news, great news, the monster is in its den on the island of Poppay. Try."

Brownsworth felt that he could not disappoint Mr Mackay, who had been so kind to him. He retired into the natural arch, from which he emerged awkwardly, his cheeks duskily blushing with embarrassment.

"Great news, great news," he mumbled. And then he gulped over and over again with a sound of corks being pulled out of his gullet one after another. He was quite unable to release the news.

"Yes, I see your point, Brownsworth," said Mr Mackay. "One or two gulps would really be quite effective, but a series of them without any words to follow might puzzle listeners. It's a pity, but it can't be helped. You'll just have to beckon me and quietly tell me the situation on Poppay so that I can make the announcement."

"If the cave is empty when Brownsworth and I go to Poppay to-morrow, would you like one of us to come over and let you know?" Carmichael asked.

"Oh, certainly, certainly, but I refuse to consider such a possibility. You're making me wonder now whether you and I shouldn't have routed out the monster last night when we heard it snoring in Uamh nan Cnàmh. Well, I must be getting back to Kiltod. The B.B.C. boys are coming over to make final arrangements with Father Macalister. What will you do, Carmichael?"

"I thought I'd take a run around Great Todday. I don't want to spend the day here in case there are any news hounds around on the look out for a tip. And I also want to tell Ben Nevis about the snoring last night. Why don't you come over with me, Brownsworth?"

"Well, I will. I want to see my friend Spinnage if I can."

Bill Brownsworth did not have to cross the Coolish to see Dick Spinnage. When they all three reached Kiltod Dick Spinnage was with Francis Urquhart and Duncan MacColl in the *Kittiwake*, which was just coming alongside the harbour steps.

The two B.B.C. men went off with Hector Hamish Mackay to visit Father James, and Carmichael asked the Biffer if he would take him over to have a look at Uamh na Snaoiseanaich in a loud voice for the benefit of various visitors who were hanging around, staring at what they felt were people in the know.

"They'll be two hours at least with Father Macalister," Carmichael said.

"Yes, yes, come aboard, Mr Carmichael," said the Biffer. "I'll take you over. Plenty time. Plenty time."

"Are you coming, Brownsworth?" Carmichael asked.

"I must talk to you, Bill," Dick Spinnage muttered to his friend. "Something frightful has happened."

So the *Kittiwake* went off without them.

"Bill," said Dick Spinnage when the two friends, remote from human company, were seated on a green knoll on the buttercup-gilded and daisy-silvered machair, "Bill, why on earth did you tell me Muriel had a coffee-coloured mole under her right ear?"

"The last thing I said to you, Dick, on the night of our picnic was to remember that, if you were in any doubt which girl was which, Elsie had a coffee-coloured mole at the back of her right ear."

"You said Muriel."

"No, you said Muriel and I said 'no, not Muriel, Elsie.' But what has happened?" Bill asked anxiously.

"What's happened? Wait till you hear what's happened. Last night, having taken particular note of this coffee-coloured mole, I asked Muriel to come for a stroll to look at the sunset."

"But if she had a coffee-coloured mole it wasn't Muriel you asked."

"You're telling me, Bill. But I thought it was Muriel, and to keep the promise I made you . . ."

"That was awfully decent of you, Dick," Bill put in affectionately.

"Oh, well, a promise is a promise. Anyway, feeling perfectly sure that it was Muriel, I suggested sitting down by the edge of the cliff and after I'd been talking in rather a gooey way for a bit I put my arm round her waist, expecting she'd freeze the way any girl just engaged to somebody would freeze if his best friend started to make the running —any decent girl that is. Well, you can imagine that I was a bit shocked when the girl I thought was madly in love with my best friend, instead of saying right out of the refrigerator 'please, don't do that' cuddled up close and put her head on my shoulder with a kind of steamy sigh. I can tell you, Bill, that shook me. It shook me from every point of view. I thought how you and I had planned this business and then I thought Bill's never going to believe that his girl cuddled up to me like this without a lot of come hither stuff on my part beforehand. You see, Bill, you've always had rather an exaggerated idea of my attraction for girls and, dash it, I didn't see how I was going to tell you that Muriel was n.b.g. as a girl to marry. Well, there was I with my arm still round her waist and her head on my shoulder, and I had a sudden feeling that perhaps it wasn't Muriel at all but Elsie. And then I caught sight of that coffee-coloured mole and knew it was Muriel right enough."

"But, Dick, I did try to impress on you that it was Elsie who had the coffee-coloured mole."

"All right, Bill, don't ride it. Riding that damn mole won't get me out of the mess I'm in. Well, to go on, there was I as I thought in the position of having tried to seduce my best friend's girl."

"I think you're putting it rather too strongly," Bill suggested modestly.

"Don't interrupt, Bill. So I said to myself, hell knows no fury like a woman scorned and it's no use my telling Muriel at this moment that I thought she was Elsie. That'll only make her vicious. I decided to take the line of having been irresistibly tempted by her and asking her to forgive me. So I said, 'you and I oughtn't to be doing this, you know,' and she cuddled up closer and said, 'why not?' 'Well,' I said, 'after all I'm Bill's best friend and I feel rather a worm.' 'What's Bill got to do with you and me?' she asked. That punch fairly made my teeth rattle and I looked again to see if I could have been mistaken about that mole. But no . . ."

"But I did keep telling you it was Elsie who had that coffee-coloured . . ."

"Don't ride it, Bill, don't ride it," Dick snapped irritably. "Do you think if I hadn't been absolutely sure it was Muriel I wouldn't have known how to handle it? Where was I? Oh, yes, 'What's Bill got to do with you and me?' And then, like an absolute ass, I lost my head and decided

to pretend I thought it was Elsie. I know, I know. I make
no excuses. Don't harp on that mole, Bill. 'Well,' I said, 'I
had an idea, Elsie, that you and Bill had an understanding.
Bill talked to me of meeting you that day in Tràigh Veck
and I got the impression that you and he had this understanding. 'Oh, no,' she said, 'there was never anything
between Bill and me. Indeed, I think he's keen on Muriel
and I'm pretty sure Muriel has fallen for him. Otherwise,
she'd have been jealous of me over you.' You can imagine
what I felt when I realised that it wasn't Muriel at all. Of
course at that moment I ought to have removed her head
from my shoulder and taken my arm from her waist and
said, 'I've no business to be flirting with you, Elsie, because
I'm already engaged to a girl in London.'"

"But you aren't, Dick."

"I know I'm not, I wish you wouldn't interrupt. Where
was I? 'I've behaved rottenly and all I can hope is that
you'll forgive me.' But instead of that I kissed her!"

"But why didn't you say you thought she was Muriel
and tell her that I'd made just the same mistake at Tràigh
Veck?" Bill asked. "That would have put everything right
both for you and for me."

"Oh, Bill, don't make me laugh. I never felt less like
laughing. Tell a girl that two men one after another have
only made themselves agreeable because they thought she
was her twin sister? But never mind what I ought to have
done. Listen to what I have done. When I kissed her she
went into a sort of doodah, and said, 'Oh, Dick darling,
you don't mind if I tell Muriel to-night that we're engaged?
I've never had a secret from my twin sister.' So apparently
I'm engaged to Elsie, and I don't see how I can get out of
it. I mean to say if old Waggett writes to Charlie Blundell
and tells him I've played pitch and toss with his daughter's
heart it might lead to my losing that partnership."

"But if he writes to tell Blundell that he's very pleased
about his daughter's engagement you'll probably be a
partner before you know where you are," said Bill eagerly.
"And you do like Elsie, don't you?"

"I'm really quite keen on Elsie, as a matter of fact. But
think of old Waggett as a father-in-law," Dick groaned.

"Well, I hope he's going to be my father-in-law too.
Really, Dick, I don't know why you're so upset. I'm tremendously pleased about this."

"Bill," said Dick sharply, "are you sure you didn't deliberately tell me that Muriel had a coffee-coloured mole at the back of her right ear?"

"Dick, I warned you that Muriel *didn't* have a coffee-coloured mole. You got it wrong once and I corrected you. I really am not to blame over this. Of course I can't help being pleased about it. I think I'll go over to Snorvig this afternoon and tell Mr Waggett that I want to marry Muriel."

"No," said Dick firmly. "Neither you nor I will say a word to old Waggett. If you think I'm going to spend the next two or three days listening to the old man talking about marriage from the time of Adam and Eve, think again. No, no, Bill, not a word until we're well out of reach of his tongue. I shall sound Charlie Blundell first. I shall tell him I want to marry Waggett's daughter and ask him what about it. Then if he makes a firm date for the partnership I shall write to Waggett."

"Yes, that's all very well for you, Dick, but I'd like to fix up things about Muriel before we discover the monster because Mr Waggett . ."

"Don't keep on calling him Mr Waggett, Bill, as if you were a small boy talking about a master to another master."

"Well, Waggett," Bill gulped, "doesn't believe this monster exists and I don't want him to be prejudiced against me."

"It won't do, Bill. We must both wait until we are out of range of the old man's tongue. I've made it quite clear to Elsie that she must say nothing to her father until I'm off the island. I'd rather he went on talking about the Normandy landings than matrimony through the ages. And if and when you and I do get married, we've somehow got to keep old Waggett safely parked in the Outer Hebrides. Well, now I've got it off my chest, Bill, I don't feel quite so gloomy, and if Charlie Blundell comes up to the scratch I believe I'll feel quite cheerful."

"You can imagine how happy I feel, Dick, and if I discover the monster and get that Readership at Norwich I shall be the happiest chap in the country. Fancy you and me being brothers-in-law."

"We won't be brothers-in-law. I've explained that to you already. You're as much muddled about our relationship as I was about our sisters-in-laws' moles. And one more stipulation, Bill."

"What's that?"

"You are not to call old Waggett 'Daddo'," said Dick Spinnage sternly.

Chapter 18

NO LONGER RIVALS

AT half-past seven sharp just as Bill Brownsworth and Ian Carmichael stepped ashore on Poppay from the *Morning Star* the doors of the Snorvig hall were closed. On the platform were Ben Nevis in his tartan doublet buttoned with silver eagles' heads; Chester Royde and Hubert Bottley in white mess jackets; Catriona and Mary MacDonald, each with a sash of Ben Nevis MacDonald tartan; Paul Waggett in a dinner-jacket and black tie, which for some reason caused a certain amount of giggling among the Snorvig school choir until Alec Mackinnon, the tall thin swarthy schoolmaster, threatened to eject them and strike their action song out of the programme; Mrs Waggett with Muriel, Elsie and Dick Spinnage, the last named also in a dinner-jacket, much to his host's gratification; Dr Maclaren, deplorably in a stained old Lovat tweed suit; the Reverend Angus Morrison and his wife; John Beaton, the burly schoolmaster of Bobanish, and his wife, demonstrating by their presence that Bobanish was not in the least jealous because the Snorvig school choir and the Garryboo school choir had been chosen to represent the juvenile talent of Great Todday; big Roderick MacRurie, Simon MacRurie, Andrew Thomson, the bank agent, and Mrs Thomson, with several more local notabilities. Donald MacRurie, from whose post-office the broadcast was being sent over the sea to the mainland listeners, remained at home, under the impression that his supervision was required for the success of the transmission. George and Catriona Campbell were down in the body of the hall giving final words of advice to the Garryboo choir. Alec Mackinnon was ubiquitous. Father Macalister was shaking his fist at the team of old, young and middle-aged women who were to uphold the fame of Little Todday at the *luadh*.

A narrow trestle-table about fourteen feet long was set out in the middle of the hall with benches on either side and on the table lay a piece of blanketing folded back on itself in the shape of a U. If the waulking had been a genuine process of shrinking and fulling, the blanket would have

been soaking in a tub of diluted ammonia; but the weaving
of tweed and blankets had almost died out in the Toddays
and a waulking to-day was only an illustration of what it
was once upon a time, and indeed unless Father Macalister
had insisted on a *luadh* from time to time in the Kiltod
hall it would have become extinct even as an illustration
of the past. The parish priest had had some difficulty in
overcoming Todaidh Beag's fear of being derided by
Todaidh Mór, but in the end he had prevailed and at half-
past six the women were all aboard Dot MacDonald's large
fishing-boat, the *St Tod*. Bean Yockey, the wife of Jockey
Stewart; Bean Uisdein, the wife of Hugh Macroon; Joseph
Macroon's daughter, Kate Anne Macdonald; Kate Anne's
friends Morag and Mairead—these were some of the party.
The older women wore long voluminous skirts of drugget
with red or green or blue lines, but the younger women
were no longer willing to wear such old-fashioned garb and
looked somewhat frivolous in printed cotton frocks. The
principal singer was Florag's grandmother, Bean Iosaiph
Sheumais, now close on seventy, but treated by her mother,
Bean Sheumais Mhicèil, aged ninety, as if she were the
same age as Florag.

The singer's duty was to sing a narrative song of innumerable verses the chorus of which, consisting of 'hiro-hivo,
huva-haro' and other sounds without meaning, was taken
up by the women who, each grasping in both hands a
section of the blanketing or cloth to be waulked, banged it
down upon the table in front of them in time with the
singer. Toward the end of the waulking what was called a
clapping song was sung, the tempo of which was much
faster and the rhythm much more exhilarating. Then like
Maenads the women sang the chorus more loudly, banged
the cloth down more and more rapidly, and induced in
themselves and in the audience a kind of dithyrambic
frenzy.

Besides the Little Todday women for the *luadh* old
Michael Stewart went over to sing a rousing *port a beul*.

"But where's Duncan Bàn?" Father Macalister asked.

Mrs Odd shook her head.

"Duncan Bang's better at home, Father James."

"Is that so? Ah, well, poor Duncan. I expect he got too
excited."

"He was very excited."

H*

"But you're coming over with us, Mistress Odd," the parish priest had said when all the women were aboard the *St Tod*. "Isn't that beautiful now?"

"And what's more, Father James, I'm going to be one of the looers myself."

"Good shooting! You'll just be knocking sparks out of them."

"Yes, Florag and me have been horoheaving away for a week and more. Talk of the Oxford and Cambridge boat-race, it's a funeral beside Florag's mother and the rest of them. 'Good land alive,' I said, 'if you bang that pore blanket about much harder it'll be a sheet not a blanket at all. Horo-hiro! Hara-hiva! Horo-hivo! Huva-hara!'"

The rest of the women were so much enchanted by Mrs Odd's rendering of a chorus that they all forgot they ought to feel sea-sick on the glassy Coolish and they were still laughing when they trooped up the steps to the pier and walked along through Snorvig to the hall. When the doors were closed a quarter of an hour before the broadcast began the Little Todday women were sitting on the bench that ran right round the hall. It had been decided to restrict admission to those who could find seats on this bench and, except for the trestle-table with the blanket, the middle of the hall was empty to give the B.B.C. equipment fair play.

"So that's Ben Nevis, is it?" Mrs Odd said to Bean Uisdein. "What's he wearing that bib under his chin for? He doesn't look a dribbler."

"Och, he's a very fine man, Mistress Odd."

"He *is* a fine man. My boy Fred thought he was the finest man he ever knew."

Father Macalister overheard this and presently went along to ask the Chieftain if he would have a word with the mother of Sergeant-major Odd, who had seen the monster.

Ben Nevis plunged down from the platform and Father Macalister brought along Mrs Odd.

"Jolly glad to meet the mother of my old friend Sergeant-major Odd," he barked, shaking her by the hand. "How is he?"

"Oh, he's in the best of pink, thanks. Has two little girls now and hoping for a little boy this September."

"Jolly good," the Chieftain woofed. "And so you saw this Todday monster, eh?"

Mrs Odd gave him an account of her adventure on Tràigh Veck.

"Well, I've seen the Loch Ness Monster twelve times."

"Have you reelly?"

"But it didn't have these long teeth, Mrs Odd."

"Well, it wouldn't do if every monster looked like the next, would it?" Mrs Odd said.

"Absolute silence, now," Francis Urquhart was calling.

"I'll get back to my seat. Jolly glad to have met you, Mrs Odd. Remember me to the Sergeant-major."

"I will. He'll be listening to us on the wireless to-night. That is if he can get Scotland in Nottingham and which he can't always."

"Please," said Francis Urquhart in a reproachful voice.

"Wireless Willie's giving us the bird," said Mrs Odd with a twinkle.

"Look out, Donald. You'll wreck the programme if you aren't careful," Hubert Bottley chuckled.

When Ben Nevis was back on the platform Francis Urquhart addressed the gathering.

"Now, listen, ladies and gentlemen. In exactly another five minutes we shall be on the air and that means that every sound in this hall will be broadcast as soon as the green light turns red. So will you please try not to cough more than you can help and under no circumstances talk to one another. Absolute silence, please. And when you are applauding the items will you please not clap until I raise my hand and will you please stop clapping the moment I drop it."

Duncan MacColl went across to the platform and asked Ben Nevis to join them round the microphone.

"It will start everything so splendidly, Ben Nevis, if you would say a few words when I give you the cue."

"What do I want a cue for?" the mystified Chieftain asked.

"To know when to speak into the microphone. And remember, please, not too close. As I suggested this afternoon, just fancy that the microphone is an old friend you've been talking to in your natural voice."

"I lay you fifty dollars, Carrie, that Donald Ben Nevis blows up the microphone," Chester Royde murmured to his wife.

Bertie Bottley began to giggle.

"Silence, please, absolute silence," Urquhart entreated. The red light glowed.

"*A Thighearna*," whispered Bean Shomhairle to Sammy MacCodrum, "it's terrible like Sahtan's eye looking at you."

"Ist, woman," her husband adjured with a nudge.

"This is the parish hall of Snorvig, the picturesque little port of Great Todday," Duncan MacColl announced, "where you are invited to join us at a *céilidh* which is being held on this lovely June evening in the land of perpetual youth—Tìr nan Òg. You will hear songs and piping. You will hear the dance-compelling *port a beul* or mouth-music when the singer takes the place of the fiddle or the pipe. You will hear an old tale or two and you will hear Hector Hamish Mackay give you the latest news of the Island Monster. And last but by no means least you will hear the women of Little Todday waulking the cloth. We are privileged this evening to have with us MacDonald of Ben Nevis, who has come all the way from Lochaber to take part in this *céilidh*. I am now going to ask him to say a few words."

"Where's this cue?" Ben Nevis asked as he stepped forward to the microphone.

"You've had it," Duncan MacColl whispered as he pointed to the microphone.

"I haven't," Ben Nevis whispered back hoarsely.

Duncan MacColl pointed to the microphone again.

"Now, now, now," he whispered.

"This is the first time I've tried talking into this wireless contraption," Ben Nevis told Scotland. "But I'm jolly glad to be here at one of our grand old Highland gatherings. I've come over to Great Todday in order to get a glimpse of this monster which some duffers believe is the Loch Ness Monster."

Francis Urquhart was signalling to Duncan MacColl to get Ben Nevis away from the microphone; he was afraid that elderly ladies all over Scotland were by now ringing up the B.B.C. to ask if the Communists were blowing up Glasgow. Urquhart tried to indicate to Ben Nevis that he was speaking too close to the microphone, but the Chieftain mistook his intention and, putting his mouth about an inch away, he bellowed into it more loudly than ever.

"They'll think the monster has gotten a hold of him,"

Chester Royde laughed. "He'll fuse every radio in the country."

It was Toker who saved the situation. He advanced with a light-footed dignity and offered his master a glass of water.

Ben Nevis looked round. Toker put his finger to his lips and pointed to the microphone. The Chieftain recognised that in Toker's opinion he had said enough and followed his butler across the hall to the platform.

"What's this for?" he muttered hoarsely, looking at the glass of water.

"Your voice was failing, sir."

"I was afraid I was talking too loudly."

"You were talking much too loudly, sir."

"How, was my voice failing then?"

"It was failing to adapt itself to the microphone, sir."

"I see," Ben Nevis murmured to himself, and then he took his seat again on the platform, wondering what difference it would have made if they had given him a cue to hold.

The *céilidh* progressed like many another *céilidh*. It was half-past eight when the *luadh* started, and a hope may be expressed here that television will reach Scotland before the *luadh* is extinct, because those who have only heard a *luadh* over the air cannot have the slightest idea of the spectacle.

"Gee," exclaimed Chester Royde, "the Carroway Indians have nothing on this. Gee, it's great. Attagirl!"

"Don't talk so loud, Chester," Carrie warned him, "they'll hear you."

"I don't give a darn if they hear me or not. Gee, this is the best thing I ever saw. Look at that big woman over there. She's shaking like a jelly."

"I say, Mary, I've a jolly good mind to go down and join in," said Catriona MacDonald to her sister

"Good-oh," Mary ejaculated. "I'm all for it."

And to loud applause from the company the two hefty daughters of Ben Nevis took their places in the team, one on either side of the table.

Thud—thud—thud—thud—thud—thud.

The bodies of the women swung to right and swung to left as they banged the blanket on the table. Father Macalister's voice was like a bourdon behind the chorus. Hirohoro! Hiro-hivo! Huva-hiva! Hive-huva!

Thud—thud—thud—thud—thud—thud.

Duncan MacColl kept up a running commentary.

"The increase in speed marks the beginning of the end of the waulking. The blanket is nearly shrunk as it should be. Oh, I wish you could see these women from Little Todday. What drive! What rhythm! They've finished. They're all breathless. One or two of them are leaning over the trestle-table as oarsmen lean over their oars at the end of a race. The audience are wildly enthusiastic. Mr Chester Royde, Jr., the American financier who is here and who was adopted by the Carroway Indians into their tribe under the name of Butting Moose, says that a Carroway war dance is a tame affair compared with this Hebridean waulking. And now I am going to call upon Hector Hamish Mackay to tell us the latest news about the mysterious visitant to these shores which is generally known as the Island Monster. Mr Mackay."

Duncan MacColl yielded the microphone to Mr Mackay.

"Good evening, everybody. We've had a wonderful evening here in Snorvig and we hope that you have all enjoyed yourselves as much as we have here with all the fine singing and piping and fiddling and that wonderful waulking you've just heard. The time is going on, but I'm told that listeners would be glad to hear from me the latest news of the monster. It remains a mystery at present, but my personal investigations lead me to suppose that the monster, which has been reported from various places right up the Long Island, has returned to Great and Little Todday, unable, perhaps like some of us, to resist the charm of these exquisite little islands which sum up in themselves all the magic of the legend-haunted West. As many of you have read, the Island Monster was first seen by Mr Kenneth Macroon between Little Todday and the much smaller and wilder island of Pillay, a mile or so north of it. It was seen again in the Snuff-taker's Cave on Great Todday by Mr Archie MacRurie; it was seen on Tràigh Vooey, the beautiful beach of yellow sand which is almost unique in the Long Island where all the beaches on the western seaboard are a dazzling white. Yes, there it was seen by the two little daughters of Mr and Mrs Samuel MacCodrum of Garryboo, a crofting township of Great Todday."

At the mention of her name Bean Shomhairle was seized with irrepressible giggles, and the more loudly she was hushed the more she giggled. Paul Waggett, who had been feeling throughout the evening that he had not been playing the prominent part in the proceedings to which as the owner of Snorvig House he felt he was entitled, and who was furious with what he considered this unwarrantable advertisement of an imaginary monster, came down from the platform with his nose in the air and told Sammy Mac-Codrum that if he could not quieten his wife he must take her out of the hall. Meanwhile, Mr Mackay, who was much too experienced a broadcaster to be upset by such a trifling incident, went on:

"The monster was seen again by Miss Jemima Ross, a teacher at Garryboo School, the performance of whose choir of boys and girls has given us so much pleasure this evening. Perhaps the most dramatic encounter was that with Mrs Odd on Little Todday, an encounter in which I myself was within an ace of partaking. Mrs Odd, who is a native of London, has taken these outermost isles to her heart and was one of that sturdy team whose waulking of the cloth has been perhaps the most notable item in a splendid programme.

"Since then I, in co-operation with three determined investigators, have established with all reasonable certainty the monster's lair or den or refuge . . ."

At this moment Bill Brownsworth entered the hall.

"One moment, please. I believe I am on the verge of being able to make a most important announcement. Could we have a tune from one of our pipers while I interrupt my talk to obtain the latest news?"

Michael Gillies, the Little Todday piper, was bidden to play and with a nice courtesy thrilled the company with the stirring strains of *Clan Donald is Here*.

"I'm getting rather fond of these Islanders, Bertie. I believe I've been wrong about them," said Ben Nevis to the laird of Cloy. "That fellah's a good piper. He must come on board the *Banshee* and have a dram with me. Angus!"

Angus MacQuat drew near.

"Who's that piper?"

"Michael Gillies, Ben Nevis."

"He's a good piper."

"He's a very good piper, Ben Nevis."

"Bring him on board the *Banshee*. I want to give him a dram."

"I'll do that, Ben Nevis."

The strains of *Clan Donald is Here* died away and Mr Mackay approached the microphone again.

"I'm sure all listeners will share in the excitement of us all here when I say that a messenger has arrived hotfoot from the little isle of Poppay off the south coast of Todaidh Beag to say that the monster is at this very moment beyond all shadow of doubt lying up in what is called the Cave of the Bones. Steam is up on the good ship *Banshee* and under the inspiring leadership of MacDonald of Ben Nevis, famed in Gaelic lore and legend as Mac 'ic Eachainn, the Son of the Son of Hector, the first Chieftain of that great line of which the present Ben Nevis is the twenty-third representative, we will immediately cross the Coolish, the strait that divides Great Todday from Little Todday. I am sure that listeners will accept our excuses for leaving the *céilidh* before it is finished. Do you hear the pipers? Led by Angus MacQuat, the hereditary piper of the MacDonalds of Ben Nevis, they are playing that grand martial tune, *Mac 'ic Eachainn's March to Sheriffmuir*. Oh, I wish you could see the scene. Ben Nevis is marching out of the hall, his head high, a noble representative of our country's most cherished traditions. He is followed by Mr Chester Royde, Jr., in this combined operation by Scotland and America. Sir Hubert Bottley of Cloy goes next; Miss Catriona and Miss Mary MacDonald of Ben Nevis follow. And now as the pipers precede the expeditionary force down to the pier I hand over to Duncan MacColl and prepare to hurry after them, conscious that listeners all over Scotland are wishing us God-speed at this tremendous moment."

Hector Hamish Mackay hurried away without seeing that Paul Waggett, with Dick Spinnage and his twin daughters, were also leaving the hall.

Duncan MacColl now came to the microphone.

"I much regret that we cannot give listeners an opportunity to share in the dramatic series of events that the announcement of Hector Hamish Mackay seems to promise, but as soon as we receive news from Poppay we shall interrupt the programme in the course of the evening to give Scottish listeners the latest information. And now the last item at our *céilidh* is an action song by the boys and girls of Snorvig School. Snorvig School are the present holders of the Shiant Shield which is competed for by schools every year at the National Mòd and they hope to defend their title at the Mòd held in Obaig at the end of September. After the action song we shall conclude the *cèilidh* in time-honoured fashion by singing *Oidche Mhath Leibh 's Beannachd Leibh*, good-night to you and good-bye, in which I hope our Gaelic-speaking listeners in the isles and on the mainland will all join us."

But we, too, must leave the *cèilidh* and follow the pipes with Mr Mackay and Bill Brownsworth.

"Now, I'm anxious to have a few more details, Brownsworth," said the topographer. "Let me have your story from the beginning."

"Carmichael and I landed at exactly half-past seven and started at once to reconnoitre. We reached the cave and listened without showing ourselves, but we could learn nothing. Then I decided to go in and I reached as far as the smaller second cave beyond, but there was nothing there. Carmichael and I decided that it would be best to return to the landing-place and give the creature a chance to retire. This summer-time rather upsets things. The sun doesn't set here till well after half-past nine at this time of year. We went back to the cave at eight o'clock. There was still nothing. Then we went back a third time at a quarter-past eight. Carmichael was slightly in front of me and as he reached the top of the slope up to the terrace he saw the back of a large body disappearing into the cave. He whispered to me and I slithered back down the slope and ran as fast as I could across the burial-ground. My knees are still burning with nettle-stings. Kenny saw me hurrying and, thank goodness, he was able to start the engine at once. You know the rest. Carmichael is going to try to cover the creature's path down to the sea so that if it leaves the cave he'll be able to get a snap of it."

"A large body is vague. Wasn't he able to give a better idea of the size?"

"He said it was definitely not as large as an elephant, but I think he was too excited to get an accurate idea of the creature. He did say that what he saw rather reminded him of a huge seal."

"That's what our friend Mr Waggett believes it is. But I never heard of a seal climbing up a steep rough path like that from the sea."

At this moment Waggett himself overtook them.

"Good evening, Mr Mackay. Good evening, Browns-worth, I couldn't help overhearing what you said, and I think it's pretty obvious that I am right. If this monster isn't entirely imaginary, it is nothing more extraordinary than a common or garden seal."

"But, Mr Waggett, you've not seen this path up from the sea. No seal could climb that."

Bill Brownsworth had dropped behind to walk with Muriel; he had no desire to argue about the alpine ability of seals with his future father-in-law.

"Oh, darling," she murmured, "I think we must tell Daddo about us. Dick wants to wait till he gets to London and then write about him and Elsie."

"I want to tell him. But I'm a bit worried about this monster. You see, it really is there and I think your father will blame me if he's wrong."

"But perhaps he won't be wrong," said Muriel. "He's going over to Poppay in the Biffer's boat. Dick and Elsie and I are going with him. Do come too, Bill."

"I'm afraid I really must stay with Mr Mackay, and he's going across in the yacht. I'll see you over on Poppay presently.

Bill Brownsworth overtook Hector Hamish Mackay, and they hurried along to where the *Banshee's* motor-boat was waiting at the pier.

"I never met such an obstinate fellow as Waggett in all my life," Mr Mackay sniffed. "His cocksureness really is nothing less than exasperating."

"He's going over to Poppay to prove that he's right,"said Bill Brownsworth. "I hope he won't get there before us and disturb the creature and perhaps make it take to the water."

"Young Carmichael will soon put a stop to that," the topographer said.

"But if Mr Waggett is the shooting tenant of Poppay he may claim that the creature is his property."

"I think not," Mr Mackay said firmly.

Ben Nevis was already in the motor-boat when they reached the pier, and Mr Mackay asked if they might come over with him to Poppay.

"This is Brownsworth, the rising young palaeontologist about whom I was speaking."

"Come aboard, come aboard. Very glad to meet you," the Chieftain shouted up.

"Be careful not to say anything derogatory about the Loch Ness Monster, Brownsworth," Mr Mackay warned him in a low voice as they went down the steps to board the motor-boat.

"So you're one of these thats, are you?" Ben Nevis woofed genially. "Did you come into contact with the Loch Ness Monster at all?"

"I was up in Inverness for a fortnight last year, sir," Brownsworth replied, "but I wasn't lucky enough to see it."

"Ah, pity. I believe I've seen it oftener than anybody. Twelve times, to be exact. It's a great sight. But I suppose Kenneth MacLennan here had the finest view of the lot. He saw it attacked by this flying saucer." Ben Nevis introduced Bill Brownsworth to the rest of the party. "Now tell us all about this Poppay business. I think we'll drop Toker and my piper. Oh, dash it, Angus, we were going to give that Todday piper a dram. Look here, I know what we'll do. We'll go straight across to Poppay and then you go back in the motor-boat, Toker, and ask Captain Gillies, with my compliments, if he'll bring the *Banshee* over and stand off Poppay, sending the motor-boat to the landing-place. And, Angus, you stay here and get hold of that piper. Good lord, what a duffer I am! We've forgotten Father Macalister. Look here, Angus, you tell Father Macalister we're expecting him to have a cold snack with us in the *Banshee* when we've solved this problem of the monster, and I'd like Sergeant-major Odd's mother to come along too, and we'd better have Joseph Macroon and Big Roderick. You see to it, Angus. I suppose I ought to ask this chap Waggett, too, oughtn't I?"

"I think Mr Waggett is going across to Poppay, of which he has the shooting rights," said Mr Mackay.

"He's jolly well not going to shoot the monster. I would never include a monster in any shooting I let. Off we go, coxswain."

"Wait a minute, Donald," said the laird of Cloy. "You haven't made proper arrangements to fetch Father Macalister and any others from Snorvig. Wouldn't it be better if we ran alongside the *Banshee* first, and told Captain Gillies the programme?"

Thus it was settled, much to the gratification of Toker, who was able to give his orders to the yacht's stewards and with a clear conscience go over to Poppay in the motor-boat with the rest of the party. The motor-boat was then to return at once to Snorvig, pick up there the invited guests, put them aboard the *Banshee* and then fetch what it was hoped would be a band of triumphant discoverers from Poppay.

The slight delay involved in these directions and preparations gave Paul Waggett time to reach Poppay at the same moment as the motor-boat. He had never known the Biffer get the *Kittiwake* so quickly on her way with such good will.

"You know, perhaps, that I am the shooting-tenant of Poppay," Waggett reminded the Chieftain. "Well, of course I'm delighted for you to land here, Ben Nevis, but I think you ought to prepare for a disappointment. I must confess I was rather shocked when I heard Mr Mackay make that announcement over the microphone."

"We will agree to differ over that, Mr Waggett," said Mr Mackay acidly. "I am perfectly satisfied that we shall not be disappointed."

"Personally, I don't believe that there is anything in the cave," Waggett maintained. "But I make one reservation. It may be a large seal."

"*A Chruitheir*, what a man," the Biffer muttered to Kenneth MacLennan.

"Well, it's no use standing here arguing about it," Ben Nevis woofed. "The sooner we get to the cave the sooner we shall find out who is right."

"Your brogues, sir," Toker said gently. "I think you will need tacks up that slope."

The ancient burial-ground had seen many a procession in the past when a Macroon Chief was borne to his last resting-place by mournful clansmen, but it had never witnessed quite such a variegated procession as moved through the rank herbage on this June evening just before sunset, such a mixture of kilts and shorts and frocks and plus-fours and dinner-jackets and whites.

"I wonder if we oughtn't to get down on our hands and knees. What do you say, MacLennan?" the Chieftain asked. "Don't you think we ought to do a little stalking?"

"I'm not going to crawl on my hands and knees through these darned nettles for any monster," Chester Royde declared.

"We're in white, Donald," Bottley protested.

"I know, that's what's worrying me," Ben Nevis replied. "I'm so afraid the monster will bolt when he sees you and Chester walking about like Dr Livingstone and all that. I don't know why you didn't both get into something quieter when we went back to the yacht."

"Young Carmichael will be close to the cave, Ben Nevis," Mr Mackay reminded him. "And if the monster had already come out he would surely have warned us."

"Yes, I suppose you're right," the Chieftain agreed, with a regretful note in his voice, for he would have enjoyed directing everybody in a stalk.

They found Ian Carmichael with his camera by the edge of the terrace on the landward side.

"I began to think you were never coming," he said. "We've only a few minutes left for a possible photograph."

Paul Waggett stepped forward.

"I propose to go into the cave by myself," he said grandly. "And when I have satisfied myself that there is nothing there, except possibly a seal, I shall come out and you will then be able to satisfy yourselves that there is nothing there, except possibly a seal."

"Daddo!" Muriel exclaimed apprehensively; under the influence of Bill Brownsworth she did not feel so confident as her father in there being nothing there. He paid no heed and with uptilted nose he and his dinner-jacket disappeared into the mouth of the cave.

"You'd better all keep to the landward side of the terrace," Mr Mackay urged. "The monster will probably make for the water by its usual path."

Suddenly they heard within the cave a noise between a bellow and a bark and a whistle.

"That's the very noise I heard on Pillay," Bill Brownsworth exclaimed.

He had hardly spoken when Paul Waggett came running out of the cave, followed by a huge form.

"Got him," Ian Carmichael shouted in triumph as his camera clicked.

"It's a walrus," cried Chester Royde. "Look out everybody. Oh, gee, why didn't you let me bring that new gun of mine, Ben Nevis? A walrus at bay is an ugly creature."

By this time Waggett was over the terrace and slithering down the slope, the walrus in noisy pursuit and slithering down, it seemed to the alarmed onlookers, rather more quickly than the shooting-tenant.

Bill Brownsworth, feeling that now was his chance to win a bride, rushed forward and slithered down the slope behind the walrus.

Waggett reached the bottom of the slope first and started to run across the burial-ground.

The walrus galumphed after him. Bill Brownsworth, shouting and waving his arms, managed to overtake the walrus and distract its attention from Waggett. For a moment as the walrus uttered again that noise between a bark, a bellow and a whistle, it looked as if those fearsome eighteen-inch tusks would be buried in the body of the devoted young palaeontologist. Then to the relief of everybody the huge beast turned away and went galumphing down into the sea. Its head and tusks and bristling moustache were presently lost to sight in the golden waters of the Coolish.

"I ought to have guessed it was a walrus," said Bill Brownsworth, "when I saw those marks on the beach on Pillay. It must have been digging up shellfish, and of course it would have used its tusks as an ice-axe to get up to the cave here."

"Well, I must admit I hadn't thought of a walrus," said Waggett to Bill Brownsworth. "But a walrus is only a large kind of a seal. So I was really right all the time. However," he added graciously, "I might have had rather a job with those tusks if you hadn't succeeded in diverting the brute's attention. Thank you, Brownsworth."

"Before the others come, may I ask you something, sir?"

"I'm afraid I never had any first-hand experience of walruses before this evening, but . . ."

"No, I didn't want to ask you anything about walruses, sir. I wanted to ask you if I may marry Muriel."

"This is rather sudden, Brownsworth."

"I love her very much and she loves me. We fell in love . . ." then the young man remembered that the father-in-law to whom he aspired did not believe in love at first sight, and he substituted "with one another."

"Well, we can't discuss this sort of thing with all these people about. You'd better come over and see me to-morrow," said Paul Waggett.

The others were now gathering round, congratulating

Paul Waggett on his escape and Bill Brownsworth on his courageous diversion.

"That wasn't the monster you saw in Loch Ness, Mac-Lennan, eh?" said the Chieftain triumphantly.

MacLennan shook his head.

"The monster I saw was a lot bigger than that. And I'm afraid he's a dead monster now, Ben Nevis. Ay, I think yon devil of a flaming machine was one too many for the poor crayture."

"I don't believe it, MacLennan, and I never will believe it," the Chieftain roared, almost as loudly as a walrus. "What do you say, Mr Mackay?"

"Oh, I'm hoping more than ever now that the Loch Ness Monster will show itself again very soon. Still, we've had a really unique experience to-night."

"Extraordinary thing, Mr Mackay," said the Chieftain, "when that brute came charging out of the cave after Mr Waggett, do you know what I was reminded of?"

"I don't know at all, Ben Nevis."

"I was reminded of my ancestor, Hector, the Fourth of Ben Nevis."

"Hector of the Tusk!" Mr Mackay exclaimed.

"That's the very chap. We've got a painting of him at Glenbogle. He used to nick felons he'd condemned to death in the back of the head with this tusk to avoid any muddle over who was and who wasn't to be put to death. This nick he used to make was called Mackickyacken's kiss. Pock-vickickyacken in Gaelic. Of course, this walrus had two tusks and my ancestor only had one, but he had very much the same kind of moustache as this walrus."

At this moment there sounded from the steep brae above the burial-ground a noise that made Ben Nevis and Chester Royde stare at one another.

"Cooee! Cooee! Wolla-wolla-wolla-wolla! Oo-hoo! oo-hoo!"

"Good lord, Chester, that's the sound of hikers," Ben Nevis exclaimed.

"It certainly is. I haven't heard that noise for some years," said Chester Royde, "but I'll never forget it. Gee, it brings back that wonderful time we had at Glenbogle before the war."

"There they are," said Ben Nevis pointing to four figures in shorts bounding with the agility of goats down the brae.

A minute or two later Ben Nevis was saluted by Mr Sydney Prew and three members of the Ealing Branch of the N.U.H.

"Good lord," he gasped.

"I hope you will let bygones be bygones, Mr Mac-Donald," said the secretary, "and allow me to offer you the congratulations of the National Union of Hikers on your successful solution of the mystery of the Todday Monster. My young friends here and I were hot on the scent, but you just beat us."

The Secretary and the three members of the Ealing Branch saluted again with their staffs, and went off to find their boat.

"Extraordinary!" Ben Nevis muttered to himself as he started off to join the others. "Well, I hope everybody will come back and have a cold snack in the *Banshee*. You'll come, Mr Waggett, and your daughters and your friend there. Where's Mrs Waggett?"

"I'll go across to Snorvig and fetch her in the *Kittiwake* if I may," said Paul Waggett, who was much gratified by this invitation.

"Yes, of course, the more the merrier, what?"

Bill Brownsworth took Dick Spinnage aside and told him that he'd broken the news to Mr Waggett about wanting to marry Muriel.

"Why don't you tell him about Elsie now? I'm sure this is the right moment, Dick. I'll come over with you in the *Kittiwake*, if you like, when we go to fetch Mrs Waggett."

And Dick Spinnage took his friend's advice.

"Your dress trousers are in rather a mess, Paul," said his wife as she finished a rapid toilet before going out to the *Banshee*. "And, oh dear, there's a piece torn out of the seat. Was that the walrus's tusks?"

"It may have been, Dolly," he said.

"Oh, Paul, I didn't realise how near I was to losing you." Her eyes filled with tears.

"Well, we're losing the chicks instead, old lady. Still, we couldn't expect to keep them with us for ever, could we?"

He put his hand to the seat of his dress trousers. "Good gracious, Dolly!" he exclaimed. "I've lost about six square inches. I'll have to put on my blue serge suit."

"Will you announce the chicks' engagement this evening, Paul?"

"I think so, old lady. They seem quite eligible young men. I shall write to Charlie Blundell at once. I'm sure he'll arrange a partnership as soon as possible. Of course, Bill's prospects rather depend on his getting this appointment at Norwich, but we must be optimistic. And we mustn't forget that he may have saved me from losing more than just a bit out of my dress trousers. Another thing I like about him is his willingness to admit that I was right about this monster all the time and that a walrus is just another kind of seal."

And Paul Waggett went on being right. Bill Brownsworth did get a Readership at Norwich University that autumn and Dick Spinnage did get his partnership in Blundell, Blundell, Pickthorn and Blundell. What is more, Bill Brownsworth was given £250 by the *Scottish Daily Tale* for the snap Ian Carmichael obtained of the walrus close on his future father-in-law's heels.

The picture had as caption:

NARROW ESCAPE OF ISLAND LAIRD
THE POPPAY WALRUS ALMOST CLAIMS A VICTIM

When Paul Waggett read about himself as an island laird he was too happy to mind about the somewhat un-dignified attitude in which he had been photographed.

It was a merry evening on board the *Banshee*, and thanks to American hospitality those who liked champagne were able to hold their own with those who preferred whisky. Everybody was happy. The engaged couples were toasted. Paul Waggett did not feel that he was playing second fiddle over the walrus. Mrs Waggett dreamed of going to live at Norwood near her sister Gladys. Francis Urquhart and Duncan MacColl were sure that Scottish Regional had provided listeners with one of the most memorable outside broadcasts since the fleet was lit up on that genial evening once upon a time. Hector Hamish Mackay was looking forward to the talk which he would no doubt be invited to give and which he might not unreasonably hope would find a place in the Home Service, possibly even in the Third Programme as a repeat. Mrs Odd had visions of disorganising the meat ration in Nottingham when she related the story of the walrus to her butcher, Mr Dumpleton.

"Though, mind you, I shan't tell him he's the walking

double of the walrus except he doesn't wear his teeth outside. I don't know why I didn't reckernise him when I saw
the walrus on Try Veck. I suppose I was a bit flustered by
those tusks. And which I certainly thought was a lot more
than two. I suppose it was the way it was chewing up the
beach. Pore thing, I daresay if we'd have fed it with winkles
it would have got as tame as young Catherine's guinea-pig."

Yes, everybody was happy; even Captain Gillies gave up
casting dark glances at marks on his deck.

But the peak of the evening was reached when Ian Carmichael, flushed with the praise he had received for the
story he had telephoned to the *Scottish Daily Tale*, came
back to the *Banshee* with a telegram for Ben Nevis which
Donald MacRurie had given him.

Few who saw the Chieftain's countenance as he read that
telegram will ever forget its expression of an ultimate, indeed
a seraphic happiness, the attainment of which is granted to
very few human beings.

"Listen to this," he bellowed. "It's a telegram from
Kilwhillie. Listen. Listen. Sent off from Kenspeckle just
about the time the walrus came out of the cave on Poppay.
Listen, everybody. Listen!

*Monster seen by me between Foyers and Kenspeckle this evening
at eight seventeen stop eight humps definite and probable ninth stop
monster was moving rapidly towards the middle of the loch where it
submerged stop am satisfied it has completely recovered from encounter with flying saucer*

Hugh Cameron

The Chieftain beamed at the company; a grateful
emotion had deprived him for a moment of speech.

"There's nobody in Inverness-shire better pleased to hear
that news than myself, Ben Nevis," Kenneth MacLennan
declared.

Then the stalker raised his glass.

"*Slàinte mhath* to the Loch Ness Monster," he said
gravely. "*A h'uile latha a chi's nach fhaic.*"

"Slahnjervaw," Ben Nevis woofed from the bottom of his
great heart.

And as the eagle-beaked Chieftain and the eagle-beaked
head-stalker gazed at one another and swallowed each a
powerful dram of Glenbogle's Pride, Angus MacQuat and

Michael Gillies piped the moving strains of *M'Eudail, M'Eudail, Mac 'ic Eachainn.*

"Och, I believe we will be having our lobster-pool for Todaidh Beag right enough, *a Ruairidh*," Joseph Macroon murmured to Big Roderick.

"Ay, I believe you will, Choseph. And we might get a grant for the road between Knockdown and Bobanish."

Then Father Macalister rose.

"*A Chàirdean*, before this glorious and beautiful evening comes to a close I want to thank our visitors for their glorious and beautiful hospitality. We wish Kilwhillie were with us at this moment, but we are glad that he has been able to give us such great news about the Loch Ness Monster. And will you now please give a thought to our Todday Monster, to Old Bill who has gone off to find himself a Better Hole. Let us wish him a safe return to his icy home."

POSTSCRIPT

About a month later Mr Hector Hamish Mackay, back
in Edinburgh, received the following letter:

Glenbogle Castle,
Inverness-shire,
July 28th

Sir,
    The memory of your recent kindness in appending your esteemed
autograph to some of your wonderful books has emboldened me to
inflict upon you the enclosed. It is the first time I have ventured to
communicate to anybody my audacious attempts to express my deeper
feelings in rhyme, and I hope you will excuse the liberty. I listened
to your broadcast about the strayed walrus with moist eyes.

Yours respectfully,
William Toker

> *Arctic amphibian of the frozen north,*
> *Who ventured far from boreal strands to roam,*
> *You have a friend beside the Firth of Forth*
> *Who wishes you a safe return to home.*
>
> *Arctic amphibian, an unerring eye*
> *Has guided Caledonia's master pen,*
> *And eke the voice of Hector H. Mackay*
> *To tell your story to the ears of men.*
>
> *Your visit to the Islands of the West*
> *Has been immortalised in jewelled words;*
> *And now, O wandering walrus, be at rest,*
> *Browsing on sea-weed with familiar herds.*

W. T.

GLOSSARY OF THE GAELIC EXPRESSIONS

The pronunciation indicated in brackets is only approximate

CHAPTER 1

page
- 12   *a Dhia* (a Yeea), O God.
- 12   *a Chruitheir* (a Crooyer), O Creator.
- 14   *Beannachd leibh* (byannak leev), Good-bye.
- 19   *each uisge* (yach ooshki), water-horse.
- 19   *Isd, a Ruairidh* (isht, a Roory), Be quiet, Roderick.

CHAPTER 2

- 28   *eich uisge* (ăch ooshki), water-horses.
- 28   *sgeulachd* (skaylack), tale.
- 28   *céilidh* (cayley), literally visit, but used for any entertainment.
- 42   *Glé mhath* (clay vah), Very good.

CHAPTER 4

- 45   *Isd thu! Bith sàmhach! Nach isd thu, a Fhlorag!* (isht oo! pe sahvach! Nach isht oo, a Lorak), Quiet, you! Be quiet! Will you not be quiet, Flora.
- 45   *a bhalaich* (a vahlich), O boy.
- 45   *Taing do Dhia* (tang do yeea), Thanks to God.
- 45   *a Choinnich*, O Kenneth.
- 46   *sgarbh* (scarrav), cormorant.
- 46   *a Thighearna* (a heearna), O Lord.
- 46   *Uamh na Snaoiseanaich* (ooav na snūsanich), Cave of the Snuff-taker.

CHAPTER 5

- 67   *Fàilte do'n duthaich* (fahlcha don doo-hich), Welcome to the country.

page

69 *tìr nam beann, nan gleann, nan gaisgeach* (cheer nam byown nan gloun nan gahsgach), land of bens, of glens, of heroes.

71 *réiteach* (raytchach), betrothal.

73 *a Mhuire Mhathair* (a Voorye Vahair), O Mary Mother.

73 *ceud mìle fàilte* (keeut mela fahlcha), a hundred thousand welcomes.

75 *mac an diabhuil* (mac an jeeol), son of the devil.

76 *bhitheadh gu dearbh* (vee-i gu jerrav), he would indeed.

Chapter 9

107 *Leodshasach* (lyosach), Lewisman.

108 *Sgiathanach* (skeeanach), Skyeman.

Chapter 10

119 *bòcain*, ghosts or bogies.

123 *am bheil Gàidhlig agaibh?* (am vail Gahlic agav), have you Gaelic?

Chapter 11

142 *eudail* (ātal), dear.

Chapter 12

152 *na bith gòrach*, don't be stupid.

161 *luadh* (loo-a, with a guttural a), waulking.

Chapter 14

172 *Uamh nan Cnàmh* (ooav nan crahv), cave of the bones.

174 *Dé rud, athair?* (jay root, ahair), What is it, Father?

174 *a Dhia na Gràs* (a yeea na grahs), O God of Grace.

178 *Obh bh'obh* (ōv vōv), exclamation of dismay.

179 *cailleachan* (calychan), old women.

179 *port a beul* (porst a bale), mouth music.

183 *tha è cho carach ris a mhadaidh ruaidh gu dearbh* (ha eh cho carach ris a vatay rooay gu jerrav), he is as cunning as a fox, right enough.

CHAPTER 16

216   *Iomradh Mhic 'ic Eachainn* (eemra Vick 'ick Eachainn),
         renown of the son of the son of Hector.

CHAPTER 17

221   *deoch an doruis* (joch an doris), drink at the door.
225   *suas thu, a Bhuttercup, suas, suas, a nighinn an diabhuil*
         (sooas oo, a Vuttercup, sooas, sooas, a neein an
         jeeol), get up, you, Buttercup, up, up, daughter
         of the devil.

CHAPTER 18

241   *Oidche Mhath Leibh 's Beannachd Leibh* (oyche vah leev's
         byannak leev), Good-night to you and good-bye
         to you.
250   *a h'uile latha a chi 's nach fhaic* (a hooly lah a chee's
         nach aik), to every day you see and every day you
         don't see.
251   *A Chàirdean* (chartjan), friends.

Fantasy, comedy, magic and high adventure in three great novels by the world-famous fantasy writer·

James Branch Cabell

"Witty, subtle and magnificently entertaining fantasy fiction" *Lin Carter*

Figures of Earth

How Manuel the swineherd set out to make a figure in the world, and ended his quest as overlord of Poictesme. ·
"So inventive, so funny and so beautiful that it is a joy to read" *James Blish*

The Silver Stallion

How the nine barons of the Fellowship of the Silver Stallion, who had ruled Poictesme under Count Manuel, came to most colourful and unusual ends.
"One of the wittiest, most delightfully entertaining of all fantasy novels" *Lin Carter* ·

Jurgen

The ribald adventures of Jurgen, who regains his lost youth and wanders joyfully through the mythical lands of Poictesme and Cocaigne, meeting the world's fairest women and dealing fairly with them all—after his own fashion.
One of the few truly comic and erotic classics: "it will amuse, bemuse and delight you" *James Blish*

Published in Tandem editions at 35p each

Best-selling fiction in Tandem editions

Elizabeth Lemarchand

Death of an Old Girl 25p
The Affacombe Affair 25p
Alibi for a Corpse 25p

Three first-class detective stories featuring Chief Detective-Inspector Tom Pollard of Scotland Yard, and sure to appeal to anyone who enjoys Agatha Christie.

"A superbly told tale of blackmail and terror"
Manchester Evening News

"A real genuine police detection story . . . a hundred per cent winner"
Sunday Times

Kate Thompson

Great House 30p   Sugarbird 25p
Mandevilla 30p   Richard's Way 25p
The Painted Caves 25p

"Family chronicles are among the most popular of novels and high on the list are Kate Thompson's stories centred on the South African family of the Derains"
Bournemouth Evening Echo

Catherine Cookson

Hannah Massey 25p
The Garment 25p
Slinky Jane 25p

Compelling and moving novels, set in the North Country which Catherine Cookson has made famous.

"In an age when so much rubbish is published and writers are two a penny, Mrs Cookson comes as a boon and a blessing. She tells a good story. Her characters live"
Yorkshire Post

Historical fiction in Tandem editions

Edith Pargeter's memorable trilogy
of medieval England and Wales

The Heaven Tree 35p
The Green Branch 30p
The Scarlet Seed 30p

Romance and history combine in a swift-moving story of border warfare, power politics and private feuds on the Welsh border in the reign of King John.

"A highly dramatic and intense story, beautifully written"
Glasgow Evening Times

Talbot Mundy

Tros 30p   Liafail 30p
Helma 30p   Helene 25p

The saga of Tros of Samothrace, warrior hero, pledged to frustrate the schemes of great Caesar, ruler of Rome and master of half the world, who would lay Britain under the yoke of the conqueror.

John James
Votan 30p
Not for all the Gold in Ireland 35p

On the edges of the civilised world eighteen hundred years ago and more, when men and gods rubbed shoulders, a wily rogue like Photinus the Greek could set whole nations to warring and emerge with some profit. Whether making kings or killing them, fathering most of the royal houses of the north, or leading an army into battle, Photinus is irrepressible.

'. . . excitement, mythology, the splendour and barbarity of the Dark Ages, and vividly imagined adventures'   *Northern Echo*

Men Went to Cattraeth 30p

It is a century or more since the Legions left Britain, and Mynydog, King of Eiddin, has raised a war-band three hundred strong who will ride south through the devastated lands beyond the Wall to combat the menace of the Saxon marauders from across the seas . . .

'Rich and fascinating and intense. . . . There is splendour in this saga'   *Western Mail*

Historical romance in Tandem editions

Barbara Michaels

Sons of the Wolf 25p
The Master of Blacktower 25p
Ammie, Come Home 30p

"Miss Michaels has a fine sense of atmosphere, of period, of humour and of storytelling"   *New York Times*

Jill Tattersall

A Summer's Cloud 25p
The Midnight Oak 30p

England is at war with Revolutionary France, and in their different ways both Henrietta Clyde and her cousin Sophia find their desire for romance and excitement more than compensated for by rumours of smuggling, revolutionary plots, and sinister strangers.

Lady Ingram's Retreat 25p

At first it seemed an exciting adventure—to play the role of governess in a great house on the Yorkshire moors. But Arabel Murray soon found that the gloomy house and her rather forbidding employer were the least of the mysteries confronting her.

Name ....

Address ....

Titles required ....

....

....

....

....

....

....

....